WORTH
KILLING
FOR

ALSO BY ED JAMES

WORTH KILLING FOR

ED JAMES

Published by Thomas & Mercer, Seattle

www.apub.com

Amazon, the Amazon logo, and Thomas & Mercer are trademarks of Amazon.com, Inc., or its affiliates.

ISBN-13: 9781503938229
ISBN-10: 1503938220

Cover design by Stuart Bache

Printed in the United States of America

For Rich.

Day 1
Thursday, 21st April 2016

Chapter One

'Oh, here we go.' DI Simon Fenchurch pulled in on Upper Street, claiming the nearest space to Chilango. The raised-up pavement was busy with early evening diners and stressed commuters heading home. A couple were tucking into burritos outside the Day-Glo frontage, torn silver foil flashing in the setting sun. He glanced over to the passenger seat. 'So, a chicken burrito, then, Mrs Fenchurch?'

Abi slumped back, the fading sunlight casting shadows over her face. She tugged her hair into a loose ponytail, just a few strands of grey compared with Fenchurch's silver suedehead, then let it go with a shrug. Her smile, dimpled cheek and raised eyebrow, still sent shivers down his spine. She leaned over and kissed him on the lips. 'It's your choice, Simon.'

'That means you'd rather get some pasta, right?'

'No, Simon, I'm saying it's your decision.' The dimple puckered deeper. 'So, go on, choose.'

'You know how I hate choosing.' Fenchurch clenched his jaw. A dirty red bus hissed at the stop just to their left, a car honking at some perceived infraction. 'Chilangos, then you pick the film.'

'Like there was ever any doubt.' She opened the door and got out onto the road.

He followed her up the steps to the pavement level. 'You're sure you want a burrito?'

'Learn to quit while you're ahead, Simon.' She strolled over and stopped just outside the Mexican, squinting at the bookshop next door. 'I could do with another one of those cheap Moleskine clones, though.'

'Get one, then.'

'You sure?' She let her handbag drop down and stared at the ground, frowning. 'Get me a prawn burrito. Maybe a chicken one.'

'Just get your book and I'll wait.' Fenchurch sat at the outside table and watched the world go by. His stomach wasn't so much growling as screaming a death metal concert.

The deep-red sky promised another hot spring day tomorrow. A man next to him took a bite of burrito and got some foil snagged between his teeth, which his girlfriend found hilarious. The street lights flickered on, lighting up the row of elms or whatever they were. Little green buds on the branches, some even having the temerity to become leaves so early in the year. At the end, the Angel tube station spewed out another trainload. Heads down, sharp elbows out, headed for the M&S or Waitrose up the back street.

Movement caught his eye. No, more than that — body language.

A girl was hurrying across the road by Boots. Red jumper under a navy jacket, pulled tight. Blonde hair cut into a wedge — long on the left, tapering to stubble by the time it got to the opposite ear. Eyes darting around at the crowd passing her, the street, the shops, but mostly behind her.

Like someone was following.

Her gaze lingered on her phone, thumbs tapping at the screen. Another backwards look then she broke into a run, her shoulder bag bobbing up and down. Heading straight for Fenchurch.

Abi got in the way, stuffing a green carrier into her handbag. 'Come on, Simon, let's eat.'

Fenchurch was on his feet, stomping across the ground. 'Wait here.'

Ahead of him, a blur of grey hoodie and black trackies on a bike bumped the kerb, getting a shout from a suited businessman talking on his mobile. Then up the wheelchair ramp to the higher level, silver wheels spinning, catching the nearby headlights.

The girl clocked his approach and darted towards a doorway.

Too late.

A flash of steel from a sharp blade glinting in the light.

The girl tumbled to the ground, desperate fingers clutching at her neck. Blood spilled through her useless hands, puddling onto the pavement slabs.

'Stop!' Fenchurch barged past shoppers and diners. Drums thundered in his head, drowning out the screaming.

The hoodie swivelled round to focus on him, like some monster from a horror film. Dark skin. Bloodshot eyes locking with Fenchurch. He started off, street lighting catching his face — just a kid, maybe sixteen at most. And he was gone, freewheeling down the ramp.

Fenchurch stopped beside the girl, tracking the cyclist on the pavement below.

Her eyes pleaded with him. 'Help me.'

'Simon?' Abi's bag skidded across the slabs, almost spinning through the growing pool of blood. 'What the hell's—'

Fenchurch grabbed her shoulders, scanning the street for the blur on the bike. There — just past the Superdry shop. A green logo on his trackies, Everlast or something. 'Stay with her.'

Abi gave a nod, her gaze on the girl as she fumbled in her bag. 'I'll call 999.'

'Call Kay as well.' Fenchurch set off, reaching into his jacket pocket for his Airwave. 'Control, this is DI Simon Fenchurch in pursuit of an IC3 male on a bike. Suspect in a stabbing on Upper Street.'

The handset crackled with office chatter and the clattering of a keyboard. 'Not got any reports—'

'It's just happened. Send as many units as you can to Upper Street. Now!' Fenchurch stuffed the Airwave into his pocket and twisted into his Mondeo. He reversed back onto the road, the engine screaming out as loud as the sharp honks. Then he squealed off, wheels spinning.

Where was he?

Fenchurch cut across the path of a bus, following the trail of the bike. There he was, standing up on his pedals as he took a right at the Green, the tall trees still in winter mode.

Fenchurch caught up with him at the bend, almost touching his wheels. Kid didn't even look round.

Ram him or don't ram him?

The hood twisted round — the dark eyes locked on to Fenchurch, widening. The bike swung a right down the lane by the Winchester pub.

Fenchurch pumped the accelerator and swerved to the right. The left wing mirror took a whack as he mounted the pavement. Then he hit the tarmac and got going again.

Up ahead, the kid took another right instead of taking the one-way street, bobbing up onto the footpath and cutting along the pedestrian side of the roadworks.

Fenchurch stomped down on the accelerator and overtook him. He hauled the car left and lurched onto the pavement, just missing the wall.

Brakes screeched out, sounding like a banshee had broken free from hell. The front wheel clattered into the Mondeo's hood. The cyclist flew over, Superman becoming Groucho Marx as he skidded along the concrete slabs.

Fenchurch tore out of the vehicle and grabbed hold of him, squeezing his fingers into his skinny arms.

'Get off me, man!' The kid wriggled, twisting his head away from Fenchurch. Bright eyes criss-crossed with rivers of red. Didn't look like he'd slept in months. Steel-toed Timberlands crunched onto Fenchurch's foot.

Fenchurch screamed. His grip slipped and the kid made a run for it, heavy feet thumping along the back street.

Fenchurch stretched out his toes and winced. His foot was already aching like he'd dropped a tractor on it. He set off at a fast hobble and crossed the road, managing to lengthen his stride. Then he jumped up the grass embankment to get some cover and a better view. The kid was maybe fifty metres away as he darted into the park, a thin strip of cherry blossom and tarmac surrounded by railings.

Fenchurch followed him in, weaving through ambling couples and dog walkers. A hipster talking on his oversized smartphone.

The kid was losing him now, the long strides of youth against cracking knees. He burst off to the right, towards the entrance shrouded by a metal fence.

Fenchurch lost him. 'Shit!' He pushed himself on, his aching foot screaming warnings back at him. He cut out of the park and stopped on the road, looking and listening, spinning around.

Fake Regency blocks of flats. More park. The canal. Shit, there was a tunnel near here somewhere, wasn't there?

Where the hell was he?

Footsteps thundered behind him.

Fenchurch twisted round and spotted him again, that loping stride eating up the middle of the road. At least a block ahead.

How had he made up so much ground?

Fenchurch lost sight of the kid again around the curve of the street. Into the Airwave: 'Control, this is DI Fenchurch. I'm on Vincent Terrace, requesting update on backup.'

'Units responding to an incident on Upper Street.'

'Send half of them to me, now!' Fenchurch passed a pub on the right and clocked the kid again.

Same Everlast trackies, same hoodie. Beside the Transport for London bike stand, fifteen or so public bikes locked in. He rushed forward and pushed a student over, the preppy teenager getting caught up in the Boris bike. The kid snatched the bike up and shot off.

'You've got to be kidding me.' Fenchurch sprinted over the road and dived at him, aiming for his shoulders. He grabbed hold of the hoodie. It slipped out of his fingers. They tumbled backwards and something clattered to the ground. His old man's knees crunched off the pavement, old man's hands stopping the rest of him doing the same. He pushed himself up as his palms burnt.

The kid was on the bike, wobbling along the road. He steadied himself with a foot and shot forwards.

A cyclist powered in the opposite direction, all yellow Lycra and focused effort.

Fenchurch waved his warrant card. 'Police, I need your bike!'

The cyclist came to a halt, rocking forward. 'What?'

'Just give me it!' Fenchurch nudged him off and rested the Airwave on the handlebars. Thing looked like it weighed less than a feather. The crossbar was too high for him — took two goes to get over. He set off, the gears far too low. A few clicks and the socket reset, the chain loosening up. He sped up, tyres grinding against the road surface, starting to close the gap. A couple of bike lengths, maybe less.

A lorry belched out of an entrance on the left. Fenchurch pumped both brakes, almost flying over the handles. The kid hadn't stopped, hadn't been hit.

Fenchurch stood on the pedals and started off again, the same slow pace as before. Airwave to his mouth: 'Control, this is Fenchurch again. I'm in pursuit heading towards the construction site halfway to City Road. Over.'

The street narrowed, the new-build flats encroaching on both sides, dwarfed by cranes.

The kid cut left onto City Road, four lanes of buses and taxis jostling for position under the shadow of a new tower block, the glass glowing in the night sky. He weaved around vans and cars into the bus lane.

Fenchurch followed, thighs burning.

The grey hoodie veered off to the left, into a petrol station forecourt, heading for a McDonald's. He swung round and clocked Fenchurch closing on him. Then did a sharp right through a tangle of vehicles at the Co-op. He bounced over the tarmac and dumped the bike by a row of lock-ups.

Fenchurch tossed his bike to the ground and sprinted off. The kid vaulted over a low wall, making for a block of flats. Fenchurch tore across a patch of grass, heading for the building the kid had entered. He stopped outside and grabbed the Airwave: 'This is DI Fenchurch, the suspect is entering Buxton Court.' Eyes scanning around for other exit points. Nothing jumped out at him. 'Repeat, suspect is entering Buxton Court. Over.'

'Alpha Papa Seven is en route.'

Fenchurch spun round, listening for the sirens, watching for the blue lights. There they were. He tore the door open and stepped into the flickering light. Dark and damp, full of cannabis fug, misting his eyes and nostrils.

Footsteps clambered up the stairwell above.

He followed, as quick as his foot let him, listening closely.

A door scraped open diagonally opposite. He sprinted up the stairs, scanning round for one swinging shut. There — fourth floor.

He pushed through it and hobbled along the corridor, felt like he had a basketball at the end of his leg.

The kid was hammering on doors, trying handles. He spotted Fenchurch and bolted towards another door, looking like it led to a back staircase.

Fenchurch sped up, far too slow.

The kid reached the stair door, fingers fumbling for the handle.

Locked, the door thudding against the frame. Not budging.

He darted over to a flat, hammered at the door. 'Let me in! The cops are trying to kill me, man!'

Fenchurch grabbed hold of his wrist and twisted him round, pushing him to the ground. The kid wriggled, fighting against it with scratching fingers and kicking boots.

Clatter.

A pile of mobiles lay at the kid's feet.

Chapter Two

Fenchurch let out a sigh of relief — his car was still there. His door hung open, the engine purring away. The racer was gone, though.

Why take a bike and leave a running motor? Bloody London.

Fenchurch thumped the squad car's roof. 'Take him to Leman Street.'

The uniformed driver nodded through his window as it whirred up. He drove off, the kid slumped over in the back seat, face lost to the depths of the hood.

Fenchurch checked his bonnet — just a slight prang by the passenger door. He got in and shut the door. Then winced as his foot pressed down the clutch. He tried to ease it out, twisting his shoe around. Bloody foot had locked. He reversed off the kerb and drove back towards Upper Street.

A row of uniformed officers cordoned it off at the Green, the traffic looking like it stretched halfway to Watford. To the left was a riot of flashing blue lights, police and ambulance out of sync. He leaned over and held out his warrant card to the uniform by the barricade. 'DI Fenchurch, I need access to the crime scene.'

'On you go, sir.'

Fenchurch jotted his name on the clipboard and trundled over, sticking to the right-hand lane.

A uniform was unrolling police tape, a rough rectangle blocking off Chilangos. Next to the off-white Scenes of Crime van mounting the kerb was a gang of bodies pulling on blue overalls.

Fenchurch parked in the middle of the road and staggered across, wincing with each step. No sign of Abi.

A blue-suited officer unfolded a crime-scene tent, struggling to erect it. Behind them, another figure was tearing off his SOCO suit and shrugging on his tweed jacket at the same time. Dr William Pratt's beard exploded from his face, almost as thick as his torso. He scattered his togs near the discard pile and marched off, bag in hand.

Fenchurch cupped his hands around his mouth and shouted: 'William!'

No response.

'William!'

Nothing.

He checked through the contacts on his phone. Just had Pratt's office number. Shit.

Inside the inner circle, the victim lay on her side, outlined in blood like a question mark, dotted by a thick pool on the pavement. Her left hand was reaching towards Fenchurch, dead eyes pleading, the sort that'd follow him. Sharp cheekbones, one side covered in her hair.

Fenchurch stopped and clenched his fists tight, fingernails digging into his palms. The back of his throat was dry and raw, starting to fill with mucus. Tears clouded his vision. Drums started hammering, heavy and steady, like they were building up to something.

A paramedic crouched down beside her, obscuring the view. His green uniform was tight over his bulky arms, less than half of it muscle. He gave Fenchurch a nod as he adjusted his hipster glasses, cream outlining the black frames. Short hair swept back over a barely concealed bald spot. 'Can I help you?' Northern Irish accent, Belfast by the sounds of it.

'DI Fenchurch.' He showed his warrant card.

The paramedic stood up and had a long look before handing it back. 'You in charge?'

'I guess so. Where's Pratt gone?'

'What are you saying, pal?' Nostrils flared, eyes narrowed. 'You calling me a prat?'

Fenchurch pointed at the receding figure, now slipping through the outer cordon. 'Dr William Pratt.'

'Right, right. I didn't know that was him.' The paramedic got up and snapped off his gloves. 'The name's Jonny Platt. Heard people call me a prat since I was this high.' He held out a hand at waist height. 'He barged in here, took a little look at her and cleared off. Didn't even give a name, said I've got to get this body out to Lewisham. Can you sign it off?'

'Did he say anything about the victim?'

'Not to me, sorry. I was here first, though. Hell of a business.'

Fenchurch tried to swallow down the lump in his throat. 'Could we have saved her?'

'Look, I couldn't and I'm trained in this.' Platt traced a line across his throat. 'Got both of her carotid arteries. Brain death was inevitable. Missed the trachea, though.'

Fenchurch took another look at her. Another unknown body . . . 'Okay, shift her once Clooney's finished.'

'Oh, come on. The SOCOs'll be ages.'

'I don't make the rules. Has DS Reed—'

'Guv!' DS Kay Reed stood in front of a mobile phone shop, an arm wrapped round Abi. Looked like she'd collapsed in on herself, shoulders hunched and staring at the pavement. Reed tilted her head up at Fenchurch as he approached, jaw clenched tight. She ran a hand over her red hair, tied back in the old Croydon facelift, an overtight ponytail smoothing out her forehead.

Fenchurch tried to make eye contact with his wife. Nothing. Back to Reed. 'Thanks for getting here so soon, Kay.'

She gave a shrug with her free shoulder. 'Did you get him, guv?' Essex accent despite ten years in London.

'On his way to the station. Jon Nelson's coming in as well.' Fenchurch tried to get Abi's attention again but it wasn't happening. Another glance at Reed. 'I saw Pratt leaving.'

'Yeah. Good thing is he lives around the corner like you. Bad thing is he's late for the theatre or something.'

'So you spoke to him? Did he give you anything?'

'You know what he's like.' Reed was barely holding it together, herself. 'She never stood a chance, guv. Looks like an expert to my untrained eye.'

'Have you got an ID for her?'

'Not yet, I'm afraid. Didn't have a purse or anything on her.' Reed let her grip go a touch.

Abi looked up from the ground, noticing him for the first time. 'Simon.'

Fenchurch thumbed behind them. 'Kay, get this place organised, would you?'

'Guv.' She set off, looking reluctant to leave them.

Fenchurch clutched Abi's hand tight and led her away from the crime scene. 'How you doing, love?'

'She . . .' Abi shut her eyes and swallowed. 'She died.'

Fenchurch glanced over at the paramedic, now humping the body onto a gurney. His stomach burnt. 'I saw. Are you—'

'Right in front of me, Simon.' Abi stared into space again. 'The girl.' She locked eyes with him. 'I stayed with her but she just slipped away. Just stopped breathing.'

Fenchurch wrapped her up in a deep hug. 'It's okay, love.'

'It's not.' She pushed back and thumped his chest, but her heart wasn't in it. 'I could've saved her.'

'Nobody could've, love. It's okay.' Fenchurch pecked the top of her head. The wild flower scent mixed with a bitter tang. 'Did she tell you her name?'

A frown appeared as she focused on him. 'She said something like camel.'

'Camel? What?'

'I don't know. Could be Kamal.'

'You sure?'

'No. I'm not sure at all, Simon.' Eyes like fire. 'She was too busy dying and spitting out blood to make sure she was clearly heard. Jesus.'

Fenchurch tightened his hug. 'I wish you hadn't seen that.'

'I should've saved her.' Clothing muffled her voice, her head stuck to his chest. 'She didn't need to die.'

'It's not your fault.' Fenchurch let her go and tried a smile on for size. Didn't really fit. 'There was nothing you could do. Nothing anyone could've done. The paramedics—'

'I hate that.' She looked up, hair plastered to her face. 'Of course there's something—' Tears were streaking down her cheeks. 'I should've . . .'

'As soon as that kid stuck the knife in her throat, that was it.' Fenchurch nodded over to the ambulance as Platt slammed the back door and trotted round the front. 'The paramedic couldn't save her. She'd need to get to hospital. University College or Royal London, both are about ten minutes from here.' Fenchurch gripped her hand tighter. 'You did all you could, love, okay?'

She brushed the hair from her face. 'Did you get him?'

'He's on the way to the station.' Fenchurch kissed her on the lips. 'Have you given your statement?'

'Kay was going to do it.' She grimaced, her pupils like red-hot coals. 'Put him away for this, Simon.'

Chapter Three

Fenchurch parked outside the back of Leman Street station, the brick grid-work glowing in the sodium glare. He got out of his car and gave a nod at the figure leaning against the wall. 'Thanks for coming in, Sergeant.'

DS Jon Nelson sucked on a vape stick and exhaled, sending a cloud of nicotine into the night air. He tugged at his suit jacket, as if drawing attention away from his belly. 'Not like I had anything important on tonight, guv.' He gave a grin as he pocketed the e-cigarette, his deep voice echoing around the tight space. 'There'll be other parents' nights.'

'Sadly, there'll be other murders.' Fenchurch swiped the back door and tucked in his ID lanyard. 'Kid upstairs?'

'Room three.' Nelson marched across the floor tiles. 'Not asked for a lawyer.'

'Let's hope he keeps it that way.'

Nelson entered first and started jogging up the stairs, losing his breath after the first few steps. 'How's Abi?'

'Not good. You and I have seen this sort of thing a few times. She hasn't.' Fenchurch opened the door to their floor and stopped, rubbing at his nose. 'Happened right in front of my eyes, Jon.'

'Jesus.' Nelson led off down the corridor, his lopsided walk getting more pronounced by the day. 'Must feel pretty weird being a witness for once.'

'A world of difference to giving them a grilling, that's for sure.' Fenchurch paused outside the interview room and rested his hand on the handle. 'Got a name from him yet?'

'Not said anything. No ID on him. No bank cards, no security, no nothing.'

'What about those mobiles he had?'

Nelson lifted up a load of evidence bags, each one containing a high-end mobile. 'Your guess is as good as mine, guv. Not sure if any of them belong to the victim.'

Fenchurch took one off him. A gleaming HTC thing, looked just like an iPhone. 'Killing someone over a bloody phone. What's the world coming to?' He shook his head and pushed into the room.

The black kid he'd chased was leaning against the table, chin resting on his wrists. He looked even younger, like a frightened rabbit more than a stone-cold killer. His dark skin almost sucked in the light. He ran his fingers along the short cornrows on his head, uneven lines zigzagging across his scalp, twirled into long strands at the back. He'd draped his grey hoodie on the tabletop, maybe to draw attention to his yellow Superdry shirt. It certainly showed off his marathon runner arms and torso, skinny to the point of bony. A wonder that a forty-two-year-old had caught him.

'Hello again.' Fenchurch perched on a chair and shrugged off his suit jacket. He started the recorder going and glanced at the clock on the wall. 'Interview commenced at seven sixteen p.m. Present are myself, DI Simon Fenchurch, and DS Jonathan Nelson.' He took his time rolling up his shirtsleeves, gaze drilling into the kid. 'You going to give us your name, son?'

He just sniffed and looked away.

'That's how you're playing it, is it?' Fenchurch scratched at his chin, rasping like sandpaper. 'See, I saw you stab a girl with my own eyes.'

'I ain't did nothing, man.'

'So you do speak.' Fenchurch tried a grin, see if that keeps him talking. 'This girl died not long after you stabbed her. We've got three witnesses on Upper Street giving statements about what you did. I'll add another once we're done here. Once you've confessed.'

Another petulant sniff. 'I told you, man. I ain't did nothing.'

'You stabbed a woman with a knife. Then you cycled away. I chased you and caught you.'

The kid gave a wink. 'You sure it was me, bruv?'

'I saw you. You don't run unless you're guilty.'

'You saw a black kid riding a bike, that's all.' The kid smirked, pupils dipping behind his sockets. 'I can't afford no bike, man. Don't got a job.'

'You dumped it when you ran into my car. Then you stole a Boris bike, which you left outside the flats on Buxton Court.'

'Call them Santander cycles, man.' The smirk widened, joined by gleaming white teeth. 'Not Boris bikes.'

'You killed that girl.'

'Weren't me, bruv.'

'So why were you running from me, then?'

'Because police brutality, man. You saw the colour of my skin.' He looked over at Nelson, still standing by the wall, and shot him a smile. 'What do you think of that, brother?'

'I'm not your brother.'

The kid sniffed again and stared up at the ceiling, bobbing his head to some silent beat.

Nelson stepped forward and dumped the bags onto the table. 'Care to tell us why you had seven smartphones on your person when DI Fenchurch arrested you?'

'Juggling a lot of girls, you know? Use all me minutes every month. Got a system to keep 'em keen.'

'Charming.' Nelson sat next to Fenchurch, the chair leg scraping off the floor. Probably deliberate. 'Heard of guys doing that sort of thing with two phones, maybe three. Not seven.'

'Them boys not getting as much as me, bruv.'

Nelson tossed another bag on the table, containing a flip-top Motorola looking like it came from the Iron Age. Smart was the last thing it was. 'This is the eighth.' He nudged it until it touched the hoodie. 'It's what we call a burner. A pay-as-you-go SIM in a disposable handset. You can toss the SIM or you can toss the mobile, doesn't matter. No contacts on the card. Memorise all the numbers you need. Input them the old-fashioned way.' He picked it up and started playing with the buttons. 'I had a look through this one. Turns out the only call made was to a number entered manually.' He gave the sort of grin a snake would before eating a mouse. 'We're tracing it just now.'

The kid stared at him, silent. Just the ticking of the clock and the hum of the digital recorder. Another sniff. 'That ain't my phone.'

'No?' Nelson pulled it back towards him. 'It was in your hoodie pocket when my DI arrested you.'

'He's planting evidence on me, man. It's racist. All cops is racist, bruv.'

Nelson pushed the smartphones over to the kid. 'Can you unlock these phones for me?'

'No way, man.'

'You just said they're yours, right?' Nelson flicked up an eyebrow, head tilted slightly. 'You should be able to unlock them, if that's the case.'

'I ain't doing nothing, man.'

'These aren't your phones, then?'

Tick. Tick. Tick. Sniff.

'You're an Apple picker, aren't you? You steal smartphones off people in the street.'

'Nah, man.'

'You nick iPhones and posh Samsungs. Fence them with some shop owner in Walthamstow or Mile End. These shops sell them on to people who don't care where they come from. People who just want the logo on the back.' Nelson held up a bagged iPhone, silver-white and looking so high-tech it could guide you to the moon if only you knew how to use it. 'How much do you get for one of these? Couple of hundred?'

'iPhones aren't worth nicking, man. Kill switch, innit?'

Nelson grinned. 'You shouldn't have said that.'

The kid jabbed a finger towards him. 'You work for the white man, bruv. Betray your *race*. Get away from me. You a *slave*.'

Nelson cleared his throat, nostrils twitching. Clenching and unclenching his fists. 'You telling me you're emancipated?'

The grin turned to a frown. 'A man say what?'

'E-man-ci-pated. It means liberated from the slave trade.'

'Go to hell. You like an Oreo cookie, bruv. Black on the outside, white on the inside, know what I'm saying?'

'Only too well.' Nelson nudged the burner back across. 'Can we look at your phone, please?'

'I don't consent to that.'

'Unlock it. Now.'

'Said, I don't consent to that.'

Fenchurch raised a hand to Nelson and leaned forward, narrowing his eyes at the kid. 'The person you killed. Who is she?'

'Don't know who you talking about, bruv.'

'Like I said earlier, I saw you on Upper Street. You cycled up to her, stabbed her in the neck and rode off. You might remember me chasing you.'

'Don't remember nothing. Where's this knife, then?'

The little shit had tossed it somewhere. But where? How could he have done it?

Fenchurch swallowed, trying to compose himself. 'Your victim looks, I don't know. Twenty? Twenty-five?'

'You're lying, bitch. Ain't killed nobody.'

'You murdered her for her bloody mobile. That's really low.' Fenchurch flicked through the bagged smartphones. 'Which one of these is hers?'

'Don't know what you're talking about. Wasn't me, bruv.'

'You severed that woman's carotid artery. Know what that means?'

'You guys trying to show me as some dumb black kid? I know what carotid means.' He tapped at his neck, just below his ear. Then repeated the gesture on the other side. 'Pair of arteries right here.'

'Impressive.' Fenchurch ran his fingers across a Sony phone, squat and shiny. 'From what I can gather, this attack was clinical. Precise. Like the killer knew what to aim for. Makes me think this might not be random.'

'Wasn't me did it, though.'

'You dug the knife into her neck. She didn't stand a chance. How old are you?'

'Eighteen, bruv.'

'Sure about that?'

'Saying I don't look it? Think all blacks look old, is that it?'

'You look like a kid to me.'

'Prefer your rent boys older, do you?'

Cheeky little sod. Fenchurch shook his head. 'When we put you away, son, you'll not get out until you're forty, I reckon. At least. Even with good behaviour. There's a big crackdown on phone theft just now. Add in a murder . . .' He tutted and left space for the kid to fill.

Tick. Tick. Tick.

'I ain't done nothing, bitch.'

'You're going away for this, son.'

'You and Oreo think that so? I want a lawyer.'

Fenchurch gripped his right bicep, his free hand stroking his chin. 'After we're done with you.'

'Lawyer.'

'I said, after we're done with you.'

'Lawyer.'

Fenchurch let his arms drop to his side. Better let the little scrote get his wish, as they didn't want someone tearing the conviction apart. He nodded at Nelson. 'Get him his bloody lawyer, Jon.'

Chapter Four

'There we go, guv.' Nelson waved a hand at the monitor in the CCTV suite. 'It's show time.'

Fenchurch moved away from the cold wall and rested against the back of another chair, fingers grinding against the fraying felt.

DC Lisa Bridge tapped at her keyboard then ran a hand through her blonde hair, resetting the spiky messiness. 'Watch this, sir.'

Grainy footage filled the screen, sharp and greyscale. The camera looked across Upper Street from the Camden Passage. Fenchurch's car pulled into a space. Seconds later, he and Abi got out and climbed up to the pavement. They chatted briefly, then she went into the bookshop. Fenchurch sat next to a couple, grinning to himself and looking like a sex pest. On the left, the victim emerged from a crowd crossing from Angel underground.

Fenchurch stabbed a finger at the monitor. 'Has she been in the tube station?'

'Maybe.' Bridge scribbled a note on her Airwave Pronto. 'I'll get someone on it, sir.'

The woman paced up the street, thumbing at her phone and glancing back the way she'd come. She tugged her bag, like it was—

'Pause it.' Fenchurch waited until the image froze then drew a circle around her arm. Looked like some expensive job, the sort that just about fit a kitchen sink in. 'We didn't get her bag, did we?'

'Not to my knowledge.' Bridge held up her Pronto, showing the Crime Scene Inventory on the case master file. 'There's not much on here, sir, but nothing about a bag.'

Fenchurch stood up tall and sucked in the old electronics musk, sharp and hot. 'So that little shit dumped it before I clattered into him.'

Bridge made a note on the Pronto. 'Shall I keep going?'

'Please.'

The bike bumped onto the pavement and sped towards the victim, almost obscuring her from the camera, just leaving a thin sliver visible. He plunged the knife into her neck and tried to remove it, pushing back against her shoulder. She tumbled onto her back, her phone and bag gone.

Then he fled, standing up on the pedals, and disappeared off the edge of the display.

Fenchurch prodded the screen as Bridge paused it. 'The little shit's definitely taken her bloody phone.'

Nelson raised his collection of retrieved mobiles. 'So it's one of the seven?'

'Hang on a sec.' Bridge wound the footage back to before the attack. The girl was staring at her phone, frozen in mid-stride. Just a white rectangle, indistinguishable from any others in the bag, save the black Sony.

Fenchurch squinted at the flat panel. 'Could it be the iPhone?'

'Maybe.' Nelson sifted through the little collection and held it up. 'It's that sort of size. Could be anything, though, guv. A Samsung, an Apple, an HTC. Even one of those Chinese makes.'

'Great.' Fenchurch put his hands on his hips and scowled at Bridge. 'Is there any more?'

'Waiting on it, sir. This is what Control prioritised.'

'Play it again.'

Fenchurch took it in again. Stab, steal, flee. 'It all happened so fast.'

Bridge stopped the footage as Abi crouched down by the victim, Fenchurch jogging over to his car. She got up and wandered over to the door. 'I'll chase up the other stuff.'

'Thanks, Lisa.' Nelson shuffled over to her seat and took out his vape stick. 'What now, guv?'

'I need more painkillers.' Fenchurch sat down and prodded at his foot through his shoe. Stung like a bastard. 'Little sod really got me.' He massaged it until the throbbing went from ten to maybe a seven. 'How are you feeling about that interview with our suspect?'

Nelson stayed focused on the display. Didn't even take a puff. 'What about it?'

'The race stuff.'

'There's nothing to feel about it, guv. Had that every day of my life since I was seven. Kids like that deserve everything they get.' Nelson returned the video back to the start and took a deep suck on his vape stick. 'I grew up on an estate. A really rough one. Strong motivation for me to work hard. I pushed through it, got into uni, then got a good job.' He chuckled. 'Then I went mad and joined the police.'

'He got to you, though.'

'They tug every lever they can. You know that. The little . . . *punk* is only eighteen, but he's been schooled. Knows how to play the system. How to game us.'

'Even so, you kept your cool. That was impressive.'

'Thanks.' Nelson stared at the monitor, chest heaving, then tapped a finger at the figure on the screen. 'You're absolutely sure it's him, guv?'

'Of course I am.'

'I mean, really?' Nelson wound it back to the attack and circled Fenchurch on the display, just watching. 'You got a good look at what happened, but did you get a good look at *him*.'

'You're like one of those plonkers with their giant iPads on Monday Night Football, Jon. Did the ref see the incident?' Fenchurch looked away, eyes narrowing. 'I know what I saw. He's through there.'

'Simon.'

Fenchurch swung round.

DCI Alan Docherty lurked in the doorway, cast in hard shadow. Bony arms folded across his chest, sleeves rolled up. His checked shirt hung as loose from his trousers as his tie from his neck. A thin island of hair at the front pretended to be a full head of hair, convincing nobody. 'A word, Inspector.' His accent was trudging around the more guttural Scots. Bad news.

Fenchurch patted Nelson's shoulder. 'Chase up a lawyer, would you?'

'Guv.'

Fenchurch limped down the corridor and joined Docherty outside a store cupboard halfway along. 'Thought you'd left for the night, boss?'

'I had. Turns out one of my DIs is involved in a stabbing so I've just driven back in.' Docherty shoved his hands deep into his pockets. Might get the bends if he brought them up too quickly. 'What the bloody hell's going on here?'

'How much do you know?'

'Enough.'

Fenchurch leaned against the doorjamb, trying for casual indifference. Probably failing. 'I want this case, sir.'

'This isn't our patch, Simon. North London are—'

'We can argue jurisdiction over them. That little bastard ran to a block of flats in our gaff.'

'Why do you want it, though?'

Fenchurch waved a hand back in the vague direction of the interview room. 'Because he killed a young woman in front of me. Stone dead. In front of *Abi*.'

'You're a witness, Simon. That's where your involvement ends. Am I making myself clear?'

'I'm not the only witness, boss. Kay Reed's got three over and above me and Abi. We'll get enough from them, you won't need me in that capacity.'

Docherty looked Fenchurch up and down. Then sighed, deep and full of disappointment, like his son had failed yet another exam. 'How old is this victim?'

'Twenties.' Fenchurch pressed his lips together. So tight it felt like he could make diamonds. 'I don't like what you're suggesting here, sir.'

'Simon, you saw a girl in her early twenties get murdered.' Docherty raised his eyebrows. 'She's not Chloe.'

'Chloe?' Fenchurch clenched a fist and tensed his arm. Stuffed it in his pocket. For now. 'Of course it's not Chloe. I'm dealing with that. Meditating and talking to a counsellor and—'

'That's all very well, but you and your buddies in the CPS are still processing those animals for that crap at Christmas. I still remember what happened, what you got up to.'

'I'm over all that.' Fenchurch took his hand out of his pockets and flexed out his fingers. 'You know I am.'

'Do I?'

'Listen, Abi saw it as well. She was there while this girl died. This is going to mess her up.'

'So go and bloody help your wife, you idiot.'

'I have to solve this case.' Fenchurch held Docherty's gaze. No chance he was going to give anything up. He looked away and sighed. Let's play this a different way . . .

He thumbed back at the interview room. 'Look. That kid did it, all right. This is open and shut. A nice tick in the box. An easy stat. We just need some more evidence to back up my statement and we'll be palming him off to the CPS.'

'Why do you keep doing this to me?' Docherty shook his head for a few seconds. A final shake, then: 'Right, Si, just leave it with me. I'll get over to the Yard just now and put us on the docket for it, all right?'

'Cheers, boss.'

Docherty gripped Fenchurch's shoulder. 'Just get me a result, okay?' He trotted down the corridor, sticking his Airwave to his ear.

'Always do.' Fenchurch slumped against the wall. His foot was still throbbing like a bastard but the shoe was barely dimpled. How could it hurt so bloody much?

'Guv.' Nelson was standing in the CCTV room doorway, vapour hazing the air. 'The lawyer's just arrived.'

A black man in his thirties sat next to the kid Fenchurch chased. He chewed on a grey Pilot pen lid as he scribbled a note in his square-boxed Moleskine. Overweight and wearing an expensive-looking suit, no tie but a purple handkerchief in his breast pocket.

Fenchurch stood in the doorway, waiting for him to look up. 'Are you the lawyer?'

'Dalton Unwin.' He took his time making another note and got up. He was shorter than his wide frame otherwise looked. 'Let's have us a nice little chat in private, shall we?' Spoke like he knew all the colleges in Oxford *and* Cambridge.

'Jon, get this started, will you?' Fenchurch waited for the door to thunk shut behind him. 'Your client's not giving us his name. I'm assuming you know it.'

'If I do, it's not a requisite that I divulge it.'

'That's stretching lawyer-client privilege a bit much for my liking.'

'All the same. I'm here to make sure you lot don't *infringe* his human rights. Which I gather you've been doing already.'

'We taped that interview.'

'And it'll be inadmissible in court given your failure to obtain legal representation.'

'Just as well all he did was racially abuse my colleague.' Fenchurch stared into his eyes. A jewelled stud glinted under the strip light. 'Nice earring. Must take a few Legal Aid cases like this to afford that.'

A hand covered over the glimmering earpiece. 'Let's get on with it. I have to get back home.' Unwin held the door open.

Fenchurch folded his arms and stood his ground. 'How did you get here so quickly?'

'Excuse me?'

'Your friend in there didn't get a chance to use his call.'

Unwin barged past and plumped alongside his client.

'—Unwin of Liberal Justice.' Nelson couldn't keep a straight face.

Fenchurch took his seat next to him and focused on the digital recorder's flashing light. Then he stared at the kid for a few seconds, taking in his eyes, his cheekbones.

Was it their killer? Definitely?

He cleared his throat. 'You said earlier you didn't murder that woman on Upper Street.'

'That's right, bitch.'

Unwin gripped his client's wrist and whispered into his ear.

Fenchurch tilted his head to the side. 'I hope the suspect's lawyer is advising him to give less offensive answers.'

'My client agrees with your statement. He didn't kill this woman.'

'So help me out here.' Fenchurch gave the kid a frown. 'If you didn't, who did?'

'Not me, bruv.'

'Where were you, then?'

'What?'

'I assume you didn't just spring into existence when you ran into my car, so you must've been somewhere.'

'I ain't telling you nothing. You stopped me going about my business, man.'

'You saying you had business in those flats?'

'I ain't saying nothing.'

'We've got you on CCTV cycling away from the murder scene.'

'Not me. Move on.'

Fenchurch puckered his lips and let go, letting his shoulders slump. 'Who's Kamal?'

The kid swallowed hard. 'What?'

Fenchurch nodded. Not camel, then. 'You just shat a brick when I said it. Who is Kamal?'

'Nobody.'

'Are you Kamal?'

'No, bruv, I ain't.'

'What is your name, then?'

The kid twisted round, eyes pleading with Unwin. He got a nod from the lawyer. 'I'm called Qasid.'

'Qasid, right. That's a new one on me.'

'It's Muslim. Means messenger.'

'Are you telling me you bow down to Mecca five times a day?'

'Hardly. Old man was. Didn't stop him leaving me and my brothers, did it? Ended up dying in prison, what they tell me. Good riddance, man.'

'You got a surname, Qasid?'

'Williams.'

'And where do you live?'

'London.'

'Which bit?'

'I'm English, if that's what you're getting at.'

'Not with that accent.'

'My mum's Jamaican.' Qasid ran his tongue over his teeth. 'Ayii?'

Fenchurch let him bask in his laughter for a few seconds. 'So. Who's Kamal?'

'Nobody, bruv. Forget him. If I was you, I'd be looking for who killed the girl, yeah?' Qasid smirked at Unwin. 'Probably did it for her phone, know what I'm saying?'

'It was you. I saw you do it.'

'Did you, bruv?' Qasid pinched his lips together. 'Did you really?'

'Where did you dump her mobile?'

'Come again?'

'You stole it and her bag as you were murdering her. We haven't found either of them yet. Or the knife you stabbed her with.'

'You must think I'm well skill, innit?' Qasid gave a belly laugh. Then shook his head, his face straight again. 'It ain't me, bruv. I ain't killed nobody.'

'Qasid, I'd like you to confess here. Is that going to happen?'

'Nothing to confess to, bitch. I ain't done nothing. Which is what you've got on me, bruv. Zilch. Nada. Zip.'

'Okay, that's enough.' Unwin dropped his pen onto the table and patted Qasid on the shoulder. 'We're done here, officers. I want my client released. Now.'

'He's been arrested under suspicion of a murder charge.'

'You're one hundred per cent certain you saw my client, are you?' Smug prick was grinning like he knew the secret to life, the universe and everything.

Fenchurch held his gaze. 'I saw Mr Williams kill that girl.'

'When you chased him, he didn't leave your sight at any point?' A wink twitched in Unwin's eye.

31

Fenchurch looked away and rubbed at his neck. The ache in his foot went back up to ten. 'We're holding him overnight.'

'You can't do that.'

'Interview terminated at two minutes past eight p.m.' Fenchurch smacked the recorder's stop button. 'Just you watch me.'

Chapter Five

Reed looked up from her burrito, chewing slowly, a hand covering her mouth. She nodded at Nelson then Fenchurch. 'Sorry, guv, I was starving.'

'Don't worry.' Fenchurch glanced at Chilangos behind the crime scene tape, shuttered and dark inside. His gut growled. 'Suspect they had a lot of food going off.'

'Abi went home after she gave me her statement. She seemed, I don't know.' A shrug. 'Like you'd expect?'

'Right.' Fenchurch took out his mobile and dialled. Thing wasn't new enough for Qasid to steal. 'Back in a sec.' He stopped and waved at Reed, already deep in conversation with Nelson. 'See if you can get me a burrito, Kay? Anything but—'

'Simon?'

Fenchurch smiled at Abi's voice and clutched the phone tighter as he leaned against a street light. 'You okay, love?'

She paused on the line. The soft cooing of Dido filled the room she was in. Never a good sign. 'I've got work to do, I'm starving and I've just put some beans in the microwave. Toaster's on as well.'

'Dinner of champions.'

'Better than Mexican.'

'You don't really mean that.' Fenchurch grimaced through his smile. It was just coming off as fake. 'Do you want to talk about it?'

'I'm trying to process . . . what happened. And I'm . . . struggling.'

'You and me both, babe. Want me to come home?'

A pause. 'Have you charged him?'

'Lawyer's with him now. We'll get him for it, don't you worry.'

'I'm not worrying. It's just . . . Make sure he doesn't get off with this. That poor girl . . .' The music in the background faded to silence. 'I'll see you when you get in, love.' Click.

Fenchurch sucked in the cool air. The almost-summer weather hadn't lingered much past sundown. He wandered back over to Reed, his foot feeling slightly better — thank God for generic ibuprofen.

She waved a silver tube at him.

He snatched the burrito out of her hands, even colder than the air. 'Lifesaver.' He tore at the foil and bit into it. Prawn. *Great.* He swallowed it down regardless and focused on the spot where the victim had lain. Just a smear of blood, the question mark still visible. Nobody'd scrubbed the pavement, despite the pair of SOCOs folding away their tent. 'I take it Clooney's finished here?'

'Done and dusted.' Reed brushed a fleck of rice from her lip. 'Pardon the pun. Not got anything on her, either. Still missing her personal possessions.'

'He definitely took a bag and her phone.' Fenchurch sighed before taking another bite. 'What about the killer? You backed up my statement yet?'

'I've taken six now, guv. Arranging an ID parade at the station just now. I'll warn you now, guv, it's very difficult to confirm. People weren't watching for someone getting stabbed. You know how it is.'

'Don't I just.' Fenchurch indicated the area behind the Victorian buildings lining Upper Street. 'What about along the route he led me down?'

'Got uniform knocking on doors, guv. Nothing yet. We need to get a press release out soon.'

Nelson appeared. 'How much can you remember, guv?'

Fenchurch chewed down another mouthful and stared back in the direction of the tube station, trying to recreate the image in his mind. Don't let the CCTV footage colour it.

The young woman walking towards him, eyes switching between her phone and behind her. Her body language sent a fresh wave of goosebumps crawling up his arms.

Was it just her body language, the fear in her behaviour?

Or was Docherty right? Was it something else in her? The way she looked, who she reminded him of? Or who she should've reminded him of, who should've been about that age by now. Who might still be.

Then just a blur of motion. A bike bumping onto the pavement. The blade caught in the light and the wheels powering away, silent.

He swallowed down the last of the burrito. 'I can't see it any more, Jon.'

'Let's retrace your steps, guv.' Nelson clapped him on the shoulder. 'Start at the end and work our way back.'

⌣

'Constable.' Fenchurch nodded at the uniformed guard then leaned against the side wall of the lock-ups, looking up at the block of flats. Buxton Court, six floors of red brick, balconies jutting out on the right-hand side, all covered in washing. Faces peered down at them, ghosted by twitching net curtains. 'How are we doing here?'

The uniform cleared his throat. Kid looked like he needed a few more weeks at Hendon Training College. Acne scars and a wispy moustache, wanting to be one of the big boys now. And failing. 'We've been going door-to-door since seven, sir.' Even his voice was trying too hard, almost cracking at the depth he was pushing it to. 'We've obtained three statements at the last count.'

Fenchurch smiled at the lad, maybe not used to such a grilling. 'And do they back up mine?'

'Em.' The uniform sniffed. 'They said he came in the building through the front door. Then you chased him up to the fourth floor and caught him. Some phones clattered onto the ground. That's all I've got, nobody got a decent look at him as he entered.'

'Have you found anything between here and Angel?'

'Afraid not, sir.' The uniform's left index finger pressed down on a giant boil hooded by his lank hair.

The Boris bike still lay on its side, next to the cycle he'd borrowed. 'Get it dusted for prints, okay?'

'Sir. Oh, and the owner wants his bike back. He's causing merry hell up at Islington nick.' Another press on the boil. 'It's a cracker, sir. Specialized S-Works. Best part of six grand, that.'

'If that goes missing, Constable, you're for it.' Fenchurch let out a deep sigh and nodded at Nelson. 'Jon, I'm off for a walk. Bring the car round.' He set off along City Road, past the rubberneckers in their Volvos and Golfs, and rounded the petrol station. Turned out it was a Texaco — he couldn't even recall that. The Co-op, yes, but not the petrol station.

He remembered a drunken night in there years ago, trying to get a pork pie from a scared Asian man after the McDonald's shut. Thought they saw that guy who covered horse racing on the telly filling up an old Range Rover. Wasn't him.

Nothing from tonight, though.

Fenchurch stopped and stared at the traffic on the main road, headlights pulsing in waves. Just one long stretch from Old Street to Angel, yet another London thoroughfare trapped between two tube stations. For once, even the Northern Line was quicker than walking between the two.

Too dark now to recover a mental snapshot. Like at Upper Street, it just happened too fast. Too many events, too little time, focusing more on avoiding lorries and buses than capturing every single detail.

Nelson pulled up in his Vauxhall Insignia, sucking on his e-cigarette, the window wound down. 'Anything, guv?'

'Lots of things, Sergeant, just none of it particularly useful.' Fenchurch walked back towards the street, scanning around for anything Qasid could've tossed on the way. Nothing.

Then he trudged back onto City Road, Nelson keeping pace in the car. A hoarding across the way marked out yet another forthcoming development.

'All change round here, guv. Remember when it was all fields.'

'Worse than fields, Jon. Feral housing estates.' Fenchurch got in. Dub techno played from the speakers — deep, minimal, lots of white noise clattering around the electronics. He reached over and turned it off. 'Always in and out of them when I was in uniform. Little bastards could hide in the rabbit warrens in these places.'

Nelson pulled out and swerved across the oncoming traffic, heading towards Angel. 'Think this is any better?' He waved his hand around ahead of them.

The new towers above them seemed to be unoccupied. More like some futuristic Tokyo film than London. Certainly didn't look like anyone was at home on this side, let alone would've seen anything.

'It's just different.' Fenchurch tried to remember weaving through the bus lane on the bike. Shiny new buildings on the right, dirty old ones opposite. Some dodgy-looking little boozer. No detail, nothing useful. Nelson got into the right-turn lane, waiting for a break in the steady stream of vehicles. 'You remembered anything yet?'

'Square root of sod all.' Fenchurch had been quite close to Qasid as he turned, almost tyre-to-tyre. Kid definitely didn't drop anything. Definitely didn't have anything to drop. So where the hell were the phone and bag? Not to mention the knife.

Nelson trundled along Graham Street. Same story — Qasid ahead of him, powering down the road. The advantages of Fenchurch's purloined racer were more than offset by his old man's legs. His thighs still burned, even though his foot was barely twinging.

Nothing dropped, nothing on his person.

Past the park and round the bend. Low-rise new-builds in among older buildings, a mishmash of eras. A sixties council block glowed across the way, the dirty thump of a bass drum accompanied by a fug of ganja.

'Stop there.' Fenchurch pointed to the bike rack. 'The little punk got on one of these, didn't he?'

'Even with his hack code, it was a bit of a gamble, guv.' Nelson pulled in and killed the engine. 'Last time I rented one, it took me half an hour to get the bloody thing working.'

Fenchurch grabbed a torch and got out. A solitary street light above the row of bike stands. Only a couple of bikes had been returned. 'You know, I've seen the ghost van redistributing the bikes across the city after dark. Lets down the environmental aspect a bit, doesn't it?' He arced the beam around the dark street and swallowed down a sigh. 'This is near where I lost him the second time.'

Nelson's vape stick hovered over his mouth. 'You *lost* him?'

'For a split second.'

Nelson took a puff, the car fumes still spilling out. 'You're not a hundred per cent certain it's him, are you?'

'Eighty, ninety.' Fenchurch flashed the light across the bike racks. Nothing.

He can't have caught the wrong kid, surely? No way . . .

Wait — there.

Fenchurch jogged over to the last stand. A tote bag lay by a drain cover. Cream with blue lettering, stained dirty brown. He extended his baton and flicked at the bag, opening it wide. Six or seven iPhones or their clones. He looked up at Nelson. 'The little shit was definitely up to something, Jon. He wasn't wearing gloves. Get these done for prints.'

'Guv. I bet they've all been nicked tonight. Maybe we can find their owners.' Nelson put on a pair of nitrile gloves and lifted the bag, keeping it arm's reach. 'If this was the second time you lost him, where's the first?'

Fenchurch was standing where he'd stopped the car in Qasid's path. Colebrooke Row bent left at the end, Regency-style flats separated by the road and a thin strip of grass. 'You got anything?'

'Five pence in coppers, guv.' Nelson got up with a groan. 'No bags, phones or knives.'

'Qasid led me through the park up there, Jon.' Fenchurch got back in the car and slammed the door.

The car growled as Nelson stuck it in gear, strapping his seatbelt on as they set off past the grass where he'd climbed up. Torchlight danced behind the railings surrounding the small park, shining off the uniform search team and catching a panting Alsatian as it sniffed in a bare flower bed. 'I had sight of Qasid for the entire time. They won't find anything.' He tapped the windscreen as they trundled along the road, heading to a pedestrian crossing. 'Right here.'

Nelson swung onto the wider street and pulled in on the double yellows behind some panda cars. The park continued on the left, bigger and less like an afterthought.

Fenchurch got out and jogged over the road. He flashed his ID at the uniformed Sergeant guarding the entrance. 'Anything?'

'Nothing yet, sir. Well, certainly not what you're after.'

'Keep me posted.' Fenchurch stared past him at the squad going through the bushes. A street led back the way they'd come and headed further west. West-ish. He paced off down the pavement opposite the idling Vauxhall. 'He went this way, Jon.'

Nelson got in front of Fenchurch, slowing him down. 'So, you lost sight of him back there at the park entrance.'

'That's what I bloody said.' Fenchurch tried to nudge past but couldn't get through. He stood tall and sighed. 'What?'

'Guv, you told me you were eighty, ninety per cent certain. If he got out back there, he could've continued onto the next bit of the park, gone down Duncan Terrace in either direction or up Duncan Street towards Angel.' Anger flared in Nelson's eyes, tempered by disappointment, maybe. 'That's five different ways in addition to the one you thought he went.'

'But I *saw* him go this way, Jon.' Fenchurch barged past him and stopped at the crossroads where a thin wood lurked across from the park. He shone his torch through the trees. 'That's the canal there, right?'

'Remember we had to fish a body out of there a few years back?' Nelson frowned as he took another suck of his e-cig. 'There's a tunnel that lets you take your barge up to Camden. Comes out past Sainsbury's, I think.'

Fenchurch tried to picture Qasid running again. Had he been carrying anything? Her phone — was it really among the batch Qasid had on him?

The torch caught something. A glint sparkled just through the railings.

Fenchurch clambered over, his foot sending a jolt of pain as he landed.

'Found something, guv?'

'Not sure.' Fenchurch crouched down and directed the light at the ground, thick with undergrowth. There. He scrabbled around at the earth, torch hanging from his teeth, and cleared some space. The buckle of a handbag. He put a glove on and picked it up. It looked new. He showed it to Nelson. 'Call Kay and get her to check the statements about the bag.'

'Guv.' Nelson held up his Airwave and turned away.

Fenchurch tore through the contents. At least six different compartments. Lipstick. White phone charger cable. Enough tampons to last a hundred years. A lanyard with a work pass.

He shone the torch against it, heart pounding. The face on the photo vaguely matched the victim's. Early twenties. Blonde hair, though longer, more normal. None of that wedge shit.

Saskia Barnett. Worked at the *London Post* newspaper, by the looks of things.

Nelson reappeared. 'Guv, Kay's got statements from a couple sitting outside Chilango. The kid did nick her bag.'

Fenchurch stood up and passed it to Nelson. 'Get me an address for her.'

'Will do. Anything else of note in here?'

'Nothing.'

Nelson spoke into his Airwave, facing away.

Fenchurch looked back the way he'd chased Qasid. Was her phone lying there somewhere? Or was it in the tote bag?

Nelson turned around. 'Just checking, guv.'

'Get a team knocking on doors round here. I need the story confirmed.'

Nelson lifted the Airwave away from his face and frowned. 'Look at this place. It's dark as hell. No chance they'll have seen anything.'

'I need them to. And I need her phone found.'

'You're definitely sure it's the same kid we've got in the interview room? He could've escaped up the tunnel.'

'It's a canal, Sergeant.'

'So? Despite popular misconceptions, black men can swim.'

Fenchurch couldn't stop laughing. 'It was him, Jon. I'm sure of it.'

The Airwave crackled. 'Control to DS Nelson. I've got an address off Upper Street. Highbury end.'

Chapter Six

'Nice place.' Fenchurch pressed the bell and took a step back. A two-window wide townhouse, the mustard-yellow paintwork distinct from the gleaming white next door. Modern mews houses lined Napier Terrace, trees rustling in the wind, drowning out the distant rumble of backed-up traffic a few streets away.

He gave the entrycom another go. 'It's the police!'

It opened with a jolt. A middle-aged man scowled out into the night. Musketeer facial hair — a salt-and-pepper moustache with a thick square of beard below his thin lips. Tweed jacket over a pink shirt and red trousers. He gave them both the once over. 'Yes?'

'DI Simon Fenchurch.' He flipped out his warrant card and held it out for inspection. 'Does a Saskia Barnett live here?'

'She's not in.'

'But she lives here?'

'That's correct. What does this relate to?'

'Can I ask your name, sir?'

'Hugo Barnett.' A frown crawled over his forehead. 'Is Sas in trouble?'

'We should do this inside, sir.'

The drawing room was bigger than Fenchurch's old flat. Expensive paintings on the wall. Designer furniture, chunky and Scandinavian. He claimed a dimpled leather armchair by a tall window overlooking the street — would feel like a goldfish bowl when the neighbours peered in. 'Does anyone else live here?'

'Saskia's mother passed away two years ago. What's happened?'

Nelson was staying by the entrance. 'You should have a seat, sir.'

Hugo didn't seem to want to leave him. His frown deepened, like his forehead was fed up of his eyes looking at things. A hand went to his mouth, covering the beard. 'Is Saskia dead?'

Nelson's gaze flashed over to Fenchurch then back to Hugo with a nod. 'I'm afraid so, sir.'

Hugo let the tears out, flowing down his cheeks. 'My God. Sas . . .' He collapsed onto a Chesterfield sofa and seemed to disappear into it. Head bowed, shoulders slumped, rocking back and forth. His head shot up, eyebrows raised, eyes drilling into Nelson. 'How do you know it's her?'

'We'll need a formal identification but we found photo ID in her bag matching the body.' Nelson snatched a box of tissues from the top of an antique chest and placed them on the arm of the sofa, tearing one off for Hugo. 'She was robbed on Upper Street this evening. Her assailant stabbed her.'

Hugo thumbed at the window. 'All that traffic was because of her?'

Nelson gave a slight nod. 'I'm afraid so.'

'Have you caught the man who did this?'

'We believe we have, sir.'

Hugo shut his eyes, his teeth grinding together. He opened them again and locked his gaze on Fenchurch. 'What do you mean you *believe* you've caught her killer?'

'We need to make sure our case against this suspect is watertight, sir.' Fenchurch gave a warning glance to Nelson. 'We're in the process of dotting the I's and crossing the T's. We think she was killed for her phone, though we're investigating other possibilities. Is there anyone you can think of who held a grudge against your daughter?'

'Not off the top of my head.' Hugo's hands were clamped around the arms of the sofa. 'She was well liked. We were close but I can't think of anyone she even had a bad word to say about, you know? She was all I had left.' His face crumpled up. 'She's gone . . .'

Fenchurch took out his Airwave Pronto and unlocked the machine. He scribbled a few notes on the screen. 'Can I ask what you do for a living?'

Hugo stopped wiping his cheeks. 'I fail to see how that's relevant.'

'It pays to paint a solid picture of the victim in cases such as this. I've seen children killed because their parents worked for a bank, for instance.'

Hugo rubbed a hand across his nose. 'I'm the professor of Economics at Imperial College.'

'Anyone there who'd—'

'It's a university, Inspector. I teach students and, when I get a chance, I write papers.' Hugo balled up the tissue and tossed it at a bin, just missing. 'And before you ask, I'm not writing about the economics of ISIS or whatever we're supposed to call them this week.'

Fenchurch exchanged a frown with Nelson, the same curiosity blossoming in his eyes. 'Why do you bring that up?'

'I'm just being flippant with you. I have no reason to believe my daughter was involved with ISIS or anyone connected to it.' Hugo let out a despairing sigh. 'I'm sorry I mentioned it.'

Fenchurch stabbed it into the device. Maybe worthy of follow-up. Maybe not. 'It would be useful if we could get some background on her.'

'Where do I start?' Hugo dabbed at his eyes with the tissue. 'She's twenty-four. Worked as a journalist at *The London Post*. She's lived here since she finished university. Very difficult for people her age to get on the property ladder, these days. Even renting. And there's more than enough space in this old house.'

'Did she study in London?'

'Edinburgh.' Hugo reached forward for another tissue and blew his nose with a loud honk. 'Then a year doing her post-grad qualification in Leeds. Made sense for her to move back in after.'

Fenchurch made a note of it. Being a receptionist or in HR would've been neater. 'How was she getting on there?'

'She loved her job. Been there two years now. It's all she would talk about.'

'What about friends?'

'Some. Most of them are in Edinburgh. Some in Leeds. There are a few down here. She didn't keep in touch with people from school, as far as I'm aware.' Hugo sucked in air, his lip quivering. 'I could give you a list, if that'd help?'

'That would be good, sir.' Fenchurch stabbed the stylus on the screen, the typing just about keeping up with him. 'Was she seeing anyone?'

'There's a man on the scene. Young chap called Liam Sharpe. Been seeing him for a while now. Lives up in Hackney.'

'Thanks, sir.' Fenchurch got to his feet and stuck his Airwave back in his jacket pocket. 'I'll get a car to take you out to Lewisham to identify the body.'

'She's what?' Liam Sharpe was barely five eight tall, though he looked up with a glinting smile. Bright eyes full of humour. 'Dead?' The grin slipped into a frown. 'What?' His thick carpet of beard was getting into an argument with his T-shirt. Four heads bobbing out of a body of water with Slint written underneath. Some band, presumably. Thinning hair kept in check with a complex comb-over. 'You'd better come in.' His generic Northern accent could've come from anywhere in Yorkshire, maybe even County Durham or Nottinghamshire. Shoulders slumped, he trudged into the flat, his skinny-fit jeans thwapping louder than his flip-flops. Hairy hobbit toes.

Fenchurch followed Liam into a kitchen area. An IKEA headache of bright-yellow units and black-marble worktops. Restaurant-grade cooker and hob. Place reeked of skunk — expensive stuff, too. Didn't seem to care they could prosecute him for that. Didn't seem right to prosecute him, either.

'Jesus.' Liam squelched into an inflatable chair. A PlayStation controller rested next to a half-drunk bottle of craft beer on a coffee table. A giant flat-screen TV hung off the wall, Batman frozen in the middle of throwing his batarang. 'How can I help you catch whoever . . . did this to Sas?'

'We can start with a few questions.' Fenchurch leaned against the divider between the kitchen and the living area. Manga posters competed with moodier comic shots. Impossibly muscled men and impossibly proportioned women, all in body-tight spandex. 'You don't live together?'

'We had talked about it but it's so expensive, even round here. All this gentrification's supposed to be good for middle-class hipsters like me, but hey.' The smile returned then was beaten away by a frown. A hand ran through his hair, exposing the depth of his baldness. 'Sorry. This is hard to take.'

'Take as much time as you need, sir.'

'I'm fine, really.' Liam's jaw was pulsing, like he was grinding his teeth together. He let out a sigh. 'I had a couple of texts, pretty nothingy.'

Fenchurch made a note to follow up on them. 'Where were you between six and seven?'

'At work. I've just got back in.' Liam tapped the PlayStation controller. 'Was going to spend some quality time with Batman.' He started resetting his hair. 'Christ, sorry. How do you begin to process this?'

'Can anyone confirm your whereabouts?'

'My boss can. I work at the *Post*. Where I met Sas.' Liam finished with his hair, not quite back to its previous elegance. His hands started tugging his beard, paying particular attention to the walrus moustache. 'Why do you think she was killed?'

'Probably for her phone. Do you know what kind she had?'

'A Samsung Note. The one with the stylus. Not the most recent model, though. It was a two or a three? Couple of years old, anyway. I don't know — I'm an iPhone guy.' Another flash of smile. 'Didn't stop her asking me to fix it all the time. Here's the number.' He held out his own mobile. Saskia's contact card filled the screen, a few numbers and email addresses. There was a cute close-up selfie of her in the top left.

'We'll check to see if we've recovered it.' Fenchurch made a note to follow up on it. 'Is it possible someone could've targeted her?'

'It's certainly possible.' Liam nibbled at a fingernail, cut way past the quick. He pinched his nose. 'God, that can't be why they've done this. It just can't.'

Fenchurch frowned. 'What, you think it's because of her job?'

'Well, it's hard to process her just being randomly killed for a *phone.*'

'I understand, sir.' Fenchurch left a gap, but Liam just sat scowling at the controller. 'As she died, she said Kamal. Does that mean anything?'

'Should it?' Liam looked up, frowning. 'You think that's who stole her phone? Who killed her?'

'We don't know. It's not the name of the suspect we have in custody. Could Kamal be someone she'd met through work?'

'Maybe.' Liam gave a one-shouldered shrug. 'Sas was an investigative journalist. Had a tendency to piss people off. Never mentioned any threats. Might be worth speaking to her boss, though.'

Fenchurch stabbed it into his Pronto. 'Do you work for him as well?'

'Afraid not. I copy and paste people's tweets into stories, pretending it's news. She worked on Features. Proper journalism. The *Post*'s a twenty-four seven thing these days, though. Mr Morgan should still be there.'

'Have you got anyone who can be with you tonight?'

'My housemate's in Cardiff for the weekend.' Liam picked up the controller. 'Batman might take my mind off it.'

Chapter Seven

Fenchurch got out onto Fleet Street, just another road now. Pretty much all of the newspaper offices were gone. St Paul's glowed in the evening sky ahead while the old London stone sprawled behind. St Bride's was similarly lit, though hidden down a lane opposite. Didn't Rupert Murdoch get married there recently?

Nelson plipped the car doors locked and took a suck on his vape stick. 'Sure that'll be okay there?' It was sitting in a police bay halfway across, letting the taxis and cars flow freely either side.

'It's night, Jon, nobody cares.' Fenchurch stepped across the tarmac and jogged over to the office building. Giant oak doors led into a monolithic Georgian building underneath a curious circular window. The *Post*'s logo was etched into the left half of the glass, the right taken up with some start-up. He pressed the buzzer and glanced over at Nelson, busy working his Airwave Pronto. 'This must be one of the last papers here.'

'Last one, according to Wikipedia.' Nelson raised his handset, a more modern rendering of the *Post* logo hazing out into the dark night. 'Just got a note from Kay, as well. Saskia's old man identified the body. Good news, right?'

'Means we're not wasting time. Not much consolation to him, though.' Fenchurch hit the button again.

The door clicked open and Fenchurch entered into a big old hall, marble tiles and oak-panelled walls. A sprawling staircase led up into the heavens, next to an old-school Paternoster lift with a grille.

Where he expected a bored security guard was a female receptionist, behind a medium-height partition covered in the *Post* logo. Perfect posture, tapping away at a high-end desktop computer, as shiny as her blue nails. 'Good evening, sir?'

———

A middle-aged black man looked up from a laptop, his dark skin was greying as much as his hair, thick silver curls shining under the spotlights. His desk was filled with years' worth of crap. Stacks of papers, folders, reference books and enough pens to write the complete works of Shakespeare by hand. A mug near the front had 'Eric' written in a comic font, steam billowing out of the top.

Fenchurch flashed a smile and his warrant card. His foot was playing up again, throbs of pain pulsing through it. 'Eric Morgan?'

That got a smile. 'Eric's my husband.' He held out a hand, ink smudges almost covering the index finger. 'Victor Morgan.'

Fenchurch shook it and sat in front of the desk, just about seeing over the junk. A square window looked across Fleet Street at the art-deco weirdness of the Daily Express Building opposite. 'We need to ask a few questions about Saskia Barnett.'

'I heard about what happened.' Victor scowled, like he was sucking on a foul-tasting mint. 'Can't believe it, though.' He pushed the laptop away, closing the lid. 'She worked for me for two years. I'm the Features editor here and Sas was one of my investigative journalists. Young and hungry. And cheap enough that I could have two of them after the last round of cuts.' He picked up his mug and slurped stale coffee, by the smell of it. 'From what I heard, it sounded like someone killed her for her phone.'

'We have a suspect in custody, but we're keeping an open mind on the why. It might be useful to know if there was anything of note she was working on and eliminate, if necessary.'

'Well, Sas had a few things on her plate. Like me in a lot of ways.' Victor tapped at his temple, flashing a grin at them. 'Juggling too many stories is the only way to keep the old brain ticking over. Couldn't keep her focused on one story at a time, so I stopped trying. Keeps us fresh, I suppose.' He let out a breath and rifled through a sheaf of papers. 'She was working on a feature on one of London's UKIP MEPs. Guy Eustace.' He grimaced at the name, like it hurt him to say it out loud. 'Just something we'd been asked to do. And when I say ask, I mean told.'

'Is that Brexit stuff?'

'The owners of this paper have . . . certain sympathies, shall we say. Britain leaving the EU seems to be one of them.'

'Is it worth us speaking to Mr Eustace?'

'Not really. He's not a player, though he thinks he is. The piece was supposed to be gushing.'

'And was it?'

Victor's eyebrows danced upwards. 'She hadn't shared it with me.'

Fenchurch settled for adding a note to the case file. 'What else was she juggling?'

'There's a piece on some flats near her home. She'd like to keep them in public hands, but there's talk of them being sold off to a developer.'

Fenchurch glanced over at Nelson, frowning as he twisted his head to the side. 'Did she annoy any property companies?'

'Not sure. Regardless, I doubt I'll be allowed to publish the story, even if I wanted to. I told Sas to keep that one on the back burner.'

Victor held up his hands. 'I'm sorry, but that's all that springs to mind as contentious among the stuff she was working on.'

'What about recently published stories?'

'I think she only had five stories printed in the last month or so. All puff pieces. Advertorials.'

Nelson left the doorway and joined Fenchurch in front of the desk. 'Nothing inflammatory?'

'There was lots of that. I just didn't publish it.' Victor smiled as he crunched back in his seat. 'Sas kept herself to herself. Sent me the finished articles, checked off her sources and that was that.' Victor nodded and scribbled on a notepad. 'How about I look out some stories for you?'

'That'd certainly help.' Fenchurch added the reminder on his Pronto. He reclined in his seat and took another measure of the man. Didn't seem like he was hiding anything, but the information was just spewing out. Was it everything? Was there anything else? He slid the Pronto's stylus onto the cradle. 'Do you know a Liam Sharpe?'

'Good kid. Saw him this evening for a coffee between meetings. You don't think he had anything to do with this, do you?'

Fenchurch gave a non-committal shrug. 'Just want to keep an open mind.'

'He's the opposite of Sas in so many ways. She was deadly serious, but I never saw him without that stupid grin. Kid's like a puppy.' Victor shook his head, eyes flickering. 'He tell you what he does all day? Copying and pasting tweets, posting photos of actresses on the beach. And their children. It's not proper journalism but it's what passes for news these days.' A tight grimace fixed his face. 'Our website is the third biggest in the US, behind the *Mail* and the *Guardian*. Can you believe it?'

Fenchurch didn't know what to make of it. 'Ever heard of the name Kamal?'

'You know, she mentioned it once or twice.' Victor looked around the rubbish on his desk, like the answer was buried around the fifth paperweight. 'Norwegian company, right?'

'I was thinking it was a name. Arabic, maybe. Kamal.' Fenchurch let it hang in the air. 'She said it as she died.'

'Christ.' Victor's Adam's apple bobbed up and down. 'Actually, now I think about it, it's Kjaer Oil. She did a feature on their greenwashing last year. Planting trees instead of clearing up a spillage.'

'So, Kamal doesn't mean anything?'

'Sorry.'

'We're trying to retrace her last movements, sir.' Nelson was dragging his stylus across his Pronto's screen. 'What appointments did she have today?'

'There was something.' Victor frowned, deepening already yawning lines. 'Let me check.' Pen between his teeth, he opened his laptop and clattered the keys. 'Here we go. I've got access to her calendar. Here's the last appointment.' He wrote it on a Post-It and handed it over. Completely illegible.

'Can you print it for us?'

'Sure thing.' Another click of the mouse then he reached through the pile of crap for an old printer as it hummed to life. He gave the warm sheet to Fenchurch. 'She was visiting Iconic Property Development at five. Their office is in Mayfair, I believe.'

The page was a calendar for the last week, filled with appointments. Fenchurch passed it to Nelson, along with a look that said 'check all of these out'. He nodded at Victor. 'Any idea what it was about?'

'Supposed to be speaking to the owner about her charitable foundation.'

Chapter Eight

'Cheers, Kay.' Fenchurch killed the call and put his Airwave in the footwell. 'They've still not found her phone yet, Jon.'

They were stopped at the set of lights at the end of Grosvenor Street. A late-night jogger bounded across the crossing. Ahead, the flags of a couple of embassies flapped in the breeze. Through the trees, the American Embassy was keeping a low profile, looking just like a normal office block.

'Typical.' Nelson gripped the wheel tight. 'What's on your mind, guv?'

'About Morgan? It's a dead end, Jon.' Fenchurch clutched the grab handle a little bit tighter. 'But me thinking it isn't enough. It needs nipping in the bud.'

'Before it blossoms?' Nelson kicked into gear and set off. A van merged in out of nowhere from the left, getting a honk on the horn for its troubles. 'What about this Kamal geezer?'

'We don't know anything about him, Jon.' Fenchurch grimaced, eyes shut. 'Could just be Abi mishearing.' Nelson pulled into the second of two disabled bays outside a thin townhouse.

Fenchurch got out and took in the building as Nelson knocked on the door. The street level looked empty, but there were lights on upstairs. The old ground-floor windows had been defaced with adverts for expensive apartments, high-end developments in the East End and lining the Southbank. All gleaming new-build things, curved steel and glass. A million miles from the old London of the Mayfair street they were in. Not that they were much cheaper.

He gave it another knock and took a step back. 'There's nobody here, Jon.'

Nelson spoke into his Airwave: 'Control, it's DS Jon Nelson. Can I get an address for a Yana Ikonnikova?'

———————

Nelson parked on Eaton Square, wedging his Vectra into a row of six Range Rovers. Walled-off gardens sat between two long rows of Regency opulence, criss-crossed by a few roads. 'Used to work round here.'

'Management consultancy war stories again?' Fenchurch opened the door and stepped out onto the pavement. Could almost see the slivers of gold in the concrete. The chinking of shattered glass and drunken laughter came from the gardens. 'Sounds like kids in there.'

'Homeless, more like. Prime location. Wake up here, head down to Knightsbridge to beg outside Harrods first thing.'

The address they had was for a townhouse spanning double the width of the rest. Ornate mouldings ran between the fourth and fifth storeys. The columned entrance on the left was repeated halfway over, but the doorway was replaced with a window, the walkway cut off and the intervening odd number deleted from existence. Railings barred the lower-ground floor. 'Saw an article in the *Standard* last year about an Arab prince owning a flat in this neck of the woods. He was trying to sell the leasehold for three and a half years. Guess how much?'

'Half a million?' Nelson gave him a wink. 'Saw the same article, guv.'

Fenchurch grunted. 'Reckoned the place was worth eighteen million or something stupid. That's just a *flat*.' He looked the building up and down again. 'Must be ten flats in there?'

'Hundred and eighty mill.' Nelson shifted his gaze around the place. 'Like a private country round here. Duke of Westminster used to own it all, but he's had to sell up, I think. Doubt there's many English tenants left.'

Fenchurch marched up to the front door and hammered the bell.

It swung open and a wall of muscle stood there, fingers pressing an earpiece. He wore the sort of suit you'd see standing a few feet behind the US President. 'What do you want?' Deep Slavic accent, maybe Russian, maybe somewhere that used to be part of Yugoslavia.

'We're looking for a Yana Ikonnikova.'

'She's not expecting anyone.'

Fenchurch flipped out his warrant card. 'Police.'

The hired muscle turned around and spoke into his sleeve. He gave a tight nod and stood up tall. 'Come inside.'

Fenchurch trotted past him into the hall.

Two similar-looking guards surrounded a shiny grand piano, standing on a chequerboard floor from a Disney cartoon. Three gleaming chandeliers hung low, surrounded by a spiral staircase, the marble sparkling in the light. Expensive-looking artwork covered the plain white walls, though the person who'd put it together had even less taste than Fenchurch.

The guard grabbed him from behind and started a pat down, another one giving the same treatment to Nelson.

Fenchurch craned his neck round. 'You know that's not legal, right?'

'Maybe not, but I assure you it is necessary if you want to speak to Ms Ikonnikova.'

Fenchurch let him finish, muscular fingers kneading up and down his arms and legs. 'You've just saved me a packet on a deep-tissue massage, mate. Cheers.'

That got a grunt. The guard led them past the staircase into a wide room, running front to back. Dark like a Paris wine bar, just a single light hanging low.

A woman perched on a stool in the middle, fondling a tablet computer. She swirled what looked and smelled like neat vodka around the crystal tumbler, the sole ice cube chinking off the sides. A dainty sip and then she looked up at the guard. 'Thank you, Yevgeny.'

'Of course.' He tilted his head and took up a position by the door. Easier to walk through the wall than through him.

Despite the late hour, Yana Ikonnikova wore a trouser suit, navy pinstripe with a lilac blouse. Salon-perfect hair framed the Slavic curve of her face, blonde curls fixed in place. She narrowed her eyes at Fenchurch, a look that could curdle milk. Or blood. 'What business do the police have in my home?' Polished Russian accent, a million miles away from the Hollywood cliché.

Fenchurch looked around for a seat, couldn't find one. 'Thanks for granting us an audience, Ms Ikonnikova.'

'I recognise sarcasm, Mr Fenchurch.'

He swallowed, drums beating a light pattern in his ears. 'You know my name?'

She gave a nod. 'My men are trained well and information flows quickly among us. Now, how can I help?'

'Does the name Saskia Barnett mean anything to you?'

Yana took a sip of vodka and nibbled at her ruby-red bottom lip. 'I gave her an interview this evening at my company's office in Mayfair. Saskia left long after six, maybe? I had to cut it short because I'm running a charity event for my foundation later and some things needed my attention.'

'What was she asking about?'

'My foundation.' A weary sigh into her vodka. 'I spend my hard-earned money on causes which support people less fortunate than me. We're having an event on my yacht in St Katharine Docks.' She smirked over the open mouth of her glass. 'You're welcome to join us.'

Fenchurch found himself grinning at her. 'I know it well but I'll pass on it just now.' He let the grin fade to a frown, heat burning in his cheeks. 'I gather from your accent you're not from round here?'

'Moscow.' Her smile slipped away, restoring the icy grimace. 'But I make a lot of money here. It's good to, how you say, give back to the land?'

'I'm sure it is.' Fenchurch tried for another smile, but it fell flat on its face. 'How did Ms Barnett seem?'

'First time I met her. She was matter of fact, yes? Just asked questions, wrote down answers. How I like it. I hate it when I get all this . . .' Yana scowled and waved a hand around in the air. 'Sugar-coating. Massaging my ego. I prefer it kept straight.' She finished the vodka and rested the glass on the table with an expensive sounding thud. 'Why so many questions about this girl?'

'She was killed this evening.'

A hand went to Yana's mouth. She swore in Russian, something harsh and guttural. 'Such a shame.'

'When did you last see her?'

Yana clicked her fingers, jaw clenched tight. 'Yevgeny, come here.'

The hired muscle prowled across the room, hands clasped behind his back. Eyes darting around, assessing targets. 'Yes?'

'When did she leave, this Saskia?'

'Seventeen thirty. Asked me which tube station to use. I didn't know.'

Yana beckoned him away again with a flick of her wrists. 'My office assistant deals with all that. I remember now.' She snapped her fingers again. 'She told her to walk up to Green Park, had to swap lines somewhere. I would've sent her in my car, but I needed it to get to my yacht.'

Chapter Nine

'A bloody yacht, Jon.' Fenchurch crawled up the back stairs and pushed onto their floor. 'I bet it's a sixty-footer.'

Nelson held the door open. 'You jealous?'

'Not really. If I had that sort of money, I'd be living in Spain or Greece, not bloody London.'

'You could sail your yacht down to the Algarve, get in some golf.' Nelson took a final suck on his vape stick then pocketed it. 'Know how much you love golf.'

'Don't get me started.' Fenchurch pushed through the door into the long corridor, Docherty's office at the end. 'Anyway, I need to get in and have a word with the DCI before— Shit.'

A wraith-like figure crept up to the office door from the side corridor, wrapping a black scarf tight around its neck. DI Dawn Mulholland.

Fenchurch ran a hand across his forehead. 'She's crawled out of the coffin early tonight.'

'Jesus, guv, you need to bury the hatchet.' The vape stick was back out. Nelson tapped it in Fenchurch's direction. 'And I mean in the earth, not in her neck.'

Fenchurch waved a hand at the closing door. 'Look at her, Jon. Sneaking in there ahead of me, just to score points.'

'Maybe you need to stop seeing it that way.'

'She'll be trying to take the case away from me, as per bloody usual.'

'I said, maybe you need to stop seeing her in that light.'

'The only light I'd like to see her in is daylight. Watch her skin burn or whatever it is happens to bloody vampires.' Fenchurch marched off down the corridor, hands deep in his pockets. 'See you later, Jon.'

———

'Right, right, right.' Docherty crunched back in his office chair and put his hands behind his head. 'Well, we are where we are, I suppose.'

DI Dawn Mulholland sat next to him. Still perma-tanned, still pouting like she had photos of Fenchurch in a compromising position. Her long dark hair was becoming one with her ever-present scarf.

Fenchurch folded his arms, narrowed his eyes at Docherty. 'What's that supposed to mean?'

'We're in a reasonably good place, I guess. Considering you've had the case, what . . .' Docherty checked his watch. The gold thing looked like it weighed more than he did. 'Four hours? Not bad. Press release has gone out and there's a proper news conference scheduled for tomorrow morning at ten. You don't have to attend, if you don't want to.'

'I'd rather not, but thanks for the invite.'

Docherty shook his head. 'So, your victim ruffled some feathers, aye?'

'I think her job's a dead end, sir.'

'Are you sure about that?' Mulholland twisted round to glare at Fenchurch. Not so much a voice that could cut glass but make the stuff from sand. 'You know what happens to assumptions.'

'Which is why I want to exclude it.' Fenchurch still couldn't look at her for longer than a few seconds at a time, in case he turned into stone. He stood up and rested his hands against the back of the chair. 'Her editor sent over links to all the stories she's published in the last month. We're tracking down her friends and we're digging into the boyfriend's background.'

'He suspicious?'

'You know me, sir. Everyone's suspicious. But I want to eliminate him.'

'We can also get CCTV of her journey from Mayfair to Angel.' Mulholland was fiddling with her Pronto. 'Looks like she came out of the tube. I want to know where she went in, which lines she took, where she was before she got on. I want everything nailed down.'

Fenchurch gripped the seat back hard. 'And we should take a look at Iconic Property. See if there's anything funny going on there.'

'Like what?' Mulholland lowered her Pronto and swung round. 'You don't like this Ikonnikova woman, I get that. But in what way was she suspicious?'

Fenchurch kept his focus on Docherty. 'She's got a private army, boss. Thinks she bloody owns this city. She's heading down to St Kath's Docks in a *motorcade*.'

'She probably does own half of London.' Docherty shrugged his shoulders and gave a laugh. 'Well, the bits you'd want to own, anyway.'

'Yeah, the bits we don't have to police.'

'You can get home.' Docherty nodded at Mulholland. 'You know the drill. Hand over to Dawn and team.'

Fenchurch still couldn't bring himself to look at her. 'I want to stay.'

Mulholland leaned forward, the pout catching his peripheral vision. 'For what purpose, Simon?'

'We've got witnesses. And all those phones we recovered. Someone needs to supervise the Forensics lads on that.'

'I know I have to keep telling you this, but I've got three DIs for a reason.' Docherty waved at Mulholland. 'Dawn's team are running the night shift. End of. You get yourself home.'

'Right.' Fenchurch got up, feeling weighed down by a load he couldn't budge. He ducked his head at her, trying to keep it civil. 'Let's catch up first thing, yeah?'

'Of course.' She raised her eyebrows, creating deep fissures in her forehead. 'From what Alan told me earlier, I suspect Abi might need you at home?'

Fenchurch flared his nostrils. 'Right.'

Mulholland got up and adjusted her scarf. Always the same one, like she was hiding a vampire bite or something. 'I'll get back to chasing up your loose ends, Simon. This case is becoming frayed already.'

'What loose ends?'

The pout appeared again, making her mouth look like a bill. 'Your suspect isn't definite, is he?'

'Oh, he did it, all right.' Fenchurch locked eyes with her. Felt like she could steal his soul just by looking. 'I need you to work with me here, not against me.'

'Excuse me?'

'Break it up, you two.' Docherty was on his feet, just a stripy shirt away from being a boxing referee. 'You're like a pair of bloody children. Dawn, give us a minute here.'

'Very well.' Mulholland left the room, the scarf billowing behind her like ink in water. Just needed a broomstick and a black cat.

'I need evidence, Si.' Docherty slumped back in his chair, bitter disappointment all over his face. He gulped coffee from his sky-blue

Rangers mug, chipped and faded from repeated assaults from the station dishwasher. 'I need something more than you telling me he did it. Show me, aye?'

'That's what I'm trying to do here.'

'Remember this is a favour, Simon. You asked me to take this case on. I've had the pleasure of spending three hours arguing the toss over at the Yard.'

Fenchurch looked at his shoes. A little scuff mark on the leather where Qasid had stamped. 'Boss, this is the only way I can cope with what I saw. He killed a woman right in front of me.' He rubbed at his forehead. 'I need to bring that little scrote to justice.'

'Scrote.' Docherty bellowed with laughter. 'Christ, Si, what are you? Something from *The Bill*?'

A smile forced its way onto Fenchurch's lips. 'We need to get evidence and snare him.'

'That's my boy.' Another slurp from the Rangers mug. 'Dawn's looking into it. The results will be on your desk before tomorrow's briefing.' Docherty grinned at him. 'Now get home to your wife. You've only been remarried a couple of months.'

'Three.' Fenchurch glanced at his wedding ring, the old gold band reworked to a fine sheen. Who knew how long that'd last? 'I'll head home after I've chased up Clooney.'

———————

Fenchurch nudged open the door to his office. Mulholland wasn't in her chair but . . . He leaned against the jamb. 'Why are you in my office?'

Mick Clooney sat at Fenchurch's desk, now covered in a tangle of IT equipment. He brushed a hand across his shaved head while the other fiddled with the ear piercings, at least one of them looked fresh and raw. The long sleeves of his Levellers T-shirt rode up, showing his other sleeves, the footballer tattoos covering his arms. 'DI Mulholland said you wouldn't mind.'

'Did she now?' Fenchurch got his Airwave out, tempted to type out a bitchy text to Mulholland. No messages from Reed or Abi, so he shoved it back in his pocket. 'Well, I've been hunting high and low for you, Mick. Feel like that guy in the A-ha video, turning into a comic book.'

'That was "Take On Me", Simon, not "Hunting High and Low". Same album, though.'

'Quite the expert.' Fenchurch walked over and tapped the bagged Samsung plugged into a laptop. 'They got you retraining?'

Clooney stretched out and yawned. 'Another string to my bow, or whatever it is.' He tossed a mobile in the air and caught it. 'Our jobs will be looking at computers and phones rather than dusting crime scenes. Five years max, you mark my words.'

'As long as you bark when I come calling, I don't care.' Fenchurch rested against his desk. 'What have you got for me?'

'Nothing.' Clooney unplugged the Samsung from his laptop and tossed it over to the others. 'They're all wiped. Reset back to factory condition. Everything's gone from them. Happens all the time.'

Fenchurch scanned through the mobiles. What model did Saskia own? Samsung something or other. 'Have you got hers?'

'Afraid not. Jon Nelson told me she had a white Galaxy Note. None in here. Just iPhones and Galaxy S5s and 6s. Got one of the Edge ones, as well.' He held up a large smartphone with a curved screen stretching to both sides. 'Not sure what the point of this is, but I imagine you pay through the nose for it. And I bet it kills the battery.'

'Pay through the nose for everything these days.' Fenchurch reached over and grabbed his West Ham scarf from the top of his monitor. He balled it up like he used to at Upton Park. The Boleyn Ground, according to his old man. He stretched it out, resetting the fabric to just the way he liked it. 'So it's definitely possible she's been killed over a theft?'

'Well, hers isn't here and she's in the morgue, so yeah.'

'Cheeky.' Fenchurch put the scarf back on top of his monitor. 'I mean . . .' He pinched the bridge of his nose. 'Actually, I don't know what I mean.'

'You found fifteen of them but her phone's still missing.'

Fenchurch stared at the mobiles covering the desk. 'So where is it?'

'Your job, not mine.' Clooney held up an old Motorola, the one Nelson had shown Qasid. 'This one's definitely a burner, though.'

'That's his, right?'

'Yup. Should be able to access the contents.'

'Jon already checked it. Just been dialling the same number by hand.'

'Like my old mum does, bless her.' Clooney stared at the mobile. 'It's not what's on here now, Simon, it's what used to be there.'

'I'm not following you.'

'By the powers vested in me, I can undelete texts and emails.' Clooney held the handset up to the light, squinting at it. 'Assuming this thing even does email.' He plugged it into his laptop.

Fenchurch walked over to the window and dialled Abi's number. He listened to the dialling tone as he stared out across Leman Street. A lone taxi trundled past. The white lights made the new student flats opposite gleam. A piss artist staggered down the opposite side, bumping into a lamp post and shouting after the cab.

It just rang through to voicemail. 'Ab, it's me. Give me a call, okay?' He pocketed his mobile and watched the drunk weave his way down the street.

Why wasn't her phone among the fifteen they'd found? How had Qasid dumped it? And where?

Fenchurch shut his eyes. *Had* he dumped it?

His Airwave buzzed. Mulholland. 'Simon, can you attend the ID parade?' No greeting or formality just wind thumping against the microphone.

'Docherty said you were to handle everything. Don't want to get in the way.'

'He also said you were still around. It starts at half past eleven.'

Fenchurch checked the time — just another ten minutes. 'Fine, I'll attend. Where are you? The crime scene?'

'That's right.'

'Well, I'm with Clooney just now. We're still missing the victim's phone. Can you prioritise finding it?'

'They've been searching between Upper Street and Colebrooke. I assume you want them to look elsewhere?'

'Please.' Fenchurch ended the call and locked the device. He went over to his desk and looked over Clooney's shoulder. Couldn't work out what the hell he was doing. He cleared his throat, making the SOCO jump. 'You deal with much phone theft?'

'A few times.' Clooney craned his tattooed neck round, pierced eyebrow raised. 'Why?'

'This kid looks like he was in a gang, right?'

'Bit of an assumption, but let's go with it. There are gangs of kids out nicking smartphones. Every night, Simon.'

'You ever deal with the team looking into it?'

Clooney let out a sigh. 'I know where you're going with this.'

'Where?'

'The Mobile Phone Theft Unit out in Mile End. Speak to them all the time.'

Fenchurch clapped a hand onto his shoulder. 'Set up some time with them, would you?'

'Sure thing.'

'Who's the DI?'

'Jason Bell.'

'Stringer? Christ, we went to Hendon together.'

'Be like old times, then. Still want me to set it up?'

'If you could. I prefer avoiding the old pal's act.'

Fenchurch opened the door to the VIPER Identification suite. The darkened room was filled with high-end computer workstations, just one analyst looking like they were doing any work.

At the far end, a window looked onto another room. Five young black men stood in a row, all wearing grey hoodies, black trackies and deep scowls. The one in the middle had cornrows. A squint showed it was Qasid. The others had a mixture of shaved heads and flat tops.

Two figures were silhouetted in the glow. 'Simon?' The one on the left turned round and a shard of light caught her face. Abi.

Fenchurch set off towards her. 'Thought you were at home, love?'

'And I came in.' Her eyes swivelled around the room, like she could feel the years of hate and anger in the building. 'No way I can sleep with this going on.'

The other figure nodded at him. 'Guv.' Kay Reed. She smiled at Abi. 'So, do you recognise any of them?'

Abi took another look at the men and shrugged. 'I can't tell. It all happened so fast. And it was dark. And the bloody hood was up.'

'We've had the hoods up and down.'

Abi shot her a glare. 'It didn't help me, though, did it? Jesus, Kay.'

'Hey, it's okay.' Reed rubbed Abi's arm. 'Don't worry. It's fine.'

'Sorry, I'm being a bitch, right?' Abi slumped back against the wall, switching her frown between her husband and her friend.

'I've seen worse from you.' Reed nodded at the analyst behind her. 'Jack, that'll do.'

Fenchurch was glaring at the men through the window. 'You don't recognise any of them?'

'Simon, I don't remember.' She shut her eyes, tears caught in the glow from the other room. 'I'm really sorry but I don't remember. I was stuffing that bloody book in my bag when he cycled past.'

'It's fine.' Fenchurch held her in his arms, tugging her close to his chest. Her hair was damp from rain, the wildflowers joined by ozone. 'I'll give you a lift home, love. Just need a few seconds, if that's okay?'

Abi broke off and looked up at him. 'Right.'

'A minute at most. Okay? Wait here.' Fenchurch nodded at Reed then the door. He followed her out, pushing it shut behind him. His eyes started adjusting to the corridor's brightness. 'Mulholland said I was to supervise?'

'See, that's what I'm always telling you, guv. She always goes over our heads. Doesn't think me or Jon can do anything.'

'I'll see what I can do about that.' Fenchurch sighed — yet more fun and games to come. 'You need anything else from—'

'Inspector?' Dalton Unwin stormed down the corridor, his jowls wobbling. Podgy fingers clutched a leather briefcase, looked as well tailored as his suit. 'My client's human rights are being ritually abused here.'

'This is due process for a murder suspect, sir. You'd know that if you'd covered one before.' Fenchurch loomed over him, trying to intimidate the little worm. 'No idea how the hell you got here but this is a restricted area. I request you leave immediately.'

'My client is innocent and I demand you let him go.'

'He's guilty and you know it.'

'You've got no evidence.'

'We're holding him here overnight and that's the end of the story. Okay?'

Unwin clutched his briefcase to his chest and tilted his head to the side. 'Want me to get Amnesty in here?'

'That won't be necessary, sir. We're operating well within the law.'

'I know people, Fenchurch.'

'Then I hope those people tell you to let us get on with our jobs.'

'My client's done nothing other than be assaulted by you. Repeatedly.'

'He was resisting arrest after he murdered a young woman. Need I remind you that we found a load of stolen mobile phones on him. With a good wind behind us, we might be able to return them to their rightful owners.'

Unwin backed off and stood up tall. 'You'll be hearing about this from your superiors.'

Reed's eyes trailed Unwin down the corridor and she shuddered. 'What a creep.'

'He's a criminal defence lawyer, Kay. Comes with the territory.' Fenchurch couldn't bring himself to look at him again. He put a hand to the door. 'Time for you to get home before you turn into a pumpkin.'

'Yeah, soon, guv. I want Dave to see what it's like managing our bloody kids when *he* works late.' She grimaced. 'But first, I need to kick someone's arse about letting Unwin up here.'

Chapter Ten

Fenchurch pulled off City Road onto Islington High Street and stopped at the lights. The traffic was now flowing freely after the incident. Just a solitary officer guarded the crime scene now. Gawkers hung around trying to see whatever they could.

He glanced over at Abi. Distorted patches of sodium yellow lit up parts of her face, the corners of her mouth downturned. 'You okay, love?'

'Thank God we're out of that place.' She ran a hand through her hair and let it settle back over her ears. 'How can you work there?'

'What's so bad about it?'

'It's just . . .' She shut her eyes and shook her head in a long, slow arc. 'I'm not okay.'

'Talk to me. That's what you always tell me, right?'

She shot him a glare. 'I can't process what happened, Simon.' She waved a hand down the street. 'I watched her die right there. Saskia.'

'I know what you saw.' Fenchurch reached a hand over and patted her knee, cold through her tights. 'Believe me, I know how bad that feels. Watching someone's life just drain away like that.' The lights changed and he set off, turning onto Liverpool Road. Not far from home now. 'It gets easier over time, that's all I can say.'

'It's now I'm worried about.'

'Did you want me to stay with you at the crime scene?'

'It's not that.' She bit her lip, looking like she'd slice all the flesh off. 'I don't know. Simon, it's . . . I couldn't do anything.'

'Neither could I and I'm trained to be able to. All I could do was chase him. I couldn't stop her dying.'

She folded her arms and looked away. 'At least you can do something now.'

'You did something, Abi. You gave a statement, you helped at the ID parade.'

She laughed, nothing like humour. 'But I couldn't pick him out. Not on the screen and not through that bloody window.' Her mouth hung open. 'I've let everyone down, haven't I?'

Fenchurch swung right just after the crowded bulk of the Business Design Centre. He pulled in outside their flat and killed the engine. 'You did the right thing. Listen, these kids wear that gear to hide themselves. Hoodies, baseball caps, baggy clothes, whatever it is. Urban camouflage. They do it to stop people recognising them.'

Dull streetlight spread across her face, showing her closed eyes. 'I should've done more.'

'I was much closer to what happened. You'd been in that shop. I watched it. It should be me beating myself up, not you.'

She sucked in air and looked up at the car roof. 'Did you ID him?'

'After what I've done tonight, I'd be breaking all sorts of rules.'

'So, you're just going to let him go free?'

'I'm not going to let that happen.'

'But he's going to get away with this, isn't he?' She looked over at him, the streetlights adding creases to her frown. 'If I told them it was that kid, he'd be going to jail for it. Should I have said I recognised him?'

'You saw what you saw. You've got to tell the truth, love. No matter what. Okay?'

'But it's my fault if he's not going away.'

'It's nobody's fault.'

'Bullshit. It's on my shoulders.'

'Hey. Stop blaming yourself, okay? You were with her when she died.' He let his hand go from her knee. 'Have we got any wine in?'

'Is that the answer? Get pissed?' She was glaring at him now. 'Is that what you were doing before we got back together? A bottle of wine every night?'

'I just wouldn't mind a glass, that's all. Give me a bit of distance.'

She bunched up her hair again. 'I opened a Merlot earlier. It wasn't any use.'

'Hopefully it'll have had a chance to breathe.'

'That's not what I meant.' She got out of the car and slammed the door behind her.

Fenchurch watched her unlock the front door, twisting the keys a bit too hard.

Same as it ever was . . .

He got out and zapped the car. Shouting came from Upper Street — drunken office boys up to Thursday night malarkey. A car alarm blared a few streets away.

He managed to catch the door before it clicked shut and trudged up the stairs towards their floor, shoulders low.

Abi was bending down outside their flat. Someone had dumped an Amazon package on their doormat. She scowled at him as she opened the door. 'Looks like it's for you.'

'It'll be those books.'

'You need to get a Kindle, Simon. There's too many books in this bloody flat.'

'I know, I know.'

The door across the hall crept open. 'Simon, can I have a word?'

Fenchurch closed his eyes and stifled a groan. Then swung round with a smile plastered on his face. 'Quentin, how can I help?'

'It's about the stone cleaning. I put three quotes through your door last night.'

'Now's not the time.'

'Listen, Simon, I don't think you understand how severe this is. This is the only block on the street that hasn't been cleaned. There could be any amount of damage being done to the brick.'

Fenchurch took a step back. 'I'll look at it over the weekend, okay?'

'There's an urgency—'

'Not. Now.' Fenchurch went into the flat and kicked the door behind him. Same as it bloody ever was. He shrugged his suit jacket and shoes off and padded through to the kitchen. Abi had dumped the package on the counter. He tore it open. Both those Edward Snowden books Clooney had been on about. He uncorked the wine and took a sniff of the deep tang. Good, even though it was Merlot. He poured a fresh glass and topped up Abi's half-empty one.

She was leaning back against the new fridge. Staring into space, nibbling her lip again.

He wrapped his arms around her and pulled her forehead into his chest. 'I love you, Mrs Fenchurch.'

'That still sounds funny. After all those years.' She stared down at her left hand. The reforged wedding band sat next to a new engagement ring, ten times the bling of the original. She looked up at him, tears welling in her eyes again. 'What happened tonight . . . I can't stop thinking about Chloe. How I couldn't do anything there.'

'Hey, hey.' Fenchurch pulled her close. 'It's okay. I know what's going on in that head of yours.'

'How the hell can you?'

'Because it's going on in mine. There's nothing we can do other than try to cope with it. That's what you told me.' Fenchurch pulled her tight again. 'Someone kidnapped our daughter from that bloody road out there. That means she's out there. Somewhere.'

She nudged away from him. 'Are you going to let it eat up your soul again?'

'It's never stopped eating me up.'

'Jesus Christ.' Abi pushed away and grabbed her wine. She rubbed away a red bead dribbling down the outside and took a long drink. 'Simon, you need to be honest with me. Are you still looking for her?'

'No. I swear I'm not.'

'You told me that before.'

'It's the truth.' Fenchurch took another drink and put the glass down. 'That wasn't Chloe lying there on the pavement but it's someone else's daughter. He's a professor at Imperial. Posh git, but he's lost his kid. I want to find out who killed her. And why.'

Thousand yard stare as she sipped more wine. This wasn't going away anywhere fast.

'Look, Ab, I've got the case now. I'm going to make sure this Qasid kid goes down for it.'

'Qasid? That's his name?'

Fenchurch slapped a hand to his forehead. 'Shit, I shouldn't have told you that.'

'I'll try to forget. Have you done your mindfulness today?'

He swallowed. 'Not yet.'

'Go on . . .'

'Come on, Abi . . .'

She wagged a finger at him. 'Now.'

'Right, right.' He set the half-empty glass on the counter. 'I'll just go and visualise a bloody spark of light in the middle of my chest.'

'Just don't fall asleep like you usually do.'

Day 2
Friday, 22nd April 2016

Chapter Eleven

'Got a little present for you, Simon.' Docherty was leaning against the Nautilus machine in the station's basement gym. His puny frame looked like he could barely lift the handle let alone any weights. 'You'll thank me for it.'

Fenchurch pulled down on the bar, grinding pain through his shoulders. 'You've sacked DI Mulholland?'

'You need to quit that. Makes you look like a petty sod.'

'I am a petty sod, boss.' Fenchurch grunted at another pull down. 'What is the present?'

'Got an extra skull for your daytime team.'

Fenchurch clamped his eyes shut. Nine, ten. He let the bar up and rested the weights against the stack. 'Who?'

'DC Lad.'

Fenchurch brushed his towel across his face. 'I've only just got shot of him.'

'Dawn thought he'd be a better fit for your team.'

'I'll bet she did.' Fenchurch ran the towel through his hair and draped it round his neck. Thank God there wasn't a mirror down here. 'The guy's a liability, boss. I need people I can rely on, not that clown.' He reached up for the handle. 'I've not got to the bottom of it, but someone made a mess of those witness interviews. Meant we lost the prosecution of that nightclub bouncer.'

'He was small fry.'

'Still, DC Lad had jam all around his mouth, if you know what I'm saying.' Fenchurch pulled the bar down again, the rough handle grinding against his palms. More callouses, no doubt.

'Look, just take him, okay? He's a good officer. Dawn wants him put in for a DS role.'

'Why can't she do that?'

'Because she's on nights.'

'Right. Fine. I'll give him to Jon Nelson.'

'That's the spirit.' Docherty slapped him on the back. Squelch. He shook his hand in the air. 'Christ, that's disgusting.'

'What's disgusting?' DC Waheed Lad appeared in the doorway, wearing designer running gear. That American brand that sponsored bloody Spurs. His shorts were almost bollock-high, his legs a gridwork of thick hair, his skin coffee brown.

'The amount your new DI sweats.' Docherty rubbed his hands on Fenchurch's towel. 'Christ, that's almost as bad. I'll leave you pair to it.' He marched off out of the room, keeping his hand as far from his face as possible.

Fenchurch got up and tried to dry his hand before holding it out. 'Welcome to the team, I guess.'

'Thanks for having me.' Lad shook it, his mouth shifting between a scowl and a grin. 'I'm happy to keep running with what DI Mulholland's had me doing overnight.'

'You should get some sleep.'

'Hey, what's coffee for, right?'

'You're working for DS Nelson, okay?'

'Cool. You finished with that machine?' Lad reached down and adjusted the weights up twenty kilos. He shot him a cheeky wink. 'I'll show you how to do it, sir.'

Twenty officers crowded the Incident Room squatting on desks, leaning against pillars. They all looked at him, waiting. The bitter tang of espresso dominated the room, overpowering the cloying odours of brown sauce and bacon, tomato ketchup and sausage. Not much chat. Seven in uniform, four borrowed from another team and nine of Fenchurch's own. Mulholland hadn't bothered to show up. Most of them were sucking on giant coffee beakers, mostly Pret or Starbucks. Nelson had his logo-less cup from the gourmet shop on Whitechapel High Street, Reed her usual Red Bull can.

Fenchurch yawned as he ran his hand through his hair, still wet from his post-gym shower. He glanced up at the clock on the wall. It struck seven — time to start. He held up his copy of that morning's *Post*, bought from the shop round the corner.

The tabloid's front page was a shot of Saskia at some awards dinner. Wearing a strapless black dress. Victor Morgan stood next to her, clutching a statue, his bowtie undone like he was Tom Jones in Vegas.

'KILLED DOING HER JOB'

'That's quite a strong headline.' Fenchurch folded up the paper and tossed it on the table behind him. 'Saskia Barnett was working when she was murdered. We don't know whether it was because she was doing her job or she was just in the wrong place at the wrong time. We do have a suspect in custody, though.'

He let out a deep breath and nodded to the right of him. 'You should all know that DC Waheed Lad is transitioning back from DI Mulholland's team and I've asked him to support DS Nelson and take a lead on the forensic analysis.' He focused on Nelson, unblinking eyes distorted by his glasses. 'We got anywhere with her phone records?'

Nelson looked around the room. 'I was hoping DI Mulholland would approve access, but we're still waiting.'

'I'll sign it after this, okay?' Fenchurch nodded at Lad. 'Given DI Mulholland hasn't shown for the briefing, can you share your overnight progress with us?'

'Sure thing, guv. Got some good news for you.' Lad grinned as he reached into the jacket pocket of his business suit, a navy chalk stripe with a crisp white shirt and bright orange tie. He pulled out a knife, bagged and bloody, and dropped it on the desk in front of him. 'We recovered this from the ground near the Regent's Canal, just by the Islington Tunnel.'

Fenchurch picked up the weapon and gave it a closer look. It was a unibody dagger, the long gunmetal blade coming to a needle-sharp point. The serrations by the hilt clearly meant business. Beneath the dark blood, the screwed-on handles were almost black. He put it back down, swallowing hard. Couldn't see it in the killer's hands, though. 'Has Pratt confirmed that's what killed Saskia Barnett?'

'Don't know yet, guv.' Lad picked it up again. 'Someone was clearly trying to lose it in the canal, though. We struck lucky.'

Fenchurch swallowed hard.

Nelson joined them at the front and crumpled up his coffee. 'I take it you've got something more about it?'

'It's a Blackhawk BESH XSF-1.' Lad smirked as he passed the knife to Nelson. 'Didn't realise that spelled out "excessive" until I said it out loud just there.' He snatched it back and set it down on the table. Fenchurch couldn't take his eyes from it. 'We've done some digging into it, guv. It's only available online. We're checking for purchases in London but that'll take weeks, unfortunately. Even then, it'll probably be inconclusive. It's also likely to be a dark web purchase. You know how much that team's time costs, don't you?'

'Well, do what you can. We could be dealing with an idiot.' Fenchurch gave Nelson a nod. 'The post-mortem's happening this morning, Jon. Can you attend for me?'

'Again?' Nelson snorted. 'Right. Can I take Waheed? He seems to know a lot about this kind of wound.'

'It's fascinating, Sarge.' Lad nodded, eyes locked on the blade. 'Our killer used almost surgical precision. One slice and she was dead.'

Nelson snatched the knife from Lad. 'We'll make sure Clooney confirms it's definitely the murder weapon.'

Clooney didn't even look up from his laptop. 'If you'll just give me it, I'll see if I can do a blood type match before lunch.'

'Didn't see you there.' Nelson was blushing. 'The guv mentioned something about prints?'

'That's going to take a bit longer.'

'Why?'

'Because our space-age strong AI is broken.' Clooney winked at Nelson. 'Look, aside from our huge backlog, you know the score. I've got to get two analysts to check it, then me and a colleague have to validate the results. Might be a week, assuming you've got serviceable prints in the first place.'

Fenchurch shook his head at him. 'That's not acceptable, Mick. We need them back tonight.'

'But—'

'We've got a suspect in custody and one of the worst lawyers I've ever encountered is representing him. This needs to be proven today.'

'I'll see what I can do.' Clooney smacked at his laptop keyboard. 'Something I don't get, though. This looks like a professional operation, right? That knife attack was a surgical strike. So why wasn't this guy you've got in custody wearing gloves?'

Fenchurch tried to stare him out. 'Because uniform would pull them over at any opportunity.'

Lad shrugged. 'Maybe they don't like wearing them?'

Fenchurch waited for the laughter to subside. 'What else has DI Mulholland been up to?'

'Right, guv.' Lad checked his notebook. 'They've done some of the checks you asked for. The boyfriend's clean, as far as they can tell. No criminal record. Nothing on file from any of our more sensitive departments. Same with the father.'

'What about Yana Ikonnikova?'

Lad flicked over the page. 'Iconic Property's going for a FTSE 250 listing. The owner is something else, though. Most of her fortune came from her father, Andriy Ikonnikov. Killed in Kiev five years ago. Poisoned, by the looks of things. She's supposed to be worth over two billion quid.'

Fenchurch raised his eyebrows. 'That's not to be sniffed at.'

'Not that much in the grand scheme of things, I suppose. Doubt she'll be buying the Hammers, guv. But there's no red flags or anything. The DI was happy with the work done.'

'Was she now.' Fenchurch frowned in Reed's direction. 'Kay, did you finish up with the CCTV footage?'

'Just received the latest batch.' Reed took a dainty sip from her can. 'Lisa's going through it just now with a fine-tooth comb.'

Fenchurch looked around. Hadn't even noticed Bridge wasn't there. 'And how are the witness interviews going?'

'Ten statements. He cycled past and stabbed her on the street. The CCTV of the chase checks out, too. Means we've pretty much backed up your statement.'

'What does pretty much mean?'

'Just a couple of black spots on Colebrooke Row. We'll close them off this morning.' Reed held up her notebook. 'Jon's passed me Saskia's calendar. We're going to go through her appointments for the last two weeks.'

'Let me know how that goes. If there's nothing, we should stretch it back a few months.'

'Will do, guv.'

Fenchurch flicked his gaze between Reed and Lad. 'Anything more on Qasid?'

'Tried every possible variation on Williams. Guy's a ghost, I'm afraid.' Lad finished his coffee. 'Same with Kamal. Just one name isn't giving us a whole heap of beans. There's a ton of Kamals in London.'

Fenchurch jotted an action on the whiteboard. 'Jon, before you go to the PM, can you check into these names? See what intel we've got. Might want to start with Trident.'

'The black-on-black guys? Doubt they'll have anything.'

'See what you can find, Sergeant.' Fenchurch waited for him to make a note. 'Anything else?'

Clooney raised a hand. 'Just finished the undelete on that phone I told you about last night.'

'And?'

He grimaced. 'No texts. Well, there were a couple relating to voicemails, but they're not on the network any more. They roll off after a month.'

'Can they get them back?'

'They're trying it for me. The most recent ones were just a series of clicks. Checked it for Morse code and a few other things, but I think it's just random. Not even anyone pocket dialling. We're tracing the numbers, but they just look like more burners.'

'Bloody hell. See what else you can dig up, okay?' Fenchurch scanned around the room. Blank faces drinking coffee. 'Dismissed.'

They all burst into life as they clattered around the room, a din rising from the silence. Mobile ringtones blaring out amid football talk.

'You okay, guv?' Reed was standing over him. She crushed her can and dumped it in the bin. 'You look like shit.'

'Difficult night.'

'Abi?'

Fenchurch gave a curt nod. 'She didn't sleep much. Means I didn't sleep much. The joys of cohabiting, right?'

'She's strong, guv, you know that.'

'Do I?' Fenchurch shook his head. 'It's just brought a few things home, Kay.'

'You're not still—' Her mobile rang. She checked the display and winced. 'It's Lisa, I'd better take it.'

'Tell her I want her to attend briefings no matter how important she thinks her work is.'

'Guv.' Reed put her phone to her head and walked off.

Fenchurch turned round and checked the whiteboard again. Took a sip of lukewarm tea and put the mug down. The gaps in the timelines were huge. Holes in his bloody statement, gaping chasms they hadn't filled yet. He'd let the kid out of his sight twice and Unwin would drive his tanks through, turning the cracks into ravines.

Someone tugged at his sleeve. Reed, eyes wide. 'Guv, Lisa's got something downstairs.'

In the CCTV suite, DC Lisa Bridge was leaning over a laptop. Low-cut blouse and tight skirt made her look like she'd been to a night-club. Her messy hair made it look like she'd struck lucky. Dark rings surrounded her eyes, hardly any of it make-up.

Fenchurch folded his arms and gave her a nod as he sat on the table. 'Nice to see you, Constable. You should attend—'

'I know, guv. Sorry but I've been up all night and I've—'

'You attend briefings, Constable. I don't want a suspect slipping through the net because you didn't know about something Jon Nelson's working on, okay?'

'Sir.'

'Now, why have you dragged us down here?'

'I've got something you'll want to see.' Bridge gave Reed a nod then flicked a switch hanging out of her laptop. 'There.'

The ceiling-mounted projector switched on and a blue box filled most of the white wall, slightly off-kilter. She hammered her thumb off the space bar. It switched to CCTV footage. A Regency street at night, sharper than the stuff from Islington the previous night.

Bridge tapped a finger off a figure at the right-hand side. 'This is Saskia Barnett walking from that house in Belgravia to Victoria tube station.'

Fenchurch looked over at Reed. 'Thought she was headed to Green Park?'

'It's six and two threes, guv.' Bridge flicked through her notebook. 'DS Nelson asked me to look into it so I checked on the TfL website. Turns out Victoria's slightly quicker. Saskia must've done the same search.'

Fenchurch scanned around the screen. The usual London rush-hour slog going on — a man with a briefcase staring at an estate agents' window, a woman on her mobile locking step with Saskia. 'You got anything before this?'

She shook her head. 'It's about a ten-minute walk to Victoria.'

The footage on the wall switched to an escalator, rush-hour busy. Bridge got up and traced a circle around a figure descending, hands tucked into a dark jacket. Then a different station, Saskia waiting in the middle of a throng of passengers. Looked like she knew exactly which spot to stand on to get a door.

'This is the Victoria line, guv.'

Then another platform, Saskia getting off a train.

'And this is Euston underground. I don't have any more until this.'

It jumped again and Fenchurch recognised the long escalator climbing out of the bowels of the dreaded Northern line. Saskia was reading an *Evening Standard* as she ascended. 'That's Angel, right?'

'Well spotted, guv.' Bridge blushed as the footage switched to Saskia, now looking behind her at irregular intervals. 'That was the lower escalator. This is the upper one.'

The video cut to the bustle outside Angel tube station. Then to Saskia crossing the road, fingers on her phone. Seconds before her death.

Bridge stopped it and rewound it to Saskia on the first escalator, lost in her paper. 'Notice anything?'

Fenchurch frowned at Reed, looking similarly mystified. 'What?'

Bridge grinned as she circled another figure with her finger, five or six bodies below Saskia. A man in a hoodie, tucked up over his head. 'This guy followed her.'

'What?'

Bridge brought up other shots from earlier in the journey. The same person was on the street in Belgravia, behind Saskia at Victoria and on both platforms. 'See?'

'Christ.' Fenchurch's acid reflux bit into his gut. 'He was following her.'

'Now watch this.' Bridge's fingers danced across her laptop's keyboard. 'This is where mobile reception cuts back in at Angel tube. Still no Virgin Wi-Fi on the Northern Line, remember.' She brought up three shots next to each other and zoomed in, grainy and pixelated, the sharpness lost.

The man had a phone to his head, the hoodie down around his shoulders. He looked a lot older than Qasid, but dressed like he thought he was the same age. His dark beard was splattered with white. Footballer hair like that Man City winger who was at Liverpool last season, shaved at the side, Afro curls piling up on top.

'Shit.' Reed locked eyes with him. 'So they weren't after her phone.'

Fenchurch swallowed hard. 'This is a bloody hit.'

Chapter Twelve

'Well, Simon, I think I agree with your assessment.' Docherty tightened his tie as he looked out of his office window. 'Why's someone targeting her, though?'

Fenchurch was leaning against the wall, too fired up to sit. He couldn't take his eyes off the photo of the man following her, the paper already crinkled around the edges. 'That's what we're looking into, boss.'

Docherty snatched it off him. 'You think this is Kamal?'

'Could be. Whoever he is, this guy followed her from Belgravia, boss. I'd put money on that phone call being him ordering Qasid to kill Saskia.'

'Supposition, Si. Any way of tracing the call?'

'Clooney's going to see what can be done but I don't hold out much hope. Must be thousands of calls in Angel at that time.'

Docherty got out his notebook and turned to a page covered in squiggles. He clicked his pen and made a note near the edge. 'So, assuming this is a hit, what are you doing to lock it down?'

'Well, there's the usual. Speak to the boyfriend again. Her father, her boss at the *Post*. But I'd rather give them some space. Let the other stuff play out.'

'Sounds wise.'

Fenchurch made for the door and clutched the cool handle. 'That us?'

'Not quite.' Docherty flicked back in his notebook. 'Does the name Unwin mean anything to you?'

Fenchurch's acid reflux started bubbling around his breakfast again. The drums tapped out a slow rhythm. 'He's Qasid's solicitor. Has he been kicking up a fuss?'

'Aye, he's making a noise, all right. He's got a bloody ghetto blaster booming out the best of Public Enemy.' Docherty curled his lip and tilted his head to the side. Looked like he could bite raw flesh off the bone. 'Anything I should be worried about?'

'Just getting people to listen to him, boss. Geezer was in here defending Qasid before anyone should've known we had him. He's poison.'

'You looking into him yet?'

'Thought I'd let him drop a bollock first. Keep our arses covered.'

'Good man.' Docherty scribbled a note on his book. 'And how's Abi?'

'Not good. I'm sure time'll heal it but . . . It's tough, sir.'

'Horrendous thing, Si.' Docherty went back to his paperwork. 'You got anything else I should know about?'

'I've got a call out to SC&O8.'

'The ex-Trident lot? Great.' Docherty groaned. 'Why do you always leave the politics to last?'

'It's not very interesting, boss. And I've not left it till last.' Fenchurch thumbed at the door. 'Clooney's supposed to be setting up some time with a DI from the Mobile Phone Theft Unit. I'm thinking the sheer number of phones we've found mean Qasid and co might be on their radar.'

'Be careful there, okay? They're Boris bloody Johnson's favourites, so don't go pissing anyone off.'

Fenchurch collapsed into his chair. The office door had swung open again. Bloody Mulholland getting the carpet fixed.

He took a slurp of tea. Lovely. Then he got out his Airwave and dialled the number.

'DI Paul Oscar, SC&O8.' Essex barrow boy accent, high-pitched. Sounded like he was in a crowded restaurant.

'It's DI Fenchurch of the East London MIT.'

'I'm very pleased for you. Now, unless you can tell me how to get a Starbucks queue to bugger off quickly, I'll get back to you.'

'I spoke to your secretary earlier. She said you'd call me back.'

'Right.' A pause. 'What do you want?'

'Intelligence, hopefully.' Fenchurch rubbed at his forehead, doubting he'd get any from Oscar. 'I'm working a case in Islington. A young woman got stabbed on the street last night. Happened right in front of my eyes.'

'Sorry to hear that. Two shots, please, love. Yeah, extra. That's fine.'

Fenchurch stuck his feet up on the desk. Nelson appeared at the other end of the corridor, his loping stride eating up the distance as he sucked on that bloody vape stick again. 'To my untrained eye, it looks like a gang hit.'

'I need a receipt. Sorry, Fenchurch. What was this girl's name?'

Fenchurch flicked up his eyebrows and leaned his head forward as Nelson pulled the door shut. 'Saskia Barnett.'

Oscar let out a sigh. 'The journalist on Upper Street?' He snorted down the line. 'Yeah, good luck solving that one.'

'Why do you say that?'

'Phone theft plus murder equals bugger all, mate. These little bastards are slippery eels.' Oscar slurped at something, no doubt some posh coffee. 'You want my advice, you should take up a healthy hobby, something that takes away the stress of this bloody job.'

'We've got someone in custody for it.'

'That wasn't in the paper.'

'That's deliberate. His name's Qasid Williams. Ring any bells?'

'Why are you telling me this?'

'Because we think it's a gang hit.'

'And yet you've got no evidence for it.'

'We've got a few pointers. How about the name Kamal?'

A long pause down the line. 'Right, I'm listening now.'

'What do you know about him?'

'Not a lot but if he's connected to this, you've got my undivided attention.'

Fenchurch locked eyes with Nelson. 'I'm sending one of my officers over. DS Jon Nelson. Please assist him.'

'Will do. Catch you later.' The line clicked dead.

Nelson took a gentle suck on his e-cigarette. 'Take it I'm heading out to Empress State Building, guv?'

Fenchurch gave him a nod. 'Report to DI Paul Oscar when you're there. Sounds like a smug prick, but you never know, I have a tendency to rub people up the wrong way.'

'Kind of implies there's a right way to rub someone.'

Fenchurch laughed before taking another glug of scalding tea. 'How'd it go with Qasid?'

'I spared you an hour of listening to the words "no" and "comment".'

'I appreciate it.' Fenchurch took a long drink. 'This Unwin's a bit of a snake, isn't he?'

'Not half, guv.' Nelson pocketed his vape stick with a last exhalation of mist. 'I bumped into Clooney on my way up. Said something like your mate Bell's in room six upstairs?'

'Bloody hell.' Fenchurch got up and drained his mug. 'He could've told me himself.'

———

Fenchurch stopped outside the meeting room and straightened his tie. He sucked in a deep breath and entered.

DI Jason Bell lurked by the window, looking a doughnut shy of Type 2 diabetes. A small peanut head gave way to a squat body, the lapels of his suit jacket distant strangers, never to meet in the middle. His trousers were overstuffed sausages just about bursting at the seams. 'Simon, mate, how's it going?' He had the sort of harsh, nasal Brummie accent people forgot about in favour of the sing-song Black Country roll.

Fenchurch took the seat closest to the door. 'Been a long time, Stringer.'

'I still don't get that bloody nickname.' Bell collapsed into the chair by the window, his shirt buttons straining against his gut. 'Where's it from?'

'*The Wire* finished years ago, String. You really should've caught up.'

'Like I've got the time with four kids.' A smirk flashed across Bell's face. 'You're clearly not that desperate for my help, are you?'

'Desperate's only a state of mind.' Fenchurch held a smile for longer than Bell would find comfortable. 'You got my email, didn't you?'

'And I spoke to Clooney.' Bell rubbed his hands together, giving a flash of a tattoo on his wrist — 'Bloodshed speculators'.

Fenchurch frowned at it. 'What the hell's that?'

'Nothing.' Bell tugged his shirtsleeve over it. 'So, you had to get Mick Clooney to do your dirty work. Couldn't call me yourself.'

'Proper channels and all that, String.'

'Do you even know what that means, Si?' Bell laughed at his joke, then folded his arms tight. 'This is about this girl in Islington last night, isn't it?' He unfolded his arms, though his suit jacket stayed crumpled. 'I don't see how it's connected.'

'String, the killer was an Apple picker.'

'Clooney didn't mention that part.' Bell's eyes scanned the corners of the room, looking for inspiration among the cobwebs. 'Our focus is on prevention rather than cure these days. Since I took over two years ago, thefts of Apple phones have fallen fifty per cent.'

Fenchurch rolled his eyes. 'Even I know that's because of the kill switch.'

'That only does so much.' Bell steepled his fingers, his brow creasing. 'Some of them carry a little netbook so they can wipe them on their bikes before the kill switch is used. Switch them off, toss the SIMs. The shops can unbrick a bricked phone, if needed.'

'Doesn't sound like you're doing a lot, though. Just waiting for tech companies to invent stuff.'

'Boris is very impressed with our progress.'

'Well done you.' Fenchurch leaned forward and rested on his elbows. 'Still, she was killed by one of your Apple pickers.'

'They're not my . . .' Bell gave his old sigh, the one he did when he knew he'd lost. 'So, you think this poor bastard you're framing is in a gang?'

Fenchurch held his gaze. 'His pockets were full of phones, String. We found a bag he'd chucked. Got fifteen in total. One of them's his, though. A burner.'

'That's a lot. They usually only ever carry a couple.' Bell got out a notebook from his cavernous suit jacket. 'I'll just say we don't get many violent crimes related to them. This isn't New York. Yet.' He ran his tongue over his lips. 'Usually there's just a punch involved. Maybe a kick. Never a stabbing. They don't tend to escalate to killing.'

'So they just leave it at brutal assault, do they?'

'Simon . . .'

The door juddered open and Reed appeared. She smiled at Fenchurch then frowned at Bell, caught in the middle of giving her the once over. Like how you'd appraise a steak at the butcher's. 'You wanted to see me?'

'I thought I wanted you to help with this.' Fenchurch got up. 'But it turns out DI Bell's got nothing for us.'

Bell cleared his throat. 'Nothing concrete, that's for sure.'

Fenchurch settled back down again. 'What about anything vague?'

'Look, there've been a couple of stabbings in the East End. Round Canning Town and Mile End, I think. One in Stratford by the Olympic stadium.' Bell flashed some needle-sharp teeth posing as a smile. 'Soon to be home of your beloved Hammers.'

'Any arrests?'

'Couldn't pin them to anyone. Eyewitnesses say it was kids on bikes. Never got a knife, never got any clear suspects. Always happens so fast. But I expect you know that.' Bell pocketed his notebook. 'Been nice catching up, Si, but I need to get back to work.'

Reed opened the meeting room door wide. 'Did you ask him about Kamal?'

Bell's turn to sit back down, adding a frown for good measure. 'What's that supposed to mean?'

'The victim's last words were that name.'

'Shit.' Bell ran a hand over his face. 'Look, there's something that might help. It's a long shot.'

'What is it?'

'It's not a what. It's a who.'

Chapter Thirteen

'We go back a long way, Kay.' Fenchurch looked out of the window at Gower Street below. A grey stone University College London building sat opposite, glowering at the new hospital they stood in, all green glass and concrete. Students milled about below, carrying rucksacks and skateboards. One was on one of those hoverboard things, a pair of Beats headphones around his head. 'He's a bit of a . . .' He looked up and down the corridor, still no sign of Bell. Or of anyone, just the ever-present reek of cleaning chemicals and boiled cabbage. 'A bell end, to be honest.'

'I got that impression, guv.' Reed checked her mobile. 'Why did you send Jon out to speak to Trident and not me?'

'Because I needed him there and you here.'

'Cos he's black?'

'Not really.' A quick glance at his phone showed no new messages, no new emergencies to attend. 'Cos he's got Waheed Lad and I want him a million miles away from me.'

'He's not that bad.'

'He's like napalm, Kay. Give him something to work on and watch it explode.'

Bell appeared from the nurses' station with a matron who looked like she could be his sister. Similar round body and tiny head. He nodded at Reed, ignoring Fenchurch. 'Good news, Si. We can look but we can't touch.'

Fenchurch scowled at the matron. 'I wouldn't mind a word, if it's all the same.'

'Wouldn't you now?' She squeaked across the corridor, her clogs marking the almost pristine floor, and tapped at a window. 'Have a look at him.'

Fenchurch squatted down to look through the blinds.

A black kid lay on the bed, all tubed up and staring into space. His arms hung by his sides, his white smock rising and falling as the incubator pumped. 'You see why you can't speak to him?'

'This is important.'

'No, Inspector. Under no circumstances can you talk to him. Am I making myself clear?' The matron strode off, the clogs squeaking up the corridor. 'Don't make me call security, now.'

Fenchurch frowned at Bell. 'What's the story here?'

'Hayden here nicked a guy's phone outside King's Cross.' Bell folded his arms, stretching out his suit jacket. 'Big Scottish guy, half-pissed and late for the train back to Edinburgh. He was calling his wife on speakerphone, holding his iPhone out. Kid swooped in on his bike, grabbed the phone and darted off through the crowds.' He scratched a patch of stubble surrounding a painful-looking boil. 'The guy went apeshit and chased after the kid, roaring his head off like he was in *Braveheart*.' He waited for a laugh but didn't get anything. 'Must've thrown Hayden here. They usually head up the back of St Pancras but he went for that road up to Islington.' He frowned, his eyebrows unsure which direction to point in. 'What's it called again?'

'Pentonville Road.'

'Should really remember that. Always slips my mind.' The frown disappeared. 'You still live up that way, Si?'

'Just moved back.'

'Doesn't Abi still live there?'

'Back with her.' Fenchurch avoided Reed's searching gaze. 'What happened next, String?'

'This big Scotch guy caught our friend just as a number thirty smacked into him. Bike got mangled.' Bell tapped the window. 'Not as bad as Hayden, though.'

'Is he going to survive?'

'Luckily for him, yeah. We'll be charging him once he's well enough. Be lucky if it's this year, though.'

'What about the Scottish guy?'

Bell winked at him. 'Didn't get a great description of him.'

'Like that, is it?'

'Won't be back in London for a while, I hope.' Bell laughed at his own joke. 'Anyway, young Hayden here had six phones on him. All broken beyond repair after his little accident. Also had a knife.'

'What kind?'

'Can't remember the name. XS something or other. Sharp point, though. Looked horrible.'

Fenchurch fiddled with his Pronto and pulled up an image from the case file. Looked like Reed was thinking the same thing as him. 'Like this one?'

'Pretty much. I'm no expert.' Another laugh. 'You'd think I would be after twenty-odd years in this bloody city.'

Reed ran a hand through her hair. 'So, you think Hayden works for Kamal?'

'That's our understanding.'

'What's his name?'

'I told you. Hayden.'

'That's it?'

99

'That's all he'll give us. Not even sure it's his real name.'

Reed's expertise at hiding her derision was slipping slightly. 'Have you found his parents?'

'Sorry, is my mouth not working? The only thing we've got from him is that name.'

Fenchurch looked down the corridor — no sign of the battle-axe matron. 'I'm going to ask him about Kamal.'

'You can't.'

'Watch me.' Fenchurch tried the door. Locked. 'Shit.' He waved at a passing nurse, a smiling black woman in a mid-blue uniform, clutching a clipboard. 'Is Hayden allowed visitors?'

She looked him up and down. 'He look okay to you, boy?' Rolling Jamaican accent.

'Matron said it was fine.'

'Did she?' The nurse shrugged and swiped a card through the reader by the door. 'On you go, sirs. Madam.'

Fenchurch put his hand on the door.

She smacked it with her clipboard. 'Use the hand sanitiser, boy.'

'Right.' Fenchurch squirted some out and rubbed, the pink gunk disappearing in a haze of alcohol fumes. He nodded at Bell as he did the same. 'You lead, String.'

'Fine, but we're keeping this low-key, right?' Bell entered the room and perched on a chair next to the bed. 'Hayden, how you doing?'

No response from the kid. His breathing looked a bit faster than before, though.

Bell leaned forward in his seat. 'We've got a few questions for you.'

Hayden focused on him, like his eyes could do the damage his body couldn't. 'Ain't saying nothing.' His voice was barely a croak, like his voice box was still on the bus. Accent was ballpark similar to Qasid's, though.

'We still haven't found your parents, Hayden.'

'They dead.'

'Is that true?'

He looked away, shrugging as much as his injuries would allow. 'True enough.'

'Hayden, my colleagues here want to ask you a few questions, okay?'

'Tol' you. Ain't saying nothing.' The voice was more fluid now. Smoother.

Fenchurch left some space between him and the bed. Kept eye contact with the kid. 'A young man on a bike took a woman's phone and handbag last night.' He held up the Pronto, still on the image of the knife. 'He stabbed her in the neck with this.'

Hayden shrugged his right shoulder again, barely lifting it from the bed. 'Wasn't me, man.'

'We know it wasn't you. Does the name Qasid mean anything to you?'

Another shrug, even less movement.

'Because of how you made your livelihood before all this, I wondered if you knew him. Should I take that as a no?'

Completely still, just more aggression through his eyes. 'Don't know him, bruv.'

'What about Kamal?'

Hayden looked away. 'Don't know no Kamal.'

'You sure about that?'

'Sure.'

'Why are you looking away?'

'Because I don't know nothing.' His breathing was harder now, not all of it machine driven. 'Know nothing, man.'

'Come on, Hayden, a young woman's been killed by someone who does what you used to.'

'I don't know him.' Faster breaths, shorter. 'I ain't done nothing.'

The door flew open and the matron squelched in, face twisted with rage. 'What in the name of God is going on here?'

Bell raised his hands. 'It's okay, April. We'll be going.'

Fenchurch got closer to the bed. 'Hayden, how do I find Kamal?'

He gave a little laugh. 'You don't find he. He find you.'

'That's enough.' The matron hauled Fenchurch off the bed and pushed him out of the room. Much stronger than she looked. She shot daggers at Bell with her eyes. She checked the kid's monitors and joined them out in the corridor. 'That was a gross betrayal of trust.'

'That kid's a lead.' Fenchurch tapped at the door. 'I'm not finished with him.'

'Look at the state of him. *You* did that to him.'

Bell dusted himself off, bright sunlight bouncing off his bald head. 'Thanks for letting us speak to him, anyway.'

'Don't come back in a hurry.' The matron jabbed a finger at Fenchurch. 'And don't bring him next time.'

Fenchurch wandered off, leaving Bell to apologise.

Reed was following in his wake. 'She's a right charmer.'

'She's probably got a point, though, Kay.'

Bell caught up by the lifts, just as Fenchurch thumped the down arrow. 'Well, did that help at all?'

Fenchurch got in the lift and leaned against the mirror. 'He bloody knows Kamal. What have you got on him?'

'Kamal? Very little, like I say. This was a long shot, Simon. Two plus two might equal five, you know?'

'Long shot or not, it's not really got me anywhere, String.' Fenchurch stared at the closing doors, the corridor disappearing. 'Anything else?'

'Why should I help you? You've just pissed her off. Who next?'

'String, this is a murder case, okay? That little shit is in custody. He might get out unless we tighten the noose around him.'

'I suppose I can take you on my rounds if you promise to behave.'

'Me, behave?' Fenchurch smirked at Reed. 'Never.'

Chapter Fourteen

'Just like the old days, this.' Bell crawled through mid-morning traffic on Bishopsgate, the towers of the City lurking on their right. The bulbous mass of the gherkin shot up less than a block away, surrounded by more new towers. He swung a right past the Heron, a pointless slab of glass scraping the clouds. 'Just like being back on the beat together.'

'That was a month, String.' Fenchurch watched the buildings switch from gentrified financial district to urban chaos, otherwise marketed as the fringe. Prets and Eats, posh salad bars and Pizza Expresses wrestled between greasy spoons, street markets and charity shops. 'Still go to Petticoat Lane Market every couple of weeks.'

'Still good, is it?'

'Brilliant food. There's a great Thai stand there. Amazing satay.'

'Doesn't sound like cheese sandwiches to me.'

'Gave those up a long time ago, String.' Fenchurch checked his phone for messages. It was like the thing wasn't even on. 'I practically live off Mexican these days.'

'Mexican?' Bell glanced over. And again, looking up and down Fenchurch's torso. 'How's that fair? All that cheese and guacamole and sour cream and you look like that?'

'You saying you live off salad and rice cakes?'

'Pretty much.'

Fenchurch could just picture him sitting on his sofa at night, wolfing down wedges of cold pizza and buckets of ice cream. 'Well, I go to the gym before my morning briefings. Every day.'

'You must've been Mother Theresa in a past life, is all I can say.'

'Don't get me started on her.' A glance in the rear view showed Reed was keeping up with them, singing along to something in her car. 'What's the plan here?'

'We're visiting a shop you might be interested in. One of a few places we've got enough budget to run surveillance on. Opens at ten o'clock.' Bell tapped at the clock on the dashboard of his pool Saab. 09.53. 'We know they handle the phones. A source says they take the bricked mobiles from the gangs and reset them to factory conditions. They box them up and send them abroad.'

'Abroad?'

'They go for crazy money in Malaysia and Indonesia.'

Bloody hell. Fenchurch shook his head again. 'Isn't that where they make them?'

'You're thinking of China. The prices over there are insane. Nicked second-hand mobiles make good money there, like four hundred quid good.'

'Christ almighty. You can see why they do it.'

'Fifty-fifty split, we reckon. Two hundred to the gang *per phone*. Just think about how many your little friend had on him.'

'Three grand for an evening's thieving. No wonder these punks aren't working in McDonald's.' Fenchurch leaned back in the seat and stretched his legs out. They were stuck behind a lorry trundling slower than his old man could walk. 'How reliable's this source?'

'Unimpeachable. Works for Trident and they gave us a heads up.'

'Trident?' Fenchurch unlocked his phone, ready to message Nelson. 'You got hooks into them?'

'Why?' Another flash of sharp teeth. 'You need some help with them?'

'Maybe.'

'Call me when they stop answering your calls, Si.' Bell pulled up beneath another sprawling City skyscraper. Spitalfields Tower or something.

The left-hand side had gone through the gentrification sausage machine. A little Sainsbury's, a branded gym, a posh pizza place and an outdoor clothing shop. The opposite side had missed it so far, still a family-run café, a battered hair studio and two cobblers, next to a shop stamped with 'Ifone Repair's'.

'Take it you're not arresting them for language abuse?'

Bell laughed, a bit too hard to be genuine. 'Not yet.'

'Isn't this City of London turf?'

'Just over the border. Heard about your little squabble with them at Christmas.'

'How the bloody hell—'

'The Met's like a village, Si. Besides, they've let us run this obbo. Bigger fish to fry, they reckon. I spoke to Boris about it. He reckons we're taking the strain off and letting them focus their resources on financial crime.'

'Did he.'

Bell let his seatbelt ride up and jabbed a sausage finger at a man with a turban sidling up to the front door. 'That's the owner. I was going to have a little word with them.'

'Slap on the wrist?'

'That kind of thing.'

'Sure that's the right play here? They know you. Might be best if I act the daft laddie, as my DCI says.'

'You can't—'

'Watch me.' Fenchurch got out of the car and jogged across the road. He entered and nodded at the owner. The place was filled with racks of video games, huge glass cases with phones of every make and model and a couple of rows of laptops. The far wall was rammed with big TVs and a pair of large iMacs, the kind John Lewis try to wow you with. An ATM machine sat near the back, stamped with 'Phone Recycling Point' in flashy green and blue.

Fenchurch rested his hands on the glass counter, another display filled with Apple Watches and old-fashioned ones. 'You the owner?'

A slight nod. 'Sir.'

Fenchurch reached into his suit pocket for his warrant card and some photos. 'DI Simon Fenchurch.'

The owner licked his lips, blinking slow and hard a few times. 'Call me Vikram.'

'Only if that's your name.' Fenchurch held up the shots. First Qasid, then the man on the escalator. 'You recognise either of these two?'

'Should I?'

'I gather they work here. Can I speak to them?'

'I work here and my brother works here.' The blinking turned into closed eyes. 'That's it.'

'You sure about that, Vikram?'

More blinking. 'Sure.'

'You definitely don't know these lads?'

Vikram pushed the photos away. 'Never seen them in my life, officer.'

'They've never supplied you with mobile phones, say?'

'Never seen them in my life.'

'That the same answer you'd give down the station?'

'It's the truth, I swear.'

Fenchurch slid the sheets back and stabbed a finger on the shot of Qasid. 'This kid murdered a girl last night in Islington. I was there, I saw it. This other guy was tailing her. You want to help me or not?'

'But I don't know them!'

Another customer entered the shop, tall and dark-skinned, wearing camouflage gear. Cheap army surplus stuff, if that was still a thing. His long dreadlocks were almost caught in the hood of a brown and cream jacket. 'Hey, Vikram, you okay?'

Fenchurch flashed his warrant card. 'Police.'

'Fascist pig bastard.'

Fenchurch got in the guy's face, forehead to forehead. And regretted it. He was *ripe*, three or four days past desperately needing a bath. The stink of infection, maybe. 'I'll deal with you later.'

The Rasta's forehead nudged forward a touch. Not quite a head butt, but enough for a six-match ban if he'd done it on a football pitch. The door tinkled open. 'Maybe I'll deal with you now.'

Fenchurch was close to losing his breakfast. 'Get out of my hair unless you want to join your friend here in custody.'

'He ain't done nothing, man. You fascist bas—'

'Easy, easy, easy.' The Rasta was pulled away by someone. Reed, handcuffs in the air, clanking off each other. 'Do you want me to put these on him, guv?'

The man took a step back and held up his hands. 'Leave me out of this, right?'

'Leave him be.' Fenchurch took another step away and looked around the place. He gestured at the displays of smart watches beneath the glass counter and smiled at Vikram. 'Want me to get trading standards in here? Reckon there's a ton of stolen goods in here.'

'It's all legitimate, officer. I have receipts for everything.' Vikram had gone back to his slow blinking. 'More than my life's worth to fence stolen items, sir. We only buy from members of our club.'

'Better hope you've got names and addresses for everyone.' Fenchurch put the photos away, then tossed a business card on the counter. 'Call me if anything jogs your memory, okay?'

'Certainly, officer.'

Fenchurch followed Reed back outside. 'The cavalry showed up yet again.'

'Easy, guv.' She shot him a wink. 'You looked like you'd lost it back there.'

Two squad cars sat either side, blocking the road. Bell was leaning against his car, shaking his head, eyes narrowed. 'You really shouldn't have done that, Simon.'

'What, forcing you to actually do something for once?' Fenchurch tilted his head to the side and raised his eyebrows as he waved at the cars. 'Best get your lads in there now before they dump the evidence.'

Bell shook his head then made a circling motion in the air. 'On you go, gentlemen.'

Fenchurch joined him leaning against the car. Reed didn't seem to know where to stand or look. 'They've got a phone recycler in there.'

'What?'

Fenchurch slumped back against the cold metal. 'Tell me you've been in there, String.'

'This would've been the first time.'

'Boris'll be disappointed with you.' Fenchurch pointed through the window. As the officers entered, the dreadlocked guy sloped out of the front door, hands in the air. Near the back, the owner was standing by the recycling machine, fiddling with it. 'I'd get that torn apart pronto.'

'Right.' Another squad car pulled up and Bell jabbed a finger towards the shop.

Fenchurch's phone blasted out. Bloody thing was still far too loud.

'Simon, I need you to stick around. This is your mess, after all.'

Fenchurch held him back with a wave then took a few steps over to the pavement. Unknown caller. He answered it, walking away. 'Hello?'

'It's Liam. Saskia's boyfriend?'

He frowned at Reed. What did he want? 'How can I help?'

'I need to speak to you. Someone's stolen her laptop.'

Chapter Fifteen

Fenchurch looked round as the lift thundered up the inside of the *Post* building. 'He didn't say anything else, no.'

'Just meet him here?' Reed leaned back against the shaking wall of the lift. 'Did they mean to take it or was it just a chance thing?'

'That's what we need to find out.' The lift clattered to a stop and Fenchurch waited as the doors took their time juddering open. The reception area looked different during the day — bright and luxurious rather than damp and cheap. He strode over and flashed his warrant card at the woman behind it. She looked like a clone of the girl downstairs, just blonde hair instead of dark brown. 'We're here to see Liam Sharpe.'

'Mr Sharpe's in here.' She got up and sashayed across the wide hall. She pulled open a glass door and stood to the side.

Liam was standing near the window, just an outline in front of the blinding glare from Fleet Street.

'Thanks.' Fenchurch nodded at the receptionist as he entered and waved for Reed to sit first. He took the seat at the head of the table and blinked at the sunlight. 'Mr Sharpe, this is DS Reed.'

Liam nodded at her and sat down. The overhead light hit his face and revealed a black eye, with a short cut just below.

'Jesus.' Fenchurch swallowed hard, his gut rumbling. 'What happened?'

'Someone attacked me.'

'Here?'

Liam shook his head. 'At my flat.'

'So why are you here?'

'I didn't know where else to go. I didn't feel safe there.'

'So you came to work instead of phoning the police?'

'I called you. Isn't that enough?'

'Where you live, you're not far from Stoke Newington or Bethnal Green. Would've been easier to just pop in there.'

'I thought it was best to come here. I just got in an Uber.'

Bloody Uber . . . Fenchurch took a deep breath and let it out slowly. 'Go from the start, please.'

Liam ran a hand through his hair, making what was left of it stick up. 'I was going through Saskia's laptop in the flat. The buzzer went and the guy said it was a delivery for next door. I let them in and waited as he climbed the stairs. When I was signing for it, he punched me. Knocked me out.'

'Did you sign one of those machines?'

'A clipboard. Should've smelled a rat. Just saw a grey uniform, that's it. Didn't even show any ID. Nothing.' Liam dabbed at his eye. 'I feel like such an idiot.'

Fenchurch wasn't going to disagree with him. 'Was your attacker black or white?'

'Black, definitely. Saw his hands when he gave me the clipboard.'

'Okay, you might be able to help me here.' Fenchurch tossed the photo of the man on the escalator onto the table. 'Do you recognise him?'

Liam scanned it for a few seconds. His free hand mercilessly combed his hair back into place. 'Never seen him in my life.'

'So it wasn't him?'

'Skin was a lot darker. Sorry.' Liam's Adam's apple bobbed up and down as he handed the sheet back. 'Who is this?'

Fenchurch glanced at Reed. Liam probably deserved the truth. 'We've identified some evidence which potentially shows someone following Saskia.'

'What? Are you serious?' Liam took another look. 'Jesus.'

Fenchurch tossed the shot of Qasid onto the desk. 'What about him?'

'Now that's the same skin colour as the guy who took the laptop.'

'Was it him?'

'Could be. Didn't get that good a look.' Liam focused on the photo, as if he could burn it into his memory. 'Who is he?'

'We think this is Saskia's killer.'

'Christ.'

'He's in custody.' Fenchurch took the shots back. 'What happened next? Were you out cold?'

Liam gave a nod. 'I woke up. Took me a while to get up. I went back through to the bedroom and saw they'd taken her laptop.' He grimaced, looking like a shiver went down his spine. 'And my mobile. Had to use my landline to call you.'

Fenchurch jotted a few notes on his Pronto. He whispered to Reed: 'Can you chase up her phone records for me?'

'I'll get his too, guv.' She got up and left the room.

Fenchurch settled his gaze back on Liam. 'What kind of laptop was it?'

'A crappy Dell thing. No, a Lenovo. You know, the CTRL key is in the wrong place?'

'But it's an old machine, right?'

'That's right. It's not a corporate job, if that's what you're getting at. We've got BYOD here.'

Fenchurch gave him a blank look.

113

'Bring your own device. Saves on IT costs, I guess. Take in our own machines. They give us email addresses and we log into the production system to post stories.'

Fenchurch leaned back in his seat. 'Why did you have her laptop?'

'She got me to take it home last night. She was going to stay over at mine and wanted to get a head start this morning.' Liam ran a hand through his hair, upsetting the comb-over. He shot a grin at Fenchurch. 'I know that look on your face. There's nothing sinister going on here, I swear.'

'I prefer to be shown things rather than just be told.' Fenchurch put the Pronto on the table. 'Mr Sharpe, who knew her laptop was at your flat?'

'No idea. Just Sas and Victor. I told him I had it, and he asked me to go through it looking for stories she was working on.'

'That should've been put into evidence.'

'Sorry. I was going to.' Liam pinched his nose, eyes locked tight. 'I looked at anything she'd had open in the last fortnight. There were tons of documents. Most of it looked like rough drafts, notes, that kind of thing.'

'So the laptop had the only copies of these stories?'

'Sorry.'

'She didn't use Dropbox, anything like that?'

Liam pursed his lips tight, turning the flesh almost white for a moment. 'I kept telling her to, but it wasn't installed.'

Reed appeared in the doorway, looking as pissed off as he was at losing a load of evidence to rank stupidity. She locked her Airwave and stayed standing.

Fenchurch focused on Liam. 'So there's no way we can get the documents back?'

Liam prodded a finger into his eye. 'Well, I'd sent some of the stories off to Victor.'

Fenchurch caught Victor Morgan outside his office. Guy looked ready to kill someone himself. 'Need a word with you, sir.'

'Not going to happen, Inspector. I'm up to here.' Victor held his hand about a foot above the top of his head.

'I understand you're up against it, sir, but I really need to speak to you.'

'Can't it wait?'

'Her laptop's just been stolen from Liam Sharpe's apartment.'

Victor focused on Fenchurch. Menace flickered in his eyes, propped up on rings a few shades darker than the surrounding skin. Then he smiled, nodding his head. 'Two minutes.' He pushed through his office door and collapsed by the tower of junk on his desk. 'Shoot.'

Fenchurch stayed by the door. 'Liam sent you the stories, right?'

'Stories is stretching it.' Victor tapped a pile of paper. 'One of the million things I'm juggling today is trying to turn this into something coherent. Saskia had a great interview technique but her writing style left a lot to be desired.'

Reed appeared in the doorway. Her nod indicated she'd got a signed statement from Liam. She leaned against the wall near the door.

Fenchurch settled his gaze back on Victor. 'Have you found anything I should know about?'

'We went through this last night, didn't we?'

'I know we did, sir, but I would've expected you to have done some more digging into her work since then.'

Victor looked at him long and hard, eyes flickering. 'I've not been through all of the files, just some stuff for tomorrow's paper.'

Fenchurch opened the notes app on his Airwave Pronto. 'We're listening.'

Victor let out a momentous sigh, the sort that could achieve escape velocity and get a good way to the moon. He flicked through a pile of junk on his desk. 'We went through most of it last night.'

'Guy Eustace?'

'Him. And I think there was something on the property developer, Iconic. You know, her last appointment?'

'I met Yana Ikonnikova last night. Was it about her charitable foundation?'

'More or less.'

Fenchurch grinned. 'Tell me about the less.'

'Saskia was criticising Ms Ikonnikova for not doing enough to help the poor, that kind of thing. She's taken millions out of London over the last five years. Meanwhile, there's a sixty per cent increase in homelessness year-on-year, rents are going through the roof and people are getting pushed out of the city.' Victor leaned back in his recliner, running his hands through his wiry hair. 'I'm sure you have some sympathy. Must be difficult to stay in London on a police officer's salary.'

'Don't worry about me, Mr Morgan. I got in at the right time. It's a lot harder for younger cops.' Fenchurch finished typing the note. He felt the thrum of his mobile vibrating in his pocket and let it ring out. 'You said something about using the stories tomorrow.'

'That's right.'

'What are you going to do with them?'

'Publish them.' Victor held his glare, giving at least as much as he was taking. 'Saskia was a great journalist. We're working on a commemorative edition.'

'I suggest you don't.'

'Why not?'

'Because, like I told you, we think Saskia was deliberately targeted. Looks like they broke into Liam's flat and stole the laptop to order.'

'Are you suggesting there's a threat against me?'

'It's possible. Until we know why she was killed, we don't know who's safe and who's not.'

'Jesus.' Victor tugged at the tight locks on the top of his head. 'Look, the cat's already out of the bag here, okay? I let my boss know as soon as Liam sent the files through. They're not going to pass up this opportunity.'

Fenchurch raised his eyebrows. 'I'm sure the opportunity relates to furthering Saskia's causes, of course.'

'I wouldn't be so sure.'

'This should've been evidence. Now it's lost.'

'I can only apologise. Do you think you'll catch who took it?'

'I doubt it.' Fenchurch passed him the shot of the man on the escalator. 'Do you recognise this man?'

Victor screwed his eyes shut. 'Never seen him, sorry.' He handed the photo back. 'Who is he?'

'We believe this man followed Saskia from her last meeting to Angel tube station.'

'Near where she was killed, right. I get it.'

'Mr Morgan, given what we've just talked about, do you have any idea who could've been targeting her?'

'Could be anyone. Nature of the beast, you know?'

'Nobody springs to mind?'

'Afraid not.'

Fenchurch nodded slowly and gave him a few seconds to think it through further. 'How did they know Liam had her laptop?'

'Are you implying something?'

'Other than Liam and Saskia, you were the only one who knew it was there.'

'Well, I haven't told anyone. Good God, this is outrageous.'

Fenchurch waited for a nod from Reed then got up. 'Okay, thanks for your time. We'll show ourselves out.' He followed Reed out and marched down the corridor towards the lifts. 'What do you make of this, Kay?'

'Buggered if I know, guv.' Reed hammered the lift's down button. 'Feels like someone's covering their tracks.'

'But who?'

'Could be anyone.' She held up her Pronto. 'I'll see if I can get some time with this Eustace geezer.'

'Thanks.' Fenchurch checked his mobile. The two missed calls he'd ignored were both from Nelson. He dialled him as the lift door ground open. 'Jon, what's up?'

'Guv, I can't make the PM.'

'Where are you?'

'I'm still out in ESB with Trident. Early doors but I think we're getting somewhere with this photograph of the guy on the tube.'

'Do they think it's Kamal?'

'Not in so many words. They're setting up some meetings with some undercover cops and a CHIS.'

'Can't we get their Covert Human Intelligence Source log?'

'Not shareable, guv. Doubt even Docherty's got clearance.'

'Right, Jon, I'll cover the bloody PM. Call Pratt and make sure he knows you're not coming.'

Chapter Sixteen

Fenchurch glanced up from the Pronto he'd been staring at for the last hour or so. 'You done yet?'

Dr Pratt hovered over the body, eyes closed as he muttered into a digital recorder. He rubbed the back of his glove across his bushy beard, the sort even a hipster wouldn't go near except on an ironic pub crawl. He locked eyes with Fenchurch. 'Well, I don't know how much you've got out of this jamboree, Inspector, but that's it nailed down now.'

Fenchurch yawned and pocketed the Airwave. 'Sorry, what's nailed down?'

'I'm absolutely certain the cause of death was that knife.' Pratt held up Clooney's exhibit, bagged and tagged but still covered in blood and twigs. 'One hundred per cent.'

Fenchurch glared at him. 'Are you winding me up? I saw her get stabbed.'

'Well, it pays to be cautious, Inspector.' Pratt dropped the weapon on a table next to the body. 'The blow severed both carotid arteries and the blood loss led to brain death within four minutes. My almost namesake, young Jonathan Platt, tried to save her at the crime scene, but the damage had been done.'

'So we couldn't have saved her?'

'It should be some consolation. She'd have died within twelve if you'd laid her on the ground. Maybe. As it was, the ambulance took twenty-two minutes to arrive. So no, there's nothing you nor Mrs Fenchurch could've done.'

Fenchurch shut his eyes and swallowed. 'Abi said she spoke to her as she died. How could she, if the arteries were cut?'

'Because her assailant missed her trachea.' Pratt caressed the throat, less like a lover and more like a butcher. 'Speech would've been entirely possible.' He removed his hand and tightened the glove. 'If only one of the carotids had been cut, there's a possibility she could've survived. One would've carried enough oxygenated blood to the brain to allow Mr Platt to do his work. The body has some wonderful coping mechanisms.' He sighed and knitted his brow as he looked down at the victim. 'But, alas, nothing could save young Ms Barnett here.'

Fenchurch felt the air squeeze out of his lungs again. Dots of light spiralled round at the edge of his vision. Blinking didn't make them go away. He cleared his throat. 'That's it?'

'For once, it's all as it appears to be.' Pratt tore off his mask as he stepped away from the body. 'While the victim was menstruating, her blood chemistry was exactly as I'd expect.' He paused to frown at a dim shape visible through the glass. 'In you come, Georgie-Porgie.'

Clooney opened the door and waltzed in, eyes dancing around the room, piercings rattling. 'Less of that, please.'

'Sorry, force of habit.' Pratt gave Fenchurch a sidelong glance then winked at the SOCO.

'I'm terribly sorry I couldn't attend, gentlemen.' Clooney thumbed at Fenchurch. 'But this frightful bore has me working my fingers to the bone.'

Fenchurch folded his arms. 'I'm not that boring, am I?'

'Maybe not, but you are frightful. Anyhow . . .' Clooney pulled out a tablet computer and cradled it like a newborn. 'There it bloody is.' He grabbed the bagged knife in his free hand. 'Good news is we've confirmed the blood type matches Saskia's. I'd say that's pretty much conclusive, though I can run DNA if you want.'

'Please.'

Clooney groaned as he tapped the screen, his long fingernail clacking off the glass. 'Noted.' He swiped across the display and frowned. 'Oh, we've not finished the prints yet.'

'But you are working on them?'

'That's right.'

'Well, that's all I ask.' Fenchurch patted Pratt on the arm, making him jump. 'We done here?'

'Indeed. I shall see you anon.'

What a bloody waste of a morning.

Fenchurch's belly rumbled as he climbed the stairs, trying to decide where to get a burrito from on the way back to Leman Street. There was that van opened up in Bermondsey he'd been meaning to try. Or the Tortilla by Borough Market at a push.

'Simon!'

Fenchurch spun round.

His old man was jogging towards him across the Lewisham concourse, his Paisley-patterned tie flapping around. He stopped by Fenchurch and hunched over, sucking in breath. His lined face was dotted with liver spots and the new Des Lynam moustache made him look like a janitor. 'What you doing out here, son?'

Fenchurch let him rest against him. 'I'm in a hurry, Dad.'

'You not got time for lunch with your old man?'

'Not today. Sorry.'

'Been a while since we had a sit-down.' Dad's breathing was just about under control. 'What brings you here? A new case?'

'A murder. Fresh one, too.' Fenchurch felt his eyes start to water. 'Happened right in front of my eyes. Ab was there, too.'

'Christ.' Dad clamped a hand to his arm. 'You okay?'

'I'll live. It's Abi I'm worried about, Dad. She was with the girl when she died.'

Dad shook his head slowly, flattening down his bushy moustache with both hands. 'I wouldn't mind a word with you.'

'What about?'

Dad sucked in a long breath. 'What do you think?'

'Chloe.' Fenchurch brushed his hand off and started off across the dimpled lino. 'You know I stopped looking. I can't do this any more.'

'Just hear me out, Si—'

'Hoping she was alive has taken years off my life. I can't keep doing this to myself. And I certainly won't do it to Abi.' Fenchurch stormed off through the front door, his fists clenched tight.

Old goat never could take a bloody telling.

Fenchurch collapsed into his seat and tore another ring of foil off his burrito as he chewed. The beef positively sang with the cumin, melted in his mouth. Worth the extra trip over to Borough Market.

A knock at the door. He looked up.

Reed stood there, eyes on Fenchurch's lunch. She sat opposite. 'That looks good, guv.'

'It *is* good.' Fenchurch finished chewing and swallowed. 'What's been going on here?'

Reed got out her Pronto and checked the screen. 'The SOCOs are done with all of the crime scenes, guv. Found nothing useful.'

'Figures. Clooney's been on blue-arsed-fly mode, or so he says. Keep close to him.'

'Will do. They're still running tests but I'm not holding my breath on anything positive coming from it.' Reed grabbed a tortilla chip from the open bag on Fenchurch's desk. He let it slide — it was one of those days and there were too many anyway. 'Been through all the statements line by line since I got back from your little scuffle. Spent a good hour putting together a lovely timeline. It's on the wall in the Incident Room.'

Fenchurch finished chewing another mouthful, his mouth in blissful agony. 'Any noticeable gaps?'

'Still a couple just before he nicked that bike. Trying to plug it, but . . .'

Nelson appeared behind Reed. 'Thought I could smell Mexican food.'

Fenchurch grabbed a handful of chips and dipped them in the tub of guacamole. 'You know how Abi and I were in Edinburgh in January after we renewed our vows? Well, had a haggis burrito there. Lovely.'

Nelson made a face. 'What's in that?'

'Offal and stuff. Mostly black pepper. Very tasty.'

'I believe you.' Nelson sat on Mulholland's desk. 'Just got back from speaking to the Trident lot at ESB. Had to make do with a prawn sandwich.' He flashed a photo through the air at Fenchurch. The man on the escalator. 'Confirmed this guy is Kamal.'

Fenchurch stared at the shot. 'Got a surname?'

'Sorry, guv. They don't know. Just got some undercover statements calling him by his first name. No photos, no ID, nothing. We're a step ahead of them.'

'How the hell don't they know?'

'Just don't. All they've got is that name. Could be a code name, could be nothing.' Nelson gave a shrug and got out his Pronto.

'They think he runs a gang of phone thieves round Shoreditch, Hackney way.'

Reed finished chewing another stolen chip. 'This was in north London, Jon.'

'Yeah, that too. Islington anyway.' Nelson tapped something on his Pronto. 'Waheed and I spoke to two CHISes. They were scared stiff of him.'

'If you think he's running kids nicking phones, speak to DI Jason Bell about it.'

'Guv.'

'God, these are good.' Reed reached over for another chip and the tub of salsa. 'Why's he on Trident's radar, anyway?'

'Stabbed a kid in Shoreditch a while back. Then another up at the arse end of Hackney.'

'So, how do we get him in custody?'

'No idea.'

'Bloody hell.' Fenchurch dumped his burrito on the desk. Some rice and peppers spilled out. 'Sergeant, I covered the PM so you could find him.'

'I left Waheed over there, guv. Believe me, they're actively hunting him.' Nelson cowered behind his Pronto. 'Problem is, the guy's just a ghost.'

Fenchurch took a sip of lemonade. 'I'm sick of hearing that.'

'Look, there's a guy undercover in a gang out in Hackney. My contact at ESB reckons I should speak to him.'

'So bloody speak to him.'

'It's not that simple, but I'll get it done.'

Fenchurch finished his burrito without too much spillage and balled up the foil. 'Let me get this straight. Saskia was running away from this Kamal kid, right?'

'That's right, guv.' Reed dumped the salsa tub back down. 'She spotted him and tried to tell Abi just as she died. Named him, meaning she knew him.'

Fenchurch spun the ball around on the desk. 'What I don't get is why she didn't call someone.'

Reed shrugged. 'She might've done.'

'Where are we with her phone records?'

'I'll check on progress, guv.' Reed's turn to hide behind her Pronto. 'Last I heard Clooney had a blocker. That RIPA wasn't sufficient.'

'Get on the rack, Kay.' Fenchurch picked up a handful of chips then thought better of it. 'Someone tell me we've found her phone?'

'It's still missing, guv.' Reed's note seemed long enough to cover a good chunk of *War and Peace*. 'It's been off since twelve minutes after the attack.'

'Bloody hell.' Fenchurch glared at Nelson as he chewed. 'Jon, I want this Kamal guy found by close of play, okay?'

'Guv, that's—'

'Stick him in a room, Jon, I don't care where. I just want me and him in it.'

'I'll try.'

'No, you'll get him. Okay?' Fenchurch stared at Nelson for a few seconds then switched his glare to Reed. 'Kay, tell me you've got something other than a timeline we can actually progress.'

'Well, I've managed to get an appointment with that MEP. Guy Eustace. Saskia spoke to him five times over the last month.'

'I'm not buying him killing her.' Fenchurch made a face. 'I don't think he's going to have paid some black kids to kill her, is he?'

'You never know.'

Fenchurch stuffed his foil in the bag for recycling. 'Right, well, I'll tag along with you.'

'As long as you bring those chips, guv.'

125

Chapter Seventeen

Fenchurch took his seat in the office. The back window looked over Laycock Green towards the health centre and the primary school where . . . He clenched his jaw. Where Chloe attended.

'You okay, guv?'

Fenchurch rubbed his eyes and looked over at Reed. 'I'm fine.'

'You don't look it. And I know why.'

'Bloody wind outside. Must've got something in my eyes.'

'Guv . . .'

'Sorry I'm late.' Guy Eustace breezed in and squeezed through a thin passageway towards his desk. He collapsed into his sprawling office chair, a mound of dimpled leather on castors, and let out the mother of all sighs. He had one of those faces you'd never tire of punching, kicking, head butting. Nothing like a chin, just a wall of flab hanging from his jawline. Tintin haircut, the smallest of quiffs gelled up at the front. The dapper sports jacket looked like it didn't care how badly it clashed with his green trousers. His eyes narrowed at Reed then darted away. 'Now, what can I do for you?'

Fenchurch slid his warrant card across the cheap laminated desk-top. Didn't want to speak too soon in case it came out as a croak.

Eustace was taking his time examining it, as if he had the Met personnel database in his skull. He tossed it onto the desk. 'Again, how can I help, Inspector?'

Fenchurch pocketed the card. 'You know a Saskia Barnett?'

'We're acquainted, yes.' Eustace grinned as he slumped back in the chair. Something clunked deep in the mechanism. 'She was interviewing me for a profile for that paper she worked for.' He raised his eyebrows at Fenchurch. 'You know who I am, of course, don't you?'

'Can't say I voted for your party, sir.'

'A shame. Well, Ms Barnett found my life story to be a fascinating one. Guy Eustace, UKIP MEP.' He grinned and shut his eyes, lost to some internal nostalgia. 'Classic rags to riches. I was a property developer in the eighties, built up from a two-bedroom flat in Covent Garden to a twenty-property empire. Lost it all in '92, of course, but I rebuilt from the ground up. The purest form of hard work. I've been out in Dubai since 2003, making a packet.'

'She found that interesting, did she?'

'Not as much as how I decided to come back and serve my community as an MEP.'

'Doesn't look like you're serving much time, sir.' Fenchurch waved a hand around the room. 'You're here in leafy Islington instead of Brussels. Is that why an investigative journalist was interviewing you?'

Eustace scowled at Fenchurch, finally cottoning on to the fact he wasn't preaching to the converted. Not even the same religion. 'You'll probably know I'm a big player in the campaign to leave the EU. Well, it seems to have made me a target for the little madam. She'd been going through my expenses, trying to find dirt. She thought she had.'

'Oh?'

'It was all above board. I declare everything.' Eustace raised his hands, the little pound sign cufflinks dangling free. 'I'd stayed at an Italian friend's house in Tuscany over Christmas last year. Put the flights through the books.'

'Thought you lot hated Europeans?'

'It's the EU we hate, Inspector.' Eustace licked his lips. 'The imperial march of German jackboots. Could've sworn we stopped that seventy years ago, but here they still are, imposing their will on this great country of ours. Opening the door to Islamic extremists. Believe you me, England will be much stronger out of it.'

Fenchurch nodded, struggling to hide the smirk. 'You mean the UK, right?'

'Well, those parts who still wish to be a part of a United Kingdom.' Eustace left it hanging in the air, dangling like his cufflinks, wobbling like his jowls. 'Listen, I have no axe to grind with Ms Barnett. Why would I? She was just doing her job. As are you.' He sat upright, frowning. 'Why are you asking me all these questions, anyway?'

'Just wondering if you had any idea why someone would want to kill her?'

Eustace blinked hard a few times. 'Kill her? What?'

'We're looking into her murder, sir. She was killed last night.'

'What?' Eustace's shaking hand ruffled the quiff. 'I assure you I had nothing to do with this.'

'Didn't say you had.'

'She was just someone I came across. Someone who took an interest in my crusade against the forces of darkness. A fascinating creature. I can't believe she's . . .'

Reed was clearly taking umbrage at the 'creature' description, her face looking like she'd drunk battery acid. 'Does the name Qasid mean anything to you?'

'Just trouble.'

'You know him?'

Eustace stared up at the ceiling, his jowls tightening to a smooth sheet. 'No, I don't. Those *ethnic* names are the ones causing trouble around these parts.'

'What about Kamal?'

Eustace looked back down, head tilted to the side. 'Why are you interested?'

'We believe Saskia was murdered by someone working for or with Kamal. Any information you had about him would be greatly appreciated.'

'He's just a myth, Sergeant. A Robin Hood folk tale for impressionable youth. The sort of youth who ISIS are radicalising at—'

'Do you know where I can find him or not?'

Eustace shook his head, jowls flailing. 'Like I said, he's a folk tale.'

Fenchurch jumped in before Reed could. 'Do you have any inkling of why Ms Barnett was murdered?'

'None, whatsoever. Our dealings were mainly about my profile, she . . .' Eustace's brow creased. 'Actually, are you aware of the Central Bar?'

Reed frowned. 'Place on City Road, corner with Moreland Street?'

'Correct.' Eustace gave her the briefest of looks. 'Right by the council flats.'

Reed stabbed a note into her Pronto. 'Why do you bring it up, sir?'

'Saskia was asking about that place at our last meeting.'

'What was the context?'

'Seemed to think I knew something about the place. I don't.' Eustace stood up and stretched out. 'Thought it might be well worth a punt.'

Reed got out of the car first, stepping onto the pavement and waiting. 'This is where you caught him, right?'

'Near here.' Fenchurch did a three-sixty, taking in the daytime drone of City Road. Delivery vans, taxis and buses queuing at the lights.

'He made my skin crawl, guv.'

'Eustace?'

'What sort of creep calls someone "a fascinating creature"? Can you believe that?'

'I saw you noticing.' Fenchurch started off down the street. A gust of smoggy breeze hit his face. 'Aside from his oiliness, did you get anything to suggest he's involved?'

'Not really, guv. Much as I'd hate to admit it.'

'Yeah, me too.' Fenchurch came round the bend and stopped.

The Central was an old brick building a couple of storeys tall and just as wide. Edwardian or late Victorian, but without much character beyond age. It stood in the shadows of an old council high-rise, flat-faced and architecturally plain. Left to fester and rot, rather than the sort of place university lecturers and the like would take over and renovate.

'I'll lead, guv.' Reed pushed the scratched brass plate on the front door and entered.

Dub reggae throbbed out of the speakers, skanking guitar buried under a wall of echo, sub bass rattling the bottles behind the bar. Given it was only just after clocking-off time, it was busy. Friday-night drinkers were already laying claim to the tables dotted around the place. More than a few still in their uniforms — courier firms, Tesco shelf-stackers and construction-work denim.

The barman stood side on, spraying polish on the burnt-wood bar. He rubbed a cloth over the surface in time with the pulse of the music, getting it to a nice shine. He wore a gangster suit, thick chalk stripes and wide lapels. His hair was fused into tumbling dreadlocks, running halfway down his spine, the strands nearest his skull looking like the stuffing of an old settee. He swung round to face them and nodded. The half of his head that'd been facing away was shaved to his scalp. Harlequin man. 'What can I get you?' Thick Jamaican accent, or the London bastardisation of it.

Reed showed her warrant card. 'Looking for anyone who's spoken to a Saskia Barnett.'

'Who's asking?'

'DS Reed. This is DI Fenchurch.' She stuffed the warrant card away and let the name settle in, waiting for the barman's face to show how much he'd taken in. 'Who are you?'

'I'm the manager.'

'Just the manager?'

'I own the place as well.' He smirked. 'Well, I own the lease.'

'And what's the name on the lease?'

'Clinton Jackson. You want my phone number as well, sweetheart?'

'You're all right.' Reed eyed the beer pumps. 'So, you know Saskia?'

'Sure I know her. She's been in here a few times.'

'What was she asking about?'

Jackson went back to spraying his bar, almost rubbing away the top layer of wood. 'I'm doing a good job with this place, like you wouldn't believe. But a lot of people round here hate me.' He looked up, wide eyes pleading with her. 'When I took over the lease, this place took in three hundred quid a week.' He grinned. 'Now it's five grand.' More polishing, more rubbing. 'I set up club nights in the basement. Dub techno, soul, house, got a reggae sound system on tonight. We brew craft beer and craft rum downstairs, too.'

Reed frowned. 'Is craft rum a thing?'

'It is now. Sell it to America. A few joints in NYC love it, man. Love it.'

'So why do people hate you?'

'Because I'm a success.' Jackson set the polish and cloth down. His clientele were keeping away from the serving area, though there were more than a few empty glasses and licked lips. 'You know how hard it is being a successful black man in London? People hate any success. *Racists*. Attacking me. Hurting me. Saying I've done this or that.'

'And have you?'

'I sell beer and rum. Let people dance. I pay my taxes, pay my staff a living wage. Lot of people round here don't.' Jackson waved at a blacked-out window on the far wall, near the door. 'You see those new buildings, how much of that money goes through this country, eh? I'll tell you. Nothing.'

Reed nodded slowly and leaned against the bar, her palms down on the shiny surface. 'Was Saskia helping you?'

'She was writing a feature about me. About what I'm achieving here. And about my . . . difficulties.'

'You ever speak to the police about them?'

Jackson gave a shrug. 'They been in here. They hassle me. Hate me as well. Police are racist, man.' He bellowed with laughter. 'You're excused, sister.'

'I appreciate it.' Reed straightened up, a slight amount of rose on her cheeks. 'So you were close with her?'

'We was tight, sister. Tight.' Jackson knitted his fore and middle fingers together. 'She's good people. Came in for a drink all the time with that boy of hers.'

'Liam?'

'That's him. They liked my rum. They in love. Deep in love.' Jackson cackled. 'So deep in love.'

'She ever mention anyone who had it in for her?'

'Nah. Not to me, anyway.'

'What about Kamal?'

Jackson stared down at the counter, like he was using the surface as a mirror, trying to work out who was the fairest of them all. 'He's barred from here.'

Reed glanced over at Fenchurch. 'You know him?'

'I tell him don't come back.'

'What did he do?'

'He's bad people.' Jackson nodded at the first customer whose desperation for a drink overcame their fear of the law. He started pouring a beer, already knowing the order. 'Opposite of Saskia. She's pure, he's . . . Yeah, dirt. Soiled.'

'You know where I can find him?'

'Hopefully in the bottom of a ditch.' The tap fizzed off and he slid the glass along the counter.

'I'll take that as a no.'

'That's a no, yeah.' Jackson pulled on a smile as he handed over the foaming pint to a delivery driver.

'Thanks for your time.' Fenchurch led Reed out onto the pavement. They'd only been inside ten minutes but the traffic had doubled, now an overflowing river, close to jamming. 'You got on well with him there.'

'Maybe. Place is buzzing just after four.' Reed skipped across the road, just avoiding a taxi. 'Did that get us anything?'

'Not sure, Kay. Feels like there's something just out of reach.'

'Back to the station?'

'Yeah, but not ours.'

———

Islington police station was a squat brick building, flags blowing in the gentle breeze, not quite slicing any of the heat off the day. The architect had clearly designed a castle but the project manager had made sure a load of bricks got chucked together.

Fenchurch started across the four lanes of suburban traffic otherwise known as Tolpuddle Street. The sort of busy back road that riddled London, always a right turn away from a high street of some description. He nodded at Reed as they waited halfway for a queue of buses to pass and pushed through the front door.

Sergeant Owen Greenhill stood behind the partition, like he was protecting the civilian receptionist. He dominated the station's entrance space, the flickering strip light above giving snapshots of his shaved head. Thin strands of beard sprouted from the tops of his ears and met under his chin. Well over six foot and the rugby-playing end of the spectrum, too. His intense stare slackened off a touch as he recognised Fenchurch. 'Uncle Simon?' His high-pitched squeak sounded like someone in a scrum had booted his testicles back into his stomach. He switched his attention back to the member of the public standing in front of him.

A haggard man with greying red hair, dancing like he needed the toilet. He gripped the counter like his life depended on it. 'You swear you've not had any screenplays handed in?'

'Not today, Pete.'

'But someone's stolen it!'

Reed got close to Fenchurch and winked. 'Uncle Simon?'

'I told you.' Fenchurch took a deep breath. 'He worked the beat for me when I was Sergeant at Brick Lane.'

'Long time ago, that.' Reed nodded over at Greenhill. 'He'd have been in nappies, then, guv.'

'Not as long ago as you'd think.' Fenchurch looked over at the customer swaying about the place. Couldn't smell any booze off him or anything. 'Owen's doing well for himself, career-wise, and wants everyone to know. Even though he's still in uniform.'

'I'll see you again tomorrow, Pete.' Greenhill smiled at the customer. 'Take care of yourself.' His gaze followed the man's slow steps across the floor until the door shut behind him, shaking his head all the way. 'Same thing every day at this time. Yet more care in the bloody community.' He gave the civilian a nod then beckoned Fenchurch through to the back. 'On you come.'

Fenchurch followed Reed through the back to a small Sergeants' room. Maybe not as much of a high-flyer as he expected. 'Did that guy mention a screenplay?'

'Really sad story, as it happens. Worked in Hollywood for a few years as a screenwriter. Did some TV and a film. Way I hear it, some bad acid kicked off some genetic psychological problems. Lives with his mum now. Poor bastard.' Greenhill shook his head as he typed something into a computer. 'Now, where were we?' A smile flickered across his lips as he hammered the keys. 'Anyway, how's my favourite uncle doing?'

'Cut that out.' Fenchurch tried to avoid looking at Reed's snigger. 'I'm fine, Owen. How are you?'

'Just came on shift. That incident on Upper Street last night seems to have scared the bejesus out of the locals. They've all been in here repenting their sins.' Greenhill shrugged. 'Happy to act as confessional, though.'

'I bet.' Fenchurch rested against the counter. 'We've just been down to the Central. Wonder if you've got any info on it?'

'That place . . .' Greenhill leaned forward, resting on his elbows, and rolled his eyes. 'Bloody nightmare and a half. We're out there every Friday and Saturday. Stabbings, assaults, you name it. Last week, we had twenty guys trying to start a bloody race war outside. Had to close City Road for an hour. Worse than your escapades last night.'

'Less said about that the better. Got anything on the owner?'

'Jackson? Guy's a nuisance. Always in here complaining about racism. About people assaulting his staff.'

'Anything ever in it?'

Greenhill drummed his stubby thumbs on the countertop. 'Never found anything.'

'What about Saskia Barnett?'

'Her.' A sigh accompanied another shrug. 'I know her. Everyone does. Cheeky little madam.'

'The incident on Upper Street that spooked your clientele? That was her.'

'That was *her*?' The colour drained from Greenhill's ruddy face. 'Christ. Like I said, I'm just on and haven't had my briefing yet. Been away in the Algarve with the boys on a stag.' His sigh sounded like it emptied his lungs. 'Rich didn't have time to brief me when I rocked on. She's *dead*?'

Fenchurch nodded at Reed, making sure she left him in his grief for a few seconds. 'I take it you knew her well?'

'Not too well. She was thick as thieves with Jackson, though. Pair of them were in here all the time, causing a ruckus. She'd always be supporting whatever his latest beef was. Having a pretty young blonde on your side's got to help, right?' Greenhill blushed as he smiled at Reed. 'No offence.'

'I'm neither young nor blonde.' She shot him a wink, leaving her prettiness uncorrected. 'You sure you want to say that out loud, anyway?'

Greenhill shrugged again. 'It might sound cynical, but my Uncle Simon taught me to be that way.'

'Leave me out of it.' Fenchurch scowled, trying to ignore Reed's flirty laughter, little giggles cut in with a nibbled bottom lip. 'What about Guy Eustace?'

'Now there's a liar and a bloody thief.' Greenhill took a step back and stared up at the ceiling, like that's where he'd hidden his inner calm. He looked back down and sighed. 'Scumbag has the cheek to take all that cash out of Dubai then try to kick any ethnics out back here.'

'Sure you should be using that word?'

'Look, you know what I mean. If bloody UKIP get in, we'll be staffing concentration camps within the first bloody week. Them or the bloody Tories.' Greenhill itched at his beard. 'Why are you asking about Eustace?'

'He put us on to Jackson.'

'Did he now? Cheeky sod. Way I hear it, he wants him to give up his lease. That pub's a bloody gold mine. Shift it and you can tear down the council flats, kick them out to Essex or Kent. Redevelop that whole stretch.'

'Tell me it's not serious?'

'Who knows? Nothing Eustace can do to shift him. He's got a twenty-year lease on the place, from what I hear.'

Fenchurch locked eyes with Reed, trying to piece it together. 'So Eustace owns stuff round there?'

'Not that I know of, but you know what that lot are like. Everything's in shell corporations and holding companies and God knows what else. I'm just a mere uniformed sergeant, I can't conjure up ownership details for you.'

'So Guy Eustace is a dead end?'

More typing. 'He is with me.'

Fenchurch took another look deep into his eyes and decided there wasn't anything else. 'Does the name Kamal mean anything?'

Greenhill stopped typing. Didn't look up. 'Kamal?'

'That's unsettled my favourite nephew.' Fenchurch handed him the shot of the man tailing Saskia in the tube station. 'This him?'

Greenhill took a long look at the photo. He closed his eyes briefly. 'I know the name, but I've never seen him.'

'Ever had him in here?'

'Once. Would've locked him up if I'd known what he did.'

'Know his full name?'

'Wish I did. Had him in for dealing. This big black lawyer turned up after fifteen minutes, went in with the CID lot and got him back out.'

'This lawyer, wouldn't happen to be Dalton Unwin, would it?'

'That's the fella.' Greenhill went back to his typing. 'I need to get on.'

Fenchurch winked at him. 'Thanks for your time.' He pulled open the door, held it open for Reed. 'After you.'

Greenhill called over: 'You have spoken to Zara Redshaw about Saskia, right?'

'Who?'

Chapter Eighteen

Fenchurch thumped the buzzer and a fake doorbell sound chimed out, like a fifteenth-generation copy of a copy. He took a step back and checked out the house again. The smallest porch in the world pimpled an eighties brick thing with tiled dormers in the attic. Part of a long terrace running all the way to the Highbury and Islington station at the end of the road. An Overground train's brakes squealed just behind the wall opposite.

The door juddered open and a woman stood there, hand on her hip. Early forties, though she clearly didn't think so. Green skirt, no tights, boots up to her knees and a white blouse. She had a page-boy haircut, looking like she was growing out the Princess Di fringe. 'Yes?'

'Zara Redshaw?'

'I've no time for Jehovah's Witnesses or whatever you're selling.'

'DI Fenchurch and this is DS Reed.' He showed his warrant card. 'Need to have a word with you, if that's okay.'

'What's this about?' Her accent might've been Hampshire, though London had hardened the country burr.

'Can we come inside?'

'No, you can't. I've asked what this is about, so please tell me.'

Fenchurch took his time folding up his warrant card and putting it away. 'We gather a Saskia Barnett interviewed you recently?'

'I've nothing to say about her.' Zara looked up and down the street. 'She comes in here, spouting a pack of lies. I've nothing to say about her.' She pushed the door shut. 'Goodbye.'

'She's dead.'

The door again. 'What?'

'Saskia Barnett was murdered last night.' Fenchurch let it sink in, watched her face fall, her mouth hanging open. 'We're trying to establish a connection between her day job and her death.'

She switched her gaze between Fenchurch and Reed. 'You'd better come in.'

———

'—and he's in custody just now.' Reed looked like she could repeat the script without engaging her brain.

The living room was somehow freezing despite the weather outside. Felt like her open patio doors were actually a secret portal to Greenland. Bookcases lined the walls, filled with lots of right-on political tomes and what looked very much like a complete collection of original Penguins. Must be worth more than the house.

'My God.' Zara hugged her arms tight around her shoulders. 'She was just sitting there a couple of weeks ago.' She nodded at Reed. 'That chair you're in.'

Reed flashed a smile. 'When did you last see her?'

'Two weeks ago, like I said. She turned up, much like you did. They used to call it doorstepping. She came in here and told me this pack of lies.'

Fenchurch raised an eyebrow. 'Would these lies have anything to do with you and your mates trashing that Cereal Killer café back in September?'

Zara scowled at the window. 'How the hell did you find out about that?'

'When you get arrested, we tend to keep a note of it.' Fenchurch leaned forward just enough to attract her attention. Gave her a raised eyebrow. 'You don't think renting out a house in Hackney to some students wouldn't be deemed hypocritical, given your actions?'

'How the hell am I supposed to pay for my family?'

'So, was she interviewing you about your hypocrisy?'

'*My* hypocrisy? They set up a café like that in one of the poorest parts of London. Five quid for some cornflakes when people are starving on the streets.' She nibbled at a fingernail, the varnish chipped and cracked. 'Listen, those bloody *hipsters* are asking for it.' She spat the word out. 'They're sucking the heart out of Shoreditch.'

Fenchurch got up and wandered over to the bookshelf, picking up a George Bernard Shaw in a plastic bag. 'Was she asking you about the Cereal Killer attack?'

'I'm not answering that without a lawyer.'

'Because you're still awaiting trial on that one?'

'That's a nonsense. It'll get thrown out.' Zara fiddled with a bead of pearls on her wrist. 'I want to keep that sort of thing out of the press because I'm standing for election to the Islington Council.'

'And she uncovered some dirt on you. Sure you're not worried how it'll look to have an anti-gentrification candidate acting as a landlord?'

'Look, she was clutching at straws. I'm just an honest woman trying to raise my kids. I need any money I can get.' Zara started combing her hair again, her gaze on the book in his hands. 'There's no story here. I told her to leave. She complied.' She marched over and snatched the paperback from Fenchurch. She carefully placed it back on the shelf. 'Now, I'm asking you to leave me alone.'

'We're just about done, Ms Redshaw.' Fenchurch nodded for Reed to back off. 'Did she ever mention the name Kamal to you?'

She tilted her head to the side. 'Should she have?'

'It was the last thing she said. Might be her killer's name.'

'Well, I've never heard of it. Sorry to be such a disappointment.'

———⌣———

Fenchurch got back in the car and looked back at Zara Redshaw's house. The curtains twitched in the living room, a thin sliver showing a slit of her face, a fraction of a scowl on her mouth. 'What do you think, Kay?'

'I don't think she's a likely suspect, guv.' Reed yanked the key and the engine started with a crack before settling into a deep rumble. 'What's she really got to gain from killing Saskia?'

'The sort of question I keep asking myself.' Fenchurch took a last look at the house. The curtain had reset now. He clicked in his seatbelt and braced himself as Reed took off. 'I don't get her. Woman's a cardboard cut-out Sloane Ranger, right? You saw that Princess Di haircut, saw what she was wearing. Why's she into all this anti-gentrification stuff?'

Reed pulled left onto the Highbury Island roundabout, her head darting around, looking for threats as she hit the right-hand lane. They cut past the thin patch of trees swaying in the breeze and swung round, back onto the outer reaches of Upper Street. One long road filled with so many memories, Fenchurch's whole career in trees and concrete and brick. Hell, his whole life since he left home.

'Sorry, guv. Bastard of a roundabout that. What were you saying?'

Fenchurch slumped back in his chair and grinned. 'I was saying, why is Zara Redshaw campaigning against all this gentrification?'

'Cultural slumming?' Reed was back in driving position, eyes front, hands on the wheel. No more jerky head movements. 'Or maybe you're judging a book by its cover. Could be she's really passionate about what's going on in London.'

'Maybe. Seems to go pretty deep with her but doesn't touch the surface.' Fenchurch focused on the traffic in the oncoming lane. A thick wedge of work vans led north out of the city. 'You could be right, but there's something I'm not getting with her.'

'Your Spidey-sense going off?'

'It's been tingling like a bastard since last night, Kay.' Fenchurch checked his phone for messages. Still nothing from anyone. 'Maybe she gains by keeping the story out of the papers?'

'I've had a look through Saskia's stories online, though. Nothing on Redshaw so far.'

Fenchurch glanced over as she gave a motorcyclist the finger. 'What if there's an unpublished story? Something Victor Morgan's sitting on?'

'I'll call him when we get back.'

They drove in silence. Lots of strands but nothing seemed to connect. Just too many loose ends and a suspect keeping quiet.

'Look at this place, guv.' Reed waved across to the right. A Costa had planted itself between a KFC and a local pharmacy, fighting a beachhead against airport taxi companies and small-time bookmakers. The old man's boozer on the corner had been reborn as a gastropub, a chalkboard on the pavement outside. 'I remember when this place was rough. I mean, it's never been Shoreditch or Hackney, but it wasn't the best, was it?'

'That's how we can afford to live here.' Fenchurch snorted. 'Couldn't now, even with selling my flat.'

'Exactly my point. The people who've lived here for years will hate all these hipsters moving in and taking over. Coffee bars and wood-fired pizza ovens. Vinyl shops. Microbreweries.'

'Sounds like you're sympathetic, Kay.'

'It's not that, it's just. I don't know. Anti-hipster movements are popular.'

'You think she's just using it as a platform to get on the council?' Fenchurch couldn't see it. While hypocrisy and politics were easy bedfellows, this wasn't the sort of shit that'd wash with the great unwashed. 'She'd need to keep up the act, if that's what it is.'

'People tend to forget what politicians say during an election once they're in power.'

'Maybe.' Fenchurch swallowed as they passed the marble-like stone registry office where they'd got married years ago. Very different place to where they renewed their vows. He'd been so unromantic back then — what changed? Other than *that*.

'Been thinking, guv.' Reed stopped to let a gang of already-drunk teens shout across the zebra crossing. 'This Saskia seemed to be pretty good at kicking hornet's nests.'

'Good old Stieg Larsson could've written about her. What are you thinking?'

'This Kamal kid's killed her because of something she did. What if it's something she did to him? Revenge. We're focusing on all these conspiracies. Stories she was writing about people. What if it's personal?'

'Maybe. Any way up, we need to find this Kamal.' Fenchurch scowled at the drunk teenager in the Jesus Christ pose halfway across the crossing. A mate twice his size picked him up and carried him across like he weighed nothing.

Fenchurch's phone throbbed in his pocket, still on silent. He got it out — Abi — and answered it. 'Hey.'

Silence.

'Abi, are you okay?' Fenchurch turned away as Reed frowned at him. They were sitting at the lights just by the Hope & Anchor pub. Lots of memories of that place. Felt like a few lifetimes ago. A gang of hipsters were drinking outside, tapered jeans and NHS specs. Still silence. 'Abi, talk to me.'

A long sniff. 'When are you coming home?'

Fenchurch released a breath he didn't know he was holding. 'Be late, I expect. Why?'

'I . . . Never mind.'

'What's up?'

'I can't stop thinking about that girl.'

'Did you go to work today?'

'I've just got home. It's been playing on my mind all day. Doubt my kids learnt anything.'

Fenchurch checked the dashboard — 18.26. 'Look, I'm not far from home just now. I'll be there in two ticks.'

'You sure?'

'Sure I'm sure. You're more important than this bloody case. Love you.' A whisper he hoped Reed didn't overhear. He pocketed the phone and let out another breath.

She looked over, her forehead creased. 'Abi okay?'

'Not coping well with what happened last night. I forget how desensitised we are to all this shit. Can you drop me at home?'

'Sure thing.' Reed grimaced. 'You'll have to brave the Northern Line in the morning.'

'Thanks for reminding me.'

'Need me to clear this with Docherty?'

'If he asks, just get him to call me, okay?'

Reed set off once the traffic lights changed, racing to get round a dawdling bus. 'Will do.'

Chapter Nineteen

Reed hung a right along Theberton Street and drove past the family restaurants — the Indian, Thai, Italian. The old pub across the way was now a wine bar. Like the bloody eighties all over again. She took a left and ploughed on down the road, mercifully quiet given the time. 'You don't talk about Abi much. What you've done is a huge change.'

Fenchurch tapped the window. 'End of the street's fine.'

Reed pulled in by the Chinese on the corner that'd been there long before they moved in. 'I take it that means "Shut up, Kay"?'

'Things are good. Genuinely good.' Fenchurch looked up at the brick building, dyed a burnt orange in the fading sunlight. 'Need to sell my flat and pay off the mortgage on this place.'

'Why not rent it out to some students and then kick in a café?'

Fenchurch couldn't help but laugh. 'Maybe. No, it's genuinely good, Kay. Christ but I've missed her. Eight years apart. Wasn't very good for me.'

'Guv, are you still looking for Chloe?'

Fenchurch opened the door and let the cooling air in. 'Abi'll cut my nuts off if she finds I have.'

'So should she be sharpening her knives?'

'No, I haven't. Genuinely. Now, piss off and find this Kamal character.'

'Sure thing, guv.' Reed was focusing on the rear-view mirror.

Fenchurch got out and leaned back in. 'Don't know why I grabbed this bloody case in the first place, it's going nowhere.'

'We're getting there. You just need to be patient.'

'Not one of my virtues. See you tomorrow.' Fenchurch smacked the door shut and waved as Reed shot off. He turned into Barford Street. Their street. Again. The fourth block over was taking a turn to have the scaffolding up. Hopefully Quentin was off to Munich or Madrid again.

He navigated his way around a Range Rover making a pig's arse of a three-pointer. The red-face driver looked like he was trying to mount the Chinese restaurant as well as the kerb.

Otherwise the street was quiet — time was, kids would've been out on their bikes or playing. Maybe hoofing a football off the back of the Design Centre.

He opened the front door and trudged up the stairs. Stuck his newly cut key in the flat door.

Same as it ever was.

The freshness had gone. This was routine now. When did that happen?

Fenchurch locked the flat door behind him and hung his coat on the rack. Then dumped his keys in the dish on top of Abi's, hers absolutely stuffed, like a prison jailer. No idea what half of them were for. He fingered the tiny USB drive hanging off his. His will and everything important about him. Jesus. 'You still home, love?'

'In the kitchen.'

He followed her voice through the flat, maybe just a bit too big for two people. Worth too much to give up on, though, in case they slip down the property ladder.

Abi sat at the kitchen table, clutching a cup of tea and staring out of the window. She looked round and gave him a weak smile, just a fleeting flicker on her lips, never touching her eyes. 'Just made a fresh pot.'

'Thank God.' Fenchurch grabbed a cup and sat next to her, easing his suit jacket off. He poured out some milk, then tipped in the tea, wisps of steam spiralling up.

'Always liked how you did that. Milk first, then tea.' She was staring into space, focusing on the vapour. 'Shows you don't come from the landed gentry, Simon. No airs and graces about you.'

'Never pretended there was.' Fenchurch took a big slurp. Hot and sweet, almost like it had sugar in it. 'How you doing, love?'

She went back to looking out of the window. Across the roof of the Business Design Centre, the City was gearing up for the Friday evening darkness. A frown teased its way across her forehead, deciding to stick there for a while. 'Can't get it out of my head.' A dainty sip of tea, the ceiling spotlights catching on the ceramic. The mug almost clattered down, not enough liquid to spill over the side. 'How do you cope?'

Fenchurch set his cup down on the table. 'Thought you said I didn't.'

That got a smile. 'Have you got anywhere with the case?'

'Yes and no. Very difficult to pin down a motive.' He took another glug and shook his head. 'Two hundred quid for a nicked phone. Can you believe it? This bloody city.'

'I can believe anything.' She fidgeted with her cup, the rim rattling off the table. 'You will get him, won't you? He won't be allowed to do it again?'

'Trust me, that kid's going away.'

Thump, thump. The front door. Thump, thump.

Fenchurch locked eyes with Abi. 'We expecting anyone?'

'Not me. Any more of your attack parcels from Amazon?'

'Nothing due for a while.' Fenchurch got up and padded through the flat. The usual floorboard creaked in a new way, a crunch rather than a squeak. Worrying. He twisted his key in the lock and opened the door.

Dad stood there, his wide smile stretching out the moustache. 'Sorry if I'm a bit early, son.'

'What?'

'For dinner. You invited me round, remember?'

———

'Better go and drain the lizard.' Dad got to his feet and cracked his spine. 'Oh, don't get old, son. It's shit.' He ambled off into the hall, one hand supporting his back, like it was doing the job his vertebrae should.

Abi leaned over, eyes cut to tight slits. 'You didn't tell me he was coming round.'

'He didn't tell *me*.' Fenchurch shook his head, scowling after his old man. 'He just pounced on us. Worse than your parents.'

'Well, I'd rather have been able to get something proper in.' She stared down at her half-eaten plate of spaghetti, smothered in pesto and sun-dried tomatoes. Just the skin of the salmon fillet left.

Fenchurch speared a chunk of her pasta and ate it. 'That was really good.'

'I need some time just with you, Simon. If I'd wanted to see your dad I would've invited him.'

Fenchurch took another sip of water. 'Can't be helped, I suppose.'

The toilet flushed and Dad strolled back through, all signs of back pain gone. 'That's better.' He sighed as he collapsed into his seat at the end of the table. 'Smashing grub, Ab. You can cook for me any time.'

'Feels like I have to.'

Dad frowned, cupping a hand over his ear. 'Sorry?'

'Any time you want to, Ian. Just a bit of warning, yeah?'

'Right, right.' Dad slurped at his tea. 'Lovely cup of tea, too, Ab. Smashing.' He shot a wink at Fenchurch. 'Did I tell you Erica called the other day, son?'

He swallowed hard. 'No?'

'She was asking after you. I said you were pretty busy but you'd call her when you got some time.'

'Thanks for putting me in it. You know I hate you setting expectations like that.'

'Listen, I bought you some time.' Dad twirled his pasta around his fork, bracing it against the spoon, and held it over his mouth. 'She's living in Sheffield now with her family. Trying to figure out what the hell to do with her life. Might go to uni, she said, but she needs some qualifications first.' He chomped at his pasta, like a fish at bait. 'Do they still have A Levels?'

Abi nodded. 'For now.'

'That's good. Thought they'd done away with it. Anyway, I told her to avoid London.' Dad dropped his cutlery and pushed his plate away. 'What's for pudding, Ab?'

Her eyes widened. 'I think there's some of that mint Ben & Jerry's in the freezer.' She winked at Fenchurch. 'Unless Simon's eaten it.'

'Wouldn't go near the stuff, your honour.' Fenchurch gave a mock cough.

Abi stacked up the plates. 'I'll just get it, then.'

Fenchurch watched her go over to the recess they'd jammed the new American-style fridge into a few weeks ago. Bloody nightmare — scraped more paint off the wall than the appliance. Wished he could just talk to her, suck all the poison out of her head.

Dad took another sip of tea and smacked his lips. 'You want to get back to it, don't you?'

'I want to put the little shit away.' Fenchurch sighed in his father's direction. 'We didn't have an arrangement for tonight, did we?'

Dad picked at his teeth, tiny black seeds stuck there. 'I need to speak to you, son.'

Fenchurch shut his eyes and let his head fall. 'You're still looking, aren't you?'

'It's not a crime—'

'Dad, I told you. It's not healthy.'

'Simon, if you're not going to look, at least let me. This case you're working—'

'Dad . . .' Fenchurch shot him a glare. 'You were the one who used to tell me off.'

'Maybe I shouldn't have.'

Fenchurch wanted to shout, wanted to scream. He leaned low and spoke in a harsh whisper: 'Are you telling me you've got something?'

'Maybe.'

Fenchurch sat back and stared at the tabletop. Pale pine artfully knotted. A little scuff where he'd dropped a beer bottle a couple of weeks ago. 'I really don't want to know.'

'Simon, twenty-three black kids have gone missing in east London in the last two years. They all match the pattern.'

Fenchurch rubbed at his left eye, just about caught the tear. 'That's a lot of kids. Someone would've noticed.'

'Yeah, me. I have. You know what it's like in the wild east. Half the kids are on crack by the time they're fifteen. That many going missing isn't going to run up any flagpoles. Especially with a Tory government.' Dad tilted his teacup and drained it. 'I linked four cases on the system. Same MO as Chloe. Then I started canvassing the area.'

'Jesus, Dad, I don't want you going out in those areas on your own.'

'Had a uniform Constable with me, son.'

'Doesn't make it right.' Fenchurch glanced over to the kitchen area. Abi was still rooting around in the freezer, half of the contents now on the counter or the floor. 'Have you got any leads?'

'Nothing solid. I've been speaking to your old mate Savage.'

'Why?'

'He's got power. And a budget.'

'Dad . . .'

Abi dumped three bowls on the table, the spoons clattering against the china. 'There's quite a lot left. Almost like Simon's bought a replacement.' She dropped the tub onto the table and ice cracked off. 'What are you two discussing?'

Fenchurch narrowed his eyes at his father. 'Dad's just moaning about how much the West Ham season tickets are going to cost at the Olympic stadium next year.'

Abi frowned. 'Thought they were going to be cheap?'

'Exactly.' Dad wrapped his hands around his empty teacup, like he wanted a refill. 'It's less than a third of what Arsenal charge at the bloody airline ground. Should put the prices up and keep the riff-raff out. Going to get loads of Orient fans pitching up if we qualify for the Champions League.'

'Don't you want the stadium full, Ian?'

'Would rather stay at the Boleyn.'

Fenchurch winked at her. 'At least Big Sam's gone.'

'Small mercies, son. Small mercies.' Dad took a bowl from the pile and grabbed the tub. 'I'll be mother, shall I?' He prised the lid off, taking a lot more effort than it should. 'Away to bloody Newcastle on Sunday, isn't it?'

'Think so.' Fenchurch's phone rattled in his pocket. Unknown caller. Take it or not? 'Sorry, I need to see who this is.' He got up and marched over to the hall. 'Fenchurch.'

'It's DS Greenhall.'

'Owen.' Fenchurch perched against the dresser. 'What's up?'

'Thought you'd like to know. There's been a stabbing down at the Central.'

Chapter Twenty

Fenchurch jogged down the back street, the same one he'd chased Qasid down just a day ago. He emerged onto City Road, a teeming sea of white and red lights. He waited for the green man and crossed over, panting heavily.

His bloody car was at the sodding station.

As he neared the Central, he felt a deep thud through the soles of his feet. Boom, boom, boom, boom. Four to the floor. Must be the basement disco.

He stopped and looked around. Not even the vaguest whiff of a police presence, other than the double-parked squad car causing hell with the traffic flow. Though there was a reek of ganja.

Fenchurch pushed through the door, the frown feeling like it'd add another line to his forehead.

The place was pretty much standing room only, old Rastas with greying dreads mixing with club girls and hipsters. Half eight on a Friday night was prime time, probably thirty or forty per cent of the weekly take. A poster on the wall indicated a dub reggae sound system on downstairs later that night.

A door opened and deep bass thudded out, loud enough you could taste it in the air. No snare, no percussion, just smooth bass and echoing keyboard sounds. Not his kind of music. The door swung closed and the noise shut off again.

No sign of Greenhill. The cheeky bastard.

Clinton Jackson was behind the bar, pulling a pint as he flirted with some white girls. Dressed like they were heading to Ministry of Sound or wherever the kids went these days. He clocked Fenchurch and waved him through to the back.

A green door was cordoned off with police tape. Fenchurch stepped over and opened it. A small office, stacked high with crates of Red Stripe, the walls covered with Ska memorabilia.

Owen Greenhill was lumbering under the full stab-proof get-up and blocking the doorway. A rare excursion from his lair at Islington nick. He turned around, his Body-Worn Video camera blinking, indicating it was recording.

Fenchurch entered the room and stomped across the small space to him. 'I would've expected this place to be in lockdown if someone's been stabbed inside.'

'You cut the call too soon, Simon.' Greenhill smirked as he thumbed at two of his colleagues behind him, dressed like they were dealing with a full-on riot. 'Kid got slotted outside.'

Between them, a black man in his twenties gripped his left bicep. Thick blood covered his right hand, dripping onto the floor, a pool forming at his feet. The angry glare on his face was just about killing the pain he was clearly experiencing.

Greenhill thumbed out of the doorway. 'Just down Moreland Street, by the flats. Got units canvassing the area. He came in here after he got attacked. Daft sod's refusing medical help.'

'I assume there's an ambulance en route?'

'Traffic's a proper nightmare at this time of night. Kid's called Lemar.'

'Got a surname?'

'What do you think?'

Fenchurch pushed over towards Lemar, who was more interested in the pub doorway. He shook his free shoulder. 'Sir, I'm a detective. Can you tell me what's happened?'

The sharp gaze switched to Fenchurch. Kid was like a walking fight, all pumped fists and snarling teeth. 'You got a big nose, man.'

Fenchurch knew the type. Such a bloody cliché. 'I'm trying to help.'

'Some prick on a bike stole my phone.'

Fenchurch's gut recoiled, wrapping tight around the digesting pasta. He caught a smug grin on Greenhill's face — see why I called you? 'Did you recognise them?'

'No, man. Cost me six hundred quid. I chased after him along the road, past the flats. Didn't see it coming, but someone else came at me with a knife.' Lemar tightened his grip on his arm and grimaced. 'I do karate, though, yeah? So I hit him, creamed the guy. Bastard caught me with the blade, man. Whole gang of them came after me so I ran off. Came in here.'

'You called the police?'

'Barman did.' Greenhill nodded over at the bar, Jackson doing his best impression of Tom Cruise in that bloody film.

'I'm going to kill them, man. Once my boys turn up, we'll get out there and do them.'

'You shouldn't be telling us that.'

'See if I care, cop. You lot need to let me call my boys. They'll hear anyway, man, and they'll come running. Hardest in Hackney.'

Fenchurch caught Greenhill's sigh. Another gang war avoided by blind luck. 'What about a name?'

Lemar screwed his eyes tight. A splodge of thick blood dripped to the floor followed by a faster trickle. It spattered on the lino. 'Nah, man.'

'You're sure about that?'

'What's it to you?' Another grimace.

'You ever hear the name Kamal?'

Lemar let out a sigh. 'They's all Kamal's boys.'

Fenchurch gritted his teeth. 'Was Kamal there?'

'Never met the dude, but heard his rep. One of the kids used that name. Think it was him with the knife, you know?'

'Did you get a look at him?'

'Pretty good.'

'I'll need to get a description from you.'

'Once I kill him, sure.'

Sirens squalled through the door, compressed by the doorway. Blue lights flashed through the bar. Outside, an ambulance had mounted the pavement, pretty much blocking the entrance.

'Listen, sir, there's an ambulance outside.' Fenchurch thumbed through the door. 'You need to get to hospital, okay?'

'I ain't going nowhere until he's in the ground, man.'

'Way you're going, you'll be there first. Once we've patched you up, my colleagues here will take your statement. We're going to get after them just now.'

'I want to get them myself, man.'

'That's not going to happen.' Fenchurch nodded at the two uniforms bookending him. 'Get him sorted out.'

One of the bar staff appeared with a bucket and mop for the bloody puddle at their feet.

'Come on, Owen.' Fenchurch got up from the tower of beer and followed Greenhill outside. The crowd cheered as the stereo crackled into life again, pumping out the same thunking bass as below. Then he pushed out of the door into the warm night air and shook his head at Greenhill. 'This place is a bloody disgrace. Kamal's bloody been here.'

'So, what's the plan?'

'Let's find Kamal.'

'Like it's that easy. I've got uniform around the corner going through the flats.'

'So come on, then.' Fenchurch marched down the road, following the wet splashes on the pavement. 'Where was it?'

'Just there.' Greenhill waved a hand at a pool of blood in front of Kestrel House. The hulking tower loomed over their heads, maybe eighteen, twenty storeys tall. Dotted with a few satellite dishes, fewer than you'd think. Most windows were lit up. The patch of grass was barely touched by the street lights.

Two female uniformed officers stood in high-vis gear, one speaking into her crackling Airwave. The other gave Greenhill a nod. 'Sarge.'

'Any sign of anyone?'

'They're like rats, Sarge. They'll just disappear when you go after them.'

'So we've not caught anyone?'

'Not likely to either.' She checked with Airwave uniform and got a shrug. 'Kate's on with Alpha X-Ray Niner. They've got a gang round the back.'

'Come on.' Fenchurch started off away from them.

A couple of cars swung past, rubberneckers gawping at them. Down at the side of the building was a playground, orange and blue swings and a slide. Three hip-hop kids were on the roundabout, slowly spinning around. A pair of male uniforms were struggling to keep them under control.

Fenchurch got on between them and sat down, not upsetting their careful balance. 'Nice night for it.'

The one in the middle inched away from him but stayed sitting. 'Get off, man.'

'Not going to do that, son.' Fenchurch moved close to him, getting the measure of the kid. Coffee skin and ginger hair. 'Wondering if I can have a word with Kamal.'

'Who?'

'You heard. Kamal.'

'Don't know no Kamal, man.'

'Sure about that?' Fenchurch thumbed towards the bar. 'He stabbed someone just down there.'

'No, he didn't, man. I did—'

The kid next to him grabbed him. 'Kiefer, man, shut up.'

Kiefer shrugged his friend off. 'I stabbed him, man. Got my knife and that.'

'This guy's five oh, man. You don't—'

'Say what I like. Free planet.'

Fenchurch held up a hand, keeping Greenhill and his uniform at a distance. 'So Kamal wasn't there?'

'Didn't say that, man.'

'Just that you stabbed that guy?'

'Punk shouldn't have been here. Shouldn't have been starting on us, man.'

'Said he got his phone nicked.'

'He lying.'

'So, if I wanted to speak to Kamal?'

'Forget about him, man.'

Fenchurch stood up and adjusted his jacket. He beckoned the uniforms over and grabbed Kiefer's arm. 'Read him his rights.' He waited until one of them had Kiefer under control then walked over to Greenhill.

'Masterful.'

Fenchurch shook his head. 'Didn't get us anywhere, though, did it?'

'So what now?'

Fenchurch started off again. 'Let's have another word with the owner.'

———⁓———

Fenchurch waved across the bar, getting hold of Jackson's attention. He beckoned him over.

Jackson nodded apologies at the white girls he was chatting up and wandered over. 'Yo, what's up?'

'Someone getting stabbed outside your bar is what's up, Mr Jackson. From what I gather, this sort of trouble happens a lot round here.'

'This is London, man.' Jackson ran a hand through the half-dreads. 'We got problems round here. They're my problems, they're your problems but they try to make me look bad in the eyes of you guys.'

'You need to tell me about Kamal.'

'I know nothing about no Kamal.'

Fenchurch raised his eyebrows. 'Sure about that, sir? You said you barred him.'

Jackson let his shoulders slouch. 'Brother causes trouble here so I bar him. He's not come back. I'm trying to run a business here and he's making me look bad.'

'The man who was stabbed reckoned it was Kamal who did it. Have you seen him around here?'

'No, man.'

'Do you know where I can find him?'

'Hell, I hope.'

Fenchurch held his gaze for a few seconds then waved him away. He glowered at Greenhill. 'Time to haul someone over some bloody coals.'

Chapter Twenty-One

'Cheers, Owen. Catch you later.' Fenchurch got out of the squad car and slammed the door. He watched it disappear down Leman Street, quiet in the late evening lull before the pubs started emptying. Nobody was kicked out any more, they just head on somewhere else, the drinking never stopping. Places always ignored the licensing laws, opening when they shouldn't.

Leman Street was a narrow road crowded by tall buildings of all vintages, tight enough to give anyone claustrophobia. He jogged up the steps of the ugliest, most brutal building and barrelled through the front entrance.

Steve was at the desk, looking like he was past the point of swearing at the drunk punter shouting the odds through the glass. 'I have made a note of your complaint, sir, and you have a—'

Fenchurch swiped through the security door and made for the stairwell. Voices echoed around, coming from above, the hearty laugh of Nelson among them.

Fenchurch stopped on their office floor and nodded. 'Sergeant.'

Nelson stuck his vape stick in his pocket and gave a naughty schoolboy smile. The female uniformed officer he'd been chatting to sloped off upstairs, sucking on her own e-cigarette. A lot less shame in her habit than Nelson. 'Guv. Thought we wouldn't see you again tonight.'

'Well, you thought wrong.' Fenchurch tugged the door open. 'You sure you should be doing that inside?'

'It's just nicotine vapour, guv. It's not harming anyone.'

'That's not what I meant.'

Nelson's cheeks tightened. 'Just a bit of friendly banter.'

'Sure your wife would see it that way?' Fenchurch raised his eyebrows and waited a beat. 'I'm just pulling your leg, Jon.'

'Well, don't. Sir.' Nelson tried to hold his gaze but looked away a microsecond later. 'You hear about a scuffle at that boozer, guv?'

'I've just been there. The stabber was Kamal.'

'Shut up.'

'According to a witness who was more interested in frontier justice than the kind we offer. Which is why I wanted you to get hold of Kamal.'

'Guy's made of smoke.'

'Bloody hell.' Fenchurch raised his hand, ready to punch the wall. 'I told you I wanted him in custody.'

'I've been running things here, guv. Street teams, all the rubbish from the press release, you name it.'

'Bloody hell.' Fenchurch shook his head as he started off down the corridor. 'How's our little friend?'

'Qasid?'

'Nobody else in custody, Sergeant.'

'Right. Kid's a pro. Getting nowhere with him, guv. Just about to head back in with him.'

'I'll join you.'

Qasid was sitting next to Unwin. The pair of them looked like they were competing in the sullen-look world championships.

Fenchurch took his time taking his seat, his foot deciding now was the time to start throbbing again. There's nothing broken but why's it hurt so bloody much? He waved for Nelson to restart the interview.

Nelson leaned across the table and tapped the digital recorder. 'Interview recommenced at eight fifty-seven p.m. DI Simon Fenchurch has entered the room.' He collapsed back with enough huff and puff to blow a house down. 'Before our little intermission, I was asking you who Kamal is.'

Qasid rolled his eyes and sniffed. 'I tol' you, man. Ain't nobody by that name.'

'Quit with that bullshit, son.' Fenchurch picked up a chair and carried it to the side, sitting next to the young man. 'We know you're in league with Kamal. It's in your best interests to help us find him.'

'Ain't helping nobody, bitch. This is police brutality. You guys are Guantanamoing me here, man.'

Unwin reached across and gripped his client's wrist. 'My client means you're still holding him without charge. What gives?'

Fenchurch gave Unwin a few seconds of glare and restored his focus on Qasid. 'I want to believe you, son, trust me.' He grinned at the kid, inches away from him. A stench wafted off him, stale sweat and rank fear. 'The problem is I just can't bring myself to accept what you're saying. I saw you stab someone in front of me. You nicked her phone and her bag and you scarpered.' He leaned back and folded his arms. 'That's why I don't believe you.'

'Ain't done nothing, bruv.'

'There's something you can do to help. We need a word with Kamal.'

'I get that, bruv. You keep asking me, man. It's all you and Oreo ask me.'

Fenchurch gave Nelson a warning glance. Keep out of it. He smiled at Qasid again. 'How can we find Kamal?'

'You don't find him, he find you.'

Fenchurch leaned back in his seat, the metal creaking as he stretched out his sore arms. 'I've heard that elsewhere.' He tilted his head from side to side, as if he was thinking where. 'Of course, we've got you on record telling us you don't know him and now you say you do know him.'

'I ain't saying nothing.'

'Inspector.' Unwin got to his feet and started forcing buttons through holes on his suit jacket. 'I'd like a word.'

'I'm very pleased for you.'

The top button slotted into place. 'Now, Inspector.'

'Come on, then.' Fenchurch nodded at Nelson and followed Unwin out into the corridor.

'Interview paused at—'

Fenchurch shut the door and rested against it. 'You've got ten seconds to have this word.'

'This is out of order!' Flecks of spit were flying from the lawyer's mouth. 'What the hell do you think you're playing at here?'

'What does it bloody look like? I'm interviewing a murder suspect.'

'It looks like you're intimidating my client into a confession. It's not the seventies, Inspector.'

'Does that kid look intimidated to you?' Fenchurch laughed and ran his tongue over his lips. 'He's, what, eighteen? He's clearly been coached in dealing with the law. Now, who could've done that?'

'Are you insinuating something here?'

Fenchurch let it hang for a bit as a pair of uniforms passed in the corridor, the uglier one giving Unwin a visual shoeing. 'I want to know how you managed to turn up here to rep him without a phone call.'

'That's none of your business.'

'This isn't pro-bono work, is it?'

'Again, my business is none of yours, Inspector.'

Fenchurch stood up tall. A good three inches above Unwin, whose slouching shoulders weren't helping him any. 'As it happens, I'm more interested in you repping Kamal.'

'Excuse me?'

'You do rep him, right?'

Unwin looked away and gave a sniff. 'I don't know what you're talking about.'

Fenchurch stared up at the ceiling, finger on his chin, and focused on the water-damaged tiles, more dirty brown than white. 'Now, what was it?' He looked back at Unwin and winked. 'Oh yes. You rep this little oik in there. He works for Kamal, who I gather you know. He got himself into a bit of trouble up Islington way and his lawyer matched your description.' He paused, watched the nerves pulse on Unwin's temple. 'Admit it, Mr Unwin, you work for Kamal.'

'I've no idea who you're referring to.' Unwin brushed a hand across his forehead, masking the twitches or at least pushing them back in the box. 'There's no story here. My office received a call to defend an unnamed black youth.'

'Qasid didn't use his. Who placed the call?'

'I didn't ask.'

'You mind asking your office staff?'

'Fine.' Unwin rested his notebook against the wall and jotted something down. 'As for the other matter, I don't know anything about him.'

'That's a lie and we both know it. Is Kamal his real name?'

Unwin let out a deep sigh. 'Inspector, just drop it.'

'Surname? First name? Is it even his name?'

'Drop. It.'

'When I bring him in here — and I will, don't you worry — I have your word you won't be representing him?'

Unwin smiled at Fenchurch, seemingly unaware of the spasms on his forehead. 'My office deals with client initiation. I deal with fascists like you.'

'Fascists, right.' Fenchurch looked him up and down. He'd schooled Qasid. They weren't getting anything out of the kid tonight. He knocked on the door and nudged it open a crack. 'Jon, wrap it up.'

'Interview terminated at—'

Fenchurch leaned back against the door. 'You're bent, Unwin.'

'Excuse me?'

'The way I see it, Kamal or whoever he is, pays you a fortune to keep him and his lads out of jail.'

'You should take up writing fiction, Inspector. I hear self-publishing can be very lucrative these days.' Unwin reached past Fenchurch to grab the handle. 'Now, do you really want to prevent me from speaking to my client?'

Fenchurch got out of the way with a sigh and let Nelson and Unwin swap places. He nodded at the security officer in the room. 'Clive, take him back to his cell.'

———

'—as a thirty-seven bob note, Jon.' Fenchurch held open the Incident Room door and looked around. A bit too quiet for his liking. Then again, he'd been the one to piss off home early. 'What do we know about him?'

Nelson leaned against the door frame. 'Who, Unwin?'

'Of course, I mean Unwin.'

'Like you say, guv, he's bent.'

'But what do we know about him? What do we know about his firm?

'Liberal Justice?' Nelson scratched at the thin stubble on his chin. 'Just a two-bit operation on Shoreditch High Street, guv. I can get someone going over their history, if you want?'

'We really need to dig deep, Sergeant. Don't throw a hundred bodies at it, but get me something I can use.'

'Guv.'

'I want a nuclear weapon in my pocket next time we go toe-to-toe with him.' Fenchurch entered the room and looked round the corner into the little nook. A hand ran through black hair above a desktop computer. 'There you bloody are.'

Lad looked up. 'Guv, thought you'd gone home for the night?'

'Well, I'm back.' Fenchurch perched on the edge of his desk. 'Which room's Kamal in?'

'Guv?'

'I said, which room's Kamal in?'

Lad's eyes darted over to the approaching Nelson. He swallowed. 'He's not in any room, guv.'

'I know that. He's just sliced someone up on City Road.'

'Shit.'

'You were supposed to get him in here.'

Lad couldn't maintain eye contact. Kept looking at the floor, the wall, the clock, anything. 'And I've been trying, guv.'

'Where are you with this undercover source?'

Lad looked away, over at the dark window. 'Still haven't spoken to him.'

'Come on, Constable, this isn't what I asked for.'

'Guv, I've been busy, you know? That's why I'm here at nine at night. It's just—'

'Where have you got to?'

'Look, there was a raid on a phone shop this morning. This source was involved.'

Fenchurch twisted his head to the side, scowling. 'Your source was there?'

'Who else are we talking about?'

'Christ on the bloody cross.' Fenchurch pinched his nose. 'I was there with DS Reed. We really need to speak to this guy.'

'His handler told me to turn the heat down until that whole thing cooled off.'

Fenchurch got up again. 'Well, we're turning the thermostat right back up.'

Chapter Twenty-Two

'Nice of you to make your way over.' DI Paul Oscar in person was different to how Fenchurch had imagined from their phone call that morning. He looked like he had trouble tearing himself away from the mirror in the morning. Thick stubble looked a good few days after a five o'clock shadow, even at quarter past nine at night. His dark hair clearly enjoyed a close relationship with a high-end barber, shaved at the sides and artfully messy on top. He had a runner's physique, wiry and thin, with longer arms than his tailor allowed for. 'So you decided on the personal touch, then?'

'Feels like the only option left.' Fenchurch got up from his seat next to Lad and walked behind Oscar, trying to intimidate him.

London twinkled through the window, a sea of street lights leading from the office in the Empress State Building towards the glowing towers in the City. Canary Wharf sprouted up on the right, a bulge of tall columns of brilliance. A couple of planes were just dots in the sky, heading to City airport in the east.

Fenchurch turned around and perched on a filing cabinet. 'Surprised you're still in. Didn't think SC&O8 needed a night shift.'

'Charming.' Oscar folded his laptop shut and swivelled his chair to look at both Fenchurch and Lad. 'I manage a budget, same as you, I imagine?' He rolled his tongue across his lips. 'We do a lot with that, but it seems to shrink every year.' He gave a slight shake of the head. 'Anyway, what can I do for you? Part the Red Sea? Turn water into wine?'

Fenchurch couldn't bring himself to even look at Lad. 'My Constable here was hoping he'd get some time with one of your undercover lads.'

'I'm sure you of all people know how controversial that kind of work is these days, right?' Oscar folded his arms, his solid-gold cufflinks dancing in the air. 'I mean, you do read the news, right?'

'Don't get cute with me, Inspector. I made a simple request. Do you need me to repeat it?'

'I can't just give up my undercover operatives. It's one of the few areas we do still get to work in. Ever since you guys took over black-on-black crime, it's been slim pickings for us. You remember that, right? Means it's your responsibility. Not mine.'

'I remember. Investigated a few myself over the years.'

'And yet here you are, cap in hand, asking for my help. You know how much of my funds that eats up?'

'I hope you get value for money.' Fenchurch got up from the cabinet, the sharp corner digging into a buttock. 'Look, we're murder squad and this is linked to—'

'I don't care if you're High Command, this is a sensitive operation. A man's life is at stake here. If you jeopardise his security in any way, you know what the repercussions would be, yes?'

'More black-on-black crimes for me to investigate?'

'Now who's being cute?' Oscar shook his head, grinning wide. 'DC Lad told my boys he's looking at a journalist's murder, right?' He waited for a nod — Lad gave it. 'Our remit is prevention. That's it. All of our intelligence is to stop these kids killing each other. We've got a whole heap of stuff, but I doubt any of it'll be useful to you.'

'Enlighten me.'

'Hits organised on other gangs. New gangs muscling in on other gangs. How can that possibly relate to your case?'

'Feels like we've got off on the wrong foot here and I can only apologise.' Fenchurch tossed a photo onto the desk. 'We think it was ordered by this guy.'

Oscar left it sitting there. 'You think this is Kamal?'

Fenchurch gestured at the shot. 'Have a look at it.'

Oscar scanned the image for a few seconds and passed it back to Fenchurch. 'Don't know him. Sorry.'

'Your subordinates do.'

Oscar glowered at Lad. 'This is what your office junior here's looking for, right?'

'Have you got anything on him or not?'

'If I did, you'd have it. I'm not a complete arsehole.' Oscar opened his laptop, the weight of his budget drawing him back. 'Now clear off. Please. I need to get this finished before I piss off home.'

Fenchurch slammed the lid, just missing Oscar's fingertips. 'I'm not pissing off until you start helping us.'

He looked like he was going to throttle Fenchurch. 'You can't do that.'

'Listen, we've got a murder case. The girl was killed in front of my eyes. Give me access to this geezer or I will escalate this through channels, okay?'

'Do you expect people to respond well to threats?'

'I've driven across central London at night. Two of my officers have spent a day over here. You need to start playing ball.'

Oscar opened his laptop again. 'Right, I'll get something arranged.'

Fenchurch trotted down the stairs running down the side of Empress State Building, the opposite windows looking across the roof of Earl's Court. 'Well, I can see why you've found it so difficult to get anything out of them.'

'It's been like that all day, guv. They're playing politics.' Lad's tap-dancing brogues clicked off the strips on the steps. 'Not what I signed up for.'

'Not what any of us signed up for. Just keep close to them, okay?' At the bottom, Fenchurch pushed into the underground car park and scanned the subterranean tunnel for their car. Where was it? He frowned at a figure approaching a ten-year-old Jag, maybe ten feet from their pool car, and cupped his hands around his mouth: 'Howard!' The sound echoed around the concrete space.

DCI Howard Savage swung round, his forehead creased. A tweed sporting jacket draped over his arm, the other hand in the pocket of his black trousers. His thin comb-over looked like it'd lost another couple of precious strands, the remaining few shimmering in the harsh light. 'Simon? Good Lord.' He met them halfway, clamping a hand around Fenchurch's. 'How the devil are you?'

'Not bad, not bad. In the thick of it, as per.' Fenchurch snorted. The place reeked of second-hand diesel and cigarette smoke. He thumbed at Lad. 'You remember DC Lad, don't you?'

'Not sure we had the pleasure. Oh, now I remember.' His expression darkened, his eyes slipping under the surface of the eye sockets' deep pools. 'Yes, you interviewed the bouncer, didn't you?'

'With one of your guys.' Lad pointed past Savage at his car. 'Nice motor. Looks expensive.'

'My brother-in-law owns a dealership in Billericay. Got me a great deal on that monster.'

'Makes it look like you're on a banker's salary, though.' Lad shot him a wink. 'Bet that has its problems.'

Savage grimaced, his jaw tightening under the loose folds of skin. 'What brings you out here, gents?'

Fenchurch waved Lad back. 'Murder on Upper Street last night.'

'I heard about that.'

Lad got out his key fob and clicked it. 'Got some calls to make, guv.' He walked off towards the pool car.

The overhead lighting glinted in Savage's eyes as he switched focus to Fenchurch. 'I thought you'd got rid—'

'He's a bloody yo-yo, that kid.'

'I see.' Savage bared his teeth as the car door slammed. Then he lightened it to a grin. 'Well, Simon, as it happens, I've been meaning to call you.'

'That doesn't sound good.'

'I spoke to your father this afternoon. He mentioned something about you investigating a gang?'

Christ . . . Fenchurch let out a deep breath. 'He did say you guys had kept in touch. I'd rather you stayed out of it, if it's all the same.'

'Your father's a good man.'

'Mm.'

'Anyway, I thought you'd given up on this hunt of yours.'

'I have. Dad hasn't.' Fenchurch turned in the direction of a squealing car. A BMW doing some Hollywood driving up the exit ramp. Looked like Oscar behind the wheel, mobile clamped to his head.

Don't report it . . . No matter how much fun it'd be . . .

He grimaced at Savage. 'Have you been helping him?'

'Both formally and . . . informally.' Savage clutched his briefcase tight to his chest. 'This thing he's working on. Someone's taking black kids off the street. North, East, Southeast. Far south as Beckenham and as far north as Romford.'

'Why are you involved?'

'One possibility is it's for the sex trade.'

'So, it's just black girls?'

'And boys. There's a bit of a gap in the market now, given what we got up to before Christmas.' Savage nodded over at the car. 'Despite your officer's best efforts. Nature abhors a vacuum and all that.'

'Just black kids?'

'Like I said.' Savage rested a hand on Fenchurch's arm. 'This isn't related to what happened to your daughter. I told your father that.'

Nice to have someone on your side for once. 'Cheers, Howard. Doesn't mean he listened, though.'

'Persistence must be a genetic trait.'

'Tell me about it. What are the other possibilities, then?'

'Well. That's where I have my people-trafficking hat on.'

'What? It doesn't make sense to take people from London, though.'

'You'd think that. Not sure sense comes into people's heads sometimes.' Savage shrugged then dumped his briefcase on the car's roof. 'But it seems like it's happening.'

Fenchurch scowled again. 'Does the name Kamal mean anything to you?'

'Christ.' Savage swallowed and shut his eyes. 'Why bring him up?'

'You know him?'

'Let's say I'm aware of his work. What's your interest?'

'Reason we're out in this Godforsaken building. This case I'm working. We reckon one of Kamal's people killed this girl last night. Got the little bastard in custody but he's not speaking.'

'They never do. Well, I'll kick some tyres and see what's what.' Savage took his briefcase from the roof and opened the door. 'Keep me updated from your end, Simon.'

'Will do. Tell Chris Owen I said "hi".' Fenchurch gave him a cheeky salute and trotted over to the pool car.

Lad was behind the wheel, twirling his finger in the air — just wrapping up. 'Yeah, cheers. I'll call you first thing tomorrow, okay?' He killed it and pocketed the phone. 'Get anything, guv?'

'Not really. You?'

'Nada. Back to base?'

———

'Howard bloody Savage . . .' Docherty sipped from his Rangers mug, eyes closing. Pleasure or pain, Fenchurch wasn't sure. He swallowed the coffee and sucked air across his teeth. 'Anyway, I hear you went home early, Simon.'

'Look, sir, Abi's not coping well with this. I needed to help her.' Fenchurch clenched his fists under the table. 'She's not used to seeing people stabbed in front of her.'

Docherty winked as he swallowed another mouthful. 'I thought she was a teacher?'

'Very good, boss. Look, I needed to make sure she's okay. I've got a good team here. I trust them.'

'I get that, believe me I do, but you made me take this case, remember?' Docherty nudged his mug over the desk, scraping against the scarred wood. 'If you don't bring this home, we'll look like a pair of fannies.'

'I will solve this, sir.'

'There's a lot of clutching at straws going on here. You giving me the short one?'

Fenchurch tapped a finger off his trouser legs in time with the thudding drums in his ears. 'We're getting somewhere, boss.'

'Really? Last night we had a kid in custody who, quote unquote, definitely did it. Now we're, what, eighty per cent certain he did it?'

'I'd say that's fair.'

'Is it going to be sixty per cent tomorrow?'

'We'll get a result tomorrow.'

'I've heard this before from you.'

Fenchurch wanted to smack his saggy face, send him flying backwards. Not the smartest move. What was, though?

The door flew open and Mulholland entered, her scarf billowing behind her. 'Sorry I'm late.' She sat next to Fenchurch, grinning at him like a mongoose about to eat a snake, then scowled at the DCI. 'This case is going nowhere, I swear.'

Docherty sighed, eyes narrowing as they locked onto Fenchurch. 'That's not what I want to hear, Dawn.'

She pouted as she glanced round at Fenchurch. 'Isn't that what Simon's been telling you?'

'No, it's not.'

Fenchurch tried to ignore Mulholland, just getting another glimpse of her impish pout. Looked like she'd been building a gingerbread house in the woods somewhere. 'Look, sir. There's a gang in that area causing absolute mischief. We're onto the leader.'

'This Kamal kid, right?'

'Right. I'm just trying to get people to take this seriously.'

'Who?'

'SC&O8 for starters.'

'Trident? Christ, Si, I told you to be careful with them.' Docherty slumped back in his seat with a deep moan. 'Those cages you're rattling have big dragons in them, you know that.'

'They seem to know something about this guy but they won't share it.'

'I wonder why.' Docherty tossed his stress ball up in the air and caught it. 'We took their remit from them, remember? They're handing out bloody pamphlets while we investigate the murders they're failing to prevent. They don't want us over there sticking our oar in.'

'Is this you telling me to stop?'

'I'm saying be careful.'

'I agree.' Mulholland reset her scarf around her neck. So easy just to choke her with it. 'This is growing so many arms and legs it's looking like a millipede.' She finished retying the knot. 'As far as I can tell, we've got nothing tying this Kamal chap to our case.'

Fenchurch glowered at her, almost added a growl. 'We've got the CCTV images. Trident tied the name to the photo.'

'It's all just circumstantial.' She splayed a sheaf of papers across the desk. 'I've been through the witness statements your team has collated today. There's very little about him in here.' She ran a crooked finger over the documents.

'That's because he's smart, Dawn.' Fenchurch stayed focused on the paperwork. 'Qasid was working for him. Kamal ordered him to kill Saskia.'

'Look, Simon, there's very little backing up this theory.' Mulholland smiled at him like a nun to a small child, deformed and ugly. 'This is more likely to be a coincidence, you know that. I bet you could pick up any number of faces from the crowd behind her on that journey.'

'Maybe, but I bet none of them are gang leaders on Trident's radar.'

'So why has he killed her?'

'I've been trying to work that out. You should be aware of the people I've spoken to today, right?'

Mulholland gave him a wink. 'I would if you'd bothered to document it.'

Fenchurch switched his focus to Docherty. His gut ached — he hated having to plead like this. 'Boss, I want to bring Kamal down.'

'A noble goal, Si, believe me but I agree with Dawn. I'm worried about the hero cop stuff here.' Docherty got up from his seat and grabbed his stress ball, pounding it with his fingers. 'I just want a result on that lassie's death, okay? Nothing more, nothing less.'

'But, sir—'

'Simon, Simon, Simon.' Docherty stopped pumping the ball and held up a hand. 'We need to focus, okay? Focus on the result, nothing else. Especially on a case which isn't even on our patch.'

'You know I want to find out why Saskia was killed.' Fenchurch positioned himself so Docherty couldn't see Mulholland. 'If we can get a kill order, we can put Kamal away. Stop more deaths.'

'We need to find him first, though, right?' Docherty collapsed into his seat and tossed the ball into the air. 'Simon, I shouldn't be having to tell you this. Like Grandmaster bloody Flash said, it's a jungle out there.'

Mulholland roared with laughter, like she'd ever heard of Grandmaster Flash. 'It's very true, though. These sorts of transient crimes just don't get solved.' She crossed her legs and smoothed down her trousers. 'I was speaking to Sergeant Greenhill up at Islington. He said he gets a few of these every year. Multiply that across our whole area and there's tens, maybe hundreds of these cases.'

Fenchurch gripped the arms of the chair. 'Dawn, are you saying we shouldn't try to solve them?'

'I'm saying I'm worried we're losing ourselves to solving something bigger than what we have in front of us.'

Fenchurch stomped his feet on the floor, readying himself to stand. No. Don't give her the satisfaction. He gave her a smile back, polite and professional. 'I'm trying to put this guy away for what he's done to Saskia.'

'And that's very noble. But, if we can't solve it, we can't solve it. Don't give yourself an ulcer.'

Fenchurch sat back in the chair and switched his gaze to burn into Docherty. 'Boss, I need you to escalate something for me.'

'Let me guess, with Trident?'

Fenchurch gave him a smile. 'Given I'm so crap at the whole diplomacy thing, any chance you can speak to them for me?'

'They're out in the Empress State Building, right? Where Savage and his crew dwell, right?' Docherty made a note on a piece of paper. 'I'll see what I can do.' He dumped his stress ball in the mouth of the Rangers mug. 'Now, I'm heading home. I suggest you do the same, Simon. Dawn, you're in charge now.'

'Sir.'

Fenchurch got out of the door first and thundered down the corridor. Who the bloody hell does she think she is?

'Simon, is all this because you think it's your daughter?'

Fenchurch stopped dead. Slowly, he turned round to face Mulholland. Fists clenched, ready to punch something. Something that wouldn't report him, like the wall. 'What did you say?'

'I think you heard?'

'You think I'm losing my edge?'

'Not the words I'd use, but that's the sentiment.' She propped herself up against the Incident Room door. 'You've got previous, haven't you? There was that thing last Christmas where you thought Chloe was—'

'Don't you *ever* mention her name again, do you hear me?' Fenchurch turned back and stormed off towards his office.

Where the bloody hell did she get off?

Chapter Twenty-Three

Fenchurch stared at himself in the mirror above the key bowl. Deep bags accompanied the lines. You need some sleep, sunshine.

The place was deathly quiet.

He strolled through to the kitchen, gloomy with just the under-counter lights on. The shared garden out back was dark, light from the flats criss-crossing the scorched grass.

'Your dad left.'

Fenchurch swung round. 'Didn't see you there.'

Abi was sitting at the table, locking her glowing Kindle. She had her dressing gown on, hanging open to show her bed vest, white and flowery. Smelled like she'd been microwaving milk until it spilled over.

Fenchurch kissed her on the top of her head and rested his hands on her shoulders. 'Thought you'd have gone to bed by now.'

'Can't sleep. Didn't get much last night. Been drinking coffee all day.'

'Ab, I don't want you getting into a vicious cycle again.'

'I'll be fine once my heart rate's below a hundred and fifty.' She leaned back into him, letting him tease out the kinks in her hair, eyes closing. 'Had a good chat with your old man, though.'

'Dad's good like that. Just wish I could do the same for you.'

She shot a glare up through half-closed eyelids. 'You don't have to do everything for me all the time, you know?'

He held up his hands. 'Sorry.'

She closed her eyes again and smiled. 'I didn't tell you to stop.'

He grinned as he restarted the combing. 'I'll be working tomorrow.'

A long sigh. Her shoulders tightened. 'A policeman's wife's lot is a lonely one . . .'

'It's not that bad, is it?'

She clasped his hand, her skin soft and delicate. 'I can think of worse people to be with, Simon.'

'That supposed to be a compliment?'

'You know what I mean.' Her left eye peeked through the eyelid. 'You know your dad's still looking for Chloe, don't you?'

Fenchurch stopped combing. 'I can't stop him.'

'You're not helping him, are you?'

'Of course I'm not.'

She grabbed his hand. 'I know when you're lying.'

'I'm not *lying*.' Fenchurch looked away. 'It's just . . . Look, I spoke to someone for him. Just a chance meeting out west this evening.' He tugged harder at her hair like he was tearing lies out of his soul. 'There's nothing in it, I swear.'

'Stop that. It's hurting.' She sat forward and propped herself on the tabletop.

'He's trying to involve me, Ab. You know what he's like. He just doesn't listen.'

'That where you get it from?' She picked up her Kindle and folded the cover back. 'Simon, you need to be honest with me. We renewed our vows on the basis that you've moved on. Are you still looking for her?'

Fenchurch's gut lurched. He struggled for breath. 'I swear I'm not looking.' He sat next to her and stroked her arm. 'I still think about her every day, Ab, but I'm at peace with it. Okay?'

'Simon . . .' She closed her eyes and rubbed her forehead. 'Look, I've been thinking. I'm thirty-nine. I'm not too old to still have kids.'

Fenchurch stopped stroking. 'What?'

'I said, we can still have kids.'

'Jesus.'

'Forget it.' She tugged her dressing gown shut and got up, nudging him out of the way. 'I'll see you when you get home tomorrow.'

'Wait.' He held out a hand.

'Simon . . .'

'Look, do *you* want to have kids, Abi?'

'I honestly don't know.'

'So why bring it up?'

'Because . . . We need to sort it out. Make a decision.'

Fenchurch screwed his eyes closed. Just him and the drumming and the thudding in his chest. He opened them again, moisture forming around the rims. 'I wasn't aware there was a decision to be made.'

'Simon, you loved Chloe. Wouldn't you like to have another child?'

Fenchurch's gut was burning. Acid reflux bubbled away. 'You want to replace her?'

'I want to fill up our lives again.'

Fenchurch collapsed into the dining chair next to her. Banged his knee off the table. Ground his teeth together. 'Look, Ab, I'm scared.' He rubbed his eyes, his knuckles pushing at the balls. 'Scared I'll just see Chloe every time I looked at her.'

'Or him.'

'Right.'

'Anyway, that might not be a bad thing, you know? Help you deal with what happened.'

Fenchurch got up and flicked the overhead light on. The room was a bloody pigsty. He reached into the fridge for a beer and tried twisting the cap like they did on films. Just got a cut on his forefinger. He grabbed the corkscrew from the counter and snapped it off. Took a deep pull from the bottle. Tasted like lemonade. 'Love, I'll be sixty by the time he or she left school.'

'Old parents are all the rage these days.'

'Abi, we live in London. If . . . Chloe taught us anything, it's not a nice place to live if you've got a kid.' Fenchurch leaned against the wall and folded his arms tight. Took another pull on the beer. 'Look, I just need to think about it. Okay?'

'Simon, if you don't want to, that's fine. We just need to talk about it and agree what we're doing.'

'It's just this world. The shit I've seen, Ab. I was twenty-four when we had Chloe. Still walking the beat, bright-eyed and bushy-tailed. What happened with her made me grow up, you know? I just don't know if I can bring another life into this world. Not in London.'

'We can move. We've talked about selling your flat. If we sell this place as well. Buy somewhere a lot bigger, maybe with our own garden. Maybe even a house. It's still marginally cheaper south of the river.'

Another tug of beer. 'It's also south of the river.'

She winked at him. 'Not sure there's any good burrito places in Elephant and Castle.'

'Well, then, we're not moving.' His grin turned to a frown as he looked out at the night sky. 'I like it here. I've just moved back to my old stomping ground. Feels like I'm back home.'

'Look, just think about it, okay?' She got up and caressed his neck. 'Just remember the clock's ticking.'

'I know.'

'You coming to bed?'

'I'm wired more than you are, love. There's probably some football on BT or Sky.'

'No more beer after that one, okay?' She pecked him on the cheek and grabbed her Kindle. 'Let me know when you'll be home tomorrow, okay?'

Day 3
Saturday, 23rd April 2016

Chapter Twenty-Four

Fenchurch took a slug of builder's tea, nowhere near enough milk for once, and stared around the Incident Room. Looked like everyone was there, finally. He put the mug down and clapped his hands together. 'Okay, come on, you lot.' He stood up and waited for them to assemble.

The drone died down, replaced with a thick silence. Tired officers slurping and chewing. Stale air. Nelson was lurking near the back with his posy coffee cup, something Lad seemed to have picked up from twenty-four hours in his shadow. Reed sat at the nearest desk, sipping on an extra-large Red Bull. Mulholland was sitting there like a cat surveying its territory.

'Right. Jon, you're up first.'

'Sure thing, guv.' A long sip through the black lid, then Nelson dumped the cup on the table next to Fenchurch. 'As you know, guv, we're still struggling to locate Kamal. DC Lad has been working with some lads from Trident but, unless there are back channels we can use, we're stuck there.'

Lad crumpled his coffee cup. 'I spent most of yesterday out there. There's an undercover officer we need to speak to urgently but they're still blocking access.'

Mulholland craned her neck to look behind at him. 'Why are we so set on him?'

'Because he's the only person we know who's ever met Kamal.' Lad couldn't help but grin. Red rag to a bull. 'Well, other than our little friend in custody downstairs and his lawyer. The undercover officer is the only one I expect to play ball, though.'

'Does this officer actually know where we can find Kamal?'

Lad blushed, his cappuccino skin turning cranberry red. 'We won't know until we speak to him, ma'am.'

'Well, I know people in the Trident team, so let's have a word after this. Not too late, I do need to disappear.'

Lad gave her a wink. 'Ma'am.'

'While we wait for hell to freeze over with Trident, DC Lad, I want you to shadow forensics. That doable?'

Lad gave a loose shrug. 'That's fine.'

Fenchurch looked around the room. Mulholland seemed like she was about to jump in. 'Okay, dismissed.'

———

Fenchurch shut his eyes. The smell of the whiteboard marker stung his nostrils. He shook his head and reopened his eyes, staring at the wall. Reed's timeline sprawled across the white paintwork, stained from spilled coffee and bashing tables. He marched over and tapped the two gaps. 'We're still missing details on her last few minutes. I want her texts and calls from the network.'

'Still waiting on Clooney, guv.' Reed loosened off her ponytail, restoring her forehead's lines and dimples. 'Not had a chance to—'

'Kay, you looking for me?' Clooney stood behind her, clutching a coffee. He waved at the timeline. 'The Sistine Chapel's looking a bit rough today.'

'Thanks for joining us at the briefing, Mick.' Fenchurch took a sip of lukewarm tea.

'Sorry, young Ms Reed here's got me working ten to the dozen.'

'*Mrs* Reed.' She tightened her ponytail again. 'Do you want to give your update now?'

'You'll be glad to know I've finished the Crime Scene Report for Upper Street.' Clooney handed a document to Fenchurch. A bit on the thin side. 'Here's your copy.'

Fenchurch flipped through it. 'There's not much here, is there?'

'What were you expecting, a third Testament or something?'

'A lot more than this.' Fenchurch dumped the pamphlet on the desk near the whiteboard. 'The fingerprint analysis on the knife? Blood-type DNA matching?'

'They'll be supplemental reports, Simon. You know that. Besides, I've got other cases on the go.'

'This isn't good enough. Fast track them. Please.'

'I'll see what I can get done while I fast track everything else.'

Fenchurch made a note on the whiteboard, twice the size of the others. 'What about Saskia's phone? Has that turned up yet?'

'Eh?' Clooney screwed up his face. 'We found it yesterday.'

Fenchurch glared at him, wishing a sandworm or something would eat him up. 'What?'

Clooney scowled at Reed then Fenchurch. 'I thought you all knew?'

Fenchurch frowned, glancing over at Reed in time to see her shrugging. 'Well, we're not aware of it. Where was it?'

'It was in the phone recycler in that place you raided yesterday morning. I told DI Bell.'

Fenchurch curled his lip. 'You bloody tell me next time, okay?'

Clooney bowed his head. 'Sure thing.'

'So, have you done any analysis on it?'

'Well . . .' Clooney gritted his teeth — here comes another wave of bullshit. 'The problem is it's been wiped.'

'Wiped?'

'I swear you've still not cleared the echo in here.' Clooney beamed at Reed. She didn't grin back. He cleared his throat instead. 'Whoever recycled it did a factory reset.' He raised a hand. 'And before you ask, these things are encrypted and the drive gets zeroed. Meaning that, even if we could undelete anything from it, it'd just be gobbledygook.'

'So how do you know it was hers?'

'She had a cheap "*Hello Kitty*" case on it. It's scratched the plastic underneath and imprinted on it. While it's not a hundred per cent, we've got no other reports of stolen Galaxy Notes matching anything like that. And it's the sort of thing people do report. Insurance companies need a crime number, right?'

'Any idea who had recycled it?'

'None. The CCTV camera on the machine was disabled. Whoever did it got fifty quid for it, though.'

'Bloody hell.' Fenchurch focused on the gaping holes in the timeline. They were getting wide enough to send coach parties to visit and open a gift shop. 'How are we doing with her phone records?'

'Tom's sending them over to DC Bridge.' Clooney tilted his head from side to side, like he was weighing up the cost of telling the truth. 'It's not the complete story, though. We're still waiting on Facebook.'

'Facebook? I've not asked for any social media searches.' Fenchurch shot a glare at Reed. 'Have you?'

'Not me, guv.'

'Forget the social stuff.' Clooney waved his hands in the air, like he was trying to cool down or take flight. 'Look, according to her boyfriend, she was on WhatsApp all the time. Lots of kids with Androids are. It's like iMessages but cross-platform. Anyway, Facebook own it.'

'Just get me the bloody messages without the excuses.'

'I'll see what can be done.' Clooney's phone rang. He looked up at Fenchurch. 'Sorry, I need to take this.'

'Be my guest.' Fenchurch focused on the timeline again as Clooney strode across the room, answering the call too loudly. 'Kay, we're solid up to the point I spotted Saskia, right?'

'That's right, sir.' Reed cradled her notebook like it was a baby. 'Even with all the nut jobs from the press conference, we still haven't got anything before she met with Yana Ikonnikova.'

Fenchurch focused on the far left of the line, completely blank. 'So we can see if Kamal had been following her before her appointment?'

'That's right.'

'Keep on it.'

Reed crumpled up her Red Bull can. She seemed to take weeks to drink one. 'People will spot a black guy hanging around in that part of town.'

'Very true. Can you get someone to dig into it?'

'Guv.' Reed checked her Pronto. 'Made some progress with the knife purchases. There are a few online dealers who'll sell in this area. Mostly American, but there's the usual eBay sellers.'

'Sounds good.'

'We've got a stack of transactions to get through. Should generate some leads.'

'I'm sensing a but here.'

Reed grinned. 'But, we're assuming the knives weren't bought on the dark net. That's a whole other kettle of fish, guv. We'll get nothing if they were.'

'Okay. Feels like a wild goose chase. Give it the rest of today and see if we've got any likely suspects.'

'Guv.' Reed stabbed her stylus on the Pronto's screen. Then frowned at it. 'Looks like Lisa's got the list of calls from Angel tube.'

'So we can see who Kamal was calling?'

'Right. Lisa's going through it just now.' Reed nodded over at Bridge near the back of the room, getting a wink in response before she went back to her laptop. 'Three thousand calls at that time to the nearby cell towers. She's reduced it to just over four hundred made to pay-as-you-go phones.'

'You're assuming he was calling a burner?'

'Just an assumption, guv. If we get nowhere with that, we can look at the others.'

'No, I think that's the right approach.'

'We'll need resource to listen to the calls, though. Assuming we can get access to them and assuming they were recorded.'

'That's not going to happen, is it?'

'Not—'

Clooney barged back in, his face having lost a couple of shades of colour. 'Simon, I need a word.' He swallowed. 'One of my analysts has just finished running the prints.'

'And?'

'Two things. Good news first. Qasid's prints are all over the bag you found by those bikes. He definitely nicked them.'

'Good work.' Fenchurch crossed his arms. 'And the bad?'

Clooney looked away. 'The impressions on the murder weapon belong to someone called Lewis Cole.'

Acid reflux curdled in Fenchurch's gut. 'Is that Qasid's real name?'

'We've checked his hands, Simon. He's got a scar on his left index finger. What we got off the knife doesn't match him.'

Fenchurch swallowed hard. The drums started playing in his ears, lazy jazz time. 'So the knife we found wasn't the one he used to kill her?'

'That's the other thing. It's her DNA markers in the blood.' Clooney scratched his neck. 'That is the murder weapon.'

The drums hammered in Fenchurch's ears, Led Zep thunder rolling. His vision condensed to a narrow tunnel. His brain started throbbing against his skull. 'What are you saying?'

'Qasid didn't kill her.'

Chapter Twenty-Five

Docherty was gazing at the middle screen in the Observation Suite, silent as the grave. On-screen, Qasid and Unwin were in quiet conference in interview room three. He shook his head again, still didn't say anything.

Fenchurch leaned against the wall, the plaster now almost matching his body temperature. The drums thudded harder and faster. 'Boss, all I can say is I'm sorry.'

Docherty looked round at Fenchurch, his eyes tiny slits. 'Simon, you are an idiot.'

'It was an honest mistake.'

'A mistake? You sure about that? Have you any idea what that wee shite could do to us?' Docherty got up and started counting on his fingers. 'Racial discrimination. False arrest. Racial profiling. Assault. And I bet you Unwin's the sort of sneaky bastard who knows precisely which bloody rules we've bent way past breaking point.'

Fenchurch let the echo in the room die down and sucked in the stale sweat smell. Not all of it was his. 'It wasn't like that, boss. Qasid and whoever this Lewis Cole is were wearing the same clothes, hiding their identities from everyone. It doesn't matter if it'd been a white kid on that bike, or an Asian kid or whatever, so long as they looked the same as the other one. They could still have played that trick.'

'You've been tricked now, have you?' Docherty slumped back in the seat and faced away from Fenchurch. He was using a blank monitor as a mirror to focus on Fenchurch. 'These little neds on the street can outwit a Met DI with some bloody hooded tops. Christ, Simon, I should stick these guys on the payroll and get them doing your job.'

Fenchurch tried a smile for size. 'They might be able to bring in Kamal.'

'This isn't funny.'

'I'm not saying it is.' Fenchurch pushed away from the wall. A pool of sweat had welled around the contact point and soaked his shirt. 'This isn't about race, boss. In any other case, we get a description and we bring someone in. This is different. I saw him do it.'

'It wasn't him, you daft sod.'

'He's involved, though, sir. That little shit had a ton of stolen phones on him.'

'Doesn't mean he's murdered that girl.'

'But it doesn't mean he doesn't know who did.'

'Bloody hell.' Docherty shook his head again, laughing this time. 'We got anything on this Lewis Cole boy?'

'Sweet Fanny Adams, sir. Another ghost. Just like Kamal and like Qasid there.'

'And he definitely isn't Lewis Cole?'

'Prints are nothing like each other.'

'Is Kamal?'

'Who knows, boss.'

On the screen, Nelson entered the room, sitting down and adjusting his tiepin. He started the recorder. 'Interview commenced at—'

Fenchurch tapped the monitor, his fingernail pinging off the glass. 'Let me lead the interview.'

Docherty shook his head. 'That can't happen, Si.'

'I've built up an understanding with the kid. If anyone can get anything out of him, it's me.'

'You've proven the opposite of that so far.'

'Ten minutes. That's all I ask.'

Docherty stared at the display for a few seconds and sighed. 'Fine, ten minutes. Then I'm taking over and you're going to work traffic or whatever.'

'Cheers, boss.'

'And Dawn'll be coming in after she's had some sleep this morning.'

Fenchurch hovered outside interview room three, sucking in deep breaths, trying to calm himself down. Eyes shut. Heavy metal drums banging away.

Count to ten. Then again. And again.

He opened his eyes, down to a slow jazz tempo now. The corridor's brightness hit him, like when the colours were popped on a photo. He swallowed down bile, acid reflux boiling in his gut. Felt like it was clawing at his heart.

Ready.

He pushed open the door and entered the interview room.

Nelson was nodding at something Qasid said. 'So you understand the situation?'

'No, man. This is police brutality. You've Guantanamoed me, yeah? We gonna take yo' badge, bitch.'

Nelson craned round and frowned at Fenchurch. He nodded then leaned towards the microphone. 'DI Simon Fenchurch has entered the room.'

'Good morning, Qasid.' Fenchurch sat next to Nelson and started rolling up his shirtsleeves. 'Who's Lewis Cole?'

Qasid smirked. 'Roofie.'

'What?'

Unwin held up a hand. 'I ask you to strike that from the record.'

'We're not going to do that.' Fenchurch locked eyes with Qasid. The little shit looked like he was at a comedy show. 'Did you say Roofie?'

'So what if I said it, bitch?' He sniffed. 'He's nobody.'

'I insist that's struck from the record.'

'Qasid, is Lewis Cole called Roofie?'

'He's called Lewis, ayiii.'

'He's not Kamal?'

'He not Kamal.'

'Inspector! I *insist* you stop this. You're infringing on my client's human rights here.'

'Mr Unwin, your client has been cleared of all charges relating to the death of Saskia Barnett. This is merely intelligence gathering.' Fenchurch waited for the lawyer to settle back in his seat and scribble a note. Then he smiled at Qasid. 'We've just discovered that Lewis murdered the girl. It looks like he's framing you for it.'

The boy sniffed again, his forehead knotted into a deep frown. Then a huge grin broke out. 'He wouldn't do that.'

'Sure?'

'He my friend, bitch. Why he do that? He ain't going do that to me.'

'That's enough.' Unwin got up and put his hands on Qasid's shoulders, trying to get him to stand. 'This interview's over and my client's walking out of here with me.'

Fenchurch slowly got up, stuffing his hands in his pockets. 'I'll be the judge of that.'

197

'You're letting him go now and we shall be seeking compensation for false arrest among a myriad other breaches of human-rights law.' Unwin stared down at Qasid. 'Mr Williams, you're coming with me.'

'He's going nowhere.'

'Inspector, you just said he's cleared of all charges.'

'Relating to the death of Saskia Barnett.' Fenchurch shot him a wink. 'Mr Unwin, your client had seven stolen phones on him, as well as his own. We found another seven where he nicked a bike. That's fourteen stolen mobiles, maybe fifteen if he's not claiming the burner as his own.'

'That's my phone, bitch. I tol' you.'

Fenchurch ignored Qasid, keeping his attention on the lawyer. 'Even you should acknowledge your client's handling a lot of stolen goods there.' A quick glance at the kid. 'While we're clearing him of the murder charge, he's not getting off. The Mobile Phone Theft Unit will be prosecuting him for this.'

'Well, we're still suing.' Unwin stood up and did up the top button of his suit jacket. 'You've got until noon to release him.' He barged past the security officer and tried the door handle.

Fenchurch gripped his arm and leaned in close. 'We're still watching you.'

Unwin shoved him.

Fenchurch tumbled backwards, struggling to stay on his feet. He slumped against the table and pretended to sit. Nobody seemed to notice his fall.

The door clattered shut behind Unwin.

'Looks like he's running rings round you plonkers.'

Fenchurch got up and went into the corridor, waiting for Nelson.

'Interview terminated at seven thirty-six a.m.' Nelson killed the recorder, nodded at the security officer and left the room. He shook his head at Fenchurch then at the door. 'You going to do Unwin for that?'

'Maybe.'

'You should think about it. Technically assault, guv. Two witnesses on your side plus it was recorded.' Nelson got out his vape stick and checked the display. 'What happened on Thursday night, guv?'

'I thought I'd caught the killer.' Fenchurch collapsed against the wall, arms crossed, drums thundering again. 'I hadn't.'

'How can that happen?'

'Like you've been trying to tell me, Jon, I let him slip out of my sight when I chased him. There's two, maybe three occasions when I could've lost him.'

'This doesn't look good, guv.'

'Believe me, I know.'

'So what are you going to do?'

'I'm going to make myself so busy Docherty doesn't know where I am.' Fenchurch started off down the corridor. 'You can come with me, if you want?'

'Would love to, guv.' Nelson was keeping pace with him. 'Problem is, Docherty's asked me to lead the case until Mulholland's back in.'

Fenchurch stopped at the doorway leading to the stairwell. 'Well, don't let me get in the way of your career, Sergeant.'

Chapter Twenty-Six

'Thanks for doing this, Kay.' Fenchurch got out of the car onto Upper Street. Place was back to normal now — light Saturday morning traffic heading to shops or kid's football or dancing or whatever. Wouldn't suspect someone had been murdered there a day and a half ago. 'I appreciate it.'

'Don't mention it, guv.' Reed got out of the driver's side and plipped the lock. 'Just so long as Docherty doesn't haul me over the coals for this.'

Fenchurch climbed up the steps to the raised pavement, his foot starting to throb again. 'As far as he's concerned, you're accompanying me home.'

'Has he suspended you?'

'Not in so many words.' Fenchurch sat at the table he'd claimed the other night. Four bouquets of flowers outlined where she'd lain and the morning dew was winning the battle with her bloodstain. 'This is where it happened. I was here with Abi.'

'And so was I, remember?' Reed wouldn't look at the spot, kept her gaze on her shoes and the shoppers milling around. 'What can you remember, guv?'

Fenchurch tried to pull himself back in time, sucking in the street smells, bitter diesel spewing from the buses. The sweet sweat smell of the tube. Onions and peppers frying in Chilango. Cigarette smoke. Coffee. Aftershave, perfume, deodorant. 'Nothing much, Kay. Just what the kid was wearing. Those trackie bottoms. The green Everlast logo. Proper Mardyke Estate stuff.'

'Takes me back a few years, guv.' Reed sat next to him, backside barely connecting with the silvery metal. 'When did you first see Saskia?'

'Her body language caught my eye.' Fenchurch looked towards the underground station. There'd been a thick crowd, Islington residents returning home to replace workers commuting in for the day. 'She was hurrying away from the tube, like someone was following her. Staring at her phone, then looking behind her. Something made her start running.'

'Did you see what it was?'

'No.'

'Then what happened?'

Fenchurch stared at the pavement just ahead of them, tried to overlay the Thursday gloom onto Saturday's glow. 'I saw Saskia running past the gap leading up to the cinema, just by the bank there. Then a flash came from over there.' He waved down at the street where two buses idled, the front one slowly swallowing a queue of passengers.

'A flash of what?'

'Must've been the knife, could've just been the bike.'

'You're not making any sense, guv. You definitely saw him?'

The black kid in the urban camouflage of the hoodie and the black trackies. Standing on his pedals, bumping up onto the pavement. A snarl in a suit shouting after him.

'I saw him. He came up the wheelchair ramp. I looked right in his eyes, Kay. Looked just like a kid.'

'And you thought it was Qasid?'

'Maybe. Could've been.'

'Was it Kamal on the bike?'

'I don't think so.' Fenchurch reached into his suit jacket for the photos. He stared at the one taken on the escalator. Stupid mushroom hair, evil eyes. He put it down on the table. 'It wasn't him. Too young.'

'You think Kamal is this Lewis Cole?'

'I don't think it's him, Kay. Too old.'

'There are bikes chained to railings all along there, guv. Could he have got one of them?'

'I don't know.'

'We don't know the first thing about Lewis Cole, do we?'

'True.' Fenchurch closed his eyes, trying to visualise things again. 'The first thing I saw was him bumping the pavement, already on the bike. Then I saw him stab Saskia.' He opened his eyes again and slumped back in the chair, the metal digging into his back. 'The way I see it, when he was on the escalator, Kamal was calling one of his guys in the area. Some kid out nicking stuff. He redirected him towards Saskia and told him to kill her.'

Saskia collapsed onto the ground, grasping her neck. Her bag fell free, clattering to the ground. What happened to her mobile?

'I can just remember the kid stabbing her. That's it. But the attacker must've taken her phone as well as her bag. Next thing we know, it's turned up in that recycling machine. How did it get there?'

'Lisa's working on it, guv. What happened next?'

Some frying steak from nearby caught Fenchurch's nose. Buses hissing. A car horn blasted out somewhere.

'I told Abi to stay with her. She told me she'd call 999.'

'Which she did. And then she called me. Then?'

'I must've lost him for a few seconds.' Fenchurch waved down Upper Street, past the bus stops and the Superdry shop. 'When he headed off that way.'

'Did you lose sight of him?'

'I glanced down at Saskia. Told Abi to call you. What was I supposed to do?'

'You did fine, guv.'

'But I lost him.' Fenchurch swallowed down bile. Drums smashed double time. Out of time. 'When I looked up again, he was cycling off, behind a bus. I called Control to get units despatched. Drove off after him.'

'Was it still him?'

'I think so. Well, I'm not definite. In his mind, he's killed someone and he's hotfooting out of there. Doesn't know a DI has spotted him. He took a right at the Green. Turned down Essex Road. I caught up with him at the Tesco.'

'And you're definitely sure it was him?'

'Sure as I am about anything.'

'So, let me get this straight. You saw a skinny black kid, right?'

'Kay, are you saying I'm racist?'

'No need to play the old "some of my best friends are black" card, guv.' Reed gave him a warm smile and patted him on the shoulder. 'You ever heard about the "cross-race effect"?'

'Sounds very much like you're accusing me of racism.'

'Hear me out, guv.' Reed flicked up her hands, all casual. 'It says people find it difficult to differentiate between different races.'

'I know what it is. Do you honestly think I just can't tell blacks apart?'

'It's saying you find it difficult. It's an evolutionary thing. A science thing.' She shrugged her shoulders. 'It makes sense to me. Our ancestors only ever saw the same race for thousands of years. Longer. So we can differentiate lots of things about other white people, but only a few characteristics of blacks. Or Asians. Or Indians.'

'Kay . . .'

'Look, guv, it's the same with Jon Nelson or Waheed Lad and white guys.'

'Still sounds like you're saying I'm racist.'

She shook her head, like she'd return to the argument at some future point, and looked past him. 'Come on, then, let's see what else you can remember.'

'Thought you were supposed to be taking me home?'

'Well, something's come up, hasn't it?'

———

Reed swerved out into the traffic and followed the route they'd taken, pulling in by the Tesco Express. 'You said you almost caught him here, right?'

Fenchurch could still see the kid on the bike just ahead of him, pedalling away without a care in the world. Like he hadn't just killed someone. 'I remember thinking about whether I should ram him.'

'Better for you that you didn't, guv.'

'True.' Fenchurch tapped the windscreen, pointing at the magnolia-painted pub on the next corner. 'Kid clocked me, though, and headed right by the Winchester.'

Reed pulled into traffic and took a right, following their route, barely hitting ten miles an hour. 'Then what?'

Fenchurch waved a hand at the pavement, clear for the whole block. 'The little shit bumped up there. There were roadworks here. Gone now.'

'You definitely saw him?'

'His head was bobbing up above the barriers.'

She pulled in, almost mounting the kerb. 'Then you attacked him with your car?'

'He attacked my car, Kay.' Fenchurch winked at her. Then he let out a deep sigh, his shoulders slumping low against the seat fabric. 'It was the same kid up to this point, I swear.'

'So you got out of the car and grabbed him. Then what?'

'The little sod stamped on my foot.' Fenchurch reached down to stroke it. Back to a dull ache now. 'Just about better now, thanks for asking.'

'Then what, he ran away?'

Fenchurch nodded as he pointed ahead. 'Through the park there.'

'Come on.' Reed let her seatbelt go and got out of the pool car. She waited for a black cab to pass then followed Fenchurch onto the tarmac and stopped. 'So he was running?'

'Very fast, too.'

'He didn't outpace you?'

'Just for a second.'

'Guv . . .'

Fenchurch waved up ahead. 'The entrance is on the right. Lost him up there.'

'How long?'

'Just a couple of seconds.'

'Guv . . .'

'Come on.' Fenchurch led back to the car and got in.

Reed waited for another cab to pass before pulling out. 'Does your statement mention losing track of him?'

'Of course it does. That's what the street team were supposed to fill in. It's why I'm so obsessed about the bloody timeline, Kay.'

'You're always obsessed about timelines, guv.' She stopped at the end of the park and got out.

Fenchurch joined her. Someone honked behind them. He turned round and gave an Audi the finger, then walked over to the gate at the side. 'This is where I lost him. Happy?' He looked up at the back of the office building. 'That road goes up to the RBS building, I think.'

'Regent's House. Dave worked there for a bit.' Reed leaned against the gate and sighed. 'Okay. This is where they did the old switcheroo.'

'What?' Fenchurch frowned at her. 'You think that's what happened?'

'Only thing that makes sense, guv. If they were wearing the same gear, they could swap. Meant this Lewis Cole got away and you focused on the wrong kid.'

Fenchurch felt something like relief surge through him. 'It's nice having someone on my side.'

'That's the only explanation, isn't it?' She patted his arm. 'They do this deliberately, guv. It's not your fault.'

Fenchurch stared at the cracked tarmac. 'I don't like this one bloody bit.' He looked around at the sound of a bike bell.

A blur powered towards them. Grey hoodie, black trackies. Young eyes lost deep in the hood.

Fenchurch stepped out into the road and grabbed the cyclist by the shoulders. Lifted him clean off the bike. Couldn't keep hold of him.

The kid rolled over a few times and the bike clattered to the ground. 'Get off me, man!'

Fenchurch turned him over, pushing his arm up his back towards his rucksack. 'Do you work for Kamal?'

The kid's face touched the pavement. 'What?'

'Kamal. Do you work for him?'

'Help, police!'

'We are police, son.' Reed was crouched down, showing her warrant card. 'He asked if you work for Kamal?'

'I don't know nothing.'

Fenchurch stood him up and frisked through his pockets. Just one mobile — a Samsung with a cracked screen, a snowflake pattern filling the display. He turned him round and got a good look at his face. Looked the same age as Qasid. His mid-black skin was a few shades lighter than Saskia's attacker. 'What are you doing here, sir?'

'I'm going to uni, man.'

'Uni? Bullshit.'

'London Met uni down in Aldgate. I swear, bruv.'

'Bit far out of your way, isn't it?'

'Long commute, but I can't afford the tube or the bus.'

'Am I supposed to believe that?'

'They tol' me it was up in Highbury but then they moved the course, man. Still, it's good exercise.'

'What are you studying?'

'Computing, man. You mind getting off me?'

'Where is Kamal?'

'I tol' you, I don't know nothing.'

Reed clamped a fist on Fenchurch's arm and whispered: 'Guv, this isn't helping. We need to get focused here. Okay?'

Fenchurch handed the phone back. 'I'm sorry. I thought you were someone else.'

He reached down and picked up his bike. 'This is all scratched, man.'

'You might want to consider wearing different clothes.' Fenchurch headed back to the car and got in. He watched the kid trundle off down the road and eased off his shoulders. 'I shouldn't have done that.'

'He didn't get your name, guv.' Reed stuck her key in the ignition. 'You're not feeling okay, are you?'

'I feel like shit, Sergeant.'

'So you want me to take you home, after all?'

'No, I don't.'

'Abi can help, you kn—'

'I don't want to bloody go home.' Fenchurch rubbed his forehead. 'Look. Like you said, Qasid probably switched with this Lewis Cole kid. That means he's someone who looks like him, someone who could pass for him.'

'So, while you were off chasing Qasid, Lewis Cole dumped the bag and the knife. Think I'm following you, guv.' Reed got out her Airwave and put it to her ear. 'Control, can you give me an update on the whereabouts of a Lewis Cole?' She nodded for a few seconds, listening. 'Well, call me back when you bother your arse. Okay?' She stabbed her finger on the screen. 'Bloody hell.'

'Take it you've still not got anything?'

'Haven't even been bloody looking.'

Fenchurch stared over at the canal. 'Me and Nelson fished a body out of there a few years back. There's a footpath running up to the other end of the tunnel, right?'

'Far as I can remember, guv. Why?'

'Let's take a little walk.'

⌣

Fenchurch followed Reed down the ramp, warm sun beating down on his neck, way too hot to be legal in April. He stopped on the towpath, busy with foot traffic. Joggers, dog walkers, hikers with backpacks. The cracked brick wall looked like it dated back to the Roman Empire.

Two boats were moored on this side, four on the other. Giant things, like houses on the water. The water surface had a green dusting of algae, surrounding the boats like ropes. To the left, the canal narrowed to the width of the tunnel. An underground mile and you were on the other side of Angel. The algae spread out around the boats, leaving the tunnel clear. Stagnant water versus flowing.

'Guv?'

Fenchurch looked over. 'You got something?'

Reed was on her knees, peering into the murky water. 'Think so. Take this.' She shrugged off her jacket and tossed it at Fenchurch. Then she got flat on her face and dipped her arm into the water, almost up to her short sleeve. 'It's bloody freezing.'

'What have you got?'

'Not sure, guv.' She stood up and threw a dark object at Fenchurch, water spraying onto the tarmac.

He caught it. A mass of fabric, almost black but mottled with green and dripping on the canal side. He snapped it out and held it up to the light. 'It's a hoodie. This'd be grey if it wasn't so wet, right?'

'Think so.' Reed pointed at the Islington Tunnel mouth, under a road bridge a few metres away. 'You lost the kid who killed Saskia at the other end, didn't you?'

'Meaning?'

'Well, after they swapped places there, Lewis Cole must've swum here. It'd be dark as hell, nobody around. No barges, nobody on the towpath. Would've taken the hoodie off to get away quicker. Barge must've dredged it up.'

Fenchurch focused on the scum on the surface, swirling slowly. 'I don't like being played like this, Kay.'

'Nobody does, guv. Another piece of the jigsaw, though.' Her Airwave blasted out. She stuck it to her head and wheeled off away from him.

Fenchurch looked around. A few old wharf buildings surrounded the canal by the road bridge. No street lights — not a chance anyone saw anything, least of all a dark figure emerging from the water.

'Send it to my Pronto. Thanks.' Reed spun round, fist pumping the air. 'Guv?'

'What's up?'

'Got the last-known address of Lewis Cole.'

Chapter Twenty-Seven

Reed knocked on the door and waited, staring at the patch of dirt in front of the house, avoiding making eye contact with Fenchurch.

Walthamstow was now just the same as every other part of suburban London. The long street was filled with two-up/two-downs climbing the gentle slope, a mishmash of roughcast, bare brick and stone cladding. The Coles' address looked like the last rundown house in a street riding the gentrification wave, dirty walls and a few slates missing from the roof. About halfway up, developed houses gave way to a flotilla of skips. Radio One, Capital FM and that new Radio X station created a hellish soundclash from the workers' radios. Some had retained their original windows though the Coles hadn't bothered to look after theirs. The rest of the street could've been a museum exhibiting 'Double-glazing: a retrospective (1967 to 2016)'.

The door opened and a black man in his late forties stood there. White vest, tartan boxer shorts, wiry white hair all over his arms and legs. Not much left on top. He looked them up and down. 'I'm not buying. Goodbye.' He started to shut the door.

Reed kept it open with her foot. 'Police, sir.'

The door opened again. Another examination, slower and more thorough. 'What do you want?'

'We're looking for a Lewis Cole.'

'He not here.' Eyes flickering. 'Not for a long time.'

'But you know him?'

'I'm his father. *Was*. We . . . lost him.'

Fenchurch saw it in the man's eyes. The years of hope tormenting you, that bastard making you think your child would come back. Made you think that something overheard in a supermarket car park could lead to something. Anything. Years of staring at the ceiling all night, listening to kids thunder about in the flat above, screaming in the street outside. Sleep just something other people did. Years of thinking you'd give anything just for another minute with her.

'—and this is DI Fenchurch.' Reed put her warrant card away and tucked a few stray hairs behind her ear. 'Can I take your name, sir?'

'Ronald. Ronald Cole.'

'And Lewis is your son?'

'Isn't that obvious?'

Reed bristled and adjusted her jacket. 'Can we come in, sir?'

'No, you can't.' Ronald stepped out onto the path and pulled the door to behind him. He wrapped his bare arms across his chest. 'It's a Saturday morning, officer. I was on late shift last night. I'm a tube driver, before you ask.'

'Mr Cole, we need to ask you a few questions about your son.'

'Why?'

'We think he's involved in an inquiry.'

'He's still alive?'

Fenchurch stepped forward and smiled. 'You lost him, didn't you?'

Tears welled in Ronald's eyes. 'You keep this from my wife, you hear?'

'I promise.'

Ronald ran a hand across his cheeks and nodded slowly. 'Someone took Lewis from right out here. This bloody street.' He waved out to the parked cars. 'Five years ago. Boy was fourteen.' His forehead creased, the confusion of hope colliding with fear. 'What makes you think Lewis is still out there?'

'That's why we wanted to do this inside, sir.' Reed pocketed her warrant card. 'We found his prints on a murder weapon.'

'What?'

'It appears he stabbed a girl on Upper Street on Thursday night.'

'No.' His head shaking was speeding up, close to matching the tempo battering Fenchurch's ears.

'Our forensics—'

'Get away from here. Get away!' Ronald pushed Reed back and yanked the door open behind him. 'You come here with these lies about me boy! Get away!'

Reed stepped forward to block the doorway. 'Sir, we matched the fingerprints on the murder weapon to those on file from before his disappearance. We understand he got into trouble when he was a boy and, had he not disappeared, those prints would've been expunged. Your son is still out there.'

Ronald ran a hand across his bald scalp. 'I don't know whether to laugh or cry.'

Fenchurch nudged Reed out of the way. 'I know what you're going through, Mr Cole. It's okay.'

'How can you? How the hell can anyone?'

'I lost . . . someone myself. Ten years ago.' Fenchurch locked eyes with Ronald, saw his torment mirrored in the deep brown as another tear slicked down his face. 'We need your help, sir. Do you have any idea where Lewis might be?

'If I did, I would've brought him back here and kept him in his room! Thrown away the bloody key!'

'You don't know where he could've gone?'

'We gave up looking long ago. The hope was killing us more than losing him did.' Ronald shook his head, his lips curled tight. 'And now you say he's not dead?'

Fenchurch gave him a smile, trying for reassuring. 'We just need to find him.'

'Get away from me!' Ronald had enough clearance to shut the door now.

Fenchurch stared at the chipped paint for a few seconds then glanced at Reed. 'Did Control give you the name of the investigating officer?'

———

'And they call this place a police office now. Not even a station, any more.' PC Dean Lawson leaned back in the chair in the tiny interview room. Long face and heroin-thin stick arms poking out of his vest. He'd somehow found a uniform small enough to fit. 'Barely a broom cupboard, I swear.'

'I know the feeling.' Fenchurch got out his Airwave Pronto, a fake smile on his face. He checked the display. No new messages. 'So, going back to Lewis Cole?'

'Yeah, sorry. Got sidetracked there.' Lawson gurned at them, his cheeks twitching with the effort. 'My partner at the time used to call him Ashley Cole.' He stared up at the ceiling and laughed. 'Shouldn't have done but he did, you know? Ged was like that.' He sniffed, rolling his tongue over his lips. 'Season-ticket holder at the Bridge for years until he carked it last March. Poor geezer.'

'Did you have any other leads on Lewis Cole?'

'Nothing much. Someone snatched him, never heard of him again. End of.'

'So he just vanished?'

'Into thin air, Inspector. I swear. Never had any leads.'

'You said nothing much?'

'Well, I meant nothing. Sorry.' Lawson scratched at the back of his neck. 'Nothing other than a pair of kids spotted in the street a few days before.'

Fenchurch frowned at Reed, the drums starting to clatter again. 'Excuse me?'

'This Cole kid. Ashley.' Lawson smirked as he winked at Reed. 'He used to play street football, yeah? Jumpers for goalposts and all that. Day before, these two kids were playing against them for about an hour.'

'Who were they?'

'No idea. We spoke to the other kids who played with them. Couldn't name this pair, though. The descriptions were rubbish, too. Once we'd taken out all the noise, we just had that they were black and kids. Nasty bastards by the sounds of things. Threatened them with a knife if they didn't let them play. Stole a kid's ball, too. Poor lad'd just got it.'

'What makes you think they took Lewis?'

'I'd put money on it. Seems like a bit of a coincidence, doesn't it?' Lawson stared at the window, the pale-blue sky streaked with jet trails. 'Problem is they're made of thinner air than young Ashley. Hell of a business. Hell of a business.'

Reed gripped the table edge. 'Well, I hate to break it to you, Constable, but it seems Lewis is alive and well.'

Lawson shot her a glare. 'Shut up.'

'As of Thursday night at half past six, he was alive and kicking.'

Lawson let out a deep breath and laughed. 'Thank God for some good news round here.' He held up the case file for Lewis Cole's disappearance. 'Can I tear this bugger up now?'

'Not so fast.' Reed stared at him, a grim expression on her face. 'Trouble is, we found young Lewis's prints on a murder weapon.'

The new-found hope deflated from Lawson just as quickly as it had appeared. 'He's murdered someone? Christ.'

'Constable, we'd greatly appreciate it if you could think of anything.' Reed left him a space. 'Anything at all that might open this up for us.'

'Hell of a business.' Lawson looked across the room at the pockmarked wall. 'I got nothing, I'm afraid. Nothing. Hell of a bloody business.' He bit at his bottom lip, looked like he tore a strip of skin off. 'Wish I'd found the little bastard before he started stabbing people, though.'

Reed grimaced at Fenchurch. 'That's what I feared, guv.'

He nodded at her then narrowed his eyes at Lawson. 'Does the name Kamal mean anything to you?'

'None of me bells are ringing.' Lawson frowned and clicked his fingers. 'Wait a sec. You're Fenchurch, right?'

'That's what I said when we gave our intro half an hour ago.'

'So where do I know you from?'

'I've been in this station a few times over the years, Constable.'

'It's not that.' Lawson looked long and hard at Fenchurch, rubbing his arms. 'Hang on, I've got it. You lost your daughter, didn't you?'

Fenchurch looked away. Blood thundered in his inner ear. 'That's not important.'

'Yeah, I remember now. Saw the story in the *Job* magazine a few years back. This isn't anything to do with her, is it?'

Fenchurch glared at him, drilling his eyes into his skull. 'I'm looking for a murder suspect.'

'Look, I'm sorry. Don't mean anything by it, sir.' Lawson frowned then wagged his finger in the air. 'There was another geezer called Fenchurch here the other week. He was asking questions about young Ashley and all.'

'That'll be my father, Ian.'

'Chip off the old block, are you?'

'Some say that. What was he asking?'

'Like I said, he was looking into cases like young Ashley's. Said this case could help him.'

'The boy's name is Lewis. Not Ashley. Okay?' Fenchurch got to his feet and leaned against the table. 'Try to treat him with some respect.'

Lawson looked away, couldn't hide the smirk. 'Yeah, sorry, sir.'

'You should send a unit round to Lewis's parents' house in Walthamstow. We just broke the news to his father.'

'Oh, thanks for nothing.' Lawson grabbed his peaked cap and stormed out of the room.

Reed slumped back in her chair. 'How to make friends and influence people, guv?'

Fenchurch was still scowling at the closed door. 'He'd've found that kid if he'd applied some bloody elbow grease five years ago.'

'Sounds like he didn't have much to go on.'

'That's what they all say. I'm sick to death of excuses.'

———

'Back to the station, guv?' Reed plipped the pool car door. 'Or are you still keeping away from Docherty?'

'The prospect of my nuts getting toasted doesn't exactly fill me with glee.' Fenchurch stared back at the Walthamstow station, a couple of upstairs units in a shoddy block of shops, across the road from a Pizza Express and a Costa. A community-facing policing initiative in brick and wood. Not that it ever solved any crimes. He leaned against the car and folded his arms. 'Think that was Kamal playing football with Lewis Cole?'

'Makes sense to me but it's still an assumption, guv.' She held her door in the open position. 'Is it worth speaking to the other kids? See what they remember?'

'If they're still around.' Fenchurch dialled a mobile number from memory. 'Just a sec.'

Indistinct office chatter cut short the ringing tone. 'Hello?'

'Dad, it's Simon.'

'Didn't think you was still talking to me after you ran away last night.'

'Relax. I'm still talking to you.'

'How can I help?'

Fenchurch stared down the high street, busy with mid-morning shoppers. A woman in a burqa dragged two feral kids behind her. 'We're up in Walthamstow speaking to Dean Lawson.'

'Worked with old Ged, didn't he? He was a lovely old geezer. Monster at the dominoes, I tell you. Shame he was Chelsea, mind. Went to his funeral. One of many, these days.'

'I can bet. Were you looking into Lewis Cole's disappearance?'

'Not one of mine. Sorry.' Sounded like Dad was in a bathroom. 'Why do you ask?'

'You mean he's not one of the kids on your list?'

'Didn't really fit the pattern. Should he be?'

'I spoke to his father. He went missing five years ago. Two older black kids played football with him the day before.'

Another long pause. Definitely in a bloody toilet. 'Got a couple like that. I'll dig into it. Bit annoyed at myself for missing it. Why you asking, anyway?'

'Long story.'

'I'm listening.'

Fenchurch chuckled. That's where he got the blind-faced belligerence from. 'Turns out his prints are all over the knife.'

'Bloody hell. Thought you had who did it?'

'So did I.'

'Right. Well, I've not been looking back as long ago as five years, son. You think it's this Kamal geezer?'

Fenchurch tightened his grip on the phone. 'How the bloody hell did you find that out?'

'Forty years' service opens a few doors, I tell you. Even now. I'll get back up there and add it to my list.'

'Make sure you get Lawson to do the actual graft, yeah? Don't want you wandering round bloody Walthamstow on your own.'

'I can still kick my fair share of arse, son.'

'I doubt it. Be careful. And let me know if you find anything.'

'Scouts' honour.' The line clicked dead.

'Dib, dib, bloody dib.' Fenchurch pocketed his phone.

Reed was ending a call of her own. 'Anything?'

'Square root of bugger all, Kay.' Fenchurch scowled. 'Other than my old man's got a mole on this investigation.'

'Long as it's just him, guv.'

'True.' Fenchurch's Airwave blasted out. Owen Greenhill. He answered it. 'Hello?'

'Simon, I've got some good news for you.'

'Go on.'

'We've found that girl's laptop.'

Chapter Twenty-Eight

Fenchurch got out of the car first. Over the road, Hackney Marshes was swamped with a children's rugby tournament. Clumps of parents huddled together dotted around the expanse of grass as their offspring got muddy. In the distance, a fat boy booted a ball over the crossbar, disinterest etched on the kids' faces, bitter rivalry on the parents'. 'Why are you asking if I'm okay?'

Reed led down a small path cut out of a hedge, heading into a triangle of trees stuck between the rumble of the A12 and two forks of the River Lea. The Olympic Park was behind, leaving its legacy of wetlands, private flats and a technology hub, like London needed another one. 'All that stuff with the missing kids. Did you know your dad's been doing that?'

'I had an inkling.'

'Take it Abi doesn't know.'

'She's got an inkling, too.' Fenchurch caught a flash of mid-blue through the trees. 'There we are.' He trotted over to a police cordon surrounding a holly bush just off the path.

Owen Greenhill stood just inside the perimeter, hands looped through the straps on his stab-proof vest, watching a SOCO work away at his feet. 'Like I say, Jim, bit of overkill for a bloody laptop.'

Fenchurch got close to him. 'It's a murder case, Sergeant.'

'Christ. Didn't see you there.'

'Keep your opinion to yourself in future.'

'Sorry.' Greenhill stuck his peaked cap back on. 'You were quick getting here.'

'Just been up in Walthamstow.' Fenchurch tried to get a view past him. 'What have we got?'

The SOCO held up the battered carcass of a laptop, already bagged and tagged. 'Someone's smashed this up with a hammer then hid it under this bush.' He held up a burnished-silver rectangle, a metallic circle sitting off-centre. 'The hard drive got the same treatment, by the looks of things, then they set it on fire.'

'Bloody overkill.' Fenchurch scowled at the device. 'Any chance you can do any data recovery on it?'

'Afraid we're not on *24*, sir. It's beyond broken.'

'Any sign of an iPhone?'

A pause. 'Not here, sorry.'

Fenchurch stepped on something that squelched. Used condoms carpeted the ground. 'Jesus Christ.'

'Lovely, isn't it?' Greenhill smirked as he waved around the cordoned-off area. 'Makes you wonder what they were doing when they found it. Bit off the beaten track, if you catch my drift.' He winked. 'Lot of lonely men out here of an evening. Remember when—'

'I remember. Have you got a name for whoever called it in?'

'Nine-nine-nine job from a call box in Dalston. Didn't leave a name.'

'Take it you've listened to it?'

'Northern accent. Probably a lorry driver up to a bit of how's your father with a rent boy. Didn't want us lot turning up at his house, asking his wife difficult questions.'

'Interesting.' Fenchurch nodded at the SOCO. 'Do whatever you can with the laptop, okay? Get Clooney to call me.'

'Fenchurch, isn't it?'

'That's right. Why?'

'Mick's always moaning about you calling him George.'

'Good to know.' Fenchurch stared at the destroyed computer on the ground, surrounded by used rubbers. He nodded at Reed. 'Come on, Kay.' He started off away from them.

Something glinted on the pinecone carpet just outside the cordon.

He bent down and picked it up with his pen, dangling it off the end. Stumpy black thing, plastic. Maybe two inches long. Looked like it'd been in the fires of Mount Doom. 'What's this?'

Reed squinted at it. 'Looks like a Flash drive thing, like you and Abi have got on your key rings.'

Fenchurch had another look at it. 'Bloody hell, so it is.' He reached into his pocket for a bag and dropped it in. He beckoned the SOCO over and handed it to him. 'Add this to the search.'

'Think it's related?'

'You sure it's not?'

'You're the boss.' The SOCO wandered off, shaking his head.

Fenchurch watched him go. 'Work with me here, Kay. One of Kamal's associates broke in to Liam's flat and stole her laptop and that USB drive. Then they dumped them here. Why?'

'So they could wipe whatever was on them, I suspect. Would've made a ton of noise, guv. Maybe thought they could get away with trashing it here.'

'Maybe. And maybe not.' Fenchurch started off down the path, fists balled. 'What I'm getting at is we've just got Liam's word for what happened, right?'

'That's correct.'

'How are those phone records coming along?'

Fenchurch perched on the edge of the kitchen counter and glared at Liam Sharpe. 'We found her laptop.'

Liam stopped fussing with his stovetop espresso maker, leaving both halves unscrewed. 'That's a relief. You can get the stories back off it, right?' He tipped some coffee grounds into the top and filled the bottom with water. Then screwed the two pieces of aluminium together and put it on the gas hob, already burning away.

'I'm afraid not. It's completely destroyed.' Fenchurch spotted a new baseball bat in the corner of the room, still in the shrink-wrap. 'And your phone's still missing.'

'Bastard.' Liam reached into the cupboard for some mugs.

'We found a USB flash drive, too.' Fenchurch dangled his keys from his own memory stick. 'Saskia ever use one?'

'All the time. That's how she backed stuff up. Never even emailed files to herself.'

'So it could've been hers?'

'Maybe.' Liam gave a shrug as he inspected the inside of a green mug.

Fenchurch shared a look with Reed. 'Makes me wonder if the laptop went missing in the first place.'

He put the mug down on the counter. 'Excuse me?'

'Well, we've just got your word that it was taken.'

'Look, it happened. They nicked my phone at the same time. My whole life's on that thing.'

'A member of the public called in to report the discovery. Anonymously. They found it not far from here.' Fenchurch let it rest, waiting for him to look up from the coffee maker. 'The caller had a northern accent, as it happens. Didn't leave their details.'

Liam finally looked round. 'What, you think it was me?'

'Tell me it wasn't.'

'You know how many northerners live in London these days?' Liam crouched down to pick up a tortoiseshell cat that waddled like a pig. 'The gold pavements still draw us down, you know?'

Fenchurch had to stop himself smiling. 'Are you swindling the insurance, Liam? Sell the old one on once you've got a replacement?'

'My girlfriend's been killed and someone assaulted me.' Liam hugged the cat tight. 'You really think I could do that now?'

'I've seen a lot of messed-up things in my time. How about you, Sergeant Reed?'

'Like you wouldn't believe, guv.' She focused on Liam, eyes narrow. 'I've just spoken to an officer who works for me. She's been looking through Saskia's call records. Turns out she made a few just before she was killed.' She nodded at him. 'Six to your number, as it happens.'

'Right.' Liam put the cat back down and leaned back against the opposite counter, arms folded. He stared at the coffee maker, as if willing it to spew out black gold. 'There's something I haven't told you.'

'Go on.'

Liam arranged three little espresso cups, gleaming white china, next to the pastel mugs, blue, green and orange. 'Sas sent me a WhatsApp message on Thursday night. Said someone called Kamal was after her.'

'What?' Fenchurch's gaze shot between him and Reed. 'Why didn't you tell us this before?'

'Because I'd been bloody playing Batman since I got in. And then you came round. My mobile was in my room, charging. I didn't see her message until yesterday morning. Hours after I'd spoken to you.'

'But we spoke to you yesterday morning. At the paper. Just after her laptop got stolen.'

'Look, I didn't know she'd texted me. I should've told you.' Liam rubbed at his thick beard. 'I was going to call you but then they took it and I felt so bad and there's no way to back up my story and . . .'

'You're an idiot, son.'

'I know I am.' Liam peered inside the espresso maker. 'When I checked my phone, I had a few missed calls from her. If I'd answered one of them, I could've saved her. Maybe. I feel bad enough about this as it is, okay?'

'So that's why you didn't tell us?'

'How would you feel if you could've stopped what happened but your bloody mobile was off?' Liam snorted, his nostrils flaring. 'She'd been trying to speak to me and I just . . . I just didn't answer. That's why she died.' He pinched his nose, eyes shut. 'I let her down.'

'It's not your fault. She was killed in front of me, not you.' Fenchurch swallowed, drums starting to clatter. 'I've been asking myself those questions since Thursday night. The answer is there's nothing anyone could've done. This Kamal character ordered someone to kill her and it just happened too quickly.' His voice was close to cracking. He sucked down bile. 'The police *were* on the scene.' He jabbed a finger to his heart. 'Me. And I couldn't stop it.'

Liam looked up from the coffee maker and nodded. 'I understand.'

'Do you know who Kamal is?'

'I've honestly no idea.'

'You expect me to believe that? It wasn't "There's someone stalking me". She told you Kamal, gave you his name. The message was very specific, like you knew who he was.'

Liam pushed the cups back on the counter. 'What possible reason would I have to lie?'

'I can think of a thousand.'

'I've never heard of Kamal.' Liam picked up the espresso maker and swirled it around, as if that'd speed things up. 'I can't think why she'd have been telling me.'

'Was there anything in the documents she was working on?'

'Not that I've found.' Liam shrugged just as the coffee whooshed up in the machine. 'Maybe she was thinking she could get the message out about who killed her.'

Fenchurch's gut started burning. 'Is that likely?'

'Her mind worked like that sometimes.'

'Liam.' Fenchurch waited for him to look up. 'I want you to go back through the files you do have and look for that name.'

'I'll need to get back to the Incident Room, guv.' Reed finished the last of her chicken salad and dumped the bag in the bin under Mulholland's desk. 'It's been fun, but I'd better show my face.'

'I'll head through once I'm done here, Kay. Thanks for the help.'

'No problem.'

Fenchurch put his feet up on his desk and leaned back. Still glorious sunshine outside the window — should really be out there. He polished off his chilli and dumped the container in the recycling. They did recycle that sort of thing, didn't they? Been ages since a cleaner'd left a note, anyway.

There were signs Mulholland was back in, but nothing indicating she'd taken over the case. No emails, texts or calls.

A knock on the door.

'Guv?' Lad stood there, hands in pockets. 'Thought you'd gone home?'

'Been out chasing down some leads, Constable. I hope this is you telling me you've got Kamal downstairs.'

'Nah, he's over at Brick Lane.'

Fenchurch jumped to his feet and grabbed his suit jacket. 'Come on, then.'

Lad held up his hands. 'I'm just joking.'

For crying out loud . . . Fenchurch slumped back down. 'That's not funny.'

'Depends on where you're standing, guv.'

'So why are you here, then?'

'Well, Mulholland's back in. Docherty's got her running the case.' Lad flicked up his eyebrows. 'I thought you'd want to know the jelly peanut's interviewing Qasid again.'

'The jelly who?'

'DI Bell.'

Chapter Twenty-Nine

Fenchurch held open a fire door, the glass zigzagged with fine mesh, and let Lad go through first. 'What're they asking him about?'

'No idea, guv.'

Fenchurch followed him down the corridor, feet thumping on the carpet. 'If they're not charging that little shit, I'll tear Stringer a pair of new arseholes.' He stopped outside interview room three and frowned at Lad. 'The jelly peanut?'

'That little peanut head and his big jelly body. Worked with him a few years back, guv. Total cock.'

'Remind me never to get on your wrong side.' Fenchurch pushed into the interview room and lurked in the far corner.

Bell sat next to a female officer, a DC Fenchurch knew of old, and gave him a nod. 'DI Simon Fenchurch has entered the room. Oh and DC Waheed Lad.' He avoided staring at the newcomers, just focused on Qasid and Unwin opposite. 'Sorry about that. Listen to me, your prints are all over those phones. All fifteen of them. We're going to prosecute you for the theft of those mobiles.'

Unwin cleared his throat and nodded at Fenchurch. 'If you charge my client, we will sue your colleague here for unlawful arrest. I'm sure there are other offences, assault maybe.'

'That's not my concern.' Bell leaned across the table. 'Are you going to change your statement?'

'The first time I saw them was when Detective Inspector Fenchurch showed them to me.' Qasid's eyes drilled into Fenchurch, his face a grim rictus. Said each word like he was reading it out, slow and deliberate. 'You have planted my fingerprints on them.'

'I'll take that as a no, then.' Bell got up and nodded at the Custody officer. 'Can you escort—'

Fenchurch lurched across the room and grabbed a handful of Bell's jacket. 'You can't let him go.'

Bell shrugged him off. 'We've not got a choice, Simon.'

'He knows who murdered Saskia.'

'I've cleared this with DI Mulholland.'

Fenchurch slumped back against the wall. This wasn't supposed to happen like this.

'You have no evidence of my client murdering anyone, Inspector.' Unwin was on his feet, helping Qasid up. 'There will be severe consequences if you don't let him go. Even more severe for you than they are at present, I suspect.'

Fenchurch held his gaze, heavily tempted to introduce the back of his head to the inside of the cavity wall.

'Right, here's what we're going to do.' Bell started shaking his head, then nodded at Unwin. 'We'll let Mr Williams go, but we need to be able to get hold of him.'

Unwin hefted up his briefcase and unclipped both catches at the same time. He got out a business card and handed it to Bell. 'You can contact him through me. Twenty-four seven.'

'Then we'll see you in court, gentlemen.' Bell smiled at the Custody Officer and watched them leave the room. Qasid walked like he'd just grown a couple of inches and wanted everyone to notice.

'Melissa, can you give us a minute, please?' Bell didn't even look at her. 'Same with you, Waheed.'

She left the room, widening her eyes at Fenchurch as the door closed. Lad's eyes were on Melissa's backside.

Bell prodded Fenchurch in the chest. It actually hurt. 'You think you can come in here and ruin my interview?'

'You were making a brilliant job of ruining it yourself, String.'

'Shut up! Shut up! Shut up! All these bloody names. Don't you ever get tired of it?'

'Are you feeling the pressure or something? Imagine what it's like when you've got a proper case, String.'

'We're doing *solid* work. We've been in the papers. My team are going places. Don't you ever forget it. Do you get to speak to Boris every month? No.'

'You know Boris'll be back to being an MP after the election, don't you?'

'So? That man's going to be Prime Minister.'

'You hope to be Minister of Tedium in his cabinet?'

Bell collapsed against the wall. Looked like all the fight had left his body. 'Simon, why the hell are you here?'

'Because I want to see some pressure applied to Qasid. He knows who killed Saskia Barnett and he knows who Lewis Cole is. I'd put money on also knowing where we can find Kamal.'

'That's nothing to do with me.' Bell dumped the business card in his briefcase and snapped it shut. 'But then I hear it's not your case either.'

The drums started pounding harder, a Nirvana stomp. 'You don't give a shit about anyone else, do you?'

'I've got my case, you've got yours. Never the twain and all that.' Bell waddled over to the door. Jelly peanut indeed. 'See you around, Simon.'

Fenchurch slumped back onto the interview room table. How to lose a case in thirty hours . . .

Lad entered the room. 'What a clown.'

'Tell me about it.' Fenchurch stared at the empty seats. 'You done any digging into Unwin yet?'

'Was I supposed to?'

'Shit, I asked Nelson, not you.'

Lad smirked. 'We all look the same to you, or something?'

'That's not even funny, Constable.' Fenchurch let out a laugh. 'Jesus Christ.'

'Why did you ask him to investigate Unwin?'

'Well, the guy's obviously bent, for starters. He's done work for Kamal. Sprang up here pretty quickly when Qasid came in.'

'You smell shit when he's around?'

'Like most lawyers. But he's worse.'

'Well, DI Mulholland was looking for you, guv.'

'Bollocks to that.' Fenchurch checked his watch. 'Have you spoken to your mates in Trident about Unwin?'

'Not yet.'

'Let's see what they've got on him, shall we?'

Chapter Thirty

'We need to sort this out, okay, Paul?' Fenchurch got up from his chair and wandered across the tiny office to stare out of the window. Just below them, Stamford Bridge was dowsed in floodlighting for the lunchtime kick-off. His old man would be watching on BT Sport. 'I'm fed up of getting nowhere. You need to pull your finger out.'

Paul Oscar sat behind his desk, looking like he'd been dragged out of bed without the fifteen minutes' shave that morning. The sunlight bleached his face, illuminating a few pockmarks and patches of stubble. 'Listen, your guv'nor was on the phone to mine. Docherty, right? He was moaning about the pair of us acting like school kids.'

'Which is why I've come out here to try and get you to play nicely on two occasions. I just need you to work with us, okay?'

'I'm thinking about it.' The sandpaper rasp of hand on stubble. 'Look, I want to help, Fenchurch, don't get me wrong. Problem is we're stretched beyond recognition at the moment. The reason I'm in on a Saturday is because my budget is so tight a gnat fancies his chances of touching both sides, know what I'm saying?'

Fenchurch rested against the window and coughed into his hand. 'Paul, I think the reason you're in on a Saturday is more to do with your own failings than mine.'

'At least you're admitting you've got some. That's progress.'

'Oh, I'm well aware of them, don't worry about that.' Fenchurch blew air up his face and shared a look of contempt with Lad, arms folded, sitting across from Oscar. He leaned back, shoulders touching the windowpane, and stuffed his hands in his pockets to stop any physical finger-pointing. 'So, will you help us?'

Oscar stared at his screen, like it could approve his actions. 'What do you need?'

'Now we're getting somewhere.' Fenchurch clapped his hands together and stood up straight. 'Let's start with one Dalton Unwin.'

'Him.' Oscar rolled his eyes. 'Let's just say we're aware of him. He led a campaign against our work back in the day, says we were treating black kids differently from whites. Seems to ignore the fact these gangs were doing that exact thing, targeting each other.' He smirked and pushed his laptop back a bit. 'Makes you think of that Krays quote. Barbara Windsor or someone. Can't remember. "They only hurt their own". It's bollocks, though, right? We don't want them hurting anyone, white or black. The fact they target other black kids is by the by. We just need to stop it.'

Fenchurch wasn't sure he'd finished his soliloquy or if he was starting on the third act. 'How much trouble was Unwin causing?'

'Kicked up a fair stink. Don't know if you remember but a few of the more liberal papers ran a campaign about it. Indy, *Guardian*, *Post. Mirror* as well, I think.' Oscar shut his laptop lid with a thunk. 'What's he done to you, anyway?'

'He's repping the kid who we caught for the murder. Just had to let the little scrotum go. And we think he's Kamal's lawyer.'

Oscar looked up at Fenchurch. 'He's repped Kamal?'

'Don't you actually do any work?' Fenchurch shook his head. 'Have a word with Owen Greenhill up at Islington nick. Kamal was in there a few years back. Unwin got him off. And he's connected with gang stuff but you lot seem uninterested in keeping him there.'

'Sounds like it's after our remit shifted.' Oscar crossed one leg over the other and started drumming on the side of his pale-brown shoe. A shaft of light from the steel plate on the sole danced a circle on the ceiling above Lad's head. 'You're going to have to leave it with me, I'm afraid.'

Fenchurch locked eyes with him, but kept his eyebrows raised. 'I'm assuming that means you'll actually do something about it, then?'

The drumming stopped. 'What's that supposed to mean?'

Fenchurch thumbed at Lad, blinking as the light hit his face. 'It means that DC Lad's been here a few times, trying to get access to your undercover officer. Feels very much like we're getting the runaround.'

'You get a lot of these feelings, Fenchurch, don't you?'

'All I want is to find Kamal. We need to speak to this officer.'

'No can do.'

'No, Paul. Here's what's going to happen.' Fenchurch leaned against his desk, spraying tea breath over him. 'You're going to get him sent to Leman Street this afternoon. By five at the very latest.'

'You don't get it do you? Sibo . . .' Oscar sighed. '*He* is under-cover.' He sat back in his chair, his gaze switching to the closed door — nobody there. 'He's not your officer and I don't report to you. His life's at risk all the time. So just quit it and move on. Do some other work. Stop making your failure my fault.'

'He's our only lead, Paul. We need to speak to him.'

'I've already done way more than I should.'

'Well, I'd hate to see you being unhelpful.' Fenchurch rested his hands on the back of Oscar's chair. 'Arrange some time with your guy and I'll let you get back to your precious spreadsheet.'

'I'm enjoying this sparring, Fenchurch. It's good fun.'

'I want him in a room at Leman Street by five o'clock.' Fenchurch marched over to the door, nodding for Lad to get up and follow him. He opened it and jabbed a finger in the air. 'And I want something I can use on Unwin.'

'Or what?' Oscar opened his laptop and focused on the screen. 'Get out of here with your empty threats.'

'Bloody wanker.' Fenchurch trotted down the staircase, heading for the basement car park. 'We keep getting the runaround from this shower, Waheed.'

'Tell me about it, guv. If I was being kind, I'd say he's just doing his job.'

'I wish people doing their jobs wasn't such a pain in my arse.' Fenchurch glanced back up the stairs. 'What info have you got on this undercover officer, anyway?'

'I thought I knew his name but Oscar's just confirmed it.' Lad gave him a wink. 'Guy's called Siboniso Xolani. Think that's how you say it.'

'Have you got a mobile number?'

'I can try.' Lad stopped at the next floor. 'Give me a second.' He pushed through double doors into a long corridor.

Fenchurch got out his phone — there was a missed call from Reed he hadn't felt. Stacked on top of the ten from Docherty he'd ignored. He tapped out a text. 'Busy, boss. Speak later.' Hope that'd do.

He dialled Reed's number, staring out of the floor-to-ceiling windows, the city pancake flat as far as the eye could see. Or as far as the afternoon fog would let it. Fewer towers out west, but just as much sprawl, some patches of grass amid blocks of flats and housing estates.

'Guv?'

'Kay, you called?'

'Did I?' A sigh exploded down the line, Reed sounding as pissed off as he felt. 'Yeah, sorry, guv. I remember now. Just wanted to let you know I'm out with Clooney's team in Lewisham. The hard drive on Saskia's laptop is completely frazzled. Way beyond us getting anything off it.'

'Just what we expected, right? Anything else?'

'Got a squad out canvassing the area around the park. Doubtful we'll get anybody to speak, assuming we can find someone who saw anything. Nobody's spotted anyone with a laptop, guv.'

'So, exactly as we expected.' Fenchurch pressed his cheek against the glass. 'So we've still got gaps in the timeline?'

'Unwin could drive a bus through them, guv.'

'What do we know about that laptop?'

Reed blew air over the receiver. 'Precious little, I'd say. We've still just got that Liam kid's word for what happened.'

'And we've already made a nuisance of ourselves with him. Worth getting him in a room?'

'You think he's actually done something, guv?'

'He kept that text message from us.'

'I don't think it's caused us any great hardship, though, has it? It just proves that she was frightened of Kamal. Poor guy must be feeling really low just now. All those missed calls and that message.'

Fenchurch almost cracked the case of the phone with his grip. 'I know what that feels like.'

'Just saying we should give him some space. If he's somehow wrapped up in this, then he'll drop a bollock at some point.'

The stairwell door flew open and Lad appeared through it, grinning.

'How's it going out—'

'I better go, Kay.' Fenchurch ended the call and frowned at Lad. 'Well?'

'Just got an address of the squat he's staying in, guv.' Lad held the door open for a burly male officer to stroll through. 'Kev here's just got a warrant to turf them out, too.'

Chapter Thirty-One

The van rumbled down some East End road, the chassis bumping along. Fenchurch caught snatches of familiar landmarks — the train station that shared his name, then St Botolph's in Aldgate, flanked by the Gherkin. In the distance, the new towers by Leman Street lurked out of the swamp of east London.

'Kev Saunders.' The burly officer held a meaty hand across the passageway, his other hand clutching a warrant. 'Good to have you on board.'

'We're just helping out.' Fenchurch glanced at Lad, unsure how much he'd shared with Trident. 'How many you expecting in there?'

'Five, maybe six.'

Fenchurch nodded. That'd be containable. 'You work for Oscar?'

'That clown?' Kev bellowed with laughter. He ran a hand over his shaved head. Definitely ex-military. 'He's just a pen-pusher. Suits S&O8 down to the ground. We do have an active investigation side, which we try to keep secret from you lot.'

Lad gave Fenchurch a wink. 'Me and Kev go back to Hendon, guv.'

'I see.' Fenchurch tightened his stab-proof vest over his suit jacket. Must look like a right muppet. 'So what's your interest in this place?'

'I've got an undercover officer in there.' Kev didn't even have to brace himself as the van juddered to a halt. He folded up his warrant and stuffed it in a pocket on his own stab-proof. 'He's given us intel on a murder out in Canning Town a month back. The lad he's fingering for it lives here.'

'You don't mind us tagging along?'

'As long as you follow my lead. Hopefully you'll find this girl in there.' Kev put his Airwave to his lips. 'Serial Bravo, are you in position? Over.'

Fenchurch frowned at Lad and mouthed: 'Girl?'

He got a shrug in response.

Kev's Airwave crackled. 'This is Serial Bravo, sir. We're in position. Repeat, we are in position. Over.'

'And we're go, gentlemen.' Kev hauled open the back door of the unmarked van and bounced onto the pavement. 'Let's do this!'

Fenchurch jumped out and jogged down the street. His stab-proof was rattling like a bastard, felt like it was going to come off. No time to fix it.

Heavy traffic trundled past them on Mile End Road, narrowing to single file beside another police van blocking the other way. Bus passengers gawped at the squad encroaching on the old building. Midland Bank Limited was cut into the stone above the door and there was still some HSBC signage in the window.

Fenchurch got on the other side of the doorway and waited for the traffic to stop, eyes on Kev. The last taxi bundled past, the passengers eyeballing him.

Kev stabbed his finger in the air three times. Three clicks on the open Airwave channel.

Fenchurch snapped out his baton, getting ready. Blood pumping hard. Drums beating out a solo, fingers patting the skins like bongos, building up to the thwack of a stick. Harder, faster. Louder, his ears thundering, feeling like they were tearing.

A uniform in riot-squad gear appeared, lugging an Enforcer battering ram. He placed it against the old door, oak thick enough to keep everyone away from the bank vault. It looked older than Fenchurch, older than his old man.

The officer fired the ram at the lock. The wood dented but stayed standing. 'Bloody hell.' He took another go and it tumbled backwards into the building.

Kev waited until it was clear and led inside. 'This is the police! Please remain calm!'

Sleeping bags filled the floor from the door to the old counter. Maybe twenty or so bodies in there — a couple with matching his-and-hers blonde dreadlocks were nearest, eyes wide. Their feet skidded on the marble as they tried to get through the empty doorway into the belly of the building. The security door was now a trestle table, a hotplate full of spitting sausages resting on top.

Fenchurch followed them through the hole in the wall, taking it slow, Lad following.

A door up ahead toppled forward, knocking a surfer dude to the floor and blocking the path for a second. Kev led a squad of officers through the gap, trapping the squatters between them and Fenchurch's team. A masked uniform pulled the door off the surfer.

Fenchurch held his baton out level but a wave of people pushed him back into the main hall of the bank. A fist connected with his cheek. Fingers clawed his forehead. He lost his footing and tumbled backwards. His baton skidded across the marble, coming to a rest on a sleeping bag. Two women fell on top of him, trapping him under their weight.

Complete disaster. Same as it ever was.

Fenchurch shrugged the women off. Or maybe they rolled off. Maybe both. He tried to get up — someone's knee cracked off his shoulder, pushing him back down again.

Over to the right, Lad was swinging his baton wildly, just lashing out with it. He battered the metal off a middle-aged man's head.

Fenchurch crawled over to the quiet of the sleeping bags and got up. At least twenty heads were bobbing up and down. Looked like they were outnumbered, three to one, maybe more, but they had the front door under control. For now.

Kev appeared in the doorway. He cupped his hands around his mouth and shouted: 'This is the police! I need you to remain calm!'

Nobody listened. Shouts and screams cannoned off the bare walls. Sounded like there were thousands in there.

'Police brutality!'

'—our home, you can't—'

'—fascist! Haven't you read *1984*? Man, you—'

Another squad of uniforms entered through the front door. The squatters tore out at them, lashing with fists and boots. A white man with dreads went down near Fenchurch. The new squad started forming a loose circle around the squatters. Then tightened it, like a noose, closing them in.

Fenchurch spotted his baton on a crusty sleeping bag and grabbed it. He got up and rushed over to plug a gap in the circle. Trained his weapon on a middle-aged man with blotchy brown skin.

Kev was next to him. He split off from the main group, letting the circle shrink further and raised his hands, almost in surrender. 'We are operating under instruction from the Tower Hamlets Council and the City of London Mayor.' He spun around, looking like he was trying to make eye contact with as many people as possible. 'Please remain calm and we will escort you to a nearby police station for interview.'

A pregnant woman stared at Fenchurch, arms guarding her swollen belly. Hair in pigtails, denim dungarees. Looked like she thought she was going to get crushed by the Death Star and Fenchurch was Darth Vader.

He wanted to tell her it was okay, they were just after one man, but he didn't. Couldn't.

He could only watch as Lad and a uniform led her out to the street, screaming.

Fenchurch leaned against the wall outside the interview room. 'I'm beginning to think this was a mistake.'

Kev Saunders clapped Fenchurch's shoulder. 'Ends justify the means, right?'

'I'm usually the first to think such Machiavellian thoughts, but . . .' Fenchurch shut his eyes. Pigtails, dungarees, hands covering a swollen belly. 'I'm struggling to see how this is a good idea.'

'We got our guy, you've got yours. Push your case forward.' Another matey clap on the shoulder and Kev was gone, loping off down the corridor.

Lad folded his arms and joined him propped against the wall. 'You just about ready, guv?'

'Give me a minute.'

'You okay?'

'I'm fine, it's just . . .' Fenchurch hissed out breath. He held Lad's gaze but had to look away. 'Never mind, Constable.'

All Lad seemed to be capable of was shrugging. 'Want me to lead, guv?'

'If you wouldn't mind.'

'No probs.' Lad entered the room and claimed the seat nearest the door. He reached over to start the recorder.

Fenchurch followed him in, and stood near the door. He immediately recognised the man at the table.

The guy who accosted him in the phone shop the previous morning. He had the same dark skin as Qasid. All this pain could've been averted if only Oscar hadn't held onto the few cards he had left.

Christ knows what he'd done or how, but he looked every inch the squatter. Worse, he smelled it, like he hadn't washed in weeks, though his dreadlocks looked recently fused. His camouflage gear was tucked tight around his torso and a cream and brown jacket was hanging over the back of the chair.

'—present is Siboniso Xolani.' Lad stretched out and yawned. 'That's right, isn't it?'

'I want a lawyer.' Clipped South African accent. 'I can give you his number.'

'Your lawyer wouldn't happen to be a DI Paul Oscar, would it?'

'Excuse me?'

'Or should I say, your boss.'

'I've no idea what you're talking about, man.'

'We staged that whole raid so we could get you in here, Mr Xolani. Your DI isn't letting us speak to you.'

'I'm not a cop.'

'Really?' Lad held up his Pronto. 'Says here your name is Siboniso Xolani. That right?'

Xolani nodded. 'My friends call me Sibo.'

'See, it looks like they missed Detective Sergeant off the start.'

A sigh as Xolani scratched at his neck. 'Fine, but you can call me DS Xolani.'

'Now we're getting somewhere.' Lad rested his Pronto on the tabletop, setting it just so. 'Never heard that name before. Is it Greek?'

'Greek.' Xolani bellowed with laughter. 'It's Zulu.' A smirk danced across his face as he sang: 'Z.U.L.U. That's the way we say Zulu.'

Fenchurch nodded in recognition. 'Leftfield, right?'

Xolani frowned at him. 'Afrika Bambaataa, man. Not some posh white kids who heard house music at one of their parents' parties.' He shook his head. 'I was born in South Africa. My parents left during apartheid and brought me to London. Feels like we should've stayed.'

Fenchurch recognised the feeling, had it crawling around his guts every month or so. 'But you're a DS in the Met now.'

'And what good is it doing me? I'm sleeping in squats. Not washing, even when I really need to. Just so I don't blow my cover. That's no life.'

'I assume it's for some end?'

'And I assume you've not got the clearance to know what that is.'

'We're protecting your cover here.'

'You think?' Xolani tugged at a dreadlock, pulling it tight like a length of string then letting it fly free. 'The others will notice I'm in here longer than the rest of them.'

'Maybe we could say it's because of the trouble you caused at that phone shop yesterday morning?'

'You shouldn't have done that, man. That guy was scared out of his wits.'

'I'm all about the result, Sergeant. But I'd also agree with you.' Fenchurch clicked his tongue a few times. 'Except for the fact we found a murder victim's stolen mobile in his recycler.'

'What?'

'Take it you don't know anything about it?'

Xolani swallowed, eyes switching between Fenchurch and Lad. 'Of course I don't bloody know anything.'

'Why were you in there?'

'The owner of that shop is a CHIS. He was giving me some info for an obbo DI Bell is running.'

Bloody Stringer and his secrets. Fenchurch scowled at Xolani. 'What info?'

'I can't tell you.'

'I'm ordering you to tell me.'

Xolani shot him a smirk. 'What level of police brutality are you going to inflict on me?'

'Let's start with some light waterboarding.' Fenchurch's grin bounced off Xolani's scowl. 'We need your help.' He waved to his left. 'DC Lad here has been trying to secure access to you so we can progress our case.'

'This murder victim and his or her phone?'

'Her phone. The name is Saskia Barnett.'

'Am I supposed to know her?'

'We're also looking for someone called Lewis Cole, aka Roofie.'

'Roofie, right.'

'Mean anything.'

'No.'

'What about Kamal?'

Xolani's mouth hung open. Then he collected himself and covered it over with a smile. 'Does this Kamal have a surname?'

'We don't know but I gather you do.'

Xolani leaned back in the chair and blew air over his face. 'I've been on the street for three years. Started off infiltrating a gang in Tottenham. Might've heard of them. They're called the Mandem.'

'Shit.' Fenchurch felt his stomach lurch. 'I can see why you're protecting your identity so closely.'

'Right.' Xolani ran his hands through his dreads. 'I'm on a tightrope, man. Every day. If they find out what I've done, who I am.' He drew a vertical line down his throat and made a hacking noise. 'You ever heard of a Colombian necktie? Well, they've got their own twist on it.'

'How does this link to Kamal?'

'I've met the guy twice.'

'Was he a member?'

'Was, yeah. He left.'

'And you followed?'

'In a way.'

'Tell me about him.'

'Guy disappeared into thin air both times. He's invisible, like he's made of smoke.' Xolani grinned and flicked up his dreads. 'Like Batman.'

'Right, Batman. Take us through them, then.'

'First time, a contact in the gang said someone needed help. Kid called Kamal. Told me to meet him near Hackney Downs. Said he'd show me the ropes. So we just wandered round Hackney and Shoreditch on a Saturday night.'

'Just the two of you?'

'Very romantic.' Xolani barked out some laughter. 'Cat was dealing to people. No, supplying to dealers. High-end stuff.'

'So, even though it's not black-on-black violence, they had you keep close to him so you could give intel to the drugs squad?'

'Right, right. Thought it was containable.' Xolani scratched at the thick stubble on his chin. 'Problem is, the cat stabbed someone. Just right there on the street. One of his dealers. Kid was running a corner at the back end of Hackney. Some white punks had stolen his stash. This dealer got in Kamal's face, right? Accusing him of this, that, the other thing. Saying he didn't need him no more. So Kamal stabbed the guy in the neck.'

Fenchurch's breath rustled over his fingers, grabbing the table tight. 'Right in front of you?'

'As far as you are from me.'

'You didn't think to arrest him?'

'Some of Kamal's other kids had turned up to watch the show. Learn from the master. There were ten of them, man. No way I'd be able to get Kamal away from them with my life intact, know what I'm saying?'

'Who was this dealer?'

'No idea.' Xolani let out a sigh. 'John something. Kamal called him Honest John, don't know if that's his name or him just being smart.'

Fenchurch gestured at Lad. 'Look out this case, will you?'

'Guv.' He made a note.

'So what happened before he disappeared?'

Xolani rubbed at his arms through his combats. 'One of his apprentice kids starts shouting at Kamal, saying he shouldn't have done that. Then someone else starts shouting at me. Next thing I know, it's just me and these kids. Kamal's gone.' He made a sweeping gesture with his hands, like a puff of smoke. 'Poof, just like that.'

Fenchurch nodded slowly. Tallied with everything they'd heard. 'What about the other time?'

'I'd been building the trust of his guys in the squat up in Islington, good friends of his. Helped out on a few things.' Xolani raised a hand. 'I'm not telling you what. Anyway, to cut a long story short, Kamal met me on Upper Street, other end from Angel. Almost where Arsenal used to play. Some posh kids were having a party. He gave me a package to take in. It was like twenty grams of coke.'

'And you just took it in?'

'This was my chance to prove myself to him, gain his trust and get in the inner circle.'

'Was it just you two?'

'I know what you're getting at here, man. I couldn't arrest him for the stabbing. It'd just've been my word against his. My partner didn't see it.'

'You've got a partner?'

'I'm not telling you his name.' Xolani gave him a wink. 'Or hers.'

Fenchurch snorted. The drums were almost drowning out the room's drone. 'So, after you dropped the drugs off?'

'I came back outside and Kamal was gone. Disappeared.'

'We haven't heard about him dealing.'

'This is a couple of years ago, man. Not seen him in all that time. Moved on to other things. Heard about him a lot since, though. Cat's baaad.'

Fenchurch shook his head and shot another glare at Lad. 'How do people contact him?'

'No idea. And that's the truth. Word gets to him and he gets in touch with you.'

'So, you're telling me you can't bring him to us?'

'I don't know what you were expecting, man. Kamal's smart, always a step ahead of people.'

'You think he's onto you?'

'If he was, I'd be dead.'

Fenchurch got up and nodded at Xolani. 'I hope you're doing what you're supposed to be doing.'

'Oh, I am. Good luck catching him. He's one evil cat.'

Fenchurch collapsed behind his desk. Someone had scribbled on a Post-it. 'Where are you?' Looked like Docherty's handwriting. He sipped at his tea and crumpled it up. 'Well, we've just abused a load of people's human rights. I sincerely hope none of them have Dalton Unwin's number.'

Lad clutched his machine coffee, steam billowing into his face. 'Sorry, guv.'

'What for?'

'That.' Lad waved at the door. 'That was all because of the intel I got. We're wasting our time.'

247

'Maybe, maybe not.' Fenchurch put his feet up on the desk. 'When we catch Kamal, we've got a murder we can pin on him.'

'Just Xolani's word against Kamal's.'

'Wouldn't be so sure. There's got to be something. Look into it for me, see if there's any forensics we can use to back up his story.'

'Guv.'

'Why haven't we heard about this drug dealing, though?'

'No idea. Want me to speak to the drugs squad?'

'Maybe.' Fenchurch finished his tea. 'Get back in with Xolani, all right? See if he passed this stabbing up the line.'

'Guv.'

'Then let him get back to that squat, okay?'

'Shouldn't be keeping him here overnight, anyway, should we?'

'No. Need to keep a few of the others in to deflect from him.'

The office door crashed open, thunking off Mulholland's desk.

Docherty burst in, Paul Oscar lurked behind him, face like a smacked arse. Docherty pointed at Lad then at the corridor. 'I need a word, Simon.'

Lad got up and whispered. 'Sounds like you want to shove some books down the back of your trousers, guv.'

Fenchurch watched Lad leave. Couldn't look at Docherty or Oscar. 'What's up, boss?'

'We're doing this in my office.'

Chapter Thirty-Two

Docherty held open his office door. 'In.'

Fenchurch entered, head bowed low like a naughty schoolboy. He sat opposite the desk and stared at his shoes. Keith Moon drumming in his ears, chaotic, erratic, heavy.

Mulholland was already in there, standing by Docherty's whiteboard. She flapped across to a spare armchair and loosened off her scarf, as dark as the rings under her eyes, pouting as she flicked her eyebrows. 'Good evening, Simon.'

Fenchurch just grunted.

Oscar sat next to him and rasped a hand across his stubble.

'What the hell are you playing at, Inspector?' Docherty collapsed into his seat and threw his notebook onto the desktop. 'I hope you've got a bloody good explanation for your behaviour.'

Fenchurch shrugged, still not looking at his superior. 'Trying to solve a murder, sir.'

'You cheeky bastard. You think jeopardising a three-year undercover obbo is the bloody way to do it?'

'That wasn't my intention, boss. We—'

'Don't you "boss" me, Simon.' Docherty reached his arms up into the air. 'Christ, this is a disaster.'

Fenchurch snorted breath through his nostrils. 'We need to find Kamal and the only lead we had was DS Xolani.'

'And you need an evidence trail that supports a conviction.'

'I've got one, believe me.'

'Look at me when I'm talking to you.'

Fenchurch stared up. He caught a glimpse of Oscar next to him, grinning his head off. Happy to tear it off.

'You're mucking about, Simon. Like you've been doing all bloody day.' Docherty tore open his notebook. 'When you told me about the latest farrago with these fingerprints this morning, I gave you ten minutes with that wee laddie you assaulted and I've been looking for you ever since.'

'We're getting somewhere—'

'No you're not. Turns out you took DS Reed off on a picnic up in Islington. Jon bloody Nelson had to tell me you'd found the girl's laptop.'

'Sorry, sir.'

'Aye, bollocks you are. You bothered your arse to come back here, but didn't even think to update me on your progress, did you?'

'Sir, I tried but—'

'Don't. Lie.'

'Sir.'

'What were you up to?'

Fenchurch glanced at Mulholland. Not in front of her. 'We chased a few leads that didn't get us anywhere, sir. Retracing my steps on Thursday night.'

'Working out precisely where you made an arse of it, right?' Docherty slapped his notebook shut. 'Care to explain why you haven't phoned me back?'

Fenchurch touched a hand to his cheek. Could melt butter on it. 'I'm sorry I haven't, sir. Not had a chance to.'

'You were up to some cowboy crap, weren't you?' Docherty waved a hand at Oscar. 'You and Kevin bloody Saunders. Anyone who's heard of Trident knows the boy's got straw for a parking space. You and him decided to raid a bloody squat.'

'Sir, he had a warrant. DC Lad and I—'

'Enough!' Docherty was panting, spit flecking his cheek. 'You know how much shit you've got us into with that? A wee crusty bird's in A&E, thinking she's lost her baby. All cos of you and your mate.'

'Sir, we've got useful intel on Kamal.'

Docherty looked over at Mulholland. 'Dawn, can you go and start the interview with Kamal, please?'

She pouted at him, her eyes long slits. 'Sir.'

Fenchurch twisted his head to the side away from her. Almost bit his cheek. 'He's not in custody.'

'Oh and why the bloody hell not? Thought you had intel on him?'

'We do, but we've—'

'—not got the bugger in custody.' Docherty slammed his fist on the desk. 'Christ on a bloody bike, Si, you're really doing my head in here.'

'Sir, this intel could get us access to him.'

'How?'

Fenchurch's mouth was dry. He ran his tongue around his teeth, trying to get some moisture from somewhere. 'I don't know, boss.'

'Aye, I bloody know you don't.' Docherty got up and stormed across the room, towering over Mulholland. 'Dawn's the Deputy SIO on this now, okay?'

'But, sir, she—'

'Simon, she's been Deputy since two o'clock this afternoon, if you'd bothered to check in with anyone.'

Fenchurch didn't have anything to say to that. Just gave a short nod.

Docherty opened his office door. 'Dawn, Paul, can you give us a minute, please?'

Mulholland got up and followed Oscar out, grinning all the way to the corridor. Her smirk was cut off by Docherty slamming the door.

'Boss, we're getting somewh—'

'Shut. Up.' Docherty sat on the edge of his desk. 'Simon, I know what's going on here. You think this is connected to Chloe, don't you?'

Fenchurch looked away. 'I don't.'

'You're telling me your old man hasn't mentioned his latest theory to you?'

'Christ. No, I don't think this has anything to do with Chloe, sir.'

'No? Well, how come he phoned me up and thanked me for the lead. What lead, I asked. Turns out you bloody told him Lewis Cole's linked to his latest wild goose chase, eh?'

'It's a dead end for us, sir. His parents don't—'

'I don't like finding out key facts on my case from your bloody father.'

'Sir.'

'Is it connected or not?'

'It's nothing to do with Chloe, sir. None of it is.' Fenchurch snorted again, fists curled tight. 'Nothing to do with what happened to her.'

'Simon, are you burning out?'

'Course I'm not burning out.' Fenchurch bit at his breath. 'Boss, I'm your Deputy SIO on this case and I aim to solve it.'

'Were you even listening to me? Dawn's taken over.'

'With all due respect, sir, she's—'

'Don't give me that shite.' Docherty put a hand on Fenchurch's shoulder. 'Look, you're not capable of dealing with this. I don't know what the hell's up with you, Si, but you're falling apart. Get yourself home, have a day off and come in here fresh on Monday morning.'

'I need to stay here and—'

'You need to get your head out of your arse and do a proper job.' Docherty squeezed the shoulder tight, like a Vulcan neck pinch. 'This was supposed to be a bloody favour, if you remember. Now there's a flashing red ball against my name. This isn't the sort of case that solves itself, you know?'

'Which is why I want to—'

'I need an officer who can focus on this. You're all over the bloody shop, Si.'

'Boss—'

'Get out of my sight.' Docherty gave another squeeze. Any more and he was getting a fist in the face. 'Dawn's team are running this from now on, okay?'

'They'll not find anything.'

'Simon, if you stay here, the way you're going you'll be locked up by morning, you stupid bastard.'

Chapter Thirty-Three

Fenchurch pushed through the door into the stairwell. Heart thumping, drums pounding. The door whistled shut behind him and he was in almost darkness, just a light on the verge of popping flickering on and off. Shards of light fell across the plastic bumps on the flooring, swallowed just as quickly as they appeared.

Bloody Docherty.

Where did he get off? Sitting there in his bloody office, never lifting a finger while Fenchurch made him look good. As soon as something happened he didn't like, he dropped him. Just like that.

There's bloody gratitude.

Footsteps boomed out from below, the click turned into a clatter by the time it reached him.

'Guv?' Reed was frowning in the flicker. 'What the hell are you doing there?'

'Just heading home, Kay.'

'What, we're working our arses off while you piss off home? You did that yesterday, remember?'

Fenchurch gripped the handrail tight, twisting his fingers around the cold metal. 'Docherty sent me home.'

'What?'

'He's given the case to Mulholland.'

'Shit.' She reached out and patted his arm. 'You okay?'

'Not really, Kay. He carpeted me in front of her and that Oscar clown from Trident.'

'You look like you need a drink.'

———

'Here you go, guv.' Reed dumped a foaming pint of craft beer on Fenchurch's side of the table, a curvy bottom-heavy thing looking more like a wine glass. 'This is the hoppiest thing they've got.'

'Good.' Fenchurch took a deep gulp. Citrus tang cut into the bitter taste. 'Lovely stuff, well chosen.'

'Brew it up in Hackney, guv. Satan's Scrotum or something.' She winked and took a sip of her own Peroni. 'You've got that look in your eyes, like you want to tear someone a couple of new arseholes.'

'Maybe I'll start with that little shit, Qasid.'

'You need to stop calling him a little bastard and a little shit.' She raised her eyebrows and looked around the pub. 'Someone will hear you.'

'Maybe.' Fenchurch stared out of the window, back across to the vulgar brutality of Leman Street's concrete front. 'Or maybe it's just Docherty I want to do it to.'

'You've got to admit you're acting a bit odd, guv.'

'How?'

'You ran away from Docherty after that evidence about Lewis Cole. We were pissing about up in Islington all morning.'

'Meanwhile, Docherty was giving my case to Mulholland.'

'What would you do in his situation?'

'Eh?'

'Say you've got, I don't know, Jon Nelson or me pissing about, off on our own, trying to sort stuff out how we saw fit. What would you do?'

'Nothing.'

'That's bollocks and you know it.' Reed took another sip of lager and tilted her head to the side. Her ponytail dangled free. 'You'd be all over us, tearing us a new one.' She clasped both hands around the tall glass, heavy with beads of perspiration. 'Like you did with Waheed in February?'

'He was out of order and he's paid for it.'

'You and him were in that raid, weren't you?'

'We were.'

'And did that get you anywhere?'

Fenchurch took another sip. Could barely taste it. 'Maybe.'

'As successful as that raid on the phone shop this morning?'

Fenchurch pushed his glass away. 'If people spoke to each other in this bloody force, we'd have had DS bloody Xolani in an interview room, spilling what he knows, instead of my bollocks being nailed to Docherty's wall.'

'You've got to admit, guv, you're no closer to finding this Kamal geezer, are you?'

Fenchurch got out his mobile and checked for messages. Nothing. 'Are you trying to help me, or what?'

'I'm trying to, guv, yes. But I'm trying to give you some perspective, as well.' She held his gaze for a few seconds. 'I'm worried you're losing it.'

'Losing it?'

'You're not acting like yourself.'

Fenchurch's throat tightened, like he had a cold on the way. Or . . . 'Kay, I think Docherty's going to boot me back to uniform.'

'Why?'

'Well, he sort of said that.'

'He doesn't mean half of what he says, guv.'

'Investigating murders is how I keep myself sane, Kay.' Another gulp of beer. 'Focusing on who did what to whoever. That's how I cope with the world.' More beer, starting to taste it again. 'That raid we were on today. They were terrified of us. How many times have those poor buggers been kicked out of a squat? Makes me wonder if we're on the right side.' He swallowed down saliva, trying to force his throat wider.

'I try not to think about it.'

'What, otherwise you'd go mad?'

'Like you're doing, guv.' She nodded at his glass. 'You ready for another?'

Fenchurch stared at the empty. Hadn't even noticed. 'I need to get home to Abi, Kay.'

'Do you want another or not?'

'What do I do?'

'About what?'

'Docherty and Mulholland. Everything's crumbling around me. Maybe I should just go back on the beat.'

'You sure about that?'

'Maybe not. Makes me shudder, Kay. I liked doing what we do. It feels good. Sometimes I worry that all we're doing is protecting property. Keeping the masses from owning it and making sure the likes of Guy Eustace keep making money off it.'

'Didn't know you were a commie. Voting for Corbyn at the next election?'

'That's not very funny.'

'Are you being serious, guv?'

'Deadly, Kay.' Fenchurch shook his head, teeth grinding together. 'You heard what Guy Eustace said yesterday. London's turning into a city state. It's so far removed from the rest of the UK. That can't be a good thing.'

'Yep, you've lost it.' She gripped his hand tight. 'Go home and have a bath.'

'I was going to spend a nice evening with Abi.'

'Well she's meeting up with me and Claire.'

'Always the last to bloody know.'

'She puts up with a lot of shit from you.'

'Is this you trying to tell me something?'

'What do you mean by that?'

'You're her friend, Kay.' Fenchurch pushed his glass away, grinding across the table. 'Has she been talking about me?'

'Yes, guv. She still loves you. Even despite all the . . .' Reed waved her hands around Fenchurch's general shape. 'You know.'

'Not really. Does she think things have happened too quickly? Me moving in again, renewing our vows.'

Reed grabbed his hand again. 'If anything, it's happening too slowly for her.' She picked up their empty glasses, foam still clinging to the sides. 'Now, go get some sleep, guv. You look like you died.'

Chapter Thirty-Four

'It wasn't him? Jesus.' Abi took another sip of wine, her lips dyed red, and let out a deep breath. She put the glass back on the kitchen table and leaned in close to him on the bench. 'I'm glad I didn't lie at the ID parade.'

'You never would've, love.' Fenchurch sipped his own wine. An intense Rioja, finally just past the breathing point. The Man United match played on the TV hanging by the window, a steamroller against a pathetic Sunderland.

'Where does this leave the case, then?'

'Docherty's pissed off with me. Worse than ever.' Another sip of wine, starting to feel a bit on the merry side. 'He's taken me off the case, love. Given it to bloody Mulholland.'

'Simon. Christ.'

'I've really dropped a bollock, Ab. Haven't handled myself at all well.'

'What've you done? This can't be because you caught the wrong bloke, can it?'

'Well, I kind of went off the reservation a bit. Didn't do anything bad, but I've not covered myself in glory.' He downed the rest of his glass. 'That little shit . . . I thought I'd caught her killer. I really did.'

'What's happening now?'

'I don't know, Abi.' He reached over for the bottle. 'Those little bastards bloody played me.' He tipped half of the remaining wine into his glass and dumped the rest into hers, filling it almost to the brim. 'Made me look like a bloody racist.'

'They didn't do that, Simon.'

'What, you think I did?'

'No, you don't look racist, you pillock. I suspect they've planned this. They get guys who look alike to hunt together in packs. Same clothes, same bikes, same age, same skin colour. If you lot get onto one of them, another can take over who's not carrying anything. Stacks the odds in their favour.'

'Maybe.'

She stared at her glass, like she could drink it through her eyes. 'Have you been thinking about . . . what we talked about last night?'

'I've not had a chance to think all day, Ab. It's full on, you know how it is.'

'But you will think about it?'

'Of course I will. Next week. We'll talk about it next week. Maybe go out for something to eat.' He smiled, then worried it was too much, too soon. 'Your choice this time.'

She took a big dent out of her glass. 'Remember Pamela who I used to work with? She moved to just outside Sevenoaks. Turned a two-bedroom flat in bloody Brixton into a three-bed cottage. We've got two flats, as well.'

'This is one of the nicer bits of London, love. I'm not moving to Kent. It'll be a bugger of a commute for you. Train in then tube across town.'

'It'll let me catch up on my reading.'

'Costs a bloody fortune, too. Forty quid into London Bridge, last time I did it from Tonbridge.'

'I could get a different job. You could, too.'

He took another sip of wine. 'Investigate garages getting turned over? I'd go mad.'

She laughed. 'Are you saying you're sane now?'

'Touché.' He chinked glasses with her, sending ripples across the surface. 'We should think about it, though.'

'This is the first big case you've worked since we got back together.' She finally took another drink and stared into space. 'I forgot all about this, you know? Losing my Saturdays to your job.'

'It's what I am, Ab. It's who I am. I can't let it go.'

'I'm not suggesting it's not. I'd just forgotten, that's all.'

'Are you saying you regret getting back with me?'

'Did I say that? Would you stop being so bloody melodramatic?' She held up her ring finger and tapped it. 'I wear this because I'm committed to you, you big idiot. Job and all. Warts and all.'

Fenchurch took another sip. Didn't know what to say to that. 'Maybe I should go to the doctor about the warts.'

'Can you stop bloody joking for a second? I'm just saying I find it difficult not knowing when you're coming back.' She stared over at the window. 'I was going to meet some of the girls for a drink. Try to take my mind off it.'

'Kay said. We went for a beer after work. You can still go out if you want.'

'And let you brood in front of the Spanish football and another bottle of wine? Hardly.'

'Do you want to go to the cinema?'

'Maybe.' She took a big gulp of wine and kissed his forehead. 'What about an early night instead?'

Day 4
Sunday, 24th April 2016

Chapter Thirty-Five

The sun climbed above the nearby buildings, bathing Barford Street in an early morning glow and crawling over their bedroom floor.

Fenchurch blinked at the alarm clock, pumping out Prince's 'Purple Rain'. The shock news still stung his gut like a knife.

Half six and no sign of Abi. Why the hell was it going off on a Sunday, anyway?

He sank back into the pillow.

Cooking smells. Bacon, egg, maybe.

He got up and padded through to the kitchen, yawning into his fist.

Abi was standing over the cooker, stirring something with a spatula, wearing trackie bottoms and a loose T-shirt.

He snuggled into her from behind, kissing just below her ear. 'Morning, you.'

'Morning yourself.' She wriggled around and spread her arms around his neck. 'How you feeling?'

'Reborn.' Fenchurch kissed her on the lips. 'Like a new man.'

'Don't get any ideas, you.' She slapped his wrist and nudged him back. 'I'm going out for a run.'

'Right.'

'I'm cooking your breakfast. Thought you might appreciate it.'

'Fry up?'

'Better than a fry up. Take a seat.'

Fenchurch did as he was told. The microwave pinged. Outside the window, the only thing out and about was a cleaning truck clearing away the mess of a Saturday night in Islington. Even the arse end of the centre had late-night bars and all-night kebab shops.

He tipped some milk from the open pint on the counter and poured some tea from the pot. Then picked up the paper. The *Post on Sunday*'s cover had some news about the Mayoral election underneath a splash of the latest Chelsea FC melodrama. Let's have a look at that.

'Here you go.' Abi put a plate in front of him. 'A breakfast burrito.' Sausage, egg, refried beans, cheese and salsa, all sort of wrapped in a tortilla, loosely secured and hanging over the edge of the plate. 'Maybe not as good as Chilangos, but that's not open yet.'

'It'll piss all over theirs.' He gripped her wrist and reached up to kiss her. 'This looks brilliant.'

'Stick the plate in the sink when you're done.' She pecked him on the top of his head. 'I'm going up to Finsbury and back down through Clissold Park, okay?' She wandered out of the room, fiddling with her phone.

Fenchurch picked up the tortilla, his mouth watering, and bit into it. He chewed and fire burnt around the tang. Heaven.

He sifted through the sections of the paper looking for the sport section, sipping tea.

And stopped dead.

The Sunday magazine's cover was a black-and-white shot of Saskia. She stared at the camera, trying for intensity, but a smile curled up her lips. Her wedge cut showed it was recent. The *London*

Post and *Post on Sunday* logos featured at the top. 'Saskia Barnett: Commemorative Edition' in white text below.

Shit.

He took another bite, reading as he chewed.

An editorial by Victor Morgan gushed over the first two pages. Her life, her achievements. He scanned through it and the last paragraph caught his eye —

'Throughout the short, short time I worked with her, Saskia produced some memorable journalism. The kind of investigative work you seldom see these days. If she hadn't been taken from us, maybe she'd eventually be up there with Woodward and Bernstein. Hunter S. Thompson. Pulitzer, Novak. Hearst and Hersh. Greenwald. Today, we're reprinting some of her best work of the last three years, helping you remember her big impact during her all-too-short time. But, we're also using this opportunity to break some big stories. New stories. Important stories. The sort of stories Oliver Kidd wanted when he founded the Post and this sister paper in 1856.'

Fenchurch flicked through the pages past some old work on Boris Johnson, Tony Blair's various new businesses, Gordon Brown's post-Prime Ministerial record and the new architecture of central London. He stopped at the first article marked with a 'New!' badge.

Halfway down the page, Clinton Jackson stood outside the Central bar, scowling at the camera in the classic tabloid style of people who'd been done over. 'Pillar of the New Community'. He skimmed the article. Saskia was defending Jackson, protecting what he was trying to achieve at his bar and castigating the authorities and the police for victimising him.

Scratch him off the list of suspects.

Over the page, Guy Eustace used his hands to block a camera as he walked away. 'Kicked Her When She Was Pregnant: Sick UKIP MEP Hounded out of Dubai After Assault on Muslim Lover, 22.' His stomach lurched as he swallowed another bite of burrito.

Looked like Eustace had knocked up a Muslim woman in Dubai in 2009. Then kicked her in the stomach during an argument before booting her out of his penthouse apartment.

Move him up the list.

Overleaf, Zara Redshaw spoke at a rally. Her arm was caught in a Nazi salute, no doubt the result of creative photography rather than fascism. 'Double Standards: Flats in Hackney Rented to Students while Campaigning Against Gentrification'. An exposé on her flat-renting business, focusing on the hypocrisy. Nothing he didn't already know, maybe, but if she'd known this was coming, could she have taken a hit out on Saskia? It hadn't stopped the story going to the press. Then again, she wasn't to know that. He'd seen enough desperate men and women over the years.

Keep her on the list.

Another couple of pages of reprints, then Yana Ikonnikova grinning at the camera, dressed in a flowing black dress. Hair shining like she was worth it. 'Stepping on the Homeless: Property Empire Kills THREE Shelters to Build Yuppie Pads.'

A damning indictment of Yana's charitable foundation. Enough to put her on the list? Maybe.

Fenchurch flicked through the rest of the paper, his stomach starting to burn as the TV listings gave way to more reprints. He burped into his hand and wiped his mouth using a serviette.

There was a closing segment by the paper's Editor, Yvette Farley. She beamed out of a stock photo, her hair neon-blue. He skimmed the platitudes until the penultimate paragraph.

'And that's why our sister paper, *The London Post*, will be printing more of Saskia's tremendous work over the next three days. Old, important stories we shouldn't forget until those in question leave public life. New, important stories where we bring the focus to bear on new faces. New hypocrites, new lawbreakers.'

And here we go again.

Fenchurch shut the paper and shook his head. He slurped at his tea, weighing up the decision. He needed a word with Victor Morgan. A long, hard word in an interview room.

'—still on the lookout for persons matching the description of Kamal.' Mulholland looked up from her notebook, the bookmark dangling just like her scarf. She made eye contact with Fenchurch then nudged Docherty in the arm.

Docherty cleared his throat. 'You should all be aware that DI Mulholland is now the Deputy SIO on this case, though DI Fenchurch will continue to support us. Okay? Dismissed.' He made a beeline for him, his skinny frame slipping through the crowd like an eel in a sandbank. 'I could've sworn I told you to take some time off.'

Fenchurch thumbed behind him. 'Need a word, boss.'

'Right.' Docherty turned round and beckoned Mulholland over. 'We're all ears.'

'Not here and not with her.'

'Beggars can't be choosers, Si.'

Mulholland appeared, wrapping the scarf around her neck like a Bond villain with a cat. 'Didn't expect to see you, Simon.'

'Bet you didn't.' Fenchurch looked around the room. The officers were thinning out, no doubt heading to the canteen or back out on the street, but there were still far too many for his liking. Sod it. He handed the Post's supplement to Docherty. 'Have you seen this?'

He squinted at the page. 'Aye, Simon, we've seen it. If that's all, you can—'

'Boss, you need to bring Victor Morgan in and put him in protective custody.'

Docherty tilted his head. 'Do you know something we don't?'

'They killed Saskia and now he's published all this shit.'

Docherty shared a look with Mulholland, like something from *One Flew Over The Cuckoo's Nest*, and passed the paper back. 'Are you aware of a threat being made against him?'

'You tell me, boss. I'm off the case.'

'Bloody McMurphy . . .' Docherty pinched his nose. 'Dawn, you got anything to add before I get stuck in here?'

'I've got a few observations, Alan.' Mulholland loosened off her scarf and started bunching it up. 'First, given your concern for these poor, poor journalists, I'm intrigued why you let them publish these stories in the first place, Simon?'

'What's that supposed to mean?'

'If you'd done your job properly, you'd have got a warrant to obtain all of their documentation and IT equipment. At the very least, an injunction preventing it until the murder inquiry was resolved. As it is, we're flying blind and I'm trying to press for access way after the horse has bolted.'

Fenchurch took a step back from her and let Lad past. He bit at his fingernail, tearing a great chunk off. 'Are you having a laugh?'

'Simon, back off.' Docherty got between them, pressing a hand to Fenchurch's chest. 'You've been speaking to all these people, right? You should've known what they were publishing.'

'We've spoken to the subjects of these stories, boss. The published works differ greatly from what Victor Morgan told me.'

'That right?'

'Speak to Jon or Kay. They'll back up my story.'

'I bet they bloody will.'

Fenchurch stepped forward, trying to crowd Docherty and push Mulholland into the margins. 'Boss, you really need to get units round to his house now. He's going to need protection.'

'I'll ask you again, Inspector.' Docherty's nostrils were flaring and his accent had gone all Gorbals. 'Has there been a threat made against anyone?'

'Not that I know of.'

'Have you even spoken to this Morgan dude today?'

Fenchurch couldn't help but grin. 'Thought I was kicked off the case, boss?'

Docherty held his gaze for a few seconds. Felt like he was going to glass him. 'I'm taking that as a no.' He shook his head with amusement. 'Simon, go and have a little chat with him, okay?'

Mulholland was trying to come in from the wings. 'Sir, with all due respect—'

'Dawn, Simon's back on the case. We're going to give him a length of rope and see what he does with it.'

'I'm not convinced—'

'Just shut up, will you?' Fenchurch got in her face. Tempted to wrench the scarf from her hands and tie it round her throat. 'Let me do my bloody job for once.'

'Don't you take that bloody tone with her, okay?' Docherty gripped Fenchurch on the shoulder, skeletal fingers gripping tight through his suit jacket. 'Dawn, give us a minute, okay?'

Mulholland pursed her lips and wrapped the scarf round her neck. Then turned to the side and called out: 'DS Nelson, I need a word.'

'Boss, you're making a big—'

'Simon, would you stop making my life so bloody difficult?' Docherty nudged him back into the corner. 'You're acting like you're going to have a nervous breakdown.'

'Maybe I am, boss.' Fenchurch leaned back, shoulder blades resting on the walls. Act like you own the bloody place. 'Saskia was killed in front of me. I don't want it to happen to anyone else.'

'Unless there's something concrete, we can't help. Okay?'

'Boss, there's a clear threat here. They've pub—'

'Speak to the dude and let me know what we're doing, okay?' Docherty dusted down his suit jacket. 'Right, is that enough incident for the Incident Room for one day?'

Grinning, Fenchurch gave him a nod then marched through the room, out into the corridor. He got out his mobile and dialled.

'Victor Morgan.' Traffic sounds, pretty busy ones at that.

'It's DI Fenchurch. I need a word.'

'We're speaking just now, aren't we? I assume this is about the stories we published today?'

'Correct. Have you had any threats?'

'Look, I've just left the office.' A pause, cut with the drone of an underground train. 'I'm just about to get on the tube and it'll be half an hour getting anywhere.'

'This is urgent, sir.'

'Well, given it's already a glorious day, how about I meet you at my favourite park?'

———

Fenchurch leaned forward on the bench, the metal studs digging into his back. He looked around Pitfield Park, a small patch of grass pockmarked with dog shit and used rubbers. Another area of northeast London between Shoreditch and Islington stuck mid-gentrification. The council high-rise nearby cast long shadows across the grass. A few bikes chained to the fence separating off the empty basketball court.

He'd brought Chloe here once, expecting swings and a roundabout. Instead, they got a load of kids swearing at each other as they played basketball, acting like they were in *The Wire*. He swallowed down mucus, meeting the broiling acid in his gut. Too much hot sauce, that's all it was.

He checked his phone — still nothing from Victor.

Shit. Someone had followed him on the tube, hadn't they?

The gate screeched open.

Victor Morgan tottered through, carrying a cardboard tray with two coffees. 'Inspector, sorry I'm late. Had to put tomorrow's Features to bed. The usual calls with the owners and their lawyers.'

'Pulling an all-nighter?'

'Thought I was done with them, but there's so much pressure on my shoulders just now.' Victor sat next to him and held out the tray. 'I brought these as a peace offering.'

'Is strong coffee a good idea before you sleep?'

'I sleep like a baby, officer.' Victor beamed wide before taking a drink. 'Screaming and wetting myself every hour.'

'I know how that feels.'

Victor held up his coffee, devoid of logo. 'You can tell good coffee from the cups they use. You see so many people strolling into the office with designer cups full of sugary rubbish. This stuff is the real deal.'

'I know how you feel.' Fenchurch took another look around. A waft of dog shit hit his nostrils. 'Why is this place your favourite park?'

'It's London in a nutshell, Inspector.' Victor nodded across the park towards a grand Victorian building, looked like an old church. 'That and we live just over there.'

The stone looked recently acid cleaned, back to its original colour. A hundred and fifty-odd years of London soot burnt off, just like bloody Quentin was trying with their less-grand building.

Victor handed a coffee to Fenchurch. 'Here you go.'

Fenchurch took it. 'Thanks.' He sipped the acrid coffee, just above lukewarm, and threw the colour supplement at him. 'What the hell's this?'

'Kenyan. Single estate according to—'

'I meant the paper.'

'It's Saskia's legacy, Inspector. What we want the whole city to remember her by.' Victor had stopped with the eye contact, just stared at the cracked tarmac at their feet. 'We're not owned by an American media mogul or a Russian oligarch. It's independent and capable of changing our little corner of the world.'

'Don't give me that bollocks. I've been through these stories.' Fenchurch rested the coffee at his feet and snatched the paper from Victor's hands. He held it open midway through. 'Our neighbourhood MEP kicked a pregnant Muslim woman in Dubai? Surprised that wasn't on the front page.' He started flicking through the rest. 'Zara Redshaw running three separate student houses in Hackney while she kicks in the window of that cereal café down the road from here?' Over a few pages. 'Iconic Property shutting down three homeless shelters despite what the charitable foundation says.' He dumped the paper on the bench and grabbed his coffee. 'Would've been useful to have known any of this yesterday.'

'It doesn't help your case, though.' Victor stuck his cup to his lips and took a drink. 'I doubt Guy Eustace is involved. Saskia was stabbed by a person who had my skin tone, not yours.' He winked at him as he slurped more coffee. 'Redshaw's small-time, just a stupid hypocrite.' Another sip, shaking his head this time. 'And Iconic? Where's the connection? Some morally bankrupt behaviour, maybe. That's it. Nothing criminal.'

'I'd still prefer to be the judge.' Fenchurch picked up his cup and let the heat warm his hands. 'Have you been threatened?'

'Of course not. What makes you think I would've been?'

'Saskia was most likely murdered because of something she wrote or was planning to write. You've just published stories about the same audience she'd been speaking to. One of them got sufficiently spooked that they got her killed.'

Victor patted his arm. 'Relax, nobody's arranged a hit on me, Inspector.'

Fenchurch sat forward and looked around the park again.

Two mixed-race kids ran across the patch of grass just ahead of their parents, white dad and black mum, walking hand in hand. A kid on a bike headed away from them, wearing similar garb to Qasid. Same as the other kid he'd assaulted the other day. Same as a million other kids. Bloody hiding in street fashions.

Fenchurch took another sip and turned back around. 'This is good coffee.'

'There's a good place just by Old Street tube. I go there every day, usually on my way in but today's a new day, right?'

'You should've come to me about these stories. Yesterday, before you printed them.' Fenchurch held up the page. 'This makes you look like you're not helping the investigation. My boss isn't happy.'

'That edition's just the owners trying to cash in on us being the news for once. It's PR bullshit, too.'

Fenchurch nudged the paper with his knee. 'Says it's going on all week. What are you running tomorrow?'

'There's a couple of things.' Victor finished his coffee and stabbed the empty cup into the tray. 'Where do I start?'

'With the subject most likely to want—'

Bike brakes squealed behind them.

Fenchurch swung round and caught a flash of steel. A knife dug into Victor's neck, catching him just below the chin.

A kid stepped off his bicycle pedals — grey hoodie, black trackies, black skin — and snatched at the handle, trying to pull it back out.

Fenchurch reached over and grasped the kid's wrist. He tugged at him, pulling him to the bench with a clatter, pinning his hips to the wood. The bike tumbled over as his hood fell away.

Qasid, panting. Frightened eyes.

Fenchurch grabbed him under the arms and hauled him over the seat, hardly any weight to him just like a little kid. His muscles burned in agony, feeling like he'd torn a bicep again, as he raised him up in the air. 'You little shit!'

'Get away from me, man!' Qasid lashed out and cracked Fenchurch in the balls. Then stuck his knee into his face.

Fenchurch screamed out and tumbled backwards onto the grass. Fire in his groin, searing his thighs and abdomen.

Qasid landed on him, squeezing his lungs like a sponge. He was up in a flash, darting behind the bench and sweeping up his bike. One last look at Fenchurch as he started to get up, then he was gone, powering across the grass.

Chapter Thirty-Six

'Stay with me, stay with me.' Fenchurch tried to plug the gaping hole in Victor Morgan's neck, the wide slash in his throat like something out of an abattoir. Fenchurch's shirt was soaked through with blood. Coffee splashed over his trousers, soaking the tarmac at his feet.

The light behind Victor's eyes died. His head tilted to the side, mouth hanging open.

Fenchurch stood up straight and looked around the park, searching for anyone in a hoodie and trackies. Bike or no bike.

No sign of anyone. The couple he'd seen earlier hugged each other tight, cuddled their kids tighter.

He got out his Airwave. Almost dropped it, his hands were slicked red. 'Control, this is DI Simon Fenchurch. I'm reporting a murder in Pitfield Park, requesting urgent assistance.'

A loud crackle. 'Receiving, over.'

'Send as many units as you can. I want them covering the area surrounding the park. Get them on the lookout for a young IC3 male in grey hooded top and black tracksuit bottoms on a bike.'

'Be about five minutes, sir.'

'And send for DS Jon Nelson and DS Kay Reed.' Fenchurch ended the call on his Airwave and stared at the body.

Victor's dead eyes drilled into his skull. Like he knew what was going on but he just didn't have enough time to tell anyone.

Fenchurch collapsed onto the bench, tears burning at his sinuses. He swallowed in air, gulping at it, trying to stop himself from crying. Just couldn't. He rested on his hands, elbows spearing his thighs. And just let it all out.

Saskia. Victor. *Chloe.*

He couldn't save all of them. Couldn't save any of them. He sucked in more air, almost choking on it.

'Sir?' A hand on his back.

He swung round, wiping at his cheeks.

A pair of uniforms stood behind him. He recognised the older one from West Ham, sat a few rows in front. 'You okay, sir?' He clocked Victor Morgan next to him. 'Jesus Christ.'

Fenchurch pointed across the park at the couple. 'Keep them here. They saw it.'

The younger one dashed over towards them, arms out wide.

'What a mess. What a bloody mess.' Fenchurch shook his head at Victor then got up, bleary eyes locked on the fellow Hammer. 'I need you to stay here, okay? There's going to be a big squad turning up soon. DS Nelson or DS Reed will manage.' He started off towards his car. 'Keep a tight lid on this.'

'Where are you going?'

'To see a man about a murderous little bastard.'

───

'Guv, we've just got to the park. Where the hell are you?'

'I waited until the uniform turned up, Kay.' Fenchurch gripped the Airwave tight. 'Get them out canvassing. I've got to go. Bye.' He dumped the radio on the passenger seat and pulled in on Shoreditch High Street across the road from a boutique hotel. Used to be some chain, but was now full of small businesses, record shops and book stores. Hipster paradise.

He got out and sucked in diesel fumes and coffee tang. Liberal Justice's office was sandwiched between a corner shop covered in Coca-Cola signage and the sort of café that kept the sixties decor they found underneath a mid-eighties refit. There was a light on inside, even though the security gate was down.

Fenchurch rapped on the steel and took a step back, trying to peer in.

He caught a flash of metal to the side. Spotted a hoodie. A cyclist bumped the kerb and powered towards him.

Fenchurch jumped and spun round, jammed his back against the shutters.

The Asian girl cycled past, her frown cut off by her black helmet. 'Jeez. Got your period or something?' American accent, west coast.

Fenchurch let out a deep breath. Focus, Simon, focus. He wiped the pool of sweat from his forehead, soaking the bloodstains on his hand.

Christ.

His phone chirped — Docherty. He let it pile up on top of the six other missed calls. No time. No time. No time.

Metal rumbled behind him. 'Inspector?'

Fenchurch swung round and stepped back.

Unwin stood in the shop doorway, dressed like he was going fighting on the seafront at Brighton. And not on the Rockers' side. Maroon Fred Perry, grey slacks and white bowling shoes, all looking like they used to fit. 'This is a Sunday, you know?'

Fenchurch gave him the up and down. 'Is Tommy in?'

'He's somewhere between Soho and Brighton.' Unwin folded his arms. A pink slash was dug out of his dark skin just above his left wrist. 'How can I help?'

'Need a word. Just as well you're at work on a Sunday.'

'Never stops, Inspector. Never stops.' Unwin frowned, eyes scanning his head. 'Are you bleeding?'

Fenchurch rubbed at it. 'It's not mine.'

'Come in, man. You can't go wandering around like that.' Unwin ushered him into the office.

It was more like a computer start-up than a law firm. Beanbags in front of a PlayStation and late-period Paul Weller played through Sonos speakers, jarring rhythms and twiddly lead guitar.

Fenchurch propped himself against the Addams Family pinball table, flashing through its attract sequence. 'See, I knew Tommy was going to be here. The pinball wizard.'

'Despite playing a mean pinball, that deaf, dumb and blind kid sure helps with our disability grants.' Unwin wet a pink paper towel from a ceiling-height water cooler. 'Here you go.'

Fenchurch took it and mopped at his brow. He scrunched the tissue up, now a deep shade of red. His throat was shrivelled up, tight. He tried to clear it. 'Where's Qasid?' Almost sounded human.

'Not seen Mr Williams since yesterday afternoon.'

'He's just murdered someone.'

Unwin swallowed. 'What?'

'I saw it happen. Just past Hoxton Square.'

'You're sure it was him this time?'

Fenchurch glared at him for a few seconds. 'It was him. I've stared into those dead eyes often enough. Call him.'

'Jesus.' Unwin got out his phone, more of a tablet than a mobile. 'I can't . . . I can't believe this . . .'

'Just bloody call him and get him here.'

'Fine.' Unwin nodded and stabbed the screen with a podgy finger. He flicked it onto speaker. Just a ringing tone.

'I'm sorry but the caller is either unavailable or on another call . . .'

Unwin killed it. He gave it another go, same result, cut dead at the second word. 'Sorry.'

'Where does he live?'

'I don't know. Just got that mobile number.'

'Jesus H. Christ. You've got no idea what you're doing. It's a bloody burner. He could be anywhere.'

'I thought it'd—'

'You're responsible for him, you dickhead!' Fenchurch jabbed a finger in his chest, dimpling the flab. 'We released him on the understanding you knew where the bleeding hell he was!'

'Look, I'm really sorry. I'll see if I can get in touch with him another way.'

'You're a bloody clown.' Fenchurch tossed the paper towel on the floor and stormed out of the office. He leaned against his car and took in the street, huffing in stale city air.

The day was starting to warm up. A few cyclists whizzed past, one doing a deadly dance with a bus. Only going to be one winner there.

Fenchurch reached inside the car and got out his Airwave. He dialled Reed's badge number. 'Kay, have you got Qasid in custody yet?'

'Hold your bloody horses, guv. No. There's a negative on the sightings, so far.'

'Shit.' Fenchurch looked up and down the street, feeling completely lost, his gut burning. 'Is there anything positive to report?'

'Well, Mulholland's just turned up. Docherty's looking for you, as well. Just firing up his nut toaster by the looks of things.'

Fenchurch clocked Docherty before he'd even parked. The DCI was sitting in his Audi, barking at someone on his mobile. Hopefully Mulholland.

Fenchurch stopped in the middle of the road, just by the SOCO van blocking the passage. Could just run away, go back home.

Too late — Docherty made eye contact and stabbed a finger in his direction. He switched his finger to indicate a minute.

Still time to run away, though.

Fenchurch got out and checked the crime scene.

Reed was in plain clothes, locked in conversation with a uniform. She nodded at him. Then her eyes widened. 'Guv, you're covered in blood.'

'Kay, just tell me what you've got.'

'What, in the last five minutes?' She couldn't take her eyes off his shirt. 'Feels like half the Met's out canvassing the area, looking for witnesses and kids on bikes.'

'Anything?'

'Nothing. Sorry, guv.'

'It's not your fault, Kay. How many units have you got out?'

'Sixty-two out and about.' She grimaced, heel tapping off the tarmac. 'The uniform Sergeant is already busting my ovaries. They're needed at the football up at White Hart Lane from eleven.'

'We'll hopefully have the little bastard back in custody by then.'

She held up a bagged knife. 'Found this, though. Not too far from the bench, guv.'

Fenchurch stared at the gunmetal weapon shining in the sunlight, sending dots of light over the grass and tarmac. Sharp point. Clean handle. 'It's the same blade they used on Saskia, right?'

'Clooney thinks so.' She waved across the park at the clump of officers surrounding the body. 'He's over there somewhere.'

Clooney and a few others milled around, all suited up. A brief gap in the crowd showed Victor Morgan, still on the seat, a puddle of milky coffee at his feet, mixing with his blood. Take away the blood and it was like he'd just fallen asleep.

Fenchurch hadn't been able to do anything. Useless. Completely useless.

'That's two dead now.' He handed the knife back, the bag crinkling in the gentle breeze. 'We need to check for bulk purchases of this across the whole Southeast.'

'Already got Lisa Bridge on it.'

'Good. Focus on London but don't exclude Essex, Kent, Berkshire—'

'—Hertfordshire, East Anglia. I know the drill, guv. Probably won't amount to anything but you never know.'

'I know.'

She frowned at him. 'Thought you were off the case? That stuff at the briefing.'

'Docherty's let me keep my ball for now. Well, we'll see how this plays.' Fenchurch nodded over at the Audi as the door tore open, clattering into a Fiesta next to it. 'Better get my nuts toasted.' He took a moment to breathe, watching Reed stomp towards the chaos of SOCOs.

'Oh, there you are, Simon. Nice of you to join us.' Docherty was on him like a terrier, nostrils flared, jaw clenched. 'What the hell are you playing at?'

'It was Qasid.'

'What?'

'This.' Fenchurch pointed back at the bench. 'He killed him. Qasid bloody Williams.'

Docherty joined him leaning against the side of the car, shaking his head. 'I've heard that before from you.'

'It was definitely him this time. I got the little shit's hood off. Stared him in the bloody eyes. He kicked me in the balls and got on his bike.' Fenchurch felt a twinge in his groin just then. Made his eyes water afresh.

'Simon, why the hell are you running around like an idiot? You don't flee—'

'I was chasing down a—'

'I'm not bloody finished!' Docherty leaned close, sickly brown-sauce breath getting in Fenchurch's nose. 'You don't flee a bloody crime scene. You saw a man get killed and you buggered off, like that was okay. Our evidence trail is up the bloody spout.'

'I waited until those two appeared.' Fenchurch waved at the pair of uniforms guarding the outer locus. Looked more like they were at the football rather than a murder scene. 'I went to see the lawyer.'

'Looking like that?' Docherty gave him the up and down then shook his head. 'So I can expect another bloody lawsuit from Dalton Unwin, can I?'

'I spoke to him, boss. He doesn't know where Qasid is.'

'He's not still in custody?'

'The Mobile Theft Unit let him go yesterday.' Fenchurch let a frown take control of his forehead. 'Didn't DI Mulholland let you know?'

'She didn't. Not that it gets you off anything. You should've let me know a lot of bloody things over the last few days, you prize pillock.' Docherty jabbed a bony finger into Fenchurch's chest. 'We let him go because you mistook him for another black kid.'

'They planned it, sir. Plain as day.' Fenchurch wrapped his arms tight round his body. 'We still need to find Kamal.'

'Him.' Docherty thumped back against the car, the chassis barely rocking. 'That shite yesterday afternoon with the undercover squatter didn't exactly get us anywhere, did it? We lost over a hundred man hours trying to make it look legit enough that your pal didn't lose his cover.'

'Boss, that was a solid lead. Our only lead.'

'Si, whatever.' Docherty gave a shrug and let out a sigh. 'Look, have you any ideas here, cos I'm on empty?'

'Thought Dawn was running the case?'

Docherty chuckled, bitter and devoid of humour. 'You know she's an admin monkey, Si. I need inspiration here.'

'If you make me Deputy again.'

'I can't take it off her, you know that. You shouldn't even ask.'

Fenchurch tried to look at Victor. His dead eyes followed him everywhere. 'He's got a husband.'

'Victor? He's gay?'

Fenchurch gave a nod. 'This isn't a hate crime, boss.'

'No, it probably isn't.'

'His husband might know why Victor was killed, though.'

'Worth a shot, Si.'

Fenchurch unlocked his central locking. 'Right, I'll have a word with him, then.'

'Not on your own, Si. Not after last time.' Docherty gave him another frosty look. 'And not covered in his husband's blood.'

Hot water blasted Fenchurch's scalp, steam misting the window and the cubicle. He stared down, lathering shower gel on his body, up his arms, as far up his back as he could manage. A wave of mint hooked his nostrils, made his eyes water. Dark-brown water swirled around the plughole, followed by soap suds, bubbling up and popping.

He shut his eyes again and let the water wash it all off.

Victor Morgan sitting next to him. The knife digging into his throat. Twisting. Qasid laughing out loud, really bellowing. Kicking Fenchurch in the balls. And again. And again. Then skipping off across the park, holding hands with the kids, spinning them round. Ring a Ring o' Roses.

Chloe loved that song when she was little.

'Simon?'

Fenchurch opened his eyes and rubbed out a clear patch in the glass. 'Abi?'

She had returned from her long jog.

'You've left the bloody extractor off again.' She tugged at the cord. Her grey T-shirt was soaked in a V-shape running from her neck. She slipped it off, showing her black sports bra and milky skin. 'Got room for me in there?'

He started lathering up his hair. 'How was your jog?'

'Fine. You're just going to ignore that, are you?'

'Look, I'm having a shit day.'

'And I was thinking we could go down to Sevenoaks and see Pamela. What do you think?'

He held her gaze through the glass. 'I need to get back out to work.'

'What are you talking about?' She stopped unhooking her bra. 'You're off today.'

'I'm working, Abi. Heading back out soon.'

She picked up his shirt, scowling. 'Is that blood?'

Water spilled over his face. Drained away more blood, as if there was any left.

'Simon, is this blood on your shirt?'

'It's not mine.'

'Then whose is it?'

'Victor Morgan's. Qasid killed Saskia's boss.'

She tugged at her hair. 'Are you okay?'

'No. I just can't . . . He was right there. That little shit on a bike stabbed him and then cycled off.' Fenchurch switched the shower off and let the water cascade to the floor, like a trail of machine gun bullets. 'The little rat boy we had in custody for a few days. Had to let him go yesterday. Victor would still be alive if it wasn't for that.'

'Sure someone else wouldn't have done it?'

'Maybe.' His eyes welled up. 'I just wanted to see you but you were out.'

'You knew I was out jogging.' She handed him a towel and stared at him, lightly shaking her head. 'I'll get you another shirt.'

'Thanks.' Fenchurch rubbed away the tears then started on his hair. 'I really can't deal with this.'

'You'll catch him, Simon.'

'You really think that?'

'I know it.'

Chapter Thirty-Seven

Eric Taylor sat on the edge of a velvet chaise longue, quietly weeping into his hands. A shaft of sunlight crawled over the stripped flooring of their apartment, the cavernous space of an old church. He was so Scottish it looked like it hurt, at least on warm days. Bright red hair and the sort of skin that would turn to melanoma as soon as the temperature hit eighteen degrees. He looked up, eyes as red as his hair. 'I just don't get it. Why Vic?'

Fenchurch clocked Docherty's nod and reached over to pat Eric on the arm. 'Mr Taylor, are you able to answer a few questions about your husband?'

'Can't believe it. I just can't believe it.' Eric shot a glare at Fenchurch. 'How could you let it happen?'

'Believe me, sir, I wish I'd stopped it from happening.' He sucked in minty musk. 'But I couldn't.'

'You need to catch who did this. Who killed him.'

'We're trying our hardest.'

'That's not very reassuring. Looks very much like you can't protect London.'

'I'm saying we're doing everything we can.'

Eric stared at the patio doors, pale decking stacked up into a sun porch. An overbred cat bleated at the door in silence, its dancing tail looking like it had tassels. He got up and slid it open. 'Come here, Patience.' He picked up the cat and hugged it tight. 'Your daddy's not coming home.' He closed his eyes again, screwed them shut. 'She's Vic's cat. I don't even like them. Now it's all I've got left of him.'

Fenchurch glanced over at Docherty. 'Can you think of anyone who had an axe to grind with Mr Morgan?'

'The usual bigots round here.' Eric sat on the settee again, flattening down the cat's fluff. 'When it became legal, we were one of the first couples to marry. It was all over the papers.'

'You think he was killed because he was gay?'

'Maybe. We didn't get a civil partnership because Vic thought it was discriminatory. We either marry or wait until straight couples can get a civil partnership. This is still a rough area, you know? Full of homophobes and religious zealots, even with all the designer coffee bars.' Eric hugged the animal tighter. 'I was worried about Vic publishing those bloody stories, you know. Especially given what happened to Sas.'

'You knew her?'

'We were like her favourite uncles. I loved that girl. Vic did too. Reminded him of his own daughter.'

Fenchurch caught a raised eyebrow from Docherty. 'I wasn't aware he'd been married before.'

'Like many of us, Victor lived a lie in the eighties. I'm sure you don't have to wonder why?'

'No, I can fully understand why. Was there a specific reason for your worry?'

'Well, Sas had been killed. It also felt very crass, you know? Running those articles so soon. I suppose if it hadn't been them, the competition would've done it. Doesn't stop it feeling so mawkish, though.'

Fenchurch checked Docherty in the corner of the kitchen. Got a shrug. He gave Eric a smile. 'Do you need anyone here to sit with you?'

'My sister's on her way, thanks.' He grabbed Fenchurch's arm as he got up. 'Just find who killed Vic. That's all I ask.' Eric hugged the cat, both staring into space.

'I'm trying my hardest, sir. I promise.'

———

Fenchurch shut Eric's front door and followed Docherty into the warm sunshine of an April Sunday.

Docherty stopped by his Audi and stared back at the house. 'Got to be something here, Si. Victor published those stories and now he's dead.'

'They've published and been damned.' Fenchurch walked over to his car and plipped the locks. 'They're not done with Saskia's work, you know? Victor said they've got another three days' worth of stories.'

'You're thinking they've been killed for what's not come out?'

'Best way to hush him up.'

'Sure it wasn't one of the stories he's just published?'

'There's no point closing the gate after the horse's bolted, right? The damage is already done.'

Docherty folded his arms, the suit flapping around him. 'Christ.'

'Could be any of them.' Fenchurch bit his lip. 'Could be none.'

'So, we speak to everyone all over again?'

'We've done that already, boss.'

'And, who killed them?'

'I don't know.'

'Smashing. You don't know.' Docherty stood up tall and dusted off the back of his jacket. 'Let's all pack up and head home, eh?'

'I'm not giving up on this.' Fenchurch tapped the roof of his car. 'I'm heading back to the *Post*.'

———⌣———

'Look, you can't just waltz in here.' Yvette Farley's PA was trying to get in the way of Fenchurch and Docherty. The paper was busy for a Sunday, reporters crammed in tight across the office floor. 'She's with someone.'

Fenchurch nudged her hand away. 'She needs to make some time for this.'

'You can't—'

The office door exploded open, clattering off a coat rack and sending it toppling over. Two hulking brutes in business suits stormed out, flanking a blonde woman. Yana Ikonnikova. She squinted at Fenchurch then gave a curt nod. 'Inspector.' She marched past towards the lifts, another guard following.

Fenchurch thumbed at the room and flicked his eyebrows up at the PA. 'Looks like she's free.'

'Fine, suit yourselves.' She knelt down to pick up the coat rack. A bag rolled over, spilling a purse and phone. 'Crap.'

Fenchurch went into the office before he was asked to help.

Yvette Farley simmered behind her desk, wearing horn-rimmed spectacles and a pink T-shirt supporting Moon Walk. Short hair, dyed pink to match the shirt. Mid-fifties, if a day. She glanced over, frowning. 'Yes?'

'DI Fenchurch.' A flash of his warrant card as he sat. 'This is DCI Docherty.'

'This is about Victor, then?' She adjusted her glasses to reach behind and rub her eye. 'Well, I'm afraid I heard what happened.'

Her cough racked out, sounding like she smoked a thousand a day. Certainly smelled like it, even under her cloak of perfume. 'Terrible, terrible business.'

Docherty was standing by the window and its breeze, letting Fenchurch take centre stage for once. Her office was four floors above the smoking zone and looked along Fleet Street towards Temple and the LSE. 'I gather you're the Managing Editor here?'

'For my sins.' Yvette dabbed at her eyes with a hanky and nodded. 'God, I can't believe this. Two of our staff taken from us in a matter of days.'

Fenchurch pointed back into the corridor. 'What was Yana Ikonnikova doing here?'

'Threatening law suits left, right and centre.' Yvette tossed a copy of that morning's supplement. 'She wasn't too happy about this. I've had Guy bloody Eustace on, threatening to get me on Andrew Marr to defend our stance on press intrusion.'

'That was all?'

'I broke the news about Victor to them. Both seemed shell-shocked.' She focused on Fenchurch. 'Tell me honestly, Inspector, do you think this is connected to their work here?'

'We're investigating that as a distinct possibility, ma'am. Are you aware of any threats made to Mr Morgan over the last few days?'

'We get about ten weird letters every day, Inspector. A hundred emails. And that's just the central mailbox.'

'Can we have a look them?'

'Are you sure you want them? They're highly deviant and I doubt they'll lead you anywhere.'

'Sometimes criminals have a need to share. If it's connected to your paper, they might've decided to write to you. Do you ever read them?'

'Like I get time for that. My assistant sorts them into a pile of junk and a pile of anything useful. We're lucky to get one useful email a month. If you really want them, you can speak to Cassie on your way out.'

'Thanks.' Fenchurch nodded at Docherty — one for Mulholland to get her fingers into. Then he smiled at Yvette. 'Did Mr Morgan say anything recently that seemed off colour?'

'You tell me, Inspector, you were with him when he died.'

Touché. Fenchurch folded his arms, waiting for the drumbeats in his ears to settle down. Frenetic jungle became hip-hop became chilled jazz. 'Any odd behaviour at all over the last week?'

'One of his protégés got killed, of course he's been odd.'

'But nothing else sticks out?'

'Victor was Victor, you know? Kept a tight counsel. He wasn't happy about how we treated Saskia's death. He expressed some grave concerns about it.' She adjusted her glasses, letting a red mark on the bridge of her nose peek out. 'That was out of my hands, though. We'd have a shareholders' mutiny if we didn't exploit it somehow.'

'Must've been a very difficult decision to make.'

'Mm.' Yvette folded her own arms. 'Now, if you don't mind, I've got to tear apart tomorrow's front page. And find someone to take on Victor's responsibilities for the short term.'

'Are these the stories you plan to publish this week?'

'Maybe.'

'Well, one avenue we're investigating is the possibility that Ms Barnett and Mr Morgan were murdered for the stories she was working on but which haven't been published yet.'

'I don't see why?'

'Let me be the judge of that, okay? Who's looking after Saskia's work in Mr Morgan's . . . absence?'

'As I said, I've not decided on a strategic appointment yet. But, given his . . . interest in what's happened, I thought it appropriate to ask Liam Sharpe to help.'

Fenchurch rapped the door again. Little bastard wasn't in. He put the Airwave to his mouth. 'Boss, he's not here.'

'So where the bloody hell is he, Simon?' Wind battered the mic on Docherty's phone. Sounded like he'd gone back to the crime scene after all. 'You find—'

The door opened to a crack, the security chain rattling as it pulled tight. An eye stared out, a thin sliver of beard just below. The door shut again.

'Boss, he's here. Repeat, Liam is here. Better go.' Fenchurch pocketed the Airwave and knocked on the door. 'Liam.'

'Go away.'

'I need to speak to you.'

'I'm not up to that.'

Fenchurch pressed his head against the door. Tried it but it wasn't budging. 'Liam, Victor Morgan's been murdered.'

Silence.

'Did you hear me?'

A pause. Followed by a sniff. 'Yvette told me.'

'I need to ask you a few questions about his death, Liam. Can you let me in? Please?'

The chain clanked and the door opened wide. 'I suppose you better come in.'

'Are you okay?'

'Not really.' Liam shut the door behind Fenchurch. 'I'm a bit paranoid, you know?'

'Paranoia's a very specific condition, Mr Sharpe.'

Liam shot him a glare. 'Do you want to leave?'

'Sorry.' Fenchurch raised his hands in apology. 'I'm thrown by what's happened, as well.'

'You're right. I'm just anxious, I suppose.' Liam leaned back against the front door. 'Victor's really dead?'

'Happened right in front of me.'

'You're making a habit of that.' Liam rubbed a hand across his forehead and pinched his nose. 'Jesus. I can't help myself. Sorry.'

'It's okay.' Fenchurch gave him a few seconds to pull himself together. 'Yvette Farley said you've got access to Saskia's stories again.'

'Well, I've been going through what Victor had. Trying to see if I could add anything.'

'And can you?'

Liam pushed away from the door. 'There's maybe something.'

'What?'

'Come through.' Liam led him into his bedroom, bare feet thwacking off the floor. The far wall was filled with a large IKEA desk, covered in computer equipment and stacks of books. His cat lay in an Amazon delivery box, deigning to look round at them. He sat down and patted the cat. 'Hey, Pumpkin.' He got a *whirr* as the cat curled up again. 'The box is a diversion. Otherwise, she's rolling all over the keyboard.'

Fenchurch perched on the edge of the double bed. 'What's all that?'

Liam started fiddling with four piles of paper. 'Victor's work. Yvette had it couriered over.'

'After you got her laptop nicked?'

'I'm a bit more security-conscious these days.' Liam stopped and gave a shrug. 'I'm just sorting through it now.' He tapped the first of the piles, the tallest. Stapled sheets in a loose heap. 'Here's what I sent Victor. The raw ideas. It's a hell of a lot.' He patted a second pile. 'He's edited the notes down to this lot. They're just working drafts really. He's thrown them around in an order, but it's still just Sas's work.' Then a third pile, the smallest of the three. 'And this is what he published in this morning's paper. You saw it, right?'

'I did. And the last pile?'

'This is what he was working on.' Liam rested his hand on it, three times the size of the already-published pile. A thin sliver at the top was at right angles. 'This is stuff he was doing all night.'

'For tomorrow's paper?'

'Front cover. He was up all night, turning them from notes into stories. Vic had a knack of being able to just churn out great copy. Comes with experience, I suppose.'

'So what have you found?'

Liam went back to the first pile and skimmed through the documents. He tore out a sheet halfway down. 'Have a look at this.'

Fenchurch scanned through the page. It was a load of disconnected notes, all tied to an 'Andrew Smith'. 'Do you know who he is?'

'No, but look at that.' Liam tapped on a mobile number near the top. 'There's a K after it.'

'You think this is for Kamal?'

'That's what I'm thinking, yes.'

Chapter Thirty-Eight

'Here you go, sir.' Lisa Bridge ran her finger along the screen and pressed down on the last column. 'Holy shit.' She drew a circle around the six rows below. 'Do you see that?'

Fenchurch leaned forward, really struggling to make out any of it. 'Not without my glasses.'

'Okay, sir.' Bridge tapped at the screen again. 'That number you gave me? Well, Saskia's called it a few times. Six.'

'Was it ever answered?'

'Three times.'

'Do you know anything about it?

'Clooney was doing all the usual "I can't do this because I'm so busy" so I just cut him out of the process.' She pulled up another screen. 'Here you go, guv. It looks like a burner to me.'

'A dead end.' Fenchurch collapsed back against the desk behind them. 'Can you trace anything on it?'

'Wish I could.' A frown flashed across her forehead and she surged into action. 'It's still live, though. Connected to the network an hour ago.'

'Can you get a location?'

'Not from this thing. I'd need to get Clooney.'

'Can you speak to him?'

'Already have. Said he's out at the crime scene till at least two. Won't get round to it until this evening at the earliest.'

'Thanks, Lisa. This is good work. I'll see what buttons I can press.' Fenchurch used her seat back to haul himself up and scanned around the Incident Room. There they are . . . He marched across the room and got between Docherty and Mulholland. 'Boss, I need to—'

'Simon, I was briefing the SIO.' Mulholland folded her arms, sending her scarf flying. 'Do you want to take a ticket and I'll call your number when it's ready?'

Fenchurch ignored her, instead locking eyes with Docherty. 'Boss, I've got a lead on Kamal.'

Mulholland scowled at Fenchurch. 'Sir, as I was saying, we're struggling to progress the grid search around the park with—'

Docherty held up a finger, cutting her dead. 'Just a sec, Dawn. What is it?'

'A burner number for Kamal.'

'The medal's in the post, Si. This bloody better be something.'

Fenchurch passed him the page from Liam's stash. 'This is how Saskia knew Kamal.'

'It says Andrew Smith here, though.'

'And the K means Kamal. Look, it all fits. She knew who he was.'

'Has Clooney traced it?'

'Lisa Bridge is doing it.'

Mulholland jumped in, getting over her disappointment quickly. 'Simon, there's a procedure in place for this. It has to go through Scenes of Crime.'

'Yeah, and there's two dead people because of this guy. We need to do something.'

Docherty raised a hand to Mulholland. 'Si, have you called it?'

'Are you suggesting I should?'

'Sir.' Mulholland snapped her pen lid back on. 'I don't think we should.'

Docherty held her gaze, daring her to look away first. 'Why not?'

'Because it's breaking with procedure. We can't just call up suspicious numbers.'

'This guy's organised two killings, we think. And counting. We can't sit on this.' Docherty handed the sheet of paper back to Fenchurch. 'Call him.'

Mulholland cleared her throat. Sounded like someone was trying to strangle her with the infernal scarf. 'Sir, are you sure?'

'I'm sure, Dawn.'

'I want no part in this.'

Fenchurch got out his mobile and tapped the number in.

Mulholland snatched it from his hands. 'Simon, you can't use your own phone.'

'Thought you didn't want any part of this?'

'All the same, you just can't do that.'

'He's not going to know it's a Met number, is he?' Fenchurch stormed out into the corridor and hit dial. He put it to his ear and listened to the ringtone.

'Yo.' A male voice, shrill, like he was at the bottom of a well.

'Kamal?'

'Yo.'

'A friend said you might be able to help.'

'What sort of help?' Had a weird accent, a ripe mixture of east coast American and street London, like he'd got lost halfway across the Atlantic.

'Like that thing on Upper Street. Our mutual friend said I could use your services.'

'How I know this is for real?'

'I'm impressed with your work so far and I can make it worth your while.'

'Need hard currency.'

'I'm flush. Believe me.' Fenchurch shrugged at Docherty, standing in the doorway. 'Can we meet?'

A long pause, sounded like booming hip-hop echoing in the background. 'Yo, one hour. Boundary Park. No funny business or there be trouble.'

———

Boundary Gardens was a circular pile in the middle of Arnold Circus. Six giant buildings surrounded it, each one six storeys of Victorian architecture, heavy bay windows carved out of red brick. Ancient trees towered over their heads, ivy climbing as high as it dared. There was a bandstand at the top of the mound, dating back to when they used such things. The railings below were clear except for two bikes at either side.

'Abi made me watch a documentary about this place a few weeks ago.' Fenchurch adjusted himself on the cold bench and sprawled out, still no sign of Kamal. 'Pretty interesting, as it happens. First proper social housing development in the world. Opened up in, I don't know, 1900 or something. Supposed to be for the poor but only the rich could afford it.'

'Sounds very London to me.' Nelson took a suck on his vape stick. 'Wouldn't know it was here, guv. Just a minute's walk from Shoreditch.' He leaned forward and pointed ahead of them. 'Here we go.'

A kid wearing a hoodie was cycling down the street facing them, long legs striding on a black bike. Big silver wheels. Taking it slowly, looking around. Cautious. He crossed the road and dumped the bike against the railings, too cool to bother with a lock. He sniffed as he started climbing the steps. His hoodie fell back.

It was Qasid. Clear as day.

Nelson whispered: 'Shall we grab him, guv?'

Qasid stopped and tugged the hood back up. Sniffed again and looked around.

'We need Kamal, Jon.'

Qasid's eyes locked with Fenchurch. Then widened. He spun around and bounded down, hauled his bike away from the railings and hopped on.

'Right, you little shit, let's see you do your disappearing trick again.' Fenchurch trotted down the steps and grabbed the bike on the left.

Qasid was pedalling hell for leather, weaving in front of a bus as he mounted the kerb.

'Little bastard's quicker than I thought.' Fenchurch started off on his bike, gliding over the smooth tarmac. He shifted the gears up and tried pushing the pace.

Qasid twisted his head round and spotted him. He wound down a side street, spiralling through the central hub of the park.

Fenchurch stood up on his pedals and rounded the corner. The cobbles started rattling his frame, putting his teeth on edge. Felt like his fillings would come out.

Qasid was bang in the centre of the road. He swerved across the path of a Golf thundering the other way and bounced up onto the pavement on the right. The Golf swept past him.

Qasid had disappeared.

'Shit!' Fenchurch looked behind him. Lost Nelson already. He reached into his pocket for his Airwave. 'Jon, I've lost sight of him and you.'

'It's okay, guv, I've still got him. He's just come onto Shoreditch High Street.'

'How's he done that?' Then Fenchurch spotted it. A little tunnel to the right. He cycled down it, catching his jacket on a street-light halfway along. He stopped at the end. Shoreditch High Street grumbled ahead of him. He was maybe a hundred metres from Unwin's office. Fenchurch barrelled up the wide pavement, dodging through the bus shelter. His heart was thudding, his breath coming in short gasps. Throat burning. Drums hammering in his ears.

He stopped by the boutique hotel opposite the office, trying to peer through a wall of idling buses.

Across the road, Qasid was hammering on Unwin's door, loud thumps rattling around like gunshots.

Fenchurch picked up his bike and ran between the buses. He jerked to a halt to let a car past.

Qasid clocked him. He jumped on his pedals and powered off along the pavement, cutting down the lane between the newsagent and a kebab shop.

Fenchurch hopped on his bike and set off, wheezing, tasting blood in the back of his throat. He weaved around the corner and stopped under the railway bridge. No sign of Qasid. Where the bloody hell was he?

A flash of steel sliced through the air.

Fenchurch ducked, using his shoulder to parry the blow. He tumbled backwards, sprawling all over a car bonnet.

Metal clattered to the ground and feet clicked away from him.

Fenchurch got up and looked around. The same model of knife used on Saskia and Victor lay on the pavement.

The little shit had been waiting for him.

Fenchurch didn't know which way Qasid went. His Airwave was lying on the opposite pavement. He crouched down to pick it up. 'Nelson, I've lost him.'

'Me too, guv.'

'Shit. Where are you?'

'Still on the High Street.'

Fenchurch looked down the lane, under the bridge. A tall block of flats made it twist to the right. 'Get round to Great Eastern Street, Jon. He's heading for Old Street.'

'Guv.'

Fenchurch jumped back on the bike and shot off, powering across the tarmac. Past the flats, a makeshift fence was supposed to have blocked the lane but it'd been kicked down. He slowed to navigate through it then sped on through a tight passageway, bright graffiti covering the walls.

He burst out onto Curtain Road, trying to push back memories of a brutal Saturday afternoon drinking around there.

No sign of Qasid.

Time for a gamble. He took a right, then the first left onto Rivington Street, another tight jam of pale-brick buildings.

A car almost clattered into him at the crossroads. His brakes squealed and he rocked forward. He didn't go over the handlebars, but only just.

Fenchurch ignored the Volvo driver's shouts and cut through the back street, emerging onto Old Street, a wide and open prairie. He took a second to get his bearings. The little shit was nowhere. He turned right then forked to the left past the Holiday Inn Express and the perpetually derelict site opposite.

Still no sign of Qasid. Or Nelson.

Fenchurch weaved around the traffic and turned right into the fast lane of the dual carriageway. A car honked behind him. Into the Airwave: 'Jon, where are you?'

'Playing a hunch, guv.' Another blast of static. 'Where are you?'

Glossy office buildings opposite a mishmash of outdated housing and shops. Up ahead, ramps and steps led down to the tube station under Silicon Roundabout.

'Just at Old Street tube.'

'Okay, I've got him. Turn right up ahead. He's on City Road, heading towards Islington.'

'Shit.' Fenchurch mounted the pavement separating the lanes and stopped between two trees, waiting for a gap.

Now.

He sprinted off then jumped on the bike, wheels spinning.

A motorbike growled round the corner, doing well over sixty, the brakes squealing as it swerved to avoid him.

Fenchurch took the ramp up and followed it round, dodging the queue of foot traffic coming up from the underground.

The lights were red, cars idling behind a section marked out for bikes on the tarmac. He bumped down onto it and cut into the traffic just ahead of a white van man, his screaming as loud as his horn.

Fenchurch swerved into the bus lane and powered on, thighs now burning as bad as his throat. Toxic fumes filled his lungs. He followed the road round to the left and raced on towards Islington. 'Jon, where are you?'

'Shit, I've lost him, guv.'

Fenchurch slowed down, keeping close to the kerb. 'Where are you?'

'Just by the Central bar.'

'What?'

'That's where I lost him.'

Fenchurch spotted Nelson on the pavement just ahead. Off his bike, Airwave to his head. He raced over and stopped just beside him. 'Where is he?'

Nelson pocketed his Airwave. Sweat poured from his head, soaking his shirt. 'Sorry, guv.'

'We've not got time for any of that shit. Where the hell is he?' Fenchurch looked down the opposing side streets. Nobody on bikes, let alone Qasid. He recognised the pair of new towers opposite, another one just a mess of scaffolding half the height. Where he'd chased the kid the other night. 'He can't just have vanished into thin air. This isn't happening again.'

'Well, at least we know he's working for Kamal. You called him and Qasid comes running.'

'Scant consolation, Jon.' Something caught Fenchurch's eye. A silver bike jammed against the railings across the road. 'That's his bloody bike!'

'What?'

Fenchurch looked around. Nowhere for him to go. Except . . . He spun round and looked inside the Central, squinting through the murky glass.

By the bar, a hooded figure was shaking his head at Clinton Jackson. Grey hoodie, black trackies, the lime fluorescent Everlast logo screaming out. He raised his arms in anger and stormed over to the staircase down. He shot a look back at the barman.

It was Qasid.

Fenchurch held up his Airwave. 'Control, I need all you can spare to report to the Central bar on City Road. Now!'

Chapter Thirty-Nine

'Come on, come on, come on.' Fenchurch stared at the back wall of the pub, clutching the Airwave tight. Ringing tone in his ear, breeze in his face, his hair thick with sweat. 'Kay, where the hell are you?'

'Just around the corner, guv.'

'Thank God. Nobody's left the pub or gone inside since. Keep it that way.' Fenchurch killed the call and jogged back round the front. His legs needed a week-long bath.

Nelson was guarding the door, getting a load of aggro off a pair of white skinheads in double denim. Must've looked out of place inside. He blocked their path. 'I can't let you back in. If you'll just follow my colleagues.' Two uniforms dragged them off down City Road towards the van.

A convoy of police cars appeared from the south. One blocked the road to the north, the other two cutting off the side streets.

Reed got out of the first one and jogged over, followed by a wave of uniforms. She handed out pages of A4.

Fenchurch took one. Qasid's mugshot. The still of Kamal from the Angel escalator was on the back.

'This is who we're looking for, okay?' She held it up and circled round to the assembled officers. 'Both men. They are highly
dangerous so watch your step. Ask around, don't take no for an
answer. Clear?'

A mumble of agreement.

'Then let's go.' Reed let the uniforms plough inside and nodded
at Fenchurch. 'Guv. He's definitely in there, right?'

'What's that supposed to mean?' Fenchurch scowled at her. 'We
followed the little bastard over here from the arse end of Shoreditch.'
He stared through the open door.

The pub was pretty busy for a Sunday lunchtime. The build-
up to the Spurs match played out on a big TV, three blokes on
the screen looking like they were at a golf club. Techno pumped
beneath the distorted voices.

Clinton Jackson was stabbing his finger into a uniform's chest.

'Here we go again.' Fenchurch entered the bar and pulled
Jackson away. 'Sir, I need a word with you.' He hauled him over to
the corner of the room.

He gave Fenchurch the up and down, recognition flooding his
eyes. 'These guys are saying I'm hiding Kamal!'

'Are you?'

'No way, man. No way.'

'I saw one of his people in here. Kid called Qasid.'

'I don't know no Qasid.'

'Well, he's in here, sir. I saw you talking with him.'

'You got a warrant for this, man?'

Fenchurch waved through the door for Reed. 'Kay, show him
the warrant.'

She unfolded a sheet of paper and handed it to Jackson. 'Here
you go, sir.'

He inspected it, his shoulders slumping as he made it down the
page. 'You think you can tear apart all I've done here? All I've achieved?'

'We're just looking for someone. Tell us where he is and we'll be gone.'

'Well, he ain't here!'

'I'm supposed to just take your word for it, am I?' Fenchurch pointed towards the door leading to the stairs. 'You mind if I have a look downstairs?'

'Course I mind, man. This is intimidation.'

'I saw Qasid go down those stairs.'

'He's not here. Get out of my bar, man!'

Fenchurch nodded at Reed. 'Get him down to Leman Street.' He marched across the bar and pushed through the door.

Cold air hit his face. A dank smell, like fungus or an open sewer. The steps were slimy. No idea how they'd passed health and safety. If they had.

The bottom of the stairs opened out into a wide corridor, a vaulted arch crawling overhead, raw brick subdividing it into two rooms.

A house DJ was setting up her decks on the right, the larger of the two. Chilled music pulsed out of the speakers. A uniform went over and interrupted her, getting a glare as she tore off her headphones.

Five or six drinkers occupied the second room, lounging on sofas, clutching unlabelled beer bottles. White kids, not even vaguely like Qasid.

Fenchurch gestured for uniformed officers to interview them.

The Gents was at the end of the corridor — no Ladies, by the looks of things. A giant bookshelf took up half of the wall, filled with paperbacks. The sign halfway down advertised 'BOOKS: £3 a pop — PAY at de bar'.

He looked around again. Where the hell was Qasid?

Nelson appeared at the bottom of the stairs. 'Guv, that's us clear upstairs.'

'No sign of him, I take it?'

'Right.' Nelson tapped at his ear, the music still blasting out. 'What about down here?'

'Nothing. Just DJs, toilets and books.'

'Thought you weren't letting him do his Batman trick again?'

'This isn't over yet, Jon.' Fenchurch waved over to the DJ. 'Can someone turn that racket off?'

A female officer wandered over to the DJ, joining the male officer. Her slit-throat action got a result. Silence.

'Thank God for that.' Fenchurch let out his held breath. Felt a slight chill in the air. 'He's not getting out of here.' He got a pair of uniforms to check each of the toilets.

'What if it wasn't him, guv? Lot of kids wearing those clothes.'

'It was him, Jon, I saw him.' Fenchurch stared at the bookshelf. Floor to ceiling, paperbacks wedged in tight, flush to the toilet door on the left. The space on the wall on the right of it was about the same size, just a bit bigger and filled with posters for upcoming club nights. Re:House, Insane in BRANE!, MetaDub.

He wandered over and had a look through the books, recognising some names. Famous black authors — Gil Scott-Heron, NoViolet Bulawayo, Eldritch Cleaver, Malcolm X, Taiye Selassi, even Barack Obama. He picked up the Obama book.

The bookcase rocked.

What the hell?

Fenchurch gripped the left edge of the bookcase and tugged it to the right. It budged a few centimetres. 'Give me a hand here, Sergeant.'

Nelson scrambled over and grabbed the other side. 'On three. One, two, three.'

Fenchurch hauled it. A little shunt to the right. Then it gave easily. Even colder air hit his face. Smell like a brazier, burning oil somewhere.

Just darkness behind the bookcase. Looked like a passage, curved into the depths of the city.

Nelson folded his arms across his chest. 'It's like bloody Narnia down here.'

———————

'Thanks, Constable.' Fenchurch nodded at Lad then clicked on his torch. Bloody thing was brighter than the sun. He looked around at the nearby officers — Nelson, Lad and six uniforms. 'Is the bar secure?'

The nearest uniform gave a nod. 'Place is on lock down, sir.'

'Good.' Fenchurch turned around and stared at the gaping hole in the wall. He shone the torch against the rounded brick walls, lighting hitting the bare stone floor, looked like it was worn smooth. He looked back at Nelson, the gang of uniform behind him itching to get going. 'You're sure this is the old City Road tube?'

'The pub's the old station building. That's got to be how they escaped, guv. Qasid just now and Kamal the other night.'

Fenchurch looked around the team. 'Ready?'

Nelson nodded in response.

Fenchurch took a deep breath and started along the tunnel. Almost lost his footing after a couple of steps and had to rock back to keep upright. His heart skipped a few beats. 'Watch out. The surface is slippery as a criminal defence lawyer.' He stopped and pointed the beam ahead of them.

The passageway curved upwards slightly, but that might just be his imagination. The light spread along the floor then disappeared into a pool of black just up ahead. He sped up, eyes trained on the gap. Light glinted off red railings. Looked like a staircase down. He flashed the torch above it. 'This is a chimney.'

'For the underground?' Nelson aimed his light at the steps. 'I take it you're going down there, guv?'

'This is where Qasid's gone, Jon. Tell me I've got another choice.'

'You need to be careful, guv.' Nelson thumbed down the staircase. 'If that does lead down to the Northern Line . . . The tracks are live.'

'Shit.' Fenchurch focused on the diagonal crisscross patternwork on the metal steps.

No idea what they were heading into down there. Best be prepared.

He nodded at Nelson. 'Last thing I bloody need is for anyone to get electrocuted.'

Nelson wheeled round and gestured at the two nearest uniforms. 'Call this in, okay?'

'Sarge.'

'Guard this area, okay? Nobody in or out.'

'Come on, then.' Fenchurch started down the steps, careful not to clank too loudly. He kept his gaze level as his gut clenched tight. Looked like hundreds of them. He hurried on, trying to ignore his vertigo. Just focus on how solid the steps feel. The bottom appeared, the path spreading off in both directions. On the ground level, he held a hand in the air, getting the squad to stop.

He could hear something. Thumping. And voices. American accents. Sounded angry.

Shiny brick walls led away in opposite directions, rounded underground tunnels looking like they were still in service.

Fenchurch stepped off the stairs onto a grimy flagstone and circled his finger above his head. Nelson paired off the remaining four uniformed officers and gestured at Lad. He shone his torch down one tunnel. The light caught sleeping bags and KFC buckets. A boombox was blasting out violent hip-hop. 'What the hell's going on here?' He aimed the beam further over and caught a tall stack of wood, gaffer-taped together. A knife practise area. 'Just like in *True*—'

Something clattered further over. He swung the beam round, the light creating circles on the walls. Some figures scurried away, like rats escaping a ship, and disappeared round the bend.

'Did you see that, guv?'

Fenchurch broke into a run, dodging past pizza boxes and Coke bottles. The tunnel came to an abrupt stop, a wall made from scarred brick. A door rattled on its hinges.

Fenchurch stuck his torch between his teeth and snapped out his baton. He nudged the door open. Nobody waiting behind. He climbed through.

Feet pounded behind him, sounded like standard-issue beat shoes.

A high-pitched squeal burst out from the right, followed by a gust of air.

'Shit!' Fenchurch pressed himself against the wall.

A train blurred past. Passengers sat reading, stood listening to music. Chatted, flirted, avoided eye contact. And it was gone, a shrinking pair of red lights.

Fenchurch shone his torch on the ringing tracks to their right. 'It is the bloody Northern Line.' He grabbed his Airwave. 'Get the bloody electricity switched off down here! Now!'

Up ahead, sheeting was piled on top of long metal poles at the bottom of a ramp. The light hit black fabric. Tracksuit bottoms, lime-green Everlast logo. He shifted the beam up and right. Six or seven men stood next to the heap of sheeting, grey hoodies hiding their faces.

'Police! Stay where you are!' Fenchurch started towards them. His ears were stinging from the train, listening for another one.

The nearest man lowered his hoodie and blinked against the light in his face. Qasid. He raised his hands in surrender. The other hoods looked around at each other, unsure what to do.

'Come with me, gentlemen. It's all over. Whatever it is, it's over.'

Fenchurch's Airwave crackled out, echoing in the tight space. 'That line will be off in a minute, sir.'

A figure behind pushed Qasid forward. He stumbled over and got a kick in the back of the head. The attacker broke ranks and sprinted off along the side of the tracks, pebbles skittering out across the planks.

Lad skipped down and bombed after him.

'Get back!' Fenchurch couldn't keep his eyes off the trail of Lad's feet on the stones, the right shoe just a bit too close to the tracks. He grabbed his Airwave. 'Get that electricity off now!'

'Still waiting on it, sir.'

Fenchurch swung around. What to bloody do . . .

The other kids huddled together like little boys on their first day at school.

Fenchurch reached down and helped Qasid to his feet. 'Got you at last.'

He was crying, dirty tears down his face, cut and bloody. 'That was Kamal, man. Can't believe he did that.'

Shit.

The second of the two figures rounded the bend, Lad's torch-light disappearing.

Two metres either side of the track to the wall. Should be enough . . .

Fenchurch twisted round and waved at Nelson. 'Keep this lot here!' He started off along the stones next to the tracks, heading round the corner. The area narrowed into a thin circle, climbing down away from them.

Fenchurch sprinted on, his legs and lungs burning. He trained his torch further down the tunnel, catching Lad and his quarry, both of them taking much longer strides than he could manage. Felt like he was pushing against the air as he ran.

Train!

He pressed himself flush to the side wall, slimy as a bath full of slugs. The torch was still pointing towards his prey. A hundred years of oil and soot stung his nostrils. Blown away by a gust of wind.

The train flashed past on the opposite track, the noise tearing at his hearing. Then it was gone.

The air pushed at him from behind, pushing him away from the wall. He stumbled forward and fell, stones digging into his knees. The live rails rose up and he pushed his hands out, aiming for the wooden boards. Caught it just right. Close call.

Stupid old bastard . . .

Fenchurch pushed up to a plank, taking his time. Then up to standing.

Up ahead, Lad was almost on Kamal, like a lion hunting a gazelle.

Fenchurch set off again, eyes on the track, making sure his feet landed at least a foot away from the rails. The ground levelled out. He'd lost them. Shit. He stopped and waved the torch around.

There, twenty metres away. Lad had the hoodie in his grasp, arm wrapped around his throat. Looked like he was trying to push him over, stones scattering around and echoing off the walls.

The wind started up again as Fenchurch set off, hissing against him. 'Waheed!' His shout was lost in the din.

Kamal swung out with an elbow, catching Lad in the gut. He staggered back, then reeled from a punch to the jaw. Right in the middle of the track.

The attacker pushed himself back against the walls. Light glowed ahead, illuminating Lad.

The train thundered down the tunnel, pushing Lad away like he was an ant.

Chapter Forty

The train's lights bled away down the tunnel. Kamal set off early, like he knew the drill. Done this too many times.

Fenchurch sprinted hard, landing his stride so he hit the slats between the rails. He crouched down by Lad.

Out cold, though still breathing. His arm was a mess, like something you'd see in the butcher's. Fenchurch pulled him off to the side and rested him away from the tracks. Up ahead, Kamal kept looking back, slowing him down.

What to do, what to do . . .

Fenchurch got up and sprinted off, following him. He reached into his pocket and fumbled his Airwave. Managed to catch it before it clattered to the ground. 'Officer down! Repeat, officer down! Get a medical unit into the tunnel now!' He stuffed it back in his pocket and tried to lengthen his stride.

Wind picked up again, blowing from behind this time. The opposite track. Why the bloody hell were the lines still live? Fenchurch kept on running, his feet rattling off the stones, keeping well away from the rails.

The light spread down the tunnel as the train whistled towards him. He struggled to keep his eyes open as it passed.

Kamal was leaning against the side of the tunnel. He clocked Fenchurch's approach and darted off, pounding away.

Fenchurch raised his baton and swung it forward. He snapped his wrist and sent it flying through the air, a cyclone glinting in the bobbing torchlight.

It clattered off Kamal's head. He tumbled over the stones and collapsed in a heap.

Fenchurch jumped on him. He grabbed his wrists and pinned him down. Then yanked his hood back and shone the torch at the face.

Black skin. Dark beard threaded with silver. Footballer hair.

'Your name is Kamal, right?'

He tried to struggle. Fenchurch kept him down.

'Get off me, man! Let me go!'

'You're going nowhere. Is your name Kamal?'

'That's me. You pleased with yourself?' Kamal spoke like a rap record.

Fenchurch sucked in stale air. Got him at last. The bastard on the escalator. The bastard who'd kept himself hidden for so long. The bastard—

A kick against Fenchurch's knee. Bent it back the wrong way. He staggered, struggled to stay upright. Managed to steady himself against the grimy wall. Then he swung a fist at Kamal's head.

Kamal dodged the blow, pushing up to parry. He swept his legs out and knocked Fenchurch's feet away from under him. His shins crashed on the tracks, metal cracking off bone, his chin clattering against the wooden slats, pain searing through his whole body.

No electricity, though. Small merc—

Boot. Boot. Crack. Kamal got on top of him, knees digging into his thighs. Fists pummelled Fenchurch's head, his chest, his hands. Longer punches, more force. Kamal dropped his knee onto Fenchurch's stomach.

Light flashed in his eyes, pain lancing his gut. Vomit caught in his throat. Fenchurch lashed out like a cat, quick and aimless, scratching Kamal's cheek.

More blows hit him — arms, chest, jaw, nose.

Kamal got up again, breathing heavily. 'You going to die!'

Fenchurch spotted a flash of light to the side, just the merest twinkle. A torch beam caught Kamal's face as he leaned over Fenchurch, fists clenched, ready for more. He punched again, blows pounding Fenchurch's chest.

He balled himself up. Bruises all over his torso and arms. Drums thudding in his ears, punk rock thunder. He tasted blood. Kamal gave him a final kick then shot off down the tracks, a shadow in the thin light from his discarded torch.

Fenchurch tried to get up, just stumbling to his knees. He pushed against the side wall and levered himself to his feet. Airwave out: 'I need units at Angel tube station, suspect approaching from the tracks. Repeat, suspect approaching from the tracks.'

He sucked in breath, trying to spot Kamal in the darkness.

Something glittered in the light nearby. He staggered over to it and bent over.

His baton.

Fenchurch gripped the handle and looked down the tunnel, Kamal striding away from him.

Bastard wasn't getting away.

He set off, his old man's legs crunching and grinding as he ran, and he started to close the gap. Then Kamal was gone.

What?

More Batman shit?

Fenchurch scanned through the pitch darkness. What was tha—

Kamal pounced from a small door cut into the tunnel and caught Fenchurch in the face, his forearm grinding up his nose.

They fell backwards onto the hard ground by the tracks. Fenchurch kept a tight grip on his baton as lumps of stone dug into his spine.

Kamal bounded to his feet again, like a puma, and loomed over him, a blade glinting in the pale light.

Fenchurch brought up the baton and smacked it into Kamal's hand. He screamed as the knife flew away.

Another swipe, cracking the baton off Kamal's skull.

He toppled over and clattered over the tracks.

Fenchurch prodded Kamal with the baton. No reaction. His chest was rising, ever so slowly. Still alive, just out cold.

Fenchurch hauled Kamal up, a dead weight not making it easy. He pushed him back against the wall and got out his Airwave. 'Control, this is Fenchurch. I have the suspect in custody. Repeat, suspect is in custody.'

———

'Guv?'

Fenchurch clamped his eyes shut, not that it made much difference. A light seared through them. He tried to wave it away. 'Get that away from me.'

'Guv, it's me.' Nelson pointed the torch at his own face. 'What happened?'

'I got him, Jon.' Fenchurch doubled over. Felt like Kamal'd taken his guts with him. 'Grab him, would you?'

Nelson unsnapped his cuffs and shone the beam on the figure leaning against the side of the tunnel. 'He's hardly got a scratch on him.'

'Whereas I look like I've been twenty rounds with both Klitschko brothers.' Fenchurch touched a finger to his face. Stung like a bee.

Lights danced around the tunnel, heavy footsteps cannoning off the sides. Four uniforms appeared in an explosion of torchlight, smudging the inky darkness.

Nelson hauled Kamal to his feet, a dead weight. He pushed him towards the nearest uniform. 'Take him down to Leman Street and arrange for a lawyer. This is urgent.'

'Sarge.' It took two of them to lug Kamal down the tracks, like a drunk on a Saturday night in Romford.

'What about the trains, Jon? We need—'

'It's cool.' A hand pressed Fenchurch's jacket. 'Won't be any trains through here for a while. The Northern Line's terminating at Old Street and Angel.'

'That's a bloody relief.' Fenchurch gasped at a wave of pain in his chest. Felt like someone was chiselling at his lungs. Hatred flashed up from the pit of his stomach. 'What about Waheed?'

'We've got him, guv. Ambulance is on its way.'

'Jesus. How's he looking?'

'Worse than you, but that's not saying much.'

'Through there, guv.' Nelson helped Fenchurch through the doorway into the Central's basement.

'Get out of my way!' A Northern Irish accent bellowed out. The same paramedic as on Upper Street on Thursday. Platt, wasn't it? He was pushing a gurney towards the stairs.

Fenchurch limped off after him and grabbed hold of his uniform. 'Is that Waheed?'

Platt stopped and looked him up and down. He pressed his glasses up his nose. 'Can I help you?'

'Don't you recognise me?'

'I'm afraid not, pal. Care to enlighten me?'

'What?' Fenchurch's suit was covered in soot and oil, torn in at least three places. Looked like a tramp. 'It's DI Fenchurch.'

'Right, and here's me thinking you're going to ask me for any old iron.'

Waheed lay on the stretcher, eyes shut, mouth hanging loose. Still breathing, but only just. His arm was like the before picture of a black pudding.

Fenchurch's gut ratcheted up a couple of notches. 'How is he?'

'Look, pal, I need to get him away to A&E and you're stopping me.' Platt adjusted his glasses and frowned at Fenchurch. 'You look like you need help yourself?'

'I'll live. Where are you taking him?'

'University College. I need to get your man here up the stairs, so if you don't mind.' Platt shook his hand through the air.

'Go.' Fenchurch let the paramedics take Waheed off and slumped against the clammy wall by the bookcase. 'Jesus, Jon. Did you see him?'

'I did, guv. We need to focus on other things now.'

Fenchurch stroked his throat in slow passes. His gut roared, most likely from Kamal's knee drop. He nodded at Nelson. 'You're right, of course.'

Reed had taken over the basement. The five men from the platform now slumped on the sofas, their hoods down. Black kids, all looking eighteen, if a day. The furthest away one was being tended to by a medic.

Reed came over and joined Fenchurch leaning against the wall. 'Was that Kamal?'

'As far as I know.' Fenchurch eased out his shoulder until it clicked. 'He's in custody now, thank God. Still doesn't feel over, though. Never does.'

Reed frowned at Fenchurch's clothes. 'Your suit's ruined.'

'Least of my worries, Kay. I'll head to Slaters bloody menswear when I get a minute.'

'Try the one up Golders Green Road.' Nelson held up his phone and snapped a photo, the flash stinging Fenchurch's eyes. He swivelled it round — Fenchurch looked like he'd just done a particularly gruelling shift down the pit. 'Might need a very long bath.'

'There's a shower in the station.' Fenchurch leaned against the brick wall and waved over at the men on the sofas. They looked even younger in the harsh light. 'What's the story here, Kay?'

'We've started processing them, guv. None of them are speaking, as you'd expect.'

'He's been doing this for years, Kay, but there's only five of them here. Where are they all?'

Reed didn't answer. Nelson just took another hit of nicotine, staring at his shoes.

'Tell me we've at least got our two suspects? Qasid and Lewis Cole.'

Reed pointed into the room at the two nearest kids, veiled by their hoods. 'That's Qasid and that's Lewis. He's only answering to Roofie, though.'

The kids looked like they were waiting to get their hair cut. Qasid and Roofie were just like brothers. Twin brothers. No wonder they'd managed to get one over on him so well. Little shits.

Fenchurch marched across the floor, just above a fast hobble, and grabbed Qasid's arm and yanked him to his feet. 'You.'

His mouth hung open as his hood fell backwards. He kept his eyes on the floor and hugged his arms around himself. Kid looked about six years old, waiting to be picked for a football team at break. He started speaking, just mumbling. Nothing made any sense.

Fenchurch tugged at the hood. 'What did you say?'

The same inaudible gibberish.

Fenchurch grabbed Qasid's chin and raised it, getting a good look at his eyes. 'Louder.'

Qasid sniffed and wiped at his cheek. 'Said, I ain't saying nothing, man.'

Fenchurch looked around at the other kids splayed around the sofas, trying to mask their fear with hip-hop nodding to an invisible beat. Then he focused on Qasid. 'You killed Victor Morgan. I saw it.'

'Wasn't me, man.'

'It bloody was you.' Fenchurch tightened his grip. Made his fingers ache. Felt so bloody weak. 'Did Kamal tell you to do it?'

Qasid looked over at the other kids. Lewis Cole glanced his way, eyes narrow as he made eye contact and got a nod back. 'Ain't saying nothing, man.'

'You're going to go to prison, son. Your prints are all over that knife.'

'Used gloves, bruv.'

'You shouldn't have bloody said that.' Fenchurch twisted his neck round and pointed him at Lewis. 'Have another look at your mate there. Lewis, right? Roofie? You'll soon be cellmates in Belmarsh.'

'Ain't done nothing, man.' Qasid was blinking hard and fast, like he didn't believe it any more.

Fenchurch beckoned Reed over. 'Get him processed, Kay. I want a full statement and a full confession from him by the time I'm back in Leman Street.'

She got a uniform to take Qasid. 'I suspect our chum Unwin will already be at the station, guv.'

Nelson took a suck of his e-cigarette, his expression showing he didn't care who saw. 'Surprised he's not here now.'

Chapter Forty-One

Fenchurch pushed open the interview room door and let Reed enter first. Clinton Jackson was staring at the table, his harlequin hair all out of whack, dreads laying across his shaved scalp. 'We need to ask you a few questions.'

Jackson glanced at his lawyer, some Legal Aid empty suit, then shrugged. 'Whatever, man.'

Reed sat opposite and leaned over to the microphone. 'Interview commenced at—'

Fenchurch stayed by the door and smoothed down the baggy shirt he'd borrowed from Nelson. Still had a layer of crap on his hand in among all the bruises. Felt like he'd been in a car crash.

Jackson reset the dreads on top of his head. Almost back to the two-way split. He craned his neck round to Fenchurch and spoke in a whisper: 'I need to get this over with, brother. I've got a bar to run.'

'That place is going to be shut for the foreseeable future.' Fenchurch waited for Reed to conclude the preamble, figuring out a plan of attack.

'—his lawyer.' Reed nodded at Fenchurch. 'Guv.'

Fenchurch sat next to Reed and cleared his throat. Felt like half a colliery was stuck in his lungs. 'Mr Jackson, thanks for joining us here. I'd like to start by asking you to describe to us what we found underneath your bar.'

'Maybe better start by telling me what you found, man?'

'So that's how you want to play this, is it?' Fenchurch cracked his knuckles. A spear of pain seared his left arm. He tried to shake it off without anyone seeing. Just about got away with it. 'Okay. There's a bookcase down there, stuffed with political paperbacks. Turns out said bookcase is movable and there's a series of tunnels behind it, which led to the Northern Line.'

'Wowee.'

'Excuse me?'

'I said, wowee. You found an old train station you knew was there, man.'

Fenchurch held his gaze. 'We found six men in those tunnels. Three of them were people we've been searching high and low for. People we've asked you to help us with.' He started counting out on his fingers. 'Qasid Williams. Lewis Cole, also known as Roofie. And, well. We still don't have a surname, but you know him as Kamal.'

'Right.'

'Kamal pushed one of my officers in front of a train.'

Jackson gasped, running his fingers against his palms like he was wiping something off. 'What?' He glanced at his lawyer, getting nothing in response. 'Look, man, I didn't know they were there.'

'That's bollocks. You spoke to Qasid Williams when he entered your bar at quarter past twelve this afternoon.'

'I didn't.'

'I bloody saw you.'

Jackson let out a deep breath. 'He told me he was going to the toilet. I wasn't happy about it.'

'Right, let's just stop this nonsense now, shall we?' Fenchurch crunched back in his chair. 'Mr Jackson, here's how I see it. You knew those kids were there and you knew precisely what they were up to. Stealing phones and killing people. And you just let them get away with it.' He leaned forward, closer to the mic. 'And for that reason, you'll lose your business.'

Jackson hammered a fist down on the table, his happy Rasta face twisting into rage. Teeth clenched, nostrils flared. 'You can't take my bar away from me!'

'We can and we will.' Fenchurch locked eyes with the lawyer, daring him to barge in. Then back at Jackson. 'Not only will you lose your business, but you'll probably go to prison. Maybe not as long as Kamal or his underlings.' He left a gap. 'Maybe.'

Jackson ran a hand through his dreads. 'I didn't know they were there!'

'Come on, you expect me to believe that bollocks?'

The lawyer raised a hand, blocking Jackson. 'Inspector, my client has given you the good grace of listening to your supposition and theorising. My problem is, we're struggling to see a shred of evidence.'

'Kamal and his gang were living underneath his bar, what more do you need?'

'Inspector, this is highly irregular. You've no proof my client knew of their presence.'

Fenchurch kept his gaze away from the lawyer. 'Mr Jackson, you were keeping a gang hidden below your bar. You've been aiding and abetting their activities. That'll mean a good five years inside, maybe longer. And I'm talking time served, not sentence.'

Jackson glanced round at his lawyer. 'That true?'

He didn't get anything in return.

'I can't go to prison, man.'

'So help us.'

Jackson stared at the desk and swallowed. 'What do you want to know?'

'Tell us everything. If it's enough to convict Kamal, we'll be able to use your evidence against him.'

'I'll still lose my bar?'

'Not necessarily. Depending on what you give us, you may be able to sell it. If it's particularly juicy, we might be able to give you a new identity.' Fenchurch waved his hand around the room, hoping he ignored the might-be-ables and the maybes. 'Means you can get out of this Godforsaken city. Maybe move back to the heat with your cash, buy a bar near the beach.'

Jackson looked at his lawyer, waiting for the eventual nod. Then a shut-eyed nod to Fenchurch. 'Want me to start at the beginning?'

Fenchurch smiled at Jackson. 'Sounds like a good place.'

'I opened my bar ten year ago. Place was a wreck. Old underground station, man. Been like that for like a hundred years. Few businesses over the years had it, let it go to ruin. I took on a thirty-year lease and my friends helped me fix it up. Used to be different round there, man, full of my sort of people. They been moved on, though.'

'When did you find the tunnel?'

'Few years ago, man.' Jackson smoothed a hand over the stubble next to his dreads. 'Had builders in sorting out the back room. They found steps down. Found the tunnel and the old underground station. Builder told me they used it as an emergency exit, but not any more.'

'So you took the rooms?'

'Course I did. Used to be the ticket halls. I started my club down there and I started brewing and distilling. Best times, man. Massive Attack did their sound system in there. Mad Professor, too. It was skanking, man.'

'Then Kamal came on the scene?'

'Then Kamal came on the scene . . .' Jackson shut his eyes and exhaled through his nostrils. 'Kamal came up to me. Heard about my discovery. Don't know how, man. Cat was big on urban exploring, said he wanted to dig further down.'

'And you just let him?'

'Didn't see any problem with it, man. Cat goes down there and finds all the tunnels. Said the old platform's gone, new line still there.'

'Then what happened?'

'I don't know, man.'

'You went from not knowing this guy to letting him camp out in your basement. Doesn't ring true, does it?'

Jackson chewed on his bottom lip.

'Okay.' Fenchurch got up, scraping the seat across the lino. 'If there's this big a gap in your tale, we're done here.'

'Sit down, man.' Jackson let his head dip and waited until Fenchurch was seated again. 'Kamal threatened me. Cat knew stuff about me.'

'What sort of stuff?'

'He knew about how I got my money to start me bar.' Jackson sighed, eyes closed. 'I used to sell ganja up in Hackney. I had enough Cheddar stuffed in my mattress to stop the dealing. Went cap in hand to a local gang and let them take my old patch. Bought the Central and everything's skanking.'

'Was Kamal your supplier?'

Jackson shook his head. 'He wasn't, no. That relationship turned . . . messy, but I got out of there.'

'Define messy.'

'I turned up at his house to get some more product. Brother was dead.'

'Did you kill him?'

'No, man. I didn't. Swear on my bar, man.' Jackson grimaced. 'But I checked he wasn't dead, man. I touched him.'

'What was his name?'

'Honest John. All I knew him by.'

Fenchurch frowned. Where did he know that from?

'Honest John, man. What a guy.' Jackson shrugged and gave a slight chuckle, lost to some romantic reminiscence. 'Had his hydroponics, grew his ganja all over the place. Roundabouts, man.'

'And Kamal knew about you finding his body?'

'Months later, man. Kamal said the police were looking for me. Said my prints were everywhere. He'd go to the cops and say I killed him. Said that wouldn't just be his word against mine. They had evidence. Cat's very persuasive, man.'

'So you just folded?'

'I folded, man.' Jackson swallowed back the tears. 'Running the bar was my big hope. I had the dream for two years then Kamal took it away from me, exploited me.'

'He moved in there two years ago?'

'That's what I said.'

'Did you ever go down there?'

'No, man, I never went down. More than my life's worth.'

'And you just let his kids come and go through your bar?'

'What choice did I have, man?'

Fenchurch glanced at Reed. Didn't see what else they could ask. 'Will you testify in court?'

'Kamal will say I killed Honest John, man. He'll say I did it.'

'We need to look into that.' Fenchurch made a note on his Pronto. 'If it does go away, will you testify?'

'Even if it doesn't go away, man.'

Chapter Forty-Two

Fenchurch stuck his phone to his ear and looked down the long corridor. Empty. Felt like he needed a new body. 'Abi, that you?'

The rumbling of a train. People chatting. The ping of an announcer.

Fenchurch sighed into the mouthpiece. 'Hello?'

'Simon?'

'Abi. Finally.'

'What's up?'

'You called me.'

'Did I?' A pause. 'Shit, I bloody pocket-dialled again.'

'You okay?'

'Just coming into Sevenoaks. Got stung for a whole seventeen quid return.'

'That's off-peak, love.'

'It's twenty-two peak.'

'Right. You heading to see Pamela?'

'Thought I might as well. You okay?'

Fenchurch leaned against the wall and felt his lungs deflate. 'We're getting somewhere, love. That kid, he's in custody.'

'I'm glad to hear it. You fancy coming out once you're finished?'

'Let me see, okay?' Fenchurch clocked Reed leaving the interview room. 'Look, I'd better go, okay?'

'Call me when you're done.'

'Be about half three next Tuesday.'

'This is unreal, guv.' Reed joined him leaning against the wall. 'Can you believe what he was up to?'

Fenchurch pocketed his mobile. 'I can believe anything, Kay.'

'We're getting nowhere, guv.'

'We've moved a little bit further forward, that's progress.' Fenchurch got out his Pronto and scanned through it. 'That dealer he mentioned, the name's bothering me. Can't find it anywhere.'

'What, Honest John?'

'Do you recognise it?'

'It was something Waheed was working on.' She shut her eyes with a sigh. 'Jesus.'

Fenchurch reached over and took her hand. 'You okay?'

'Not really, guv.' She brushed a tear away. 'Still no word about him.'

'You want to head to the hospital?'

She shook her head. 'I want to get to the bottom of this.'

'Good.'

'I'll get Lisa checking into that Honest John thing, guv.'

'Good idea.' Fenchurch pointed at the three interview room doors. 'Behind each of these doors is a young, murdering punk. Who should we tackle first?'

'Kamal?'

'Not so sure we should. Let him stew for a bit first.'

'So Qasid?'

'Nope.'

'You killed someone, Lewis.' Fenchurch cleared his throat and glared at Roofie. 'Saskia Barnett. I was there, I saw it. You're going to prison for that.'

'No comment.'

Same as it ever was. 'That's how you're dealing with this?'

'No comment.'

Fenchurch got up and stormed over to the door. Legs on fire. 'I'm going next door, Kay. See if Qasid's interested in the deal.'

Roofie just sniffed.

Reed leaned over to the machine. 'Interview terminated at—'

Qasid was alone apart from the Custody Officer. He was slumped in the chair, playing with the toggles on his hoodie, staring into space and running a hand over his crow lines. He looked up at Fenchurch then down again. 'Bitch.'

Fenchurch sat opposite him. 'Qasid, I need to ask you a few questions.'

'Lawyer.'

'You were found under the Central—'

'Lawyer.'

'I see.' Fenchurch grunted as he got to his feet. 'And who is your lawyer?'

'You know his name, bitch. Dalton Unwin.'

Fenchurch stopped in the corridor, trying to ignore the burning in his gut, and stopped a passing Custody Officer. 'Is Unwin about?'

The lump of pecs and gristle thumbed behind him, back down the corridor. 'Getting a drink from the kitchen.'

The bitter tang of machine coffee came from the end of the corridor, accompanied by a hissing and a booming voice resonating. Unwin's, sounded like he was talking on a mobile.

Fenchurch turned into the little nook. The machine dribbled out the last of its facsimile latte.

Unwin looked up and pointed at the phone. He still wore his mod gear, the collar on his Fred Perry now upturned. 'Yeah, we'll have to pick up again tomorrow, Dave. The fascist empire are calling on my services.' He stabbed at the screen and glared at Fenchurch. 'Yes?'

'Grab your coffee, you've got your first interview.' He set off the way he'd come.

From behind: 'Whose human rights are you abusing this time?'

Fenchurch stopped in the corridor and jabbed a finger at the Fred Perry wreath on Unwin's shirt. 'How many people are you repping, Dalton?'

'I've got six here.'

'How do you sleep at night?'

Unwin sipped at his coffee, smirking over the rim. 'Vodka, painkillers and a lot of tears.'

'Well, we've magicked up Qasid Williams, no thanks to you, and we need him to cooperate. Can I trust you to help me out here?'

'Not my business to help you.'

'You know precisely what he's been up to. And he's guilty as hell, Dalton.'

'They're allegations, Inspector. Nothing's been proven yet.'

'Do I need to get a Legal Aid lawyer in here to replace you?' Fenchurch left a long pause. Unwin didn't fill it. 'Because I will. When one of those kids starts spilling, and they will, how's that going to look for you?'

'So do it. See if I care.'

Fenchurch held up his mobile. 'I'll just get the ball rolling, shall I?'

'Let's leave it as is.' Unwin set off down the corridor and followed Reed into interview room four.

Fenchurch joined them, pushing the door shut behind him.

Qasid looked round at Unwin and held his hand up high, ready for a fist bump. 'Dalton, my man.'

Unwin bumped it and dropped his briefcase on the table. He started unpacking half of Ryman's stock. 'Have they been kind to you?'

'Can't complain, man.'

———

Unwin's pen scratching across the paper was the only sound in the room. He looked shell-shocked. Blinking a lot. His left arm propped up his head.

Qasid slumped against the desk, forehead against the wood. Tears flowed down his cheeks, made him look like a little boy in the rain, lost and alone. 'I ain't done nothing, man.'

'It's not just my word against yours. We've got statements from other people in the park. There was a couple there. They had twin boys, aged five. Those kids saw what you did. That'll be with them the rest of their lives.'

Grown-up Qasid returned, steel covering his eyes and supporting his quivering jaw. 'Not me, man.'

'I saw you.'

'Yeah, but you tol' me you saw me kill that girl the other night, bruv. Wasn't me, was it?'

'We know who it was. Lewis Cole. You call him Roofie.' Fenchurch leaned across the table. 'You swapped places with him and tricked me. Tried to save him from prison. He's in custody now, though. Your little plan didn't work, did it?'

Qasid smirked. 'Think we all look alike, bruv?'

'You look alike when you choose to, Qasid. You dressed the same and you pulled up your hood to hide your face. You and Lewis have the same physique, exact same skin colour. And I don't mean you're both black.' Fenchurch waved a hand over at Unwin. 'Your pigmentation is the same as your lawyer's. Very different to Kamal's, his is a lot lighter. Same with Clinton Jackson.'

'*Bored.*'

Cheeky little shit.

'Here's how I see it.' Fenchurch sat back in his chair and folded his arms. 'Kamal ordered Lewis to kill Saskia. He got you to support him in case anyone saw it. Problem is, he didn't factor on a serving officer being there, did he?'

'You got it all figured out, right? What help do you need from me?'

'We can reunite you with your family, Qasid.'

The little boy face returned. 'What?'

'We spoke to Lewis Cole's father yesterday morning. His parents are on their way in now.' Fenchurch let every word hang there. Let Unwin intervene. Didn't seem to want to. 'We knew who he was from the prints on the knife. We can't find you, though, Qasid. I assume you've got a family out there, though?'

He just shrugged. 'Like I care.'

'I think you do care. You murdered Victor Morgan. Then you assaulted me. You're going to prison, Qasid, for a long time.'

'If you're expecting me to help, bruv, this ain't the right way to go about it.'

Fenchurch drummed his thumbs on the table. 'You live in an old underground station. You wear cheap trackie bottoms from Sports Direct. What are they, five quid a pair?' He waited for a shrug. 'Trouble is, you're getting loads of cash for the killings. Why does Kamal live like that?'

'Only just started that.'

Unwin looked up from his note taking. 'Please strike that from the record. My client means he's only started on his answer.'

'No, bruv. Cut it out.'

'Excuse me?'

'Kamal's branching out. Those were the first hits.'

Unwin raised his hands. 'You can't say this, Qasid.'

'Say what I like, bruv. Free country, innit?'

'You won't be free for much longer, though.'

'Like I care. Cop here says I'm going on death row, man, what do I care?'

'You're not going on death row.' Unwin sighed and shut his eyes. He dropped the pen onto the table. 'Look, I advise you to keep your counsel.'

'Keep my what?'

'Never mind. Just don't speak.'

Qasid nodded at Fenchurch. 'Sorry, man. We was just starting, eh?'

'What's your story, Qasid?'

'Not an interesting one, man.'

'Here's a thing. When I spoke to Lewis's father, he said someone abducted him from Walthamstow. This was two years ago. The day before, two kids were playing football with Lewis. I'm thinking one of them was Kamal and he took Lewis. It all ties together.'

Qasid just shrugged.

'Were you the other kid?'

'Not me, man.'

'How do I know that?'

Snot bubbled in Qasid's nose. He rubbed it away, smearing up his arm. 'Because Roofie was already there when Kamal took me.'

'He abducted you, did he?'

'I didn't want to go, man. Didn't have no choice.'

Fenchurch stared at Unwin. Why wasn't he butting in? 'Start from the start.'

Qasid focused on the desk, rubbing at his nose. 'I lived in East Ham. Went to school there. Then got into a gang.'

'So how did you get in with Kamal?'

Qasid gave a slight shrug. 'We friends, bitch.'

Fenchurch folded his arms, watched Unwin's shaking handwriting scrawling across the page. That was all he was going to get. 'This morning, when you killed Victor Morgan, Kamal told you to do it. Right?'

'You're not listening to me, bruv. I ain't saying shit.'

'How did he know Victor was going to be there?'

'I didn't ask. Learnt a long time ago not to ask him anything.'

'Do you know who he did it for?'

'Ain't saying shit, bitch.'

Fenchurch leaned over to the recorder. 'Interview terminated at—'

⸻

Fenchurch stuck his head against the wall in the corridor. 'Jesus Christ, Kay, I thought we had him.'

Reed patted him on the back. 'So did I, guv.'

'He was going to spill. Bloody Dalton buggering Unwin.'

'Any chance we can get shot of him?'

'Not without a ton of shit falling on our heads, Kay.'

'What now? The other three kids?'

Fenchurch stared at the interview room across the corridor from them. Felt like Room 101, all the shit in the world in one place. 'Time we spoke to Kamal.'

Chapter Forty-Three

'Mr Unwin, you need to let your client speak.' Fenchurch got up and prowled around the interview room. 'Kamal can't get a word in edgeways.'

'Please respect my client's right to silence.'

'He's not being given a chance to exert any rights. You keep cutting in.'

'Fine.' Unwin folded his arms and leaned back, shaking his head. He swept an arm forward. 'Fire away, then.'

Fenchurch crouched in front of Kamal, just about ignoring the searing pain in his knees. 'I'm going to charge you with a few crimes. You're going to prison for a very long time. This is your chance to start clearing your conscience.'

'So why should I speak to you?'

'To clear your name. Suggest any mitigating circumstances.'

Kamal laughed. 'You offering me a deal?'

'Maybe.'

'Let's hear it, then.'

'I can only go so far, Kamal. You ran a gang of kids who stole mobile phones, which you sold to various shops for money. I don't think you shared many of the spoils, did you?'

'This supposed to be getting my cooperation?'

'You kept the cash for yourself, didn't you?'

'You see where I lived, man. See the clothes I wear. These sweatpants ain't Confederate or even Grimey, man. I ain't no high roller.'

'So where is it? Stuffed in your mattress?'

'Ain't no Cheddar, man. Ain't no nothing.'

'Then I can't help you.' Fenchurch got up, his thighs burning and clicked his tongue against the roof of his mouth as he sat next to Reed. 'Let's talk about the other stuff you've been doing. Maybe see if we can bring your sentence down.'

'What's this other stuff?'

'You're killing people for money, Kamal.'

'Where is this cash? I ain't seen any of it.'

'You've murdered two people so far.' Fenchurch didn't let his gaze wander from his dark eyes. 'You arranged for your people to kill Saskia Barnett and Victor Morgan.'

'Never heard them names, bro.'

'You know a Qasid Williams and a Lewis Cole?'

'Sure, they my homies.'

'They killed these people.'

'If they did, why am I here? Why you not speaking to them?'

'We've spoken to them. But they work for you. Means you're complicit in this.'

'That right?' Kamal slapped Unwin's arm. 'You want to show my lawyer here the evidence?'

'We've got some evidence of you murdering someone in Hackney a couple of years ago.'

'Evidence. Right.'

Fenchurch ignored the look Reed was shooting him. Eyebrows standing upright, eyes wide. 'Iron-tight.'

'Why am I not in jail, then?'

'Because of your tendency to disappear.'

338

Kamal stared at Unwin, tongue slowly circling his lips, getting a pinched brow from the lawyer. Then he shrugged at Fenchurch. 'Evidence, bro.'

'You know Saskia Barnett, right?'

'Not saying nothing.'

'Sure you don't know her? Your name was her last word. She died saying your bloody name.'

'I don't know she.'

'That right? We've got a recording of her calling a burner phone. Quite a few times, as it happens. I called it myself and someone who sounded a lot like you answered it, said to meet at Boundary Park. Your little friend, Qasid, turned up there. You saying that's not connected to you?'

'Then he must be doing stuff behind my back. This is nothing to do with me, man. Better speak to them.'

Kid was good. Kid, ha. He was thirty if a day.

Fenchurch couldn't help but grin. 'Seems like you're dropping them in it.'

'Ain't dropping nobody in anything, man.'

'Where are the rest of them?'

'What?'

'There were six of you down there. Your gang should be a lot bigger. We've got reports of over twenty kidnappings.'

Kamal raised his hands in the air. 'Nothing to do with me, man.'

'Kamal, your part in this is over. Don't you get that? You're going away for a long time. Some judges might throw away the keys.'

'You're fitting me up, man.'

'This is your last chance to help us.'

'I doubt it is, man.' Kamal pursed his lips, rocking his head slowly. 'Good night, sweetheart.'

Fenchurch stormed into the Obs Suite.

Docherty looked up from the monitor and bowed down, fanning his arms like Fenchurch was Cleopatra. 'All hail DI Fenchurch.'

'What's that supposed to mean?'

'That's you getting a conviction, is it?' Docherty leaned back in his seat and stuck his feet on the desk. 'You big, soft shite. Practically let him walk out of the door.'

Fenchurch jabbed a finger at the screen Kamal was on, lost in conversation with Unwin. 'I've seen two people stabbed to death and that . . . animal pushed Waheed in front of a bloody train.'

'Aye, and he's keeping himself quiet. Christ's sake.'

Fenchurch rubbed a hand down his arm, igniting the pain-pleasure release from the bruises. 'Do you want to have a go?'

'Not sure what else we can get out of him.' Docherty got up and patted Fenchurch's arm. 'We should just let him stew.'

'Stew?' Fenchurch glared at him, his gut churning. 'Boss, I've been to hell and back on this case. I don't want him getting away with it.'

Docherty gripped his shoulder tighter. 'You've done all you can. That's all I ask, okay?'

Fenchurch swallowed hard and sunk back onto a desk. 'How's Waheed doing?'

'Still in surgery, last I heard. Dawn's up there just now. His wife's there as well.'

'Christ.' Fenchurch collapsed against the desk. His body ached and drums clattered in his ears. His acid reflux was climbing up his throat. 'Feels like a game over here.'

Docherty shrugged. 'We'll put in the man hours, we'll put in the time.'

'Is that enough, though?'

'What else can we do, Si? We'll get him for what he's done. Mark my words.'

The door clattered open and Reed stormed in, clutching a wad of paperwork. 'Guv, you need to—' She nodded at Docherty. 'Sir.'

Fenchurch got up. 'What is it?'

'I had Lisa looking into that story Clinton Jackson told us about this dead dealer, Honest John. She checked with that Oscar guy in Trident. It was part of their investigation when they still had it.'

'So they know about it?'

She nodded. 'Xolani was investigating it for them. They know Kamal did it, guv. Got his prints on the knife, got Xolani as a witness.'

'So Kamal had Jackson wound up over nothing?'

'Looks like it.' Reed jabbed her thumb towards the door. 'Your old man's looking for you, by the way.'

Fenchurch looked up. 'What?'

'Him and Savage are mooching around. Said the operation to prosecute Kamal is their remit.'

Fenchurch shot a glare at Docherty. 'Are you letting them, boss?'

Docherty raised his hands, palms up. 'I don't really care. Could do without losing the resource but as long as someone puts him away and gives the kids back to their parents, I couldn't give a shit.'

'Well I bloody do.'

———

Fenchurch's dad sat facing the door, DCI Howard Savage next to him. He frowned at his son. 'Simon?'

Across the table, Ronald Cole glared out at Fenchurch. His wife cuddled into him, rocking with tears. Straight black hair and a bright-blue dress.

Fenchurch closed the door behind him and nodded at Ronald, his expression as sombre as the cuts and bruises would allow. 'Mr Cole.'

His wife looked up, bloodshot eyes blurry, mascara running down her cheeks. 'Where's my boy?'

Fenchurch patted his dad on the shoulder. 'I just need a word with my colleagues.'

Dad got to his feet and nodded at the Coles. 'We'll just be a minute.'

Mrs Cole tugged back at Savage. 'When do I get to see my boy?'

'We'll be discussing that now.' Fenchurch held the door open for Dad, leaving Savage with the parents. He shut it and rested against the steel.

A couple of DCs clutched coffees further down the corridor, looking shell-shocked.

'What are you doing here, Dad?'

'Howard's borrowed me for a bit. We're working together to help sort this mess out.' Dad prodded a finger across Fenchurch's face, digging into the fresh wounds. 'Simon, what the bloody hell have you been up to?'

Fenchurch batted his hand away. 'Catching robbers and killers, Dad.'

'I worry about you, son.' Dad stared at the door. 'I was with them when the call came in about their boy. They just want to see Lewis. More than anything. Sure you know the feeling?'

'Dad. Don't.'

'Can't imagine what's going on in their heads, though. How'd it feel if Chloe just turned up.' Dad swallowed, his eyes bulging. 'How'd it feel if she was a murderer?'

Fenchurch held his gaze until he looked away. The old goat wouldn't take no for an answer. He clenched his fist, ready to punch something. The wall, Dad, himself. 'We only found five of these kids. There's at least twenty in your little hunt.'

'Howard's got a team going down other abandoned stations. Maybe they'll find them and maybe they'll speak.'

'Sounds like a bloody long shot to me.'

'It's worth a shot, son. York Road's a good punt. Not far from there.'

'Make sure you keep away from the stations. They're not in that good a nick. City Road was one of the best.'

Dad cackled. 'Like I'd get my hands dirty, son.'

The door burst open and Savage stepped out into the corridor. 'Ian, which room is Lewis in?'

Fenchurch used an arm to block his progress. 'I need a word before you speak to him, sir.'

'Excuse me?' Savage frowned at Fenchurch. 'They've just been reunited with their son. They need—'

'I don't care what they need. Their son has murdered someone. I need him to start speaking.'

'You'll get in there when I'm done with him, Inspector.'

'We need to get their son talking.'

'Put the Fenchurch blunderbuss back in its case. We're playing this softly, softly.'

'This isn't the time, Howard. They're the carrot I'm dangling. That kid needs a stick right up his arse.'

'Inspector, you've not got the authority to—'

'Go and chase up Docherty, if you can be bothered. I'm heading back in there and I'm using them as bait.' Fenchurch turned back to the room and smiled at the Coles. 'Now, if you'll just follow me?'

Chapter Forty-Four

Fenchurch locked eyes with Roofie. Lewis Cole. Yellower whites than Qasid, very different bone structure on his face. Not that similar when you spend time with both of them. 'You know what you've done, don't you?'

A shrug. Then a sniff. 'Ain't done nothing.'

Unwin looked up from his legal pad, the yellow page almost covered in arcane scribbles. 'My client—'

'—murdered someone.' Fenchurch tossed a photo on the table. 'Saskia Barnett. You stabbed her on Thursday night. I was there, I saw it.'

'Sure it's not Qasid you saw?'

'You can only do that trick so many times.' Fenchurch tossed over a copy of the Crime Scene Report. 'Lewis, we've got your prints on the knife.'

'Would help if you wasn't a racist, bruv.'

Fenchurch glanced over at Reed, his nostrils feeling like they were going to pop. 'Your parents are outside.'

'What?'

'You heard.' Fenchurch collected up the sheets of paper. 'They're outside, just waiting on me letting them speak to their pride and joy. You do remember them, right?'

Lewis blinked away tears. 'No, man, no.' He shook his head in a wide arc, eyelids flickering.

'They're so proud of what you've achieved with your life. Everything they ever dreamed of. Killing people. Stealing phones. Living in a bloody tunnel.'

'Man . . .'

'I spoke to Qasid earlier, just after we interviewed you. He said you helped Kamal abduct him.'

'He didn't, man. No way.'

'Don't get smart with me.' Fenchurch dropped the pages onto the desk. 'Looks like Kamal's been abducting kids off the street for years, then forcing them to commit a string of crimes.'

'Shut up, man.'

'Just imagine what your parents went through, Lewis.' Fenchurch puckered his lips and blew out. 'Problem I'm having is, well, Kamal's got thirty people working for him. At least. I don't get how one guy can hold so much sway over that many people, no matter how brutal he is. He needs lieutenants, people to keep the rank and file in check.'

'It ain't me, bruv.'

'Was it Qasid?'

'No, man.'

'You're part of a criminal conspiracy. That'll be added to your charge.'

'Come on, man, I ain't speaking.' Lewis paused and looked at the door. 'Can I see my parents?'

'Tell me first.'

'Can't tell, man. He'll kill them.'

Fenchurch stared at his eyes for a few seconds. Kid definitely knew something. Maybe time to hang up the stick and use the carrot. He got up and waved at the camera. 'Interview suspended at sixteen twenty-three.'

The door opened and Savage led the Coles in. They stood a few metres away from their son, wary and unsure.

Lewis's face cracked, tears slicking his cheeks, his mouth losing all motor control. 'Mum. Dad.'

Ronald Cole raced over and grabbed his son in a bear hug, almost knocking him off his seat. 'My boy.'

His wife joined in, wedging her body between the men, arms pressed against their backs.

Fenchurch watched the reunited family, tears flooding three faces. Just that one moment where they reconnected, where all the wrongs of the past and the recriminations of the future flew out the window. Thick mucus filled his throat, his sinuses. It stabbed at his gut, stung his heart.

Dad patted Fenchurch on the arm and winked. 'Makes it all worthwhile, doesn't it?'

Fenchurch just nodded. His breath came in fits and starts. 'He's a murderer, Dad.'

Unwin was still sitting there, writing away as though nothing was happening. Reed looked like she was trying to decipher his shorthand, upside down.

Ronald left his wife with his son. 'Is there nothing we can do to stop this?'

'I wish there was.' Fenchurch swallowed. 'Your son murdered a young woman. He might've been coerced into doing it but he still did it.' His lip quivered, close to losing it. 'It's not for me to decide what happens to him.'

'Can we at least spend more time with him?'

'That can be arranged.'

'Thank you.'

Fenchurch held his hand. 'If he helps us.'

Ronald looked at him for a few seconds then gave a curt nod. 'I'll see what I can do.' He limped over to his son and whispered in his ear. Roofie — *Lewis* — blinked hard and slow, teary eyes gleaming under the strip lighting. More whispering then Lewis locked eyes with his father. Then he nodded, eyes shut. 'Okay.'

Unwin looked up from his paperwork and waved a hand in the air. 'I need some more time alone with my client.'

Lewis shook his head, strong and defiant now. 'They need to hear the truth, man.'

Unwin grabbed his wrist. 'You need to keep quiet.'

Lewis pushed the lawyer's hand away. 'I don't want you here no more. Leave.'

'You're taking the side of a corrupt police officer against—'

'Excuse me?' Fenchurch got between them. 'Corrupt?' He focused on Lewis. 'Your lawyer isn't doing you any favours, Mr Cole.'

'How dare you?'

Fenchurch glared at Unwin. 'How dare I? You're the one suggesting I'm corrupt.' Back to Lewis. 'It's your call.'

'Get out, man! I don't want you here!'

'Lewis, you don't—'

'Get! Out!'

Unwin collected up his stuff, shaking his head. 'This isn't the end of the matter.' He stormed out of the room, slamming the door behind him.

Fenchurch waited until Dad and Savage had taken Lewis's parents out then nodded at him. 'Do you want a Legal Aid lawyer to be appointed?'

'I just want to help.'

'Do you want a lawyer?'

'You want to hear or what?'

Fenchurch let out a breath. 'Please.'

'Then start that tape, man.'

Reed hit the recorder's button and leaned forward. 'Interview recommenced at sixteen thirty-six. Dalton Unwin has left the room.'

'This is just shit I hear, man. Might not be true.' Lewis patted down his cornrows, a mirror image of Qasid's except for the seashell spiral by the ear. 'Kamal used to be Mandem up in Tottenham. Big guys. Got into some shit, though. They after him, say he a dead man. This is his stab at freedom. Building up a gang of us so we'd take them out. Trained us with knives.' His face was as red as his skin colour would let it. 'He's brutal, man. Nobody could beat him. Always armed. Seen him kill six brothers.'

'Jesus.' Fenchurch gave him a nod. 'Andrew Smith, right.'

'Right.' Lewis leaned forward. 'That's his name. Andrew Smith. Grew up in Harlow.'

'In Essex?'

'You know another one, man?'

'Why Kamal?'

'Andrew Smith sound gangster to you?'

'When did this falling out happen?'

'Five years ago, maybe more. He been on the run so long, man. So long.'

'Tell me about when he abducted you.'

'This was two years ago. May, I think. We were playing football. Arsenal versus Chelsea, you know?'

Fenchurch shrugged. 'I'm West Ham.'

'Man, I love West Ham.' Lewis smacked his right hand's fingers off his left palm. 'So we was playing in the street. Then Kamal and this kid turned up. Hayden.'

Fenchurch frowned. 'Did you say Hayden?'

'Sure. He was Kamal's right-hand man. When you ask me about who's his lieutenant, Hayden was one of them. Nasty man.

Ain't seen the brother in a few weeks, know what I'm saying? Kamal must've got him.'

'No, I know precisely where he is. I'll need you to identify him.'

'I can do that.'

'So what did Kamal say when you were playing football?'

'He say he'd get me an iPhone 5S, man. That's like eight hundred quid.'

'So you joined his gang for a mobile?'

'I said no.' Lewis nibbled at his bottom lip. 'But he took me, anyway.'

'Kidnapped you?'

'Said I couldn't go back. Said he'd kill my mum and my dad if I didn't steal a phone for him. Took it from some chump by Leather Lane, this big ponce in a suit just coming out of an office.' Lewis rubbed at his eye. 'Kamal, he videoed it man. Had my hood down. Said if I ever ran my mouth, he'd send the video to the police.'

'You've done a lot worse now.'

Lewis rolled his shoulders. 'Didn't got no choice, man.'

'Everyone's got a choice. You could've just run away.'

'You don't understand, man. Two days ago, Kamal killed a kid who just spoke to his folks to let them know he was okay. Stabbed him right there. Twenty times, man. Said if anyone did the same, we'd be dead men. And our families be dead, too.'

'Where's the body?'

Lewis sniffed. 'Under the tarp in the tunnel.'

Reed got up and left the room, slamming the door behind her.

'How many kids are in this gang, Lewis?'

'Twenty. Twenty-five. Kamal brings new ones in all the time.'

'We only found five of you, six including Kamal. Where are the rest of them?'

'I don't know, man. He kept it a secret from us. We worked in teams, five or six. I never went anywhere else, man.'

'But Hayden was one of the leaders?'

'Damn straight, man.'

Reed came back into the room and whispered in his ear: 'The uniform at the Central found that body, guv. Dead a couple of days, by the looks of things.'

Fenchurch focused on Lewis, rubbing a finger across his eyebrows. Poor kid never had a chance. The odds were stacked so hard against him from the moment he was born until he stabbed Saskia Barnett. A chain of events he had little or no control over. Taken from his home and forced to do what he was doing now.

Fenchurch felt tears form behind his sinuses, sting at his nostrils. Not now.

Not. Now.

'Did Kamal order you to murder Saskia?'

'He did, man.' Lewis splayed his hands on the table, pale palms facing up. 'Said just kill the bitch. I didn't ask who she was. Tol' me to grab her phone and bag.' He nodded at Fenchurch. 'Then you chased after me. Hit me with your car, man.' He rubbed at his leg. 'Still sore. Feels like . . .' He grinned. 'Like you ran a car into it.'

'How did you give me the slip?'

'You a lot older than me, man. It was easy. Qasid met me at the end of the street. You followed him. I got away.'

'How?'

'I jumped into the canal. People say black kids can't swim. I was a champion in my school, man. Love swimming. Love it.'

'You tossed her bag, didn't you?'

'Sure, man. Threw it into the canal.'

'You missed.'

'Damn.'

'What did you do with her phone?'

'Took it to Kamal. Same as the little thing.' Lewis held his fingers a few centimetres apart. 'Little thing for computers.'

'A thumb drive?' Fenchurch reached into his pocket for his keys and held it up by the USB flash drive. 'Like this?'

'Sure. One of them.'

'What did Kamal do with the phone?'

'He got it unlocked. Don't know how. Next thing I know, man, he asks me to break into this kid's flat.'

'Liam Sharpe?'

'Never got his name. Hipster. Looked like he run a coffee shop.'

'Did Kamal say why?'

'You never asks why.'

'But it was after he saw what was on her phone?'

'Said something about some texts this girl sent to him. Didn't ask, he didn't tell.'

'What happened to the flash drive?'

'Burned it when I destroyed the laptop in the park. Hit it with a hammer.'

Fenchurch stood up and stretched out. Seemed like everything. 'Thanks for that.'

'What do I get for that?'

'You're going to go to prison for murder, Lewis. There's no way round it, I'm afraid. I can put in a good word with people I know and see what we can do. It might mean a reduced sentence, you never know.'

'Appreciate it, man.'

Fenchurch leaned over to the mic. 'Interview terminated at sixteen thirty-seven.'

***

Fenchurch poured hot water on the teabags and let them sit. 'When we were up in Scotland just after Christmas, you had to mash the teabag against the side of the mug for bloody ages.'

351

'Weird.' Reed plonked the milk on the counter in the canteen area. 'Why's that?'

'Soft water or something. No lime in it.' Fenchurch took the bags out and dumped them in the bin. Then poured in some milk, just a spit in Reed's. 'There you go.'

'Cheers.' She held it up to her nose and let the steam waft up. 'You okay, guv?'

'Things are starting to come together, Kay. We know Kamal ordered her death.'

'Still missing the why, though.'

'This USB stick, though.' Fenchurch shut his eyes, practically pulled his forehead down to his cheeks. 'That can't be why she was killed, can it?'

'Kamal told Lewis to take it and it ended up burnt next to her laptop. It's got to be connected.'

Fenchurch got out his mobile and hit a button. He got in before it was answered. 'Liam, it's Fenchurch.'

'Right. Was that stuff any use?'

'Very useful. Thanks.' Fenchurch wrapped a hand around his mug, almost searing the skin. 'Do you know anything about a USB drive Saskia was carrying?'

'You asked me about this when you accused me of lying about the laptop.'

'We think it might be why she was killed.'

'Shit.' A pause. 'Oh, shitty bollocks. Bugger.'

'What's up?'

'Meet me at her old man's house.'

Chapter Forty-Five

Fenchurch knocked on the door and took a step back. A light glowed in the townhouse's upstairs. 'This better bloody lead to something.'

The door opened and Hugo Barnett peered out. His musketeer facial hair was drowning in a sea of stubble. His dapper attire had given way to the sort of red tracksuit a seventies Liverpool manager would've worn. He gave a curt nod and spun on his heel. 'In you come.'

Fenchurch let Reed enter first. In the wide hall, the table was covered in pizza boxes. A couple of half-drunk whisky bottles lay on the parquet. 'How are you coping, sir?'

'How do you think I'm coping? My daughter's been killed by some black scumbag. How the hell am I supposed to cope with that?' Hugo had to rest a hand against the sitting room door. Alcohol fumes wafted off him. 'What's going on? Why are you here?'

'Liam said he'd meet us here, sir.'

Hugo bellowed up the stairs: 'Liam? It's the police.' He shrugged at them.

'Do you mind if we go up?'

Hugo frowned at a bottle, then smiled at it as if he'd just met an old friend. 'Be my guest.' He picked up the bottle and went into the living room.

Reed started up the staircase, the boards crunching under her feet. The cream paintwork was glowing in the late afternoon sun. 'Poor guy. Can't even begin to . . .' She stopped halfway and screwed up her face. 'Shit, sorry.'

'You don't have to tread on eggshells all the time, Kay.'

'Just most of the time, right?' Reed marched up to the first-floor landing. A clatter came from a room at the end of a long hall. She stomped off towards it. 'Liam?'

A small girl's bedroom, the pink walls filled with Hannah Montana and Justin Bieber posters. In the middle was a double bed with plain white sheets, dimpling around a silver laptop. At the far side, a dresser was groaning under the weight of makeup and piles of paperwork.

Someone was rooting around under the bed. Tight jeans giving the Billericay smile.

'Liam?'

He crawled out and nodded. 'There you are.' He was carrying a treasure chest, the sort of thing a pirate would have stuffed with gold. 'This is a long shot, but . . .' He reached into his pocket for a key. 'Sas used to stick important stuff in here. Completely forgot about it until you mentioned that thumb drive.'

'And?'

'Let's see.' Liam twisted the key in the lock and opened it, like that elf kid in that game Chloe used to play. Zelda or something. He picked out her passport and some paperwork. Then froze. 'Shit.' He held something up. 'This look like it?'

Fenchurch squinted at it. Another USB stick. 'The one we found was burned to a crisp.'

'Right, right.' Liam sprang to his feet and grabbed the silver MacBook, stuffing the drive in the side. 'Let's have a look at this, shall we?'

Fenchurch wasn't going to stop him — he'd know what he was looking for. 'What's it got on it?'

'A spreadsheet.'

'That's it?'

Liam tapped the trackpad then his eyes darted around the screen. 'Holy crap.' He swivelled the computer around.

Didn't mean anything to Fenchurch. 'What is it?'

Reed picked it up and stared at the data. 'These names . . . They're all councillors.' She handed the laptop to Fenchurch. 'Look, they're all in Islington.'

'Shit.' Fenchurch scanned through the list as best his eyes would let him. The last column read: 'Ms Hughes made no comment as to the source of the donation. [NOTE — Forensic accountant might be useful here]'

'I don't get it.' Fenchurch dumped the laptop on the bed. 'She found evidence of corruption. Why not publish it?'

Liam sat next to the computer, roughing up the pristine sheet. 'Sas went to a few Islington council meetings. She said they were tied on a big issue at the moment. There's a proposal to shift people out of the flats on Buxton Court.'

Fenchurch frowned — where he'd collared Qasid the first time. 'On City Road, right?'

'That's the badger. They want to move them all over the borough. Up to Highbury, a few houses over this way.' Liam flicked through to the last page. 'Sas had spoken to some of the councillors who were against it. They reckoned some business had bought it up.'

'And you think this is who paid them?'

Liam tapped the screen. 'Look at the size of those bungs. That's over two hundred grand. Each.'

Fenchurch nodded. 'I take it this is from the developers?'

'Got to be.' Liam scowled at the display, fingers doing double time on the trackpad. 'The name Purple Heron is all over this.'

'Who are they?'

'Something I spotted in her documents.' Liam collapsed back onto the bed, knees bent together. 'If I remember right, Sas checked it out but it's one of those businesses hidden behind loads of shell companies.'

'And she never found out who owned it?'

Liam shut the laptop's lid and tapped it. 'Victor never got funding for the forensic accountant.'

Fenchurch dialled Nelson's number. 'Jon, can you look into something for me?'

The Incident Room was empty. Most of them must still be up at the park. Nelson was prowling around the area near the whiteboard, chatting to two DCs.

'Jon.'

Nelson waved off his colleagues and wandered over, a laptop under his arm. 'Mulholland's doing my bloody head in, guv.'

Fenchurch rolled his eyes and leaned against a desk. 'You getting anywhere?'

'Sort of.' Nelson opened the laptop and held it up, just far enough that Fenchurch could make out some of the text. 'Here you go, guv. Had to pull a few strings with the City police but we traced those bribes to a UK limited company.'

Fenchurch scanned down the screen. 'This is all very impressive but we need to know who bloody owns it.'

'That's going to be a bit harder. Steve's checking for me.' Nelson switched to another tab. 'Good news, though, is their registered office is in Canary Wharf.'

———

Canary Wharf was deadly quiet, Sunday evening pretty much the quietest it would ever get.

Reed followed two uniformed officers inside, one of them lugging an Enforcer. 'Thought this place turned into a pumpkin on a Friday night, guv.'

Fenchurch pushed the door shut behind him. 'Place is a bloody disaster, Kay.'

A series of business logos were etched onto the wall above a glass reception desk. Look at one from the right angle and it was a purple heron.

Space for only one receptionist. Two leather couches against the walls, coffee tables filled with Finance-y magazines and Friday's *FT*. The window at the end overlooked the Thames, a thin slice of the Isle of Dogs just visible. His old flat was just below, a couple of city playboys no doubt smashing the place up, doing coke and God knows what else. The O2 sat in the distance, like someone had planted an alien jellyfish on Greenwich. It'd been years since he'd seen what was left of Led Zep play there.

'Guv!' Reed was by the reception area, footsteps echoing around the vast space, waving the warrant around.

Fenchurch charged over.

A security guard tugged at his bulbous nose, the skin red and cracked. Looked like it was fighting a losing battle against its owner's whisky habit. 'What are you lot after?'

Fenchurch gave a flash of his warrant card. 'Looking to speak to someone in Purple Heron?'

The guard thumbed behind him. 'Right. Nobody's in, not that there ever is, mind.'

'What's that supposed to mean?'

'It's a front address. Most of them in here are the same. Lucrative business, not that I get a cut of it.' He did a big tug at his nose. 'One of the banks owns it, I think. Purple Heron rents a unit from them.'

'Whose name's on the lease?'

The guard sniffed. 'I'd need to check on that, sir.'

'Go on, then.'

'Right you are.' The guard unlocked a computer and dragged the mouse around half of the desk. Another sniff. Then some single-finger typing, his left hand scanning around the keyboard for the correct letter, his right not shifting. He hit return and squinted at the monitor, moving closer to it. 'Something called "Purple Heron 2015 Ltd" owns that suite, sir.'

'I asked for the name.'

'That's all I've got on them, sir. Other than some number. Code for something, God knows what.'

'Let me see that.' Fenchurch swivelled the screen round and jotted the number down. 'Back in a sec, Kay.' He grabbed his Airwave and trotted away from the desk. He dialled Nelson.

'Jon, it's a dead letter drop.'

'Guv, can I call you back?'

'Are you with your mate in the City police yet?'

'That's why I need to call you back. DI Clarke's come in especially and we're busy with— Just a sec, guv.' The line went dead for a few seconds then Nelson cleared his throat. 'There are two owners, guv. Both companies. One is "Dubai Investments (UK) Ltd". Just checking into them now.'

'I've not got all day, Jon.'

'Nothing I can do here, guv.' Seconds that seemed to last for hours. 'Here we go. The owner is one Guy Eustace.'

Chapter Forty-Six

Fenchurch hammered the horn again and wound down the window to get a better view. A voice boomed out further down Upper Street, cannoning off the buildings. Either through a megaphone or a PA, Fenchurch couldn't tell. He checked his phone — still nothing from Nelson. 'Bollocks to this.' He pulled in and mounted the pavement. Then got out, leaving his Mondeo in among the stalled traffic, and stormed off.

Reed jogged after him, struggling to keep pace. 'Guv, wait!'

Fenchurch was marching down the street, the drums drowning out the honking of car horns and the squealing feedback up ahead.

A crowd had formed around Chilango, maybe three hundred people spilling out over the road and blocking the traffic, swamping the Superdry shop. Tattoos and shaven heads.

Fenchurch barged past two skinheads, more interested in their burritos than in politics.

Guy Eustace was standing on a box by the scene of Saskia's death, bellowing into a microphone, distorting his already shrill voice. He was dressed like he was going shooting, though it was unclear whether he was hunting game or immigrants.

'A young woman was murdered here the other night. You all know this, that's why you're here. You've all seen the newspapers this morning, cashing in on her death, selling the lie that a girl in her twenties has a legacy. I met Saskia a few times. She was a nice girl, kind-hearted and warm. She had an eye for a story, that's what they say. The problem was, she missed the real story.'

Fenchurch waited for Reed to catch up then jostled ahead through the crowd, pushing towards the front.

Eustace locked eyes with him, holding his gaze as he spoke. 'The police . . . The police are spending a lot of time investigating Saskia's death.' He looked away, across his audience. 'But the real crime here is they're missing the story that's killing people.' He held up a copy of his election manifesto, a glossy brochure like you'd get selling luxury holidays. 'In this city, there's a campaign of social cleansing. People are losing the homes they grew up in or they've raised families in. They're being kicked out, just so Syrian migrants can move in. They're disrupting communities and for what? I'll tell you.' He let it hang in the air. 'Political correctness. We're losing, guys. This used to be Great Britain but it's lost its greatness. Saskia was killed by black men. Sons of immigrants. How long until your children or your wives are murdered by immigrants?'

That got a cheer. A half-eaten burrito landed near Fenchurch, thrown by a supporter just behind Reed.

'This is getting worse, not better. The government want to open our doors further. The EU want to include half of the world. Turkey is next? How long before we're letting Islamic extremists just walk through the door?' Eustace paused to look around, eyes narrowing. 'I'll tell you, shall I? It's now. It's happening now. It's always been happening, since we sold our country to the Germans and the EU.'

A lone dissenting voice shot up near Fenchurch. 'You're worse than Trump!'

'Trump? There's a man with the right idea.' Eustace laughed to himself. 'What can be done to stop this social cleansing?' He raised his left hand in the air, waving like he was a Presidential nominee. 'Vote to leave the EU! Vote for English control for English people! Thank you and God bless!'

A huge roar went up. The burrito couple applauded more than anyone else he could see.

Fenchurch raised his eyebrows at Reed then pointed at the TV cameras at the far side. 'Their opponents haven't had time to mobilise but the press have.'

'We can do him for inciting racial hatred, guv.'

'Not a bad idea.' Fenchurch nodded at her and she slipped off towards their uniform cover.

Eustace made his way to Fenchurch, reaching out to kiss a baby on his way. 'Didn't think you were interested in politics, Sergeant.'

'Inspector. And yes, I am interested. I read *Private Eye*, anyway.' Fenchurch waved at the crowd around them. 'How long have you planned this?'

'Not long. Why?'

'Take it you heard Victor Morgan was murdered this morning?'

'Who?'

'Features Editor at the *Post*. Saskia's boss.'

Eustace clasped a hand over his mouth. 'Oh my God. What happened?'

'Stabbed in broad daylight. You didn't have anything to do with it, did you?'

'Why on earth would you think that?'

'That's not answering my question. I saw what she published this morning.'

'That's all lies.' Eustace stepped closer to him, as if that would quieten him. 'Look, if you're here to intimidate me, I know absolutely nothing about either death.'

361

'I don't believe you.'

'It's the truth. Now, I need to speak to the Press. Good day.'

Fenchurch tugged at the sleeve of his Barbour jacket. 'Does the name Purple Heron ring any bells?'

'Sounds like a pub in Hackney.'

Fenchurch let him have his joke, watching the crowd for a few seconds. He clocked Reed's approach, accompanied by some uniform, then snapped out his handcuffs and gripped Eustace's wrists. 'Guy Eustace, I'm arresting you under the—'

'—and Guy Eustace, who is representing himself.' Fenchurch locked eyes with the MEP, aware of the digital recorder flashing away. 'Are you sure about that, sir?'

'I've passed the bar, Inspector. Better than some Pakistani oik on Legal Aid.' Eustace brushed some fluff from his shoulder. 'Sooner we get this over with, the sooner I can get out doing my bloody job.'

'Mr Eustace, do you recognise the name Purple Heron?'

'No comment.'

'Who owns it?'

'No comment.'

Fenchurch pushed a sheet of paper over. 'Says here it's co-owned by "Dubai Investments (UK) Ltd". That business is, in turn, owned by yourself.'

'No comment.'

'Who are you in league with?'

'No comment.'

'This'll come back to bite you, one way or another, Mr Eustace. We'll find out who else's behind it.'

'What, so you can publish that in the press?'

'Like Victor Morgan did? Is that you admitting you ordered his death?'

'No comment.'

'Look. Either way, you're finished. Your glittering career in Brussels will be in tatters.'

'I've done nothing. You need to let me go.'

'Victor Morgan had more stuff on you, didn't he?'

Eustace stomped down, kicking a boot heel off the floor. 'He already published a tissue of lies.'

'That's not quite what I said.' Fenchurch shook his head. 'I believe Mr Morgan had something else on you. Something unpublished.'

Eustace flicked his reptilian tongue. 'What?'

'Two hundred thousand pounds worth of help to a load of councillors.'

Eustace looked away, desperate eyes searching the walls. 'I don't know what you mean.'

'Saskia Barnett found payments you'd made to Islington borough councillors. Something to do with planning permission for Buxton Court, right?'

'Excuse me?'

'We know what you're planning, Mr Eustace. A team is going through the transactions just now.' Fenchurch grinned at him. 'It'll look better for you if you come clean.'

'There's absolutely nothing to come clean about, I can assure you.'

'Just tell me who you're working with and we're done here.'

'Seems like you already know.'

'I don't. I'd appreciate it if you told me.'

'No comment.'

'Back to that, are you?'

Fenchurch kicked his bin, sending a stream of crap all over the floor. Burrito foil, lemonade cups, Mulholland's scarf. 'He's not getting away with this, Kay.'

'And you're not either.' She stared at the pile of rubbish. 'Is that Mulholland's scarf?'

'Maybe.'

'Guv . . .'

'Kay, it wasn't me. Okay? Like I've had time to be so bloody petty.' Fenchurch picked up a soggy foil ball and dumped it back in the bin. 'We need to link Eustace to Kamal.'

'Yeah, like that's going to be easy.'

'Come on, Kay . . .'

'Well, Lisa Bridge is pulling his phone records and bank accounts.'

'We should get Liam Sharpe in here. There might be something in that pile of shit he's got.'

'Guv.'

'You know what you said last night?' Fenchurch ran a hand through his hair, thick with sweat. 'Am I losing it?'

Reed looked up, eyebrows standing to attention. 'What?'

'This case. What the hell's going on?'

Reed clapped him on the shoulder. 'You're not losing your mind, guv.'

'I meant my touch.'

'Right. No, you're not. Things are escalating, guv. You know what it's like. They'll get worse before they get better. These kids aren't like anything else we've ever dealt with. Guerrilla tactics.'

'More like gorilla. Strike hard and fast.'

Nelson appeared in the doorway, phone clamped between his ear and shoulder. 'It's guerrilla, boss.' He pronounced it like he was using the original Spanish.

'It's bloody not.' Fenchurch pinched his nose. 'What do you want?'

'Charming.' Nelson handed him a sheet of paper. 'That's the results of the company checks. Eustace is the sole owner of this Dubai company.'

'Just him?'

'Just him, guv. Steve's looking at the co-owner of Purple Heron just— Just a sec.' Nelson turned away, nodding. 'Cheers, Steve. That's superb.' He grinned at Fenchurch. 'It's a charity, guv. That's why it took so long. Different database. Something called the Iconic Foundation.'

Chapter Forty-Seven

'Well, then you need to bloody hurry up.' Fenchurch leaned against the black railings and clutched his Airwave to his chest. 'Bloody uniform.' He gave the Belgravia townhouse another once over. Didn't look like anyone was in, but then that never proved anything.

Eaton Square was quiet for a Sunday evening. Just an elderly couple walking a yapping ball of anger, keeping their distance from the police officers. The flags at the embassy flapped in the gentle breeze. He still hadn't worked out who was in there. Chile? Bolivia? Just the one Range Rover this time as opposed to the six.

To his left, Nelson had paired off with uniformed officers. Another team stood to the right.

Fenchurch put his Airwave to his mouth. 'Have you covered the back yet?'

'Affirmative, sir.' Heavy panting. 'Both ends. Eccleston Mews is under our control.'

'Then we are go. Hold your position until I tell you otherwise.' Fenchurch waved a finger at Nelson then jogged over the road, bounding up the steps. He thumped at the door and waited.

Nothing.

He looked around, locking eyes with Nelson, and spoke into the Airwave: 'Any movement out the back?'

'Negative, sir.'

Another thump on the door. 'Ms Ikonnikova, it's the police! Open up, please!'

Nothing, again.

Fenchurch kicked it this time, his size elevens thudding against the black wood. 'Ms Ikonnikova, we have a search warrant to enter your property!'

The door opened to a crack. A woman peered out. Latte-coloured skin, black hair, hazel eyes. Nothing like Yana Ikonnikova. 'Yes?'

'We're looking for Ms Ikonnikova.'

'She not here.' Spanish accent. She wore a cleaner's uniform, clutching a St Christopher around her neck, mouth twitching as if she was reciting incantations. 'She not here!'

Fenchurch let out a sigh. 'Where is she?'

'I told you. She not here.'

'Where is she?'

'Out. Men took her.'

Fenchurch's pulse shot up a few BPM. Drums skittered in his ears. 'Men took her?'

'In cars. Her men.' She slid back the chain and pulled the door open wide. 'Her guards? Yes, yes. Guards. Yevgeni. He nice to me.'

Fenchurch stepped forward and stuck his foot in front of the door. 'Where did they take her?'

'I just clean the house.'

'Is there anyone else—'

'Stop!' A man wearing a towel stomped across the chequer-board floor, leaving puddles behind him. Rippling muscles, big rather than toned. As bald as if he'd just been born. 'You are in charge, yes?' Thick Russian accent.

'That's right.' Fenchurch gritted his teeth, pushing fillings together. Didn't fancy his chances against him. 'And you are?'

'Dmitri. You call me Dmitri. Who are you?'

'DI Fenchurch.' He handed him his warrant card. 'We need a word with Ms Ikonnikova? I'd rather speak to her directly.'

Dmitri involuntarily flexed his pecs. 'She out.'

'Can you get a message to her?'

'Do I have to?' Dmitri folded his arms across his chest. 'I don't think I do.'

'You will tell me where she is. We can do this down the station, if you'd rather.'

'You're threatening me?' Dmitri held out his hands, crossed at the wrists. 'Then take me instead.'

'I'd rather you put on some clothes first.' Fenchurch waved to a nearby uniform, beckoning him over. 'Make sure Dolph Lundgren stays here, okay?' He turned round and put the Airwave to his ear. 'Anything out the back yet?'

'Still a negative, sir.'

Fenchurch killed the call and dialled Reed's badge number. 'Kay, I need an update.'

'We're just at the office, guv.' She was breathing hard. 'Hold on a sec.'

'Anybody there?'

'Place is empty, guv. Sunday empty. It's not like they've cut and run.'

'So where the hell is she?' Fenchurch groaned, his gut sinking deep. 'She's got a yacht moored at St Katharine Docks.'

Dmitri's eyes were widening.

'Kay, get out of there and head to the yacht.'

St Katharine Docks were a mix of an ancient wharf, an old brewery and new-build flats surrounding a chaotic grid of a marina on four sides, just a thin channel leading out to the Thames. Tower Bridge loomed over to their right.

Nelson stopped on the steps and pointed at a boat, just one among many. 'That's it there, guv.'

Brilliant white in the sunshine, the murky water below was calm enough to give some sort of reflection. Maybe thirty metres long, the yacht looked like the sharp bow could spear the water. The stern was open and backed onto the mooring. A viewing platform jutted out of the top, just a couple of bodies up there. Lights shone through the windows below deck even in the midday glow.

Fenchurch scowled at it. 'It's hardly Roman Abramovich's yacht, is it?'

Reed winked at him, a cheeky smirk on her face. 'She doesn't need a penis substitute, guv.' She held up her Airwave Pronto. 'Anyway, according to this, she's got a three-hundred footer moored out near Poole.'

'She better not be on that one.' Fenchurch stormed down the gangplank towards the boat, the wood creaking beneath his feet. Something swarmed in the dark water below.

A group of men stood near the back of the boat, suited and booted. Probably armed.

Fenchurch stepped onto the deck. The boat wobbled more than it should. 'Afternoon, gents.'

A hand gripped his shirt. 'Stop.' Yevgeni, the guard from Ikonnikova's house on Thursday night. The same suit, a bulge just over the heart. A handgun. 'I'm going to ask you politely. Get off this boat.'

Nelson stepped next to Fenchurch, three uniforms behind him.

'We're looking to speak with Ms Ikonnikova.' Fenchurch craned his neck to look round him. 'Is she here?'

'She's here.' Yevgeni took a step forward, towering over Fenchurch. 'Get off this boat.' The two others fanned out into some military formation. Just as big and broad as him. Same suits, same telltale bulge. Yevgeni put a hand to Fenchurch's chest. 'I can't let you on board.'

Drums clattered in Fenchurch's ears. He tapped Yevgeni's chest. Definitely a gun. 'You got licenses for those firearms?'

'What firearms?'

'So, it's a copy of the Bible, is it? A cigarette case?'

'You funny guy.' Yevgeni's grin switched to a scowl. 'Now, get off the boat. Sir.'

'Can't do that.' Fenchurch reach out and gripped Yevgeni's wrist. He twisted it hard.

It didn't move.

Yevgeni countered, steel fingers clawing at Fenchurch's forearm. He pulled his arms wide, wrenching Fenchurch's shoulders, sending him squirming to his knees. Yevgeni let go and Fenchurch's arms dropped. He tried to kick out but nothing was stopping the monster. The Russian picked him up and grabbed him in a bear hug, squeezing the air out of his lungs. Felt like he was drowning.

'If I let you go, you promise to get off the boat, ah?'

Fenchurch pulled his head back and drove it forward. His forehead cracked into Yevgeni's nose. He lashed out with his knee and crunched it into his groin. The guard collapsed into a heap at his feet, clutching his balls and squealing like a pig.

'That's how we do it in London, sunshine.' Fenchurch waved at a stunned-looking uniform. 'Cuff him.'

The uniform snapped a cuff on the groaning man's wrist. Another knelt next to him, keeping him secure.

Fenchurch nodded at the other two hired muscle. 'Are you pair going to cause me any trouble?'

They stood back, leaning against the designer-brown walls of the yacht's interior, and raised their hands.

Fenchurch made for the staircase, a sharp left bend off the entranceway. He stopped halfway down and sucked in air. 'Christ.'

Nelson put an arm round his shoulder. 'You okay, guv?'

'Feel like I'm dying, Jon.' Hard, deep breaths. Didn't seem to make any difference. 'That ugly bastard's stronger than he looks.'

'Looks pretty strong to me. Where'd you learn that move?'

'Our little friend, Qasid. Pulled it on me after he'd . . .' Fenchurch grimaced. 'After he killed Victor Morgan.'

'You want me to supervise the search?'

Fenchurch sucked in a final breath and stretched out. 'No, I'm fine.' He trotted down the stairs like he owned the place, hand skirting the oak banister.

A side lamp shone to the left, recessed into the wood panelling covering the walls. Looked like an open door led to some bedrooms. Smelled like the other was a kitchen.

To the right, three windows looked out across the docks, a reassuring police presence visible in all of them. Sixteen chairs huddled round a dark wood dining table in the middle of the room. Three cream sofas sat beyond, arranged in a U-shape, matching sidelights on inset tables behind them.

Yana Ikonnikova reclined on the left one, flicking through a magazine. Her black dress shimmered in the spotlights, a toned thigh crossed over the other leg. She sipped at an iced vodka. 'Yevgeni, what is all this noise?'

'Ms Ikonnikova, I need to have a word with you.'

She looked up at Fenchurch, eyes wide. 'You?'

'Come on, ma'am. We'll do this somewhere a bit less comfortable.'

Fenchurch nodded at Reed, holding the station's front door open for them, and pushed Yana inside. 'Steve? Here's another one for you.'

The desk sergeant looked up from his computer terminal. He left the counter and limped over.

'What's up with you?'

'Started a Metafit class at the gym last night. Absolutely broken myself.'

'Better late than never, I suppose.' Fenchurch let go of Yana's wrist and let Steve take her. 'Get her upstairs and get her lawyer in here, okay?'

Steve nodded at one of the uniforms then followed Reed over to the counter. He tapped at his computer and snorted at the screen, running a finger along a line. 'There's a Giles Langerman upstairs for you, guv.'

'Who's he when he's at home?'

'Looking after some Russian. Yana something.'

Fenchurch shook his head. 'That was bloody quick.' He nodded at Reed, then started up the staircase. 'I'm fed up of psychic lawyers, Kay.'

'Must've been what those muscle boys were up to when you were making sure Yevgeni couldn't breed.'

———

Giles Langerman looked like he'd been built at the same factory as Yana's security guards. Tall, shaven head, dark suit, red tie and he worked out, big time. He just failed on the accent — lisping Oxbridge RP instead of pinched Slavic. 'I ask you to respect my client's wishes and accept her statement. She has no knowledge of the crimes and misdemeanours these allegations pertain to.'

Fenchurch switched his gaze to Yana, picking at something stuck between her teeth. 'During her work, Saskia Barnett discovered a few items I'd like to discuss with your client. Let's start with your charitable foundation, shall we?'

'My father, God rest his soul, said we can't exist in isolation. No man is an island, yes?' Yana dabbed at her eyes. 'He set up the foundation to help improve this city in the right way. To help communities come to terms with progress.'

'I think I know how you're doing it.' Reed pulled out a sheet of paper, the product of Nelson's activities with the City cops that evening, and pushed the page across the table. 'We've found a series of payments made to councillors in the borough of Islington from a company called Purple Heron.'

'Which is?'

'You denying knowledge of it?'

'I just can't understand your accent. Is it Australian?'

'Essex.'

'Let's try it differently, then, shall we? Purple Heron is co-owned by your charitable foundation.'

Yana gave a loose-shouldered shrug, eyes staring into space. Like she had a million and one better places to be, that this was a mere hindrance.

'My client's position as CEO means she's not party to the deepest workings of the business.' Langerman smoothed down the lapel of his suit jacket. 'She can't be expected to have knowledge of all the activities undertaken by the myriad businesses under her purview.'

'Ms Ikonnikova, how close are you with Guy Eustace?'

'Who?'

'You know who he is.'

Yana flicked her hair again. She fluttered her eyelashes, puckered her lips. 'Guy's a businessman. Made a lot of money in property, like I have. We want to give back to the community so we work together with our charities, yes?'

'That's very noble of you.' Fenchurch fetched another sheet of paper from the pile on his leather document pouch. 'You co-own Purple Heron with him. It looks like a holding company for the flats on City Road? Buxton Court?'

She glanced over at Langerman. Even he didn't have anything to add.

'Our understanding is the pair of you plan to tear the whole lot down and rebuild them.' Fenchurch gave a thin-lipped smile, showing his teeth. 'The only fly in the ointment is a left-wing council who want to build more social housing, maybe even buy back ex-council stock. Their problem is they're deadlocked with their more monetarist colleagues. So you and Eustace hatched a plan. Pay them off and you swing the vote in your favour.'

'No comment.'

'Are you sure you just want to leave it like that? It's a fairly strong accusation. If it was me, I'd be denying the hell out of that one.'

'No comment.'

'That your final answer?'

'Inspector.' Langerman steepled his fingers on the desk. 'My client wishes to remain silent, as is her right.'

Fenchurch nodded slowly, casually dragging his gaze from Langerman back to Yana. 'Ms Ikonnikova, why are you killing people?'

She spluttered. 'Excuse me?'

Reed drilled her eyes into Yana, practically head butting her. 'Come on, we know you had Saskia Barnett and Victor Morgan killed.'

Langerman waved a hand at the pile next to Fenchurch, eyes open wide. 'Can I see the evidence, please?'

Fenchurch ignored him. 'The way I see it, if anyone gets in your way, Ms Ikonnikova, you smite them down. Saskia Barnett on Thursday night. Victor Morgan this morning.'

'Evidence, please.'

'You use a gang of black youths to do it. That about right?'

'Can I see this evidence, Inspector?'

Yana hung her head low. 'No comment.'

'How do you get in touch with Kamal?'

Her head jerked up. 'Who?'

'You know who he is. He's the leader of this little gang you pay to bump people off. Nasty piece of work by all accounts.'

'I don't know what you're talking about.'

Langerman put a hand in front of Yana, trying to shush her. 'I really need to see your evidence.'

Fenchurch leaned forward. 'Just shut up and let your client speak. Okay?' He glared at Yana. 'Saskia and Victor were both murdered. Why? Just so you can make another few quid from throwing up some dodgy flats?'

'Inspector, you've got nothing on my client.' Langerman was getting to his feet, fingers splayed on the desk. 'I suggest you stop this charade now.' He fiddled with a cufflink. 'I have to return to my offices and arrange for a formal complaint to go to the Met Commissioner this evening. I'd appreciate it if you could wrap this up tout de suite.'

Fenchurch stood up and did up his jacket. Looked straight into Langerman's eyes. 'She's going to remain in custody until I get to the bottom of this, okay?'

Chapter Forty-Eight

Fenchurch dumped his jacket on his office desk and collapsed into his chair. It swung back and his stomach lurched. Some bastard had flipped the catch off. He sighed and reached down to adjust it. 'Where does that leave us, Kay?'

Reed was shutting the door, pissing herself laughing. 'Want me to get her for knackering your seat, as well?'

'Fiver says it's bloody Clooney.' Fenchurch tried it again — still not quite right. Another notch. There we go. 'Here's what I still don't get, Kay. Why did she kill Victor now?'

Reed sat opposite the desk and crossed her legs. 'This news-paper story, maybe.' She picked the supplement up and flicked through it. 'Victor Morgan published a story about Eustace kicking this Muslim girl in Dubai. Maybe he arranged it, not her.'

Fenchurch started scanning through to the story about Eustace. 'That's out there already, Kay. Killing him now means it's the stuff still to come.'

'Liam Sharpe didn't have anything, did he?'

'No, he didn't.' Fenchurch stared at the window, like it could show what they needed to do next. 'You think it's this property on City Road and those bungs?'

'Must be millions locked up in that deal.'

Fenchurch perched on the edge of the desk and pinched his nose. 'Assuming she's behind all this, we've got this big gap between her and the killers. It's like money laundering.'

Reed nodded. 'Murder laundering.'

'There's absolutely no evidence linking her to this, other than the circumstantial shit we've got.' Fenchurch shook his head. 'It's a bloody mess in a monkey shop.'

'A what?'

A knock on the door. Bridge stood there with Liam, the pair of them looking like an advert for a unisex hipster hairdresser. 'Sarge?'

Reed couldn't rouse herself. 'What's up, Lisa?'

'Been going through the call records, like you asked.' Bridge dumped her laptop and phone on the desk then handed her a sheet of paper. 'Yana's calls are clean, same with her guys.'

'Figures.' Reed put the page down again. 'And Eustace?'

'Doesn't even have a phone.'

'What?'

'I didn't believe it either, so we asked him.'

Liam bunched his face up. 'He says the EU surveillance state is monitoring important men like him.'

'Where does he get off?'

'Saturn, I think.' Liam held up a document. 'I found this among Sas's stuff. She got a freedom of information request from Eustace's office. His appointment book. We've been going through it and one thing jumped out at us. 12/11/2014, Hayden.'

———

'What do you bloody mean I can't see him?' Fenchurch shook his head, hands on hips. 'Do you know what's at stake here?'

The matron gave an unblinking stare. Five seconds, ten. 'I remember what you did the other day.' She thumbed behind her at the closed door. 'We've just got poor Hayden's blood pressure back under control.'

'You know what he's done? Who he's working for?'

'Not my concern, officer.'

'He's been murdering people. I need to see him.'

'Look, if you want to speak to the lad, you need to clear it with the doctor.' She checked her watch, sighing. 'He'll be on duty in half an hour.'

'Fine. Where's his office?'

'Not so fast.' She raised a finger. 'It has to come through DI Bell.'

'Simon, you know the score, don't you?' Bell's voice sounded even worse down the phone line. 'Besides, it's bath night.'

Fenchurch pushed his free hand on the barrier and stared out of the window. London lay in darkness, disconnected lights glowing in the evening sky. 'String, I need your help here. We're onto something big.'

'You always are, Si. Still can't help.'

'Jason, I need your help here.'

'Not often you call me by my real name.'

'Shows how desperate I am.'

A sigh distorted the phone line. 'Right. I'll see what I can do.'

'Cheers.' The line was already dead.

Reed was checking her Airwave, sipping on a tea. He caught her eye. 'Guv?'

'He's on his way in.' Fenchurch wandered over and picked up his cup from the table. 'How's Waheed?'

'Not good, guv.' She took a sip and grimaced. 'Doc says we should be able to get in there in five minutes.'

'Right.' Fenchurch had a glug of tea. Tasted like chicken soup. Wouldn't be having another one.

Reed finished her drink and dumped the plastic cup in the bin. 'That stuff with Kamal taking kids, you okay with it?'

'Why do you think that, Kay?'

'It's close to what happened to—'

'It's nothing to do with Chloe, Kay. She's gone. Whatever happened to her, it just happened. It's horrible and it's wrecked our lives, but we've got to move on.'

'Sorry to bring it up.'

'It's fine, Kay. Glad someone's looking out for me.'

A doctor appeared, clutching a tablet computer tight to his white coat. He smiled at Reed. 'Inspector?'

'That's him.' She thumbed at Fenchurch. 'I'm just a Sergeant.'

'Right, of course.' The doctor tapped at his tablet, frowning. 'Blasted things. Prefer clipboards. Anyway, Mr Lad is out of surgery and is awake.'

'How is he?'

'He's recovering from a general anaesthetic, Inspector. But he's survived a potentially fatal accident.' He waved at the door. 'You can see him just now, if you wish.' He held the door open for them.

'Thanks.' Fenchurch followed Reed into the room.

Waheed lay on the bed, covers pulled up to his chin. His eyes were shut and his mouth was obscured by a mask. A tube stretched over to a ventilator.

Reed sat on the chair next to the bed. Her smile inverted to a frown. 'Shit.'

Fenchurch clocked it. His stomach lurched.

Waheed's right arm was just a stump, severed halfway up the bicep and covered in thick bandaging.

Jesus Christ. Fenchurch struggled to get his breathing under control, panting like a clapped-out lab. He glared at the doctor. 'Why didn't you say?'

'Sorry, I thought you knew.' The doctor frowned at Reed. 'I thought DI Mulholland here would've told you?'

'I'm DS Reed.' She brushed a hand across her forehead.

'Right, yes, of course. DI Mulholland took Mrs Lad to the canteen for a break.'

'How is he?' Fenchurch's throat felt raw, even rawer than chasing a gang leader down a train tunnel.

The doctor peered at his tablet. 'Mr Lad has broken six ribs, his femur, and we had to perform a trans-humeral amputation on his arm. And that's getting off lightly, I'm afraid.'

'Jesus.'

'He'll be in here a while.'

The door slid open. An Indian woman in her late twenties stood there, frowning. Her eyes were ringed with deep pools of black. 'Who the hell are you?'

Fenchurch tried for a benevolent smile, his forehead creasing in a painful way. 'Mrs Lad?'

'That's right. I asked who you were?' Cut-glass accent, voice full of steel.

'Noopoor, this is DI Fenchurch.' Mulholland breezed into the room, scarf-less for once. 'He is your husband's line manager.'

'You.' Noopoor lashed out with a hand, slapping Fenchurch's cheek. Sounded like a drumstick on a snare. Felt like she'd tore open the skin. 'You did this to him!'

Fenchurch dabbed at his face. 'Your husband acted heroically, Mrs Lad. He caught a multiple murderer.'

'You see what you've done to him! You've made him like this! He won't be able to work!'

'He'll be taken care of.' Fenchurch hovered his hand in the air, unsure whether to try and stroke her arm. 'I'm truly, truly sorry for what's—'

'Get out.' Noopoor pointed at the door, her hand shaking. 'Get out!'

Mulholland gripped Fenchurch's bicep, her talons tightening around a patch of bruises. 'Simon, you should leave her in peace.'

'Mrs Lad, I'm sorry.' Fenchurch bowed his head and left the room. He powered off down the corridor, wishing the lino could swallow him whole. He brushed past a nurse and stopped by the lifts. Hammered the button for the ground floor.

'Guv, you okay?' Reed caught up with Fenchurch and started massaging his arm.

'I'm pretty bloody far from okay. This is my fault.'

'You said he ran off, guv. That's not your fault.'

'It's the sort of shit I'd do, though, right? Cowboy shit.'

'You're not a cowboy, guv, you just care.'

'He's lost his bloody arm because of me.'

'And he knew the risks. It's not your fault. If it's anyone's, it's his.'

Fenchurch rubbed his forehead, felt like he was growing scales over the skin. 'Doesn't make it any easier.'

His Airwave chimed out. He scanned the display. Bell. 'I better take this, Kay.' He wandered over to the window, the first spots of rain starting to appear. 'Hello?'

'Simon, it's Jason Bell. I'm on my way. I've got the doctor's approval to speak to Hayden.'

Hayden had bunched up the bedsheets between his fingers, almost tugging them off the bed. 'Don't know what you're talking about, man.'

'Bollocks you don't.' Fenchurch got up and put a knee on the bed. 'You were Kamal's lieutenant, weren't you? Helped him abduct kids off the street, assimilate them into your gang.'

'Who tol' you that?'

'I'm not going to tell you.' Fenchurch looked behind him. Reed was guarding the door, stopping anyone getting in with them. 'Kamal is finished, okay? He's being done for murder.'

'What?'

'This whole gig is over. We're onto you. If I were you, I'd give it up now. I need you to help us here.' Fenchurch leaned over the boy. 'One of my officers has lost an arm because of Kamal.'

'So? Why should I care.' He lifted a shoulder. 'So glad I'm not you. You's nowhere.'

'You're the one who's got nowhere to go, other than prison. It's all over. We're charging you with phone theft, you know about that. But now we've got evidence linking you to murder, kidnapping, entrapment and a whole host of other crimes. Twenty years is what you're looking at. Add conspiracy on and it'll be double that. Wave goodbye to good behaviour, not that I expect it from you.'

Hayden swallowed. 'You offering me something, pig?'

'Give me Kamal and we'll see what we can do.'

'No, man.'

'Kamal can't protect you any more. You need to give him up.'

Hayden dug his heels into his eye sockets. He coughed. Hard, like his lungs were going to come up. Then nodded. 'What you want to know?'

'Guy Eustace called you up just over a year ago.'

'Right. Coke.'

'Cocaine?'

'Give the man a hand.' Hayden rolled his eyes. 'He call me up about some coke. He was having a party or something. Needed forty grams in a hurry, heard I could get it. This was what me and Kamal were doing at the time. Gave it all up.'

'You gave him the drugs?'

'Sho' thing. Said to him, anything else he needed we could help.' Hayden got into another coughing fit. Rasping hard. 'So, two weeks ago, he calls me up again. Out of the blue, man. Says he's got a problem.'

'This is before you got hit by the bus?'

'Right. Says he's got something he needs sorted. Some*one*. I gave his number to Kamal, don't know nothing else about it.'

'Will you go on the record about that?'

'You get me off, sure. I'll do whatever you need.'

Chapter Forty-Nine

'This is completely unacceptable. You need to let me out of here.' Guy Eustace ran a hand across his ruddy face, brushing at the five o'clock shadow. 'I've been in here for hours and nobody's telling me what's happening.'

'You can blame your solicitor for that.' Fenchurch drummed his fingers on the table. 'Oh, hang on, it's you.' He left a pause, enough for Eustace to snort three times. 'Do you know anything about the murders of Saskia Barnett and Victor Morgan? Of course you do, I saw you on Upper Street, milking Saskia's death for all it's worth, spreading your hatred.'

Eustace just looked away, arms hugged tight around his body.

'Now, I want to know if you knew anything about them *before* they happened.'

More silence.

'You need to talk to us. We know you and Ms Ikonnikova have been killing people to make money.'

Eustace looked like he was being kept up. He yawned, his tonsils dancing a jig. 'I've done nothing of the sort.'

The door burst open and Bell entered the interview room. He stormed over and whispered in Fenchurch's ear: 'Hayden's statement checks out, Si. His burner got a call from a phone box outside Eustace's office.'

'Stupid bastard.' Fenchurch grinned at Eustace. 'Well, well, well. Coke, eh?'

Eustace woke up, like he'd tooted a couple of grams of coke in one go. 'Excuse me?'

Fenchurch made to look up Eustace's nostrils. 'Bad for you, you know? Does funny stuff to your heart. Lines it, makes you more susceptible to a heart attack.'

'What are you talking about?'

'We believe Ms Ikonnikova's been using a gang of kids to do these killings.' Fenchurch rubbed his hands together. 'Problem is, I don't know how she was contacting them. Her phone records are clean. Same with her men. Yours aren't, though.'

'What?' Eustace spluttered the word out, his cheeks going as ruddy as his tongue, hanging out of his mouth. 'My phone records are immaculate.'

'Quit with the bullshit, Mr Eustace. How do you know Hayden?'

A frown flickered on Eustace's forehead, on and off like a light bulb on the blink. 'You've lost me.'

'The twelfth of November, 2014. You had a meeting with him according to your diary.'

Eustace's neck bent forward and he let out a deep sigh. 'Christ.'

'The game's over.' Fenchurch shrugged then left a space, watched Eustace crumple and rest on his arms. He handed him the printed spreadsheet. 'Let's start with the payments from Purple Heron.'

'This is nothing . . .' Eustace shook his head against his forearm, skin sliding across Egyptian cotton. 'Look, it's not what you think.'

'Do you admit to making these payments?'

'I did.' Eustace's tongue flicked like a snake. '*We* did. But it was at Yana's insistence. We needed to progress that matter.'

'The flats on City Road?'

Eustace rubbed at his eyes, staring into space, his breathing short and sharp. 'What would you do in my situation? Just let that opportunity slip through your fingers?'

'I'd try and do the honest thing.' Fenchurch gripped the table edge, his knuckles whitening. 'I certainly wouldn't kill people.'

Eustace pinched the skin over his throat. Didn't say anything.

'Why did you give Kamal's number to Yana?'

'She had a problem, I thought I could solve it.'

'This problem being Saskia Barnett?'

Eustace stared at the floor and clenched his jaw. 'I thought Yana wanted drugs from him.' He ran a hand through his hair, tiny flecks of gel catching in the harsh light, and leaned back in his seat. 'But that's not what she was after.'

'She wanted Saskia killed.'

'Correct.' Eustace held up his hands. 'You must believe me, I had no part in this.'

'Well, I don't believe you.' Fenchurch fixed a hard glare on him, let it seep into his skull. 'London's going to rack and ruin because of people like you and Ms Ikonnikova. She owns a yacht and her house is worth two hundred million quid. She closed her homeless shelters so she can build more houses to sell to rich people.' He got up and buttoned up his suit jacket. 'You're forcing the people you're supposed to be helping out of the city. Just for some bloody money.'

'What do you want from me?'

Fenchurch killed the recorder. 'I need you to write that all down in a statement for me, okay?'

'I can't do that.'

'Why? You're going to prison, Mr Eustace. I'd say at least twenty years, served. You can wave goodbye to your office, your Brussels expenses, your career. You might want to do the decent thing and give your flat in Dubai to the mother of your child.'

Fire burnt in Eustace's eyes. 'How dare you?'

'Statement, please.'

The coals went out, replaced with steely frost. 'Look, I can't go to prison.'

'You got into bed with the devil. I hope you got a fair price for your soul and invested it wisely.'

Eustace reached over and gripped Fenchurch's wrists. 'The prisons are full of . . . blacks and Poles. Belarusian rapists. *Muslims*.' Sweat beaded his forehead, now blotchy like the skin of a peach. 'They'll kill me.'

'Much as I hate to admit it, I suspect you'll be protected from the worst elements inside.' Fenchurch folded his arms tight across his chest. 'Of course, there's got to be *some* time when the guards turn their backs. You probably won't be alone then.'

'I will do whatever it takes to stay out of prison.'

'Should've thought about that a while ago.' Fenchurch snapped his fingers at the Custody Officer and beckoned him over. 'Get DC Bridge in here and get her to take Mr Eustace's statement, please.'

Eustace looked up, head still on the table. 'So you'll keep me out of prison?'

'I'll be honest with you. You're going to prison.' Fenchurch watched Eustace slump forward again. Didn't feel anywhere near as good as he thought it would. Maybe nothing could.

'But.' He waited till Eustace looked up. 'If you help secure the conviction of Yana Ikonnikova, we'll see what can be done about the level of accommodation you'll enjoy at Her Majesty's Pleasure.'

Eustace sat up straight and smoothed down his shirtsleeves. 'Give me a pen.'

Giles Langerman adjusted his tie and grinned across the interview room table. 'I'm terribly sorry, but it appears you've wasted your time.' He scraped the chair back across the lino. 'I'll bid you adieu.'

'Just a minute.' Fenchurch tried to hold up his arm but the bruises flared in his shoulder. He'd definitely torn something. 'I want to hear what she's got to say.'

'She's saying nothing.' Langerman stuffed his papers back in his briefcase. 'Now, good day.'

'This is over when I say it's over.'

'No, it's over now. You've come in here and made unfounded, baseless allegations against my client. I'm telling you to desist.' Langerman closed his briefcase, the catches thunking shut. He made great show of hefting up the Swiss timepiece on his wrist, closer to a grandfather clock than a wristwatch. 'Now, if you'll excuse me, I have an appointment at Kensington Palace Gardens.'

'Excuse me?'

Langerman got to his feet. 'The embassy of the Russian Federation.'

Fenchurch motioned for him to sit again. 'As you were, Mr Langerman.'

'I beg your pardon?'

'We just had a very informative chat with Guy Eustace.' Fenchurch slid a sheet of paper across the table. 'This is his statement.'

Langerman glanced at Yana, her eyes practically out on stalks. He sat back down and scanned through the contents.

Fenchurch waved a hand at it. 'I've highlighted the interesting bits for you.'

Langerman tore through the document, running a finger through certain paragraphs. He flapped it down on his briefcase. 'These are nothing more than the confused ramblings of someone suffering from paranoid delusions. It proves nothing.'

Fenchurch flashed a grin. 'I trust you've got evidence to support that claim?'

Langerman shook the paper in the air. 'You really expect this story to stand up in court? I'll tear it to shreds in seconds.'

'Your client is going to be charged with two counts of conspiracy to murder.' Fenchurch rubbed his hands together. 'This is her chance to set the story straight.'

'My client is a respectable businesswoman. She has no—'

'She paid someone to kill for her just so she could buy another bloody yacht.'

'We're done here.' Langerman stuffed the statement into his briefcase and got up again. He took a step towards the door and leaned against the table, his face inches from Fenchurch. 'I shall return with the Ambassador.'

'Then I'll google the Russian for "piss off and stop wasting my time".' Fenchurch snorted in his face. 'Your client's guilty. She can't buy her way out of this.'

'The ambassador won't take too kindly to a *Rossiyanka* being charged with frivolous crimes.' Langerman pronounced the Russian in a perfect accent.

'I very much doubt he'll help a *Rossiyanka* such as Ms Ikonnikova. Her father was killed by agents of the government, wasn't he?'

The lawyer backed off, shifting over to massage his client's shoulders as her breathing sped up.

'What do they call the KGB these days? Ah, yes, the FSS, right? Read a book about them a few months back. Proper nasty bastards, by the sounds of things. Don't take too kindly to enemies of the state, do they?'

'You keep my father out of this.' Yana had narrowed her eyes, deep sockets hiding a laser-guided glare. 'He was good man!'

'Whatever. He avoided spending his days in some Siberian gulag.' Fenchurch lifted his hands, not labouring the point. 'Of course, HMP Holloway isn't anywhere near as bad.' He coughed. 'Nowhere near as secure, either, mind you. I know they're shutting it down, but it's where you'll end up. It's a dated place, very difficult to keep locked down.'

'Are you threatening me?'

'I'm not, no. Why would I?' Fenchurch shrugged, flaring up some pain in his shoulder. 'I don't need anything more from you. You'll rot in that jail. Or its successor, I don't care. Thirty years. That's if the FSS don't get to you in there. No yacht, no vodka or caviar, no Yevgeni and his troupe of muscle-bound dancers. You'll be in a single cell, most likely, but that eight-foot square will become your world. You'll miss both of your yachts. Your hair will go back to its natural colour.'

Yana shut her eyes, jaw clenched, and stared at the table. Fast breathing, tears streaking her sharp cheeks. 'I am innocent.'

'No, you're guilty.' Fenchurch got up and opened the door, settling his gaze on Yana, rocking with tears, then Langerman, steely to the last. 'I'll see you both in court.'

Liam Sharpe leaned against the office window, looking out across Leman Street. He spun round and beamed at Fenchurch. 'This is a surprise. Thought you'd be busy.'

'I've learned to delegate over the years. Not everything, but some things.' Fenchurch collapsed behind his desk. 'We've just charged Yana Ikonnikova and Guy Eustace with the deaths of Saskia and Victor.'

'I just wanted to say you've done a good thing, you know?' Liam rested against the window ledge. 'You stopped Kamal doing this again. No more deaths.' He swallowed a sigh. 'You've given Saskia's old man closure. They'll throw the book at whoever did this to her. And Victor.'

'Thanks. Wish I shared your hope.'

'What?'

'Nothing.' Fenchurch put his feet up on his desk. 'I've just seen the other side of the coin. I shouldn't be telling you this, but these kids weren't doing it voluntarily. Kamal was forcing them. He'd kidnapped these kids.'

'Jesus.'

'Saskia's killer is called Lewis Cole. Not much more than a kid, really. Kamal abducted him two years ago.' Fenchurch shut his eyes, the sting of tears still present. He focused on Liam, arms folded in the window frame. 'I lost my daughter ten years ago. Never found her.'

'I didn't know.'

'How could you?' Fenchurch snorted through his nostrils. 'It's the hope that kills you, you know that? It lingers there every day. Makes you think she could just reappear. I thought I'd found her last year. Wasn't her.'

'How do you cope?'

'You just do.' Fenchurch wiped away the tears. 'Why am I telling you this?'

'It's okay, I'm happy to help.'

'That stuff on the payments, that got us the connection. I appreciate it.'

'Kamal's going down, though, isn't he?'

'It's too easy to convict a black kid in this city. That's the problem. The deck's stacked against them. People like Yana Ikonnikova and Guy Eustace, they just take, take, take, and they don't give a shit who suffers. Just so long as they've got their yacht. People like Saskia and Victor get caught in the crossfire trying to do the right thing.'

'Just make sure Saskia's death wasn't in vain.'

Fenchurch nodded at Liam. Kid had a point. 'That's all exclusive, by the way. You've got a few hours before the official press release goes out. Take it as thanks for helping me out. Might get you off copying and pasting tweets.'

Liam got up from the windowsill. 'I appreciate it.'

'Don't mention it.'

'Can I interview you about your daughter?'

Fenchurch rocked forward on his chair. 'Why?'

'It might help find her.'

Fenchurch shook his head and sighed. 'Piss off out of here and write your bloody story.'

'Think about it.'

Fenchurch held his gaze until he had to look away. 'Maybe.'

'Good evening, Andrew.' Fenchurch stared across the table, the digital recorder blinking away. He grinned at Kamal, relishing the frown crawl across his forehead. 'That is your name, right?'

Kamal turned to Unwin, jabbed a finger at him. 'Tell him to shut up.'

Unwin gave a shrug. 'I can't do that.'

'Andrew, we've got witnesses who'll testify against you. You're going away for a very long time.'

'Who are these witnesses?'

'This is your chance to confess, Andrew. You can help take down who you were working for.'

'I don't name names.'

'Well, that's your decision. There's not a jury in the land won't prosecute you, sunshine. We've got a pretty solid evidence trail against you and Ms Ikonnikova.'

'So get out of my face and put me away, man.'

'Andrew, I'm giving you the chance to help us here.'

'Not doing that. I'm going away, you said that. Doesn't matter if it's four years or life. Same difference.'

Fenchurch sighed. 'We're prepared to drop the charges relating to conspiracy to murder if you help us secure the convictions of Yana Ikonnikova and Guy Eustace.'

'Who?'

'You're not interested in getting the charges dropped?'

'Why should I be?'

'The phone stuff's maybe two to four years, depending on the judge. One to two with good behaviour.' Fenchurch tilted his head from side to side. 'Maybe less if you let us know who you sold the phones to.'

'Drop the other charges.'

'I can't do that.'

'Then we got no deal.' Kamal ran a hand along his lips, zipping them together.

'Last chance, Andrew.'

'Quit it with that.'

'You prefer Kamal?'

'It's my name. The name I chose. Not Andrew Smith.' He snarled at the name. 'Get your white ass out of here, boy.'

'If that's what you want.'

'Get out.'

'I'm going to stand up two seconds after I stop talking. I'll walk over to that door and leave this room. That'll be the last you see of me until you're in court.' Fenchurch counted in his head — one Mississippi, two Mississippi — and got up. Headed for the door, grabbed the handle.

'Wait.'

Fenchurch turned slowly. 'You going to help?'

'I know *your* name, Simon.'

Fenchurch frowned. 'That supposed to be a threat?'

'No, I know it of old, man. Years back.'

'What are you saying? Did I pick you up when you were a kid in Harlow?'

'No, man.' Kamal sneered and rubbed his hands together. 'But I know what happened to your girl.'

Fenchurch stared at him. Heart thudding, drums battering his ears, mouth dry. 'What?'

'Lovely girl.'

'You're talking shit.'

'No way, man. Definitely her. Said she was called Fenchurch. Thought I knew your name from somewhere.'

Fenchurch's mouth was drier than the Sahara. Was the prick lying? Worse, was he telling the truth? 'Tell me what happened to her.'

'No way, man.'

'You're lying.'

'Bullshit, man. I know all about her.' Kamal smirked. 'Just wanted to see if you were—'

Fenchurch lurched at him. He pushed him right over. Kamal's skull cracked against the wall, denting the plaster. He grabbed his T-shirt, bunching the fabric around white-knuckled fists. 'Where is she?'

Kamal just laughed.

A hand grabbed his shoulder, hauling him back. 'You need to let him go, sir.' The Custody Officer.

Fenchurch let one hand go of the T-shirt and balled up his fist, hovering it over Kamal's face. 'Where. Is. She?'

Kamal lay back on the floor, laughing. 'I'm not going to tell you. You'll never see her again. I pumped that white ass.'

Fenchurch let the fist go, smashing into his face. Kamal's head cracked off the wall again.

The Custody Officer pushed Fenchurch over, arm round his back, face on the carpet.

Kamal sat up, still laughing, face covered in blood.

Fenchurch wriggled round. 'Tell me what happened.'

Kamal spat at him. 'I'm never going to tell you, bro.'

Chapter Fifty

Docherty slammed his office door and stomped across the carpet, thundering into his chair. 'Simon, you are a bloody idiot.'

Fenchurch kept his focus low. His shoulder felt like it was lying on the floor, severed from his body. 'I want five minutes in a room with him. Alone.'

'You'll get your wish in Belmarsh, you stupid bastard.'

Fenchurch looked up at him. 'Come on, boss.'

'Once Unwin's finished with you, you'll be lucky to be issuing speeding tickets in the bloody Dartford tunnel.'

'He knows what happened to Chloe.'

'And I thought you were over that?'

Fenchurch brushed the tears from his eyes. 'He said he knows what happened to her.'

'More like he knows how to play you.'

'How does he know what happened? How did he know Chloe was missing?'

'It's not exactly a secret, is it? All that press you've done over the years. And all the shite you've been up to with Unwin. A guy like him will be googling your name before you can fart.'

Fenchurch looked away, let the tears flow. 'I just want to know what happened to her, boss.'

'Does Abi want that?'

'She wants to know. Needs to know.'

'You're going to get into this all over again, aren't you? I can see what's going to happen. Abi'll kick you out by summer. You move back into your bachelor's pad in the bloody Isle of Dogs. Spending an hour a day looking over her bloody file. Drinking cheap wine to get to sleep. Tormenting your old man with it all.'

'He's been tormenting me.'

'Aye, well things bloody change quickly, don't they?' Docherty ran a hand through his hair, letting out the mother of all sighs. 'Listen, I'll sort this out, okay? You've somehow got Unwin on side, he's not pushing an assault charge. He knows the lay of the land.'

'The Complaints will come after me.'

'I know people there. Favours due.'

'You sure you want to cash them in on me?'

'What's the point in favours if you don't use them? Same with the Russian embassy. I've been onto the Foreign Office already. Don't worry about it.' Docherty snorted. 'Simon, I need you, okay? You're the only cop I've got who isn't a complete idiot.'

'Thought I was.'

'You know what I mean.' Docherty flashed a smile. 'You're the only one who gets results.'

'I don't want special treatment.'

'We'll sort this out. Okay?' Docherty picked up his Rangers mug and had a look inside. 'Nelson and Reed are interviewing him. We've charged the little shit, so there's no upper limit, okay? Whatever he knows, we'll get it out of him.'

'I want to get in there.'

'Not going to happen.' Docherty took a sip from his mug. 'Look, he's probably playing you, okay? The Mandem weren't kidnapping girls. They're big time, but they're not doing that. He's just messing with you. And it bloody worked.'

Fenchurch rubbed his fist, felt like the tendons had unravelled. 'If he knows something, boss, I want to find out.'

'He doesn't know anything, okay?' Docherty pointed at the office door. 'Now, get the hell out of here before you lamp anyone else.'

Fenchurch kicked off his shoes and padded through the flat. The lights were off in the kitchen and the living room. A crack appeared under the bottom of the bedroom door. He nudged it open.

Abi looked up from her Kindle, reading glasses perched on the end of her nose. 'You've remembered where you live, then?'

'Just about.' Fenchurch sat on his side of the bed and leaned over to kiss her.

'Jesus, Simon.' She caressed his cuts and bruises, plasters and gel. 'What the hell happened to you?'

'You should see the other guy.'

'Who?'

'Kamal. The guy who had Saskia killed. We got him, love. And the arseholes who paid for it. The bloody one per cent . . .'

She put the Kindle down. 'Sounds like he didn't do the killing.'

'We got them both. Poor little bastards were kidnapped. He took them off the street.'

'Jesus. Like Chloe?'

Fenchurch looked away, focusing on the painting on the wall, the dim light bouncing off the glass. 'I reunited them with their parents. For how long, I don't know. They'll be going away for a long time.'

'They were kidnapped?'

'He has a gang of kids. Little assassins on bikes.' Fenchurch flicked on his bedside light. 'They were getting paid to kill people.' He let out a deep sigh, feeling like it wouldn't stop coming out. 'Kamal said he knows what happened to Chloe.'

'What?'

'He stared at me and said he knows what happened to "my girl".'

'Do you believe him?'

'He seemed pretty sure of himself. Doc reckons he's just playing me.' Fenchurch rubbed his forehead. 'What if he's telling the truth, though, Ab?'

'He's just messing with your head.'

'I went for him. Pushed him right over. It was all I could do not to kill him.'

'What's going to happen?'

'Docherty reckons it'll all blow over, but I'm not so sure.' Fenchurch collapsed onto the bed. 'I couldn't take it if she's out there. The kid who killed Saskia . . . His parents lost him a few years ago. Qasid, too, the one he swapped places with. It's the same as Chloe. They were just stolen from the street.' He could just picture Ronald Cole in his tartan boxers, blank eyes pleading with them. 'It's maybe not worth knowing.'

'Tell me you're not going to start looking for her?'

'After ten years, we've finally got a lead.'

'Simon . . .'

'Look, whatever we do, we're doing it together, okay? I'm not going to drive another bloody wedge between us. If you want to drop it, I'll drop it. Okay?'

'I want you to drop it.'

'That's fine. I'll make sure Dad doesn't find out.'

'That's for the best.' She stroked his shoulder. 'Have you thought about having another child?'

Fenchurch lay back on the bed, let her play with his hair. He looked at her, glasses now on her head. 'How can we bring a new life into this world, Ab?'

'She might save it, Simon. You've got to have hope.'

'I'm fed up of feeling it's going to kill me.' Fenchurch nodded. 'Maybe you're right.'

Abi stared into his eyes, so deep she could probably see the back of his skull. 'Do you want another child?' Her voice was soft, like an angel whispering.

Could they replace Chloe? Did they have to? A new life would put a full stop on all the pain, all the bullshit. But it'd bind them together, might even be the start of something new.

Fenchurch sighed, and let his shoulders go. It was time to move on.

'Yes. Yes, I do.'

Afterword

As some of you know, I worked in London for a few years, returning to the fresh coldness of Scotland in December 2013 and a new career as a full-time writer. Towards the end of my stay there, I was out with a few friends for some beer. On our way to get something to eat, I had my iPhone nicked. By a kid on a bike. On Upper Street.

Crime number 2720204/13 in Islington.

Wasn't much fun and kind of tarnished London for me in a lot of ways. The idea for this came back to me last time I was down, as I got flashbacks to that, admittedly drunken, night. I remembered the idea last October and the rage swelled up again. I wrote the first draft of this book in six days. It just poured out, all the bile and hatred and anger and fear, like a long hangover. Took my time editing it, though, by which time the anger had subsided. I feel a lot better about it now.

Anyway, whoever nicked my phone — well, I hope you got a nice meal out of my trauma. You gave me a book.

To the undercover cops out on the town, thanks for stopping me doing something stupid and giving us solid advice.

And Rich, thanks for helping me deal with it — this book's for you.

Acknowledgements

The most amount of thanks ever go to Al Guthrie for brilliant agenting and editing before anyone else saw the first draft.

Special thanks again to Jenny Parrott, for helping me through January 2016's editing hell and then pushing me to improve the book further.

Doffed caps to Emilie, Sana, Eoin and all at Thomas & Mercer for continuing support and just being brilliant.

And, finally, thanks to Kitty for all the help and support as I wrote and edited this book, which isn't much compensation for how grumpy I am, I know.

About the Author

Photo Kitty Harrison © 2014

Ed James writes crime fiction novels. His Scott Cullen series features a young Edinburgh detective constable investigating crimes from the bottom rung of the career ladder he's desperate to climb. *Worth Killing For* is the second novel in his latest series, set on the gritty streets of East London and featuring DI Simon Fenchurch. Formerly an IT manager, Ed began writing on planes, trains and automobiles to fill his weekly commute to London. He now writes full-time and lives in East Lothian, Scotland, with his girlfriend and a menagerie of rescued animals.

28657361R00244

Printed in PolandPrinted in Poland
by Amazon Fulfillment
Poland Sp. z o.o., Wrocław